FAMILIAR
WARS

FAMILIAR WARS

Julietta Harvey

MICHAEL JOSEPH
LONDON

First published in Great Britain by
Michael Joseph Ltd
27 Wrights Lane
London W8 5TZ
1987

British Library Cataloguing in Publication Data
Harvey, Julietta
   Familiar wars.
   I. Title
   823'.914[F]   PR6058.A6989
   ISBN 0-7181-2823-0

Typeset in Janson 10/12pt by Goodfellow & Egan, Cambridge
Printed in Great Britain by Billings & Sons Ltd, Worcester

Στή μνήμη τοῦ πατέρα μου καί τῆς μητέρας μου.

*To my husband John Harvey and
my daughter Katerina.*

Τοῦ δ'ὥλετο νόστιμον ἦμαρ.

The day of the return home was lost to him.
Homer, *The Odyssey*, *I, 168*

· CONTENTS ·

·PART 1·

· 1 ·
The Unredeemed

LIKE HIS father and his grandfather, Gregoris Gregoriou wanted to be a merchant. He sat on a high stool at the corner of the shop and watched his father unfold, with the speed and artistry of a juggler, lengths of beautiful fabric: he would touch them delicately, turn them over to examine the weave, carry them with affection and pride to the entrance of the shop to appreciate the colour in the sunlight. Gregoris liked to watch his father sell his merchandise, wrapping the material round women's bodies with quick eyes and hands, or letting it drape from their shoulders, lowering his own body as if to kneel in adoration in front of them as they stretched upward with new dignity. He teased and tempted – and Gregoris felt the thrill, and also a small secret sorrow, when the lovely fabric was finally sold.

When the sales were good his father would wink at him and slip a new shiny coin into his pocket, and Gregoris felt pleasure linger in the shop till the end of the day. Was it the light weight of the new coin in his pocket, the faint traces of scent left behind by the lady clients, the tinkle of excitement carried from father to son? It was a feminine sensation mixed of rich colours, soft touches, ripples, curves, and smiles.

In the evening, they locked the shop, and he was carried home on his father's shoulders. Gregoris didn't talk to his mother about the shop – he felt, with pride, that there was a secret alliance between himself and his father, and he sought his father's eyes through the evening to confirm their secret. But the father's eyes remained innocent.

Father was different at home. Gregoris observed him put on the slippers and housecoat his wife handed to him – she had made them herself, and in her son's eyes they had a secret power over him. He would settle with a sigh of comfort against the intricately embroidered

3

cushions on the kitchen sofa, and every now and then take his eyes from his shop accounts to glance at his wife with quiet pleasure. She moved about the room with easy grace, humming popular love-tunes to herself and carrying the rhythm of her movement into all the things in the room. Gregoris saw there were loves and alliances that left him outside.

But he waited for his moment. For all the tiredness of the day he kept himself awake till his younger brothers had been put to bed; then, when his mother went to sit on the sofa next to her husband, he squeezed in quietly between them, stretched his arms round her waist, and let his head rest on her lap. As she undressed him to put him to bed, a brand-new shiny coin rolled on to the floor, which she picked up and, smiling, returned to his pocket.

Business flourished in Mouryes in the summer, and overflowed into the streets and alleys. The merchants sat cross-legged on low benches at the entrance of their shops, under wooden shutters propped up precariously to provide shelter from sun and rain. Their fingers told amber worry-beads as they invited inside shy hanoums and coy Circassians. The taciturn old Turk across the street was absorbed in the pleasures of his hubble-bubble. Gregoris, barefoot and pantalooned, ran in and out of the shop on small errands. He liked helping his father hang bright cloths round the entrance, so the shop looked like an exotic tabernacle; then he sat like a real merchant, cross-legged and dignified in the midst of his fabrics, crying his merchandise in a thin young voice, now and then popping roasted chickpeas into his mouth.

The cobblestoned alley leading to the market place was a hot, noisy confusion of different costumes, merchandise, tongues, smells. Donkeys, burdened with fresh vegetables and flowers, brayed their interminable complaints; ox-carts blocked everyone's way; camels with moth-eaten fur rocked their long necks forward with slow superior indifference. Every day there were fights between camel and mule drivers in Greek, Turkish, Armenian, Kurdish. Old, corpulent Osman walked with slow dignity, balancing gracefully on his head a large tin tray of halva, shouting thunderously at the boys racing past him with their trays of pastelia. The barefooted hamals, bent double under towers of merchandise, zig-zagged past obstacles, cursing them in breathless rasping voices. The waterman arrived with well-calculated timing in the heat of midday.

In the cool of evening, life became sweet. The streets were sprinkled with water, the smell of damp earth mixed with the familiar smells of grilled meat – spiced karamanli sausages, soudsoukakia 'à la Smyrna', donner kebab, shish kebab, sucking pig on the spit turned all evening by bored, flushed-cheeked boys. From the high balcony of the minaret, the muezzin's prayer to Allah travelled the entire valley: the faithful Moslems joined him in prayer, and the Christians attended with respect.

In the cool dusk there was a new spring in the women's gait and a sparkle in their eyes. The hanoums' veils became secretive and their embroidered slippers curled temptingly. The breeze carried a sudden scent of jasmine, undulating voices and unexpectedly a woman's laughter that was music to the ear.

This was the best time for Gregoris to run errands. Most of the shop-owners of the village were Greek, and they liked Gregoris' quickness, and good memory, and sharpness. 'He will go far,' they predicted. 'He will be known all over Asia Minor. He will sell silk in Smyrna.'

With the generous baksheesh in his pocket, Gregoris took the long way back to his father's shop. He liked the noise, the business, the quarrels, the bargaining, the easy jokes of the market place. As soon as a woman appeared at the corner of the street the fishermen started in exuberant chorus:

'What a plump lovely mullet I have for you today! What a delicate sardine, what a delicious little anchovy! Aman what freshness, aman what beauty, aman manoula mou! Look how it moves, how it writhes!' With active hands they stirred the mounds of acquiescent fish.

Gregoris arrived at his father's shop full of pleasures and business – requests for samples of the new cottons from Konstantinopolis, the brocades from Smyrna, for so many yards of raw silk, for so many pairs of lace curtains; greetings for Mr Vangelis, regards to his charming wife, they would hope to pay their respects next Sunday after church . . .

With the fall of darkness, the market place grew quiet. The shop-keepers gathered outside their shops in small groups – Greeks with Greeks, Turks with Turks – for a drink of raki and good company. Gregoris liked to sit among them and listen to their unhurried talk. The discussion moved from business through local politics to world crises and old histories. They fell respectfully silent when they were joined by the schoolmaster, Mr Iakovides, who had been educated at the Evangelical School in Smyrna and knew his Greek history by heart, and was full of moving stories and anecdotes. He spoke in a sweet voice, with emotion and drama, in perfect archaic katharevousa Greek.

He talked about the Greeks who had moved to this coast three thousand years ago, and had civilised it and created the Greek language and Greek art; and about blind Homer, admired all over the world, who was born and raised on this very soil – he stamped with enthusiasm on the ground, raising a cloud of red dust – and about the Trojan War, the wiles of Ulysses, the prophecies of Kassandra, the tears of Hecuba and Andromache. He talked about the Golden Fleece which Jason and his sailors came to steal, about Medea the witch who followed them and cut her brother into pieces, and scattered the pieces in the sea to break her father's heart and stop him from pursuing them. He then drew moral lessons from these stories: the treasures of Troy and the Golden Fleece were the envied wealth and riches of this land. The merchants listened in silent wonder and shook their heads with understanding and agreement. The schoolmaster also talked about the fall of Konstantinopolis and brought tears to their eyes. And about the brave deeds of 1821: the young priest Athanasios Diakos martyred at the hands of the Turks; the brave women of Soulli singing and dancing on the cliffs of Zalongo and hurling themselves down one by one with their babies in their arms . . . His voice became low and elegiac, and the listeners' hearts trembled with fear and pride. He talked about the Great Idea; one day, with the help of God and the Tsar and Holy Russia – the brave defender of Orthodoxy – Greece would win back Konstantinopolis, and the lands of the Black Sea, and the Ionian Coast, all that was once hers. One day, poor suffering Mother Greece would embrace her scattered, persecuted children . . . one day . . . A reverent nostalgia filled their hearts. By and by they all became silent, listening, as the scent of jasmine soothed the night, to the sweet, swooning wail of a distant baglama.

Gregoris and his family spent August with relatives on the coast. He loved those summers by the Sea of Marmara. The large leisurely picnics on white tablecloths spread in the shady orchards; strumming on his cousin's mandoline while the others lay in the dappled shade; admiring his mother dancing with her sister and cousins in the garden in the late evening; lying on the beach with relatives and friends in the moonlight listening to the waves and saying little; watering the vegetable garden in the cool of the morning; going night-fishing with his father, the excitement of the tug at the end of the line, struggling to keep awake as the dying fish gave sudden breathless jumps about his feet, finally falling asleep to the gentle rocking of the stars. Playing all day with his brothers in the shallows, and learning how to swim in the blue deep – 'trust the water', his father would say as he held them lightly under the chin – and his mother calling from the shore, calling and waving to them with her white silk scarf, 'Come back, time to come back . . .' But father and the boys were enjoying themselves, and took their time.

The family returned home for the grape harvest. The entire village moved out to the vineyards: the houses and shops stood startled by the loss of young life, while on the terraced hillside the familiar noises of birds and crickets were hushed by the abrupt invasion. The yellowing vines waved their tendrils blindly, delivering their gathered colour and flavour, their year's life, in the midst of such unfamiliar mirthfulness. The women cut the bunches of grapes and attentively filled the baskets; the men loaded the crop on mules and donkeys; the children moved from vineyard to vineyard offering help and spreading havoc.

The over-ripe grapes went to the local presses where mothers and children joined in mysterious merriment. Gregoris loved his mother in the grape season. He was filled with rare delight watching the women, with their skirts tucked up, dancing with abandon in the red juicy pulp, while he and the other children stomped wildly in the midst of those happy women, falling with unrestrained shrieks of laughter into the grapes, until they dripped with their red sweet juice.

In the sweet warmth of the early evening Gregoris and his mother walked home barefoot through the harvested vineyards. He watched his own and his mother's grape-stained feet move unhurriedly, almost in one rhythm, kicking up as they went a small, noiseless cloud of fine warm earth. He felt her hand hold his securely, and felt with pleasure the light swing of their arms. To right and left the empty vines rested lightly on their supports. The large orange circle of the sun hung low, above the distant sea; on the hillside the village, surrounded by orchards and olive groves, lay in a warm haze. Gregoris walked with eyes half-closed into the unstable sun-dazzle. Before them and behind them were companies of women and children: a varying hum of voices, with occasional laughter or a brief tune, travelled through the vine-yards. Naked feet made a soft feathery sound on the tilled earth. He felt through his hands the free rhythmical movement of his mother's body: 'Sing, will you sing?' he asked her, and she, smiling with pleasure and mischief, started his favourite song, 'My son, my cherished son . . .' The syllables hung on a note, then sprang and danced into lasting tremulous words; and he lost himself in the trembling and rippling of her voice, and the smell of crushed grapes.

The companies of mothers and children stopped at the spring outside the village to wash. The children pushed and shouted and splashed water at each other. He looked at his mother's naked wet limbs – the drops of water on her skin caught the light of the disappearing sun. He stood in the failing light abandoning his small, tired body into her familiar hands.

The autumn of 1913 was sober. Greeks and Turks didn't work together at the vineyards that year, visits between them became less frequent. The long mouhabetis between the women at their front doors had stopped.

Gregoris' father came back from a shopping trip to Smyrna with exciting news: the Greeks were fighting the Turks in Macedonia; they were winning, and pushing the Turks out of Macedonia and Thrace, soon they might even retake Konstantinopolis – soon Greece might take possession of all of its unredeemed lands. But there was also fear of reprisals by the Turks against the Greeks of Turkey; the Young Turks were spreading hate against the Greeks; the Sultan had opened his prisons, and let out all the thieves and murderers – the scum of the earth – and given them guns; the mountains were now full of tsettes, murderous brigands, waiting for the word to start pillaging Christian villages.

Although it was well into October, the weather was warm and mild, and everyone came out on Sunday afternoon to catch a last glimpse of summer. People looked satisfied after their big midday meal and afternoon rest. The Gregoriou family wore their new Frankish clothes from Smyrna. Father and sons had a similar look of solemnity and restraint in their dark suits and white shirts; the boys took heavy awkward steps in their new, unbending, patent-leather shoes. Their father looked proudly at their mother, beaming in her Greek jewellery and the new European dress that showed her thin waist; but he was displeased with the low décolletage and told her to cover herself with her shawl. She would have none of that – this was the latest fashion, you could see it in the magazine, there was no question of wearing a shawl in this heat. They walked up and down the road meeting friends and acquaintances. The men walked ahead discussing business and politics, the recent fighting in Macedonia, and its repercussions for the Greeks of Asia Minor; the women followed, complimenting each other on their dresses; the children lagged far behind complaining of blistered feet. They finally sat at the cafeneion at the square and waited for '*les attractions*'. By sunset, the taverns at the square were full of people, the smell of grilled meat made mouths water, the waiters whirled like dervishes trying to please an entire impatient greedy village, keeping everyone happy with raki and oriental delicacies while the assistants patiently turned young pigs and lambs on the spit. The musicians soon started playing karsilamades and zebekika – some in Turkish, some in Greek, to please everybody. On that Sunday, the few Turks of the village sat separately.

The Greeks celebrated the latest victories in Macedonia: they danced arm in arm, in a circle, to the Greek songs; and they danced in pairs to the languid Turkish amanes. The Turks looked serious and displeased, but said nothing. Two young Greeks, who had had several glasses of raki, got up and danced a Turkish karsilama with exaggerated feminine gestures, moving sensuous hips and coy shoulders, rotating their bellies, and rolling their eyes and hiding their faces in mimicry of coy hanoums, behind invisible veils. The Greeks laughed, an angry Turk got up and stopped the music. There was an ominous hush when the musicians started playing, at the Greeks' request, the Macedonian sword dance. A group of young Greeks walked defiantly to the centre, tied scarfs round their foreheads, and unsheathed their swords. They danced with vigour, agility, grace – now tearing the air with their swords, now clashing them, jumping over them. Greeks and Turks listened to the blades clanging, grating, scraping together in an enduring caress. The clashes were accompanied by small explosions of breath and sound, of effort and pride – 'hoppa, yassou'. The other Greeks joined in; the Turks looked dark, unforgiving.

The village crier, Iordanis, walked proudly to the centre of the square clanging his cowbell; the children teased him but he paid no attention. He cleared his throat noisily, waiting for all other sounds to subside.

'Aman yavroum, stop the mouhabeti and give me your attention. I have great delights in store for you. Your eyes will look upon wonders and miracles tonight. We have the good fortune to have amongst us – a great, a world-famous artist. Who pierces girls' bodies with huge sharp scimitars, without shedding a drop of blood! Who swallows fire, and stays cool as the evening dew!' Iordanis' voice rose with emotion. 'Who sticks needles and knives into his body without a sigh or moan of pain! He will make your hearts go pata-kiouta pata-kiouta with terror.' Children were crying 'pata-kiouta, pata-kiouta' in chorus. 'He is the renowned Greek magician from Poli: none other than the great Policleitos Politis. And – be quiet, be patient, yavroum – and with him the fearless, the beautiful houri, who fills all hearts with ach kai vach, the sweet as honey – Leila.'

General exclamation: children fainted into each other's arms shrieking 'ach kai vach, ach kai vach.' A black-browed, black-bearded man in clothes that were an odd mixture of European and oriental was bowing low to the excited population while a few steps behind a plump, sallow girl wrapped in a flimsy embroidered veil was curtseying and smiling wearily in all directions. They were soon surrounded by boxes, pigeons, knives, hats, colourful scarves. Everyone was awe-struck when the scimitar passed through the box, and the girl hopped out heavily, unscathed; or when flames jumped out of the magician's mouth, and needles went through his cheeks. People approached and made sure. The astonishment was followed by noisy pleasure when in the finale the girl made her belly wriggle and writhe.

Iordanis clanged his bell. 'Aman yavroum, be quiet, I have more delights for you. Prepare your souls for wonder, prepare your hearts for fright. You will have the rare good fortune to witness a meeting that will give heart attacks to old women and abortions to young mothers – a meeting between the famous Turk, the official wrestler at the court of the great Sultan himself, the unbeatable Efendi Hasan – otherwise known as Boulderhead! And against him, his only worthy opponent, the greatest Greek wrestler of all times, the glory of Ionia, the pride of Hellenism, the son of proud Koutali, our own Panayis Koutalianos.'

Among shouts and whistles, the two men stomped towards each other, slow, heavy, threatening – huge men with shaven heads, wild looks, and layer upon layer of oily fat flesh. They came together and were locked in slow, slippery, long embraces, that made their faces go red and their eyes bulge. They parted with sudden jumps and groans, but came together again, pawing at each other like huge toddlers, grasping and clinging passionately to each other, held in tortuous love-holds, until with growls of pain they flung apart and, trium-phantly, back together. They lie and roll together on the dusty ground. Now the Turk is on top and the Greek down, now the Greek is on top hitting the Turk who lies on his back, groaning like a wounded boar. Frightened children cling to their mothers, but still watch. The crowds shout in Greek, in Turkish. Panayis the Greek is down, covered in dirt, the Turk is sitting on top of him striking his face, his chest, his windpipe. People get up from their seats, call out, 'Enough.' He goes on. People shout, 'You will kill him, stop.' The Turk does not stop until Panayis stops resisting, his dusty fat body lying flabbily under the weight of the Turk who now jumps on him with all his strength. The women shriek, 'He's killing him, stop him, someone stop him.' It took several men to get hold of him and push him away.

Spirits were low for the rest of the evening. As the tired families prepared to go home, a small company of Turks, young and most of them strangers, strutted through the square, ostentatiously carrying new rifles. The Greeks recognised amongst them a criminal from the neighbouring village who was meant to be in jail. He and his friends sat noisily at the cafeneion and ordered the sleepy musicians to play.

The following morning, a young Greek, twenty-two years of age, was found stabbed to death on the outskirts of the village. His two elder brothers armed themselves and joined a Greek guerilla band in the hills. War had arrived.

Gregoris looked through the shop window at the endless, slow procession of people, animals and vehicles: exhausted men and women pulled carts and wheelbarrows loaded with household furniture, kitchen utensils, babies and grandparents; hordes of children ran alongside, with goats and sheep, the odd cow. They were Turks from Macedonia and Thrace looking for a new home in Turkey. On the first days the Greeks sold or gave them food, drink and clothing; later they felt the threat to themselves and to their homes, and stayed inside locked shops and houses, watching the menacing army of hungry people move through the deserted streets. There were rumours now that the Greek communities on the coast would be deported to the interior of Turkey to make room for the Turkish refugees.

On his way from school to his father's shop one afternoon, Gregoris met an alarmed crowd of people in the village square. Iordanis the town-crier was clanging his big cowbell. He waited until everyone was quiet – so quiet that you could hear the rasping noise of his chest as he prepared for his announcement.

'Moslems and Christians, Subjects of the Ottoman Empire,' he started in a quivering but loud and solemn voice. 'I have black tidings, they make my heart ache. A great war is shaking the foundations. Europe will crack. Austro-Germany has proclaimed war against the Ingleterra, Frangia, and the Holy Russia, Mother of our Orthodoxy. And our Great Sultan, long be his life, has taken the decision to side with the Kaiser.'

Everyone was stunned and silent – then a bombardment of questions, guesses, predictions. Iordanis clanged his bell again:

'Aman yavroum, be quiet, I haven't finished; worse is to come. Our great Sultan has issued a firmani: it is his wish and order that all his subjects – I repeat, all his subjects – Moslems and Christians, from the age of twenty-two to the age of forty, join the army.'

11

More bad news arrived. The Greeks who had joined the army were not given uniforms, or guns. They were not trusted, and were not sent to fight. They were sent to the Amele Tabour, work camps which had suddenly appeared in the far depths of Turkey, where not even thistles grew. The Greeks were sent there to break mountains and make roads – roads for whom? Roads for what? – out in the wilderness.

Gregoris' mother was inconsolable. 'Ah! Who knows on what mountains my love will spend the winter!' Her husband comforted her, as if the disaster had fallen more heavily on her than on anyone else.

'It's the quickest way to get rid of us,' Gregoris' father confided to his brother-in-law. 'This is not a Turkish idea, Panayioti. The Turks! The Turks are naive, they haven't woken up yet. This is a German invention. They were spreading their propaganda in Turkey even before the war broke out. Smyrna was full of German specialists when I was there, financial advisers they called them. And you know what they told our Turkish bumpkins? You know what ideas they sold them? Look at this!'

He took out of the drawer an old yellowed newspaper and several leaflets, and showed his brother-in-law, who looked at the documents in thorough confusion.

'Get rid of the Greeks and the Armenians. Get rid of the parasites, who enjoy the wealth of your country. Get rid of the leeches, who suck your blood.

'And the question, Panayioti mou, is why? Would the Kaiser have a bellyache for the Turks? No! The Kaiser wants all this for himself – our wheat, our olives, our silks, our wine. Because, Panayioti, there is wealth in this country.' He pronounced the words slowly, emphatically. 'Real wealth! And it's not only what you see, the grapes, the oil, the wheat. The real wealth, Panayioti,' he came near the amazed Panayioti and whispered, 'the real wealth is – underneath. Underneath this very ground, underneath the entire Aegean.' He stamped his foot on the floor. 'Oil, Panayioti mou, oil! That's why I'm buying all that land on the Marmara coast. And the stupid Turk hasn't a clue. Because that land will be a gold-mine one day; but gold without this' – he pointed to his forehead – 'is bok, shit, with your sympathy. Where would the Turks be without the Greek wits and know-how? Look at them – their hubble-bubbles, their houris, their pilafs, their arati. That's all they want. That's life, that's happiness. If it was not for us they would still be in the Middle Ages – they are in the Middle Ages. They have no crab in here' – he beat his chest – 'no crab.'

He shook his head, overcome suddenly by exasperation – that he had in him all these possibilities, these plans, the cleverness, the foresight, the appetite: and he was bound for where? For what? Breaking stones at the Amele Tabour! He became silent, depressed.

Uncle Panayiotis shook his head pensively, and Kyr Vangelis continued in a quiet, philosophical vein, recalling now the schoolmaster's stories.

'We are basking on the Golden Fleece! You know the story of the Golden Fleece, Panayioti? A very true, very wise story. Germany,' he started slowly, thoughtfully, 'Germany is like Jason, who came to these shores to steal the Golden Fleece – its treasures, its riches, its gold.'

'But Jason was Greek . . .'

'Of course he was Greek, but let's pretend he was German for the sake of the allegory. And Medea, the traitor, the witch, she helped him steal it, just like the Turks now giving everything away. She betrayed father, and brother, and country, to a foreigner. She gave him the Golden Fleece and sailed away with him. But wait, when her father sailed after them, she – the murderous witch! – she cut her little brother into small pieces, and scattered them in the Aegean Sea. Just like the Turks do to the Greeks. By the time the old father gathered the pieces, she and her lover were gone.' The two men paused, absorbed by the terrible story.

'She came to a bad end, the bitch!' Kyr Vangelis concluded with venom.

Gregoris listened, transported, to his father's peroration. He was moved by the story of the Golden Fleece, and impressed by his father's shrewdness and confidence, and proud to be this clever merchant's son. He knew that he would be as good a merchant as his father and grandfather – the excitement and animation had gathered into something alive in his chest. The crab – he understood perfectly what his father meant by 'the crab in here': a small, quick life right in the middle of his being, restlessly clawing.

Gregoris' father managed to avoid for a while the Amele Tabour. The local Turkish official, an acquaintance of the family, paid them a visit late one evening; husband and wife were surprised and pleased to see him.

'Hoş geldin, Efendi.'

'Hoş bulduk, Vangeli Efendi.'

The two men had a brief quiet conversation, then Kyr Vangelis came out of the room, and exchanged a few words with his wife. He unlocked the linen chest, took out a wad of money wrapped up in newspaper, and carried it back into the room where the Turkish official was enjoying his raki. When he left, Kyr Vangelis embraced his wife and children with relief.

'We have bought some time. I don't know how much, months, perhaps a year, who knows what will happen? Perhaps the war will be over by then.'

But the war did not end soon. Again Iordanis clanged his bell. Greece had come into the war, and she was on the enemy side. What would the Greeks of Turkey do now? Could Greeks fight against Greeks? What would happen to them, now that they found themselves living in enemy country and were seen as spies and traitors? The war had come home, but home was no longer home. Greeks and Armenians from Trebizond were moving west along the coast of the Black Sea: they reported pillaging and massacres. Greek men from Gregoris' village disappeared every day: they hid in caves by the coast and waited to be picked up by caiques at night, and taken across to Greece to join the Greek army.

Gregoris was woken up one night by a noise in the kitchen. He saw a man in rags at the kitchen table devouring a bowlful of blegouri; between noisy spoonfuls the man talked to his father, who listened pensively. His mother was heating up water in the big copper basin. Gregoris saw the large glazed eyes, the dark stubble on the hollow cheeks, the bones protruding under the eyes and at the sides of the jaw, barely covered by thin sallow skin. The man kept scratching his head and chest. Gregoris shut his eyes to make the sight of the dreadful night visitor disappear: but he could hear the noisy sipping of the blegouri and the unfeeling voice reporting, uninterruptedly and incessantly, a catalogue of deaths – diseases, beatings, starvation, the freezing cold.

'They are not work camps, they are death camps. They are finishing us off.'

The man hid in their attic for a day and a night, and a further day. Gregoris was told that the man was a deserter from the Amele Tabour, and that he was not to whisper a word to anyone. In the night he listened with fear to fits of coughing that came through the wooden ceiling.

He woke up one morning and the house was quiet. He could see in the faces of his mother and father that the man was gone; life was again peaceful at home.

Every day deserters from the Amele Tabour came through the village. Their reports of defeats, victories, deportations, and persecutions were translated into a confusion of threats and predictions in the dim crowded cafeneion. Gregoris listened to the noise of worried and argumentative men, gathering fragments of fear and hope under the unstable light of the paraffin lamp.

'The Russian fleet are in control of the Black Sea,' the café-owner announced triumphantly. 'They have put the fear of God into the Turk, and he runs and cries, "Moskof gelior, Moskof gelior."' He was encouraged by smiles. 'The Russians will protect us, they must protect their orthodox Christian brothers.'

'As they protected their brothers the Armenians?' the schoolmaster asked quietly, bringing the evening to a close.

It was the schoolmaster who a few months later brought the news of the fall of the Tsar, and threw everyone in the cafeneion into bewilderment. The older men crossed themselves to exorcise the blasphemous words.

'The holy Tsar fallen! Who could raise a hand against the Father of our Holy Russia!'

'Who are these . . . Bolsheviks? Are they a new nation, a new race?'

'Are they going to side with the Germans?'

'And who is this new Tsar, Lenin? Is he a German lackey, or what?'

'If God willed the end of Holy Russia, then He must be preparing the end of the world.'

'Bolsheviks! What Bolsheviks? What new breed of devil is this?' they asked each other, as they spat out noisily the accursed name, and ground it into the floor.

But the schoolmaster and the younger men were talking with secretive animation about a revolution and the end to oppression. Gregoris saw in his teacher's eyes the same exhilaration as when he talked to them about the Great Idea and a Great United Greece.

They heard that evening of new victories by the Entente and Greece, which were forcing Germany and Turkey to their knees. That news they all understood and shared – the old men and the young men clinked their glasses and drank in unison.

Mother was taken ill with a fever. She lay in bed, quiet, obedient, her cheeks flushed, her thick braid of hair lying on her shoulder, her eyes turned with expectation towards the door.

The children were not allowed into the room. But Gregoris stood at the door; he waited for her to spring up out of bed at any moment and, smiling at him mischievously for having stayed in bed so late, stretch her body out of her feverish slumbers, and come over to him with a sudden thirsty shower of kisses. But she remained in bed. She sent him, occasionally, a weak, shy smile, and then was lost to him as she became wrapped in secret dreams that filled her with dread.

He came back from school one afternoon and found the room empty of all its furniture, except for the sick-bed; she lay all alone in the middle of the empty room, looking like a young child, so still, so quiet, so removed, except for the occasional distant smile. He wandered aimlessly from room to room. The house was empty and foreign now, all its life had gathered in the bare room where his mother lay ill. He stood at her door so he could be with her. Her eyes travelled about the empty room wondering – where was all the furniture? Where were her children? She was restless, perplexed: frightened. Gregoris was seized by amazement at this small, young, frightened mother.

At night he heard her cries. With pain and jealousy he watched his father hold her and talk to her and look after her as if she were his child – caressing her hair lying now all loose in dark, damp strands on the pillow, holding her hand, rocking her in his arms, calling her 'my girl, my heart, my soul, my life', and she leaning upon him and sometimes looking calm and at other times taken by fear. Her sleep was troubled by apparitions which made her cry with weak, young whimpers and made father cry silently, stifling all sound and movement.

One morning the children found her lying still and quiet in deep slumber. A clean white sheet followed the light curves of her body, her face was tilted to one side, the frown between the brows had disappeared; Gregoris thought he could see the slight lift of the upper lip that gave her a familiar, coyly plaintive expression. Her hair had been brushed smoothly as if by a mother's hand, and a small posy of flowers and herbs was lying on her pillow. The scent carried his mother's loved face into him.

He found his father out in the backyard, sitting under the mulberry tree with his head between his knees, and their aunt Demetra embracing him and speaking to him comfortingly as if to her child. The woman from next door was looking furtively through the window.

The funeral was hasty and desolate: neighbours and friends watched and crossed themselves from behind half-shuttered windows. There were frequent funerals in the village in the following days, and weeks. People spoke with horror of a typhus epidemic; the deserters from the Amele Tabour had brought typhus to the village. They shut themselves in their houses, avoided each other, and whitewashed everything – walls, backyards, streets, alleys. They covered the wells and carried water from the springs. They hung garlic on their doors and kept an oil lamp lit day and night in front of the icon of the Virgin Mary – the healing Mother.

Father shut his shop, and stayed in the shuttered house. Aunt Demetra looked after him and the boys who wandered round the house, stunned by the loss. They followed their father secretly, curiously, and watched him from dark corners, through half-shut doors. He sat on the kitchen sofa – where he used to lie in the evenings with his head resting on his wife's lap – with his body bent down, his head buried in his hands.

Gregoris remained curled up, a drowsy worm, feeling the desolation surround him like heavy waterlogged soil. He was unwilling to move or speak or listen, for fear that any sign of life might waken unbearable pain. In the night he was startled from sleep by a recurrence of his mother's death.

Bad news from the war brought Gregoris' father bitter relief, as if a Great War, a World War, was the only proper funeral, and consolation, for his wife's death. When a new order was issued for the Amele Tabour, he appeared at the army office. Gregoris spent the day outside the warehouse where the Greeks were quartered, but no one was allowed near the building. In the evening one of the guards let him approach a small window. He gazed at his father's tired, thin, unshaven face – there were grey hairs in his short stubble of beard – and was surprised to see his father look suddenly old. He couldn't find words.

'You are big now, Gregori,' his father said finally. 'Look after your brothers and the shop.'

Gregoris started to speak, but as his lips parted they trembled, and instead of words he gave a whimper. Someone pushed him away abruptly; he stumbled as he looked back at his father watching him.

Gregoris and his brothers went to live with Aunt Demetra and her husband Panayiotis. The two younger boys accepted shyly, unsmilingly, their aunt's motherly tenderness. They didn't mention their mother, and when they visited her grave with Gregoris and their aunt every Sunday afternoon, they placed their small posies of flowers on the stone, as they were told, and then sat and watched quietly the other visitors strolling through the cemetery. Once they asked Gregoris when their father was coming back.

Gregoris was fond of his aunt. She reminded him of his mother, in the way she braided her hair, with quick, deft movements and furtive glances in the mirror; in the coy raising of her shoulders; her voice. He watched her stooping over her sewing: she would lift her head, give a slow deep sigh, wipe her tears with the edge of her apron and bend down again to her needle. He wanted to rest his hand on her back and say something comforting, as he had seen her comfort his father.

Gregoris' young brothers succumbed easily to the capricious mothering of their girl cousin. She was their age, but she pretended they were her babies, or dolls, and fussed over them with a businesslike confidence, feeding them, dressing them, putting them to bed, singing them lullabies. But at night she lay still, in fear of the dark silence of the room and the moving shadows on the walls. The small pale face resting on the pillow, surrounded by long disorderly strands of hair and the frightened eyes, made Gregoris think of his mother.

Gregoris grew tall and thin suddenly, and moved with haste and impatience, as if he lived solely in anticipation, or in bewildered escape. 'Where do you run to, Gregori?' his easy-going uncle teased him. 'Who is after you?' Gregoris got impatient, as he had seen his father get impatient, with the temperate unworried way his uncle ran his life – his long rests after large meals; his extended taciturn evenings with his friend Sonylem-Aga over a bottle of raki and the choicest pickles; the shared satisfied silences during which both men held, supportively, protectively, their generous bellies as if they contained the secret of salvation.

Gregoris would disappear for hours at a time. He did not say where he went, but the neighbours saw him creep into his father's shop, and heard him move boxes and furniture. Sometimes he remained quiet in the dark shop for long stretches of time. He came home looking preoccupied and restless, and when his uncle asked where he had been, he said he had been putting the shop in order.

He pretended, as he pottered about the shop, that his father was there, in the back room or in the basement sorting out last year's stock; or that he would walk into the shop as if he hadn't been away at all. He waited for his father's return, and as he waited he rehearsed his own future in big leaps and strides. He saw himself becoming his father's partner one day soon, when the war was over and he came back; or he saw himself going to Smyrna and working there as an apprentice and one day starting his own shop; or even going to America, the land of opportunity – New York, Vancouver, where other Greeks had gone and made fortunes. He bought a textbook and started learning his first English words. Or he might start his own silk business: he would buy hundreds of mulberry trees and grow silkworms, manufacture and sell the silk himself, cut out the middle-man and keep all the profit.

He stayed awake at night, weaving about him a silken cocoon of plans and expectations to ward off tears of motherlessness – till they flooded his face, bringing him a warm melting sorrow that put him to sleep.

As the Great War in Europe came to an end, Iordanis' cowbell clanged stronger than ever, his voice screeched and cracked with patriotic fervour as he shouted the victories of Greece, the defeats of Turkey. He would climb on to a table from the cafeneion, the hero of the day, and read in archaic Greek long proclamations, embroidered with foreign names which had joined the Greek Pantheon, the company of the Saints, the heroes of the Revolution: with the thunderous crowd-gatherer Iordanis – interpreter of destinies, speaker of languages, from whose lips the entire village hung – at the top.

'Greeks, Christians, inhabitants of Mouryes – give me your attention. The great men of Europe and heroes of the war, Loid Dzordz of Ingleterra, the Great Empire; Clemantzo of the glorious Frangia; Cavour from the land of the Serenatas, the beautiful Italy; and our own hero, and saviour, Eleftherios Venizelos, God bless his name, they have put their heads together to see how they can bring back to our Motherland Greece its old glories, how they can return to her the lands that the Turk and the Bulgarian grabbed from us; the lands that Alexander the Great won; the lands of our Byzantine Empire. To put it in plain Greek, kouzoum, they are cutting the Turk into pieces, a piece for each, but the biggest piece goes to the Greeks.'

'Iordani, you are telling us fairytales,' a young merchant who travelled back and forth to Smyrna shouted. 'The great allies will take the lion's share and give Venizelos the bones to shut him up. The glories of Greece! You think the Powers have nothing else to do than sit around worrying about the glories of Greece?'

'Aman Yavroum, you blaspheme, and cause me a lot of pain. Of course the Powers will want their portion; they are human like everyone else; they are not doing all this only for the sake of their mother's soul. But you were always a faithless, loud-mouthed dog, Papadopoule. Oust! Qut of here! Trundling my nerves on a day like this! Kiopoglou Kiopec, Kiopoglou Kiopecler!'

The men were returning from the Amele Tabour and from their hideouts on the mountains. A few shops opened, there were gatherings in the square and the schoolchildren sang patriotic songs on Sunday afternoons; the cafeneion was filled with noise in the evenings. Gregoris went about asking for news of his father.

'He probably settled with a plump hanoum from Anatolia,' someone joked.

He listened to the stories of war, which the survivors repeated with passion so they knew they had survived. He hadn't imagined death had so many voices and faces.

The end of the war: but while the countryside about them still lay numbed and war-wounded, and thoughts of peace had not yet rooted, nor leafed, a threat of new war sprang up from ancient roots. The victorious Greek army landed from the warship *Patris* in Smyrna: the proclamation travelled the shore – Greece had arrived to reclaim its ancient rights. Iordanis' bell rang as loud and clear as the bells of Agia Sofia.

News of the arrival of the Greek fleet and army brought Uncle Panayiotis and Aunt Demetra out on the streets, hugging each other and their neighbours. Still in his pyjamas, Panayiotis grabbed the big portrait of Venizelos hanging in the front room and ran towards the square. Aunt Demetra took down the biggest of the icons of the Virgin Mary and, embracing it tightly as if it were her baby, ran after her husband. Gregoris and his brothers and cousin followed behind holding a Greek flag by its corners, making it flap and billow as they ran. Their neighbours joined the procession, carrying flags, branches of olive and bay, and nursing long ornamented Easter candles whose light was paled by the strong Ionian sun.

The square hummed with animation. The cafeneion-owner broached a new keg of wine, and glasses and bottles travelled from hand to hand as slogans passed from mouth to mouth – 'Freedom to the Unredeemed Greeks', 'Long live the Great Idea', 'Long live Venizelos!' Gregoris, light-headed from the wine, joined in the patriotic noise. As he had seen his father do, he swung his glass down so it struck the table and raising it high, still full of wine, cried 'Long live the Liberation! Long live Greece!'

The village priest sprinkled holy water and blessings, the crowd talked loudly of making the Turks pay for the Amele Tabour, and the persecutions, and the humiliations.

'We shall take Konstantinopolis back,' someone shouted.

'Konstantinopolis is not in the Treaty,' the schoolmaster reminded them.

'Treaties! Now that the army is here, who cares about treaties! Did the Turks think about treaties when they took Konstantinopolis from us?'

An old woman, known for her prophetic dreams, began announcing loudly that the time had come: she had seen the signs, and had been given the message by the Virgin herself – Konstantinopolis would become Greek again on the Day of the Virgin – 15 August. Women and children listened with wonder to her dramatic account of her dream. A huge white boat sailed towards the coast from the Aegean; for sails it had blue and white Greek flags and on the bow, instead of a mermaid, was the Virgin Mary, looking fierce and vindictive, and guiding the ship towards Victory. She said in slow prophetic tones: 'Konstantino-polis will become Greek on my Day – remember my words!' They all crossed themselves and prayed. Another woman remembered the old prophecy, that Konstantinopolis would be retaken by a six-fingered king. Other women said they didn't need any kings to take Konstanti-nopolis back, they had their protector and saviour in Eleftherios Venizelos, who would live up to his name and would regain their City with only five fingers. Another old woman remembered that just as the fish jumped from the frying pan back into the sea at the news of the fall of Konstantinopolis four hundred years ago, so the fish will jump back into the frying pan when Polis becomes Greek again, and she swore that while she was frying fish the other day, her three fish had suddenly become five. The children laughed, but she waved her stick at them and shrieked that God punishes those of weak faith.

'I don't like this news,' a well-to-do merchant confided to Uncle Panayiotis. 'We have good business here; there are troubles, but on the whole we get on with the Turks. Why risk our properties, our families, for a Great Greece – for a Greek Smyrna, a Greek Ionia? What good will that be to us? Why bring such upheaval into our lives? And what if they start another war? And what if there are more reprisals?'

But the sceptics kept their voices low, while the news of the warship's arrival travelled along the Ionian coast like a sea breeze, bringing back to life ancient memories and hates, forgotten expecta-tions. All else was in suspense while this immense family of scattered, unredeemed children of Mother Greece, raging with other-worldly pride, prepared to conquer what they deemed their rightful home. The past was within reach, time at its climax, history concentrated into story, consecrated into legend. The season was sweet and full of revelations.

On the highest slopes of Mount Ida, Zeus lies with Hera on a bed of wild asphodels, and in their playful love-making he grants her victory for her beloved Greeks. Their senses fill with the scent of crushed flowers. On the plain, the marble hearts of the ruins of Troy underneath the wild flowers echo with the shrieks of Hecuba. Will they now come to life to break once again?

When a small army detachment came through Mouryes, the villagers waited outside the village with wreaths of laurel, and bunches of May flowers and sweets. Even the men had tears in their eyes, and as they embraced the soldiers they called them brothers. They bombarded them with questions about the motherland where they had never set foot.

'Where do you come from, palikari? From Psara? My grandfather fought at Psara.'

'And you must be a northerner. From Thessaloniki? Ah, the Bride of Thermaikos! I have relatives in Thessaloniki – spice merchants, well-to-do, an old family, Vafeiades is the name. Is the White Tower still there?'

Gregoris approached a group of young soldiers and asked them about Piraeus, Athens, Saloniki, about the large buildings and ancient monuments he had seen in pictures, the two-storey shops, the paved streets, the gentlemen with the high hats and golden chains. The soldiers wanted to talk about the Liberation, the fighting, but Gregoris did not want to think about war. He liked to imagine armies parading along broad avenues in front of important politicians, and happy, well-dressed crowds throwing flowers at them, he liked the bands and the patriotic songs, the immaculate, expensive officers' uniforms; but not the war. And when the officers talked about volunteers amongst the young men from the village, Gregoris, barely of age, remained hidden in his father's shop for hours.

There was a special celebration in honour of the Greek officers in the school hall. Gregoris' brothers and cousin were taking part in it, and Aunt Demetra had stayed up all night sewing their clothes.

The Greek officers were offered seats in the front rows. The school orchestra played the Greek national anthem slowly and solemnly, with hardly any mistakes, and everyone sang. The curtains were drawn, and revealed a tableau made by the schoolchildren. On the left side of the stage, on top of what looked like a pedestal, stood a tall slender girl with long black hair, dressed in blue and white and with a laurel wreath on her head – she was Motherland Greece. A group of small children were kneeling round her, and she had her arms stretched out over their heads, protecting and blessing them. They were dressed in different colours, and each wore a ribbon with the name of a Greek territory. They were the freed, redeemed lands of Greece: Peloponnesos, Sterea Ellas, Epeiros, Macedonia, Crete, the Islands. On the right side of the stage, the unredeemed children of Greece were crouching in fear under a huge Turkish scimitar, made of cardboard, held by a ferocious-looking Sultan. Gregoris' brothers were the tiny islands of Imbros and Tenedos, and his cousin Eleni, prominent in the centre, was the glamorous, gay Smyrna. Gregoris had never seen her so happy, so full of smiles and poses. She was next to a serious girl in rich reds and golds and royal blues, who was Konstantinopolis.

From behind the curtains, a voice resonant with emotion recited the heroic history of Greece. But the younger children could not keep still; they looked for their parents in the audience and made excited, furtive signals. Finally, the voice called out the names of the unredeemed lands with solemnity, and the children jumped away from under the Sultan's suspended scimitar and walked in well-practised measure to Motherland Greece on the other side of the stage, and joined with kisses and embraces their redeemed brothers. The audience applauded when smiling Smyrna sailed across the stage, and they applauded again when shy Imbros and Tenedos, hand in hand, shuffled across the stage before their turn. The rest of the children got excited and started kissing and embracing and shoving each other and shrieking, while the school-master was whistling and trying to restore order; one of them got a bleeding nose from someone's elbow and started hitting wildly to right and left. The curtains were drawn in a hurry while the familiar tune of the Greek national anthem, made up by unsynchronised instruments and voices, announced the finale.

The army squadron moved on; several Greeks from the village went with them. The Turks had left to join Kemal Ataturk's new army. The village was once again occupied by women, children and old men. The Greek and Turkish women greeted each other with lowered eyes; their children still played together, but got more often into fights. The market place was quiet, almost deserted; in torn smudged posters on walls the images of Venizelos and Kemal Ataturk were locked in a permanent wordless stare. Silent, pensive old men sat outside the cafeneion drowsing in the warm sun: occasionally one of them read slowly and carefully from an old newspaper, or from a letter from the front, while another listened, leaning forward upon his stick or contemplating its end lodged in the earth, as if in slow difficult preparation to stand up and walk away. But they stayed in their places, in the same position, gravely shaking their heads as they pieced the news together, until the sun set and it got chilly. Then they moved indoors and, silent, joined the others round the dim noisy oil lamp.

Gregoris prowled the empty market place, stayed long hours in his father's dark shop, waiting and preparing for his father to arrive or send a letter, a message. Perhaps he had joined the Greek army, or one of the armed bands in the mountains; or maybe he was still in the Amele Tabour. He recollected his father's face at the small window, pale, unshaven, sad, and tried to read in it his fate, and the fate of this war. He tried to remember his mother's face, and found, painfully, that he could not; he tried, with pain, not to think of her face, and then her face appeared to him as if she had died only yesterday. He remembered the fear in her eyes. He covered his eyes to escape from his apparitions, and dreamed of splendid cities.

He thought of Smyrna, the rich, elegant, cosmopolitan Greek Smyrna, with the European shops, theatres, dance-halls; buzzing with the sounds of foreign tongues – French, Italian, English, American – bathed in electric light, criss-crossed with noisy telephone wires, surrounded and protected by fleets from all over the world. The Paris of the East. That was the city of his dreams, his destination.

He lay, held by the warm embrace of a dream, and didn't dare move or open his eyes, for fear he might lose it. He was running, hardly touching the ground, towards Smyrna. On the way he saw a house surrounded by a rose garden, and there were people on the verandah; he made out his father sitting on a pile of cushions in his light summer clothes and his slippers that had been embroidered by his wife, and looking up lovingly, longingly, like a child at his mother, at his wife watering the flowers. She said something to him that made him smile – he looked at that moment just like Gregoris himself, young and thin, almost a child. His two brothers and young cousin Eleni were playing at the other end – she, in white laces and frills, was mothering them and telling them not to cut the flowers. Gregoris was surprised, happy to see them all – 'How could I have thought my mother had died?' And yet, somewhere in him was a pain, that had to do with the cut flowers – a tiny speck of sadness, a minute moment of loss. He ran to make a place for himself among them, as if in an old family photograph, but woke up holding on to and held by the dream, and by a fathomless longing.

Cousin Demos stood at the door in the middle of the night, unable to speak. He stood, the ends of his mouth pulled down in frozen anguish.

'Aivali. Aivali has gone. The Turks attacked. Killed all the men. Took them out to the fields and killed them all, all. The women and children they took away. Not a soul left. Not a soul.'

Terrifying stories arrived with deserters and panicked survivors. Kemal's army was gaining ground, the Greek army was in disarray, there had been defeats. The Turkish irregulars, the tsettes, were on the loose killing and burning Greek villages. Greeks from Karaman and the Black Sea and all over Anatolia were moving towards the coast.

'We must go,' Uncle Panayiotis announced to the family. 'The day of exodus is here, may the Lord guide and protect His children.'

· 2 ·
Smyrna, 1922

BEHIND LOCKED doors the Greeks of Mouryes were preparing, incredulously, to leave. They hid their daughters' trousseaus in chests, counted their coins, packed silver, jewellery, icons, and wondered where to go. 'To Smyrna,' they advised each other, 'where the Patriarch is, and the Greek fleet.' Others were thinking of Konstantinopolis. 'At least it's Europe, and Agia Sofia will not let us perish.'

Uncle Panayiotis tried to sell what he could, but who would buy at such a time? Everyone wanted cash. He tried to collect debts owed him; people gave excuses, postponements.

'How could we know it would come to this?' He quarrelled with the world. 'The Great Idea! A Great Greece! They've sold us, they've betrayed us to the Turks, our great European allies! They get us into the war, they sign documents, treaties, territories, we shed our blood for them, and when the war is over and they don't need us any longer, what do they do? They tear up the treaties – "We're sorry," they say, "We changed our mind!" Changed their mind! And they pick up their hat and walking stick and go for a stroll!'

He tried to console Aunt Demetra: 'Don't worry, my heart. It's not such a big journey. We can visit your cousins in Euboia, whom you haven't seen in years. We always said we would visit your cousins one day, and the sea air might do you good. And when things have quietened down, we'll come back . . .'

Aunt Demetra went about the house lamenting to herself. 'And what is going to happen to my household, my dowry, my mother's rugs, my grandmother's furniture? And who is going to look after my parents' and my sisters' graves? How can I let them be covered with weeds?' At that thought she dissolved in tears. She looked sorrowfully at her vegetable garden, her potted plants. She took the family

26

photographs down from the wall and placed them carefully among her linen.

'Pack and go! Go where? With four children and a husband who is no longer young. And do what? Beg?' With a wistful look on her face, she folded slowly her daughter's pretty dresses and her own embroidered waistcoats and pinafores, and colourful scarves; her best embroideries. 'Refugees!'

The younger children played quietly at home, afraid to ask questions, looking with hushed curiosity towards the windows.

Uncle Panayiotis announced that he had decided to send Gregoris to Kalamoti, a few hours down the coast, to collect the money that Berberian the Armenian owed him. Gregoris would also visit his godfather, and ask for his advice, his blessing, perhaps for some help in these difficult days.

Aunt Demetra was full of misgivings. 'I have bad premonitions, Panayioti. He's only a child – my sister comes to me in my dreams. And with all the killings in the interior . . . We can manage without the money.'

'You are always full of premonitions, Demetra. Gregoris is almost a man. At fifteen they start looking for a wife nowadays. He is clever, grown up, and the coast is secure – safer than we are.' He stood before the icon in his nightshirt and crossed himself mechanically several times.

'If the Armenian doesn't give us the money now, he never will,' he said decisively. 'The boy will stay with his godfather, he'll be looked after as if he were in his own home.'

They had little sleep that night.

'Are you awake, Panayioti?'

'Yes. Try to get some sleep, Demetra, my heart. The boy will be all right.'

Gregoris was up at dawn so as to travel before the August heat descended on the plain. He felt grown up – a real merchant on his first real job. He put on his best trousers and white shirt, wetted his hair and combed it back with care. He looked at his face in the dim mirror in the kitchen – he would have to start shaving any day now. He kissed his brothers who were still asleep on the big mattress in the family room, and shook them lightly, but they didn't want to wake up.

'Dionysi, Achilea, be good boys. Do what Aunt Demetra tells you. Don't play out on the streets. Don't go near the Turkish neighbourhood. What do you want me to bring you back from Kalamoti?'

Aunt Demetra came to the door in tears and kissed him on both cheeks. 'The Holy Virgin be with you, Gregori. Be careful. Look after yourself, my child. Have a safe journey.'

Uncle Panayiotis walked with Gregoris to the edge of the village. They said little. When it was time to part they kissed each other on both cheeks.

'The Virgin be with you, Gregoris.'

'Your blessing, uncle.'

Gregoris walked with a quick light step. He inspected the melon patches on the sides of the road – the plants were yellow and dried up, but the melons were big and juicy, and ready to be picked. He heard the young crowing of a rooster persist with unfaltering bravado on the high notes, before it faded slowly and gently into silence. A donkey woke and burst into a series of loud, wild, breathless sobs. The familiar sights and sounds brought a tightening to his chest. But his step got faster with nervous determination, and he didn't look back.

He looked with misgiving at the landscape lying quiet, open and innocent in its warm freshness. The melons seemed content and thoughtless. There was no human sound. He came to the end of the plain and started walking uphill with agility. From the top he took one last look at his village, and started the descent. The endless feeling of loss always trailing behind him made him go faster. Stones were dislodged as he gained speed and rolled downhill before and after him, in animated sympathy and competition.

He walked between vineyards and saw the vines bending down with the weight of the large ripe bunches of grapes. The lower bunches rested on the ground, some had been savaged by birds. What a rich crop, he thought, and cut a bunch as if to relieve the plant of its burden. He ate a few grapes, mechanically, without hunger, each grape crushed in his mouth filling him with unbearable sweetness, and sadness. He thought of his mother. He liked to think of his mother in the grape season. Walking with her, hand in hand, through the vines, in the smell of crushed grapes, in the late, last sunlight, in the ripple of her voice – 'My son, my cherished only son.'

He looked at the over-burdened, unsupported vines. What a waste! he thought, and then he realised. They're all going away. They're leaving everything behind and going away. What a pity, what a waste!

The sun was high and hot when he arrived at Kalamoti. He found the Armenian's shop with the shutters half-closed. Mr Berberian came to the entrance and looked at Gregoris suspiciously. He was a big man,

28

everything about him was large and coarse: dark eyes shaded by thick black eyebrows, a thick, humped nose surrounded by generous folds of flesh. When Gregoris introduced himself and mentioned the money, Berberian nodded to him to come into the shop. 'Cup of coffee, halva, loukoumi?' he asked sullenly, not inhospitably. Gregoris felt at home in the dark coolness of the shop. He liked shops in the summer: they were cool, shady refuges, from where you could see the hot, dazzling flood of sunlight rushing into the entrance, but stopping short and quickly toning down to gradations of soothing dimness, hardly reaching the protected, dark corners. Gregoris recognised the familiar mustiness in the air and the different shop smells: of mothballs, fabric dye, new leather, spices, olives, vine leaves in brine, the sharp smell of new wine. As he chewed the slow cloying sweetness of the loukoumi, he took in the shop in quick examining looks. It was a large and well-stocked general store, with haberdashery, ladies' embroidered slippers and scarves, men's woollen undershirts, fezes, and barrels of cheese, olives and pickles.

The Armenian was wearing several layers of shirts in spite of the heat and gave off a strong smell of stale sweat. He asked Gregoris about his uncle, his family, the shop, the village. He complained about his business. 'With all this upheaval, all this patirdi, who wants to buy! Everyone is trying to sell, everyone is after cash. The clever ones turned everything into gold and jewellery – easy to carry, easy to hide.' He spoke with a strong nasal accent in a mixture of Greek, Turkish and Armenian. He moved to politics: the village was quiet now – it hadn't always been quiet, half of the population had been Armenians before the massacres of 1913, now only two or three families were left. 'But the people are frightened, kouzoum. They have seen a lot, a lot of savagery, a lot of butchery. The Turk looks quiet, but there is a wild beast in him and when that wakes up . . . ach aman! God protect the Christian heads.'

Gregoris tried to move back to the money. Berberian shook his head.

'Where will I find money all of a sudden, yavroum? Everyone needs money these days. It's difficult, very difficult.'

Gregoris pleaded, bargained; the Armenian finally mumbled a half-hearted promise to try to put together a small sum to tide them over for the time being, and for the rest, he was sorry but it would have to wait until things quietened down.

As Gregoris prepared to go, the Armenian suddenly remembered. 'Your godparents, Kyr Yiannis and Kyra Kyveli from Marmara – they've gone.'

'Gone? Where?'

'I don't know – to Marmara, to Poli? The whole family – son, maid, grandmother. They locked up the house and shop and went.'

After a pause, he offered, kindly, 'You can come and stay the night with us, Mrs Yeranoui will be pleased to see you.'

At the door he said, 'Your father was a good merchant. I had great respect for him.'

Gregoris found his godfather's house locked and shuttered. He walked through a narrow passage to the back of the house and like a thief climbed up the stone wall and stole a few glances at the secluded garden. It was neat and tidy, full of roses in full bloom; someone might have been sitting in the dappled shade only minutes ago. That thought, and the scent of the roses, and the honeysuckle rampaging along the wall, held him.

'They've gone away,' said a man's voice behind him. Gregoris jumped in confusion from the wall and started explaining that he was a relative. The man scrutinised him with shrewd curiosity. Gregoris noticed the small lively blue eyes peeping through his tanned, lined face; he seemed to be old, but strong for his age. His donkey, loaded with sticks, waited for him patiently. He took his tobacco-bag out of his pocket and started rolling a cigarette with weak, experienced fingers.

'One by one, they up and go, like rats.' He laughed coarsely. 'They lock up houses, shops, and go. Where do they go? How will they live? Who will look after them?' He raised his brows and spread his arms in a gesture of complete ignorance. 'Who knows?' He tried to light his cigarette, the matches went out one after the other. 'They expect our brothers across the Aegean to look after them?' He gave a short snigger. 'They haven't got enough to feed themselves – it's all mountain and rock, I've been there.' He finally lit his cigarette, took a few deep puffs. 'You should have seen them when the Greek fleet arrived. Strutting around in their new breeches, sashes round the waist, like whores from Konstantinopolis. Full of words, full of threats, full of swagger.'

Gregoris sat down on a stone, the old man remained standing, shifting his weight from one leg to the other. 'I told them. I am not stirring an inch. Where I was born, there I will die. I've got my donkey.' He stroked his donkey on the neck; the donkey stirred, preparing to go, then gathered that they were not going and remained in his place. He started chewing on a thistle. 'I've got my donkey, I've got my shack. There's only one person I miss. My wife, God rest her soul.' He took a deep puff. 'When you lose your mate, believe me, no one, nothing, can make up for that – not children, not grandchildren,

30

not women, not money. She was a saintly woman.' He shifted his weight. 'I could have married again if I wanted. There was a certain person, a widow, but I said, and I made it clear to everyone – no more marriages for me. Because once you are married, you are always married. And I would remain loyal to her memory, God forgive her sins.'

He started rolling another cigarette. 'My sons. Two of them. Big, strong, handsome men. Brains? Not an olive stone! Quarrel, quarrel, quarrel – they never stop. I had some land: a few hundred olives, a few acres of tobacco, a couple of vineyards. I said to them: "I've got only two children. I'll keep some of the land for myself – one soul, I don't need much. The rest is for you. Take it, divide it." I haven't seen one bright day since. It's a miracle they haven't knifed each other. Their poor mother will be watching them and shedding bitter tears.

'I raised them, I educated them as best I could. They didn't finish school, but they learned the basics, their Alpha Beta and more. I was not a rich man, after all, never learned any letters myself, but I have worked hard in my time, and, with God's help, I have put together enough to leave something to my children, and my grandchildren even. Hm! Children! Dogs are better than these children.

'They've gone. Full of big words, about freedom, and victory. And how they'll join the army and fight the Turks. "Hot air," I told them. "You can't even look after yourselves and your families, you can't keep your own breeches clean, and you will fight the Turks." Boudalathes! They wanted me to go with them. I said to them, "You must have lost the little mind God gave you. Leave my shack and drag about like a hungry dog? Become a beggar at my age, after sixty years of hard-working, self-respecting life? I am going to die where my wife died and was buried. The Turks – if they want to kill me let them kill me. I never exchanged an angry word with a Turk. I've worked side by side with him. I have eaten my bread with honesty and pride."'

He paused. Gregoris waited. 'They're all at the church now. They run together like sheep. As soon as they hear of a miracle they run. What miracles can they expect now? As they made their bed they will have to lie on it. Have you heard about the miracle? Hm, he got his comeuppance, Karamano's son. He got his lesson. He was a friend of my sons – the same kind of breed, loud-mouthed, good for nothing. He went on and on about God, about the Virgin, about the Saints. If there is God and Christ and all the rest, why do they let Christians be killed by the infidels? Why do they let people have wars? The smartass! The blasphemer! So, to make a long story short, his friends – a no-good

31

bunch like him – dared him to hold the icon of the Virgin in his lap. You have heard of our icon. Famous for her miracles. At least one a year, on her nameday. Well, she almost killed him. She jumped out of his hands, and heavy with silver and gold as she is, she started hitting him with the corner of the icon – on the face, on the chest, on the head, on the arms. She hit and hit until the poor bastard was covered in blood. "Forgive me, forgive me" he cried, "I believe." Stupid bastard! They carried him home half dead. His poor mother almost had a heart attack. He had his lesson. That's what my sons need.' He turned to his donkey. 'Time to go, my friend.'

'Life,' he mused philosophically, as he patted his donkey on the back. 'Deee,' he said to the donkey. 'Life,' he repeated, and started with his donkey up the alley. 'God be with you,' he waved to Gregoris.

Gregoris followed the dispersed companies of people on their way to the church, a few minutes outside the village. He thought he should light a candle for his mother's memory; and for his father's return; and for his family's and his own safety. He thought he should pray. His meeting with the old man made his thoughts turn to his father and mother. The terrible story about Karamanos' son filled him with fear. Crowds of people came and went, carrying flowers, candles, holy bread, offerings to the Lord and the Virgin Mary; they related to each other in frightened whispers the story of the miracle. Was it a bad omen? Was the Virgin angry with the Greeks? Gregoris wondered what the miracle augured for him. What could he offer to appease the angry Mother? He felt the power of God the Father travelling with the breeze from tree to tree, touching everything, punishing and rewarding, avenging, protecting, perhaps forgiving. What were His plans for these unredeemed children of Greece?

He entered the dark overcrowded church with trepidation. Holiness was near at hand, and pressing from all sides. The serious gaunt faces of the saints and martyrs on the walls, and the Pantocrator from above, were closing in on the congregation in a relentless circle of eternal promise or threat. The congregation, untouched by the smiles of the angels and the torments of the saints, attended to their own fears. They prayed quietly to themselves, 'Give victory to the Greek army. Save us.' Gregoris joined them: one amongst many poor suppliants at the portals of a powerful Lord, waiting for Him to appear, waiting for a sign. But the famous, miraculous icon, having performed its yearly miracle, stared darkly from its corner. The Mother of God was covered with gold, silver, precious stones and votive offerings: wedding rings, brooches, bracelets, crosses, small silver legs, arms, eyes, hands; reverent offerings plundered from disease and bereavement; tokens of her unquestionable might, questioning tokens of her mercy. The icon was covered with metal except for the face, which was dark and serious, and looked through austere almond-shaped eyes.

Gregoris closed his eyes to avoid her look, and like a good merchant's son gave a proper account to the Father. With trembling lips he kissed the corner of the icon, and hurried out of the church. He tried to think of his mother. The warm afternoon light playing through the plane leaves, the ruffling noises of the breeze, and the memory of his mother walking with him through the vines, dispersed his fears. He had appeased the powers. He took a deep breath and filled his lungs with the sweet, clean air. He touched his sides firmly, holding and containing this new, strong self.

An assortment of crippled and blind men were stationed in the churchyard selling candles, incense, icons, trading on people's fear and faith. A small group of them were comparing their earnings with animation. The congregation lingered outside the church, still discussing the details of the miracle. They stayed together to draw reassurance from each other. Gregoris joined a group of men discussing the latest news from the front; each one had his own story to tell about Greek victories and losses. They argued with the force of thwarted pride and the fever of unadmitted ignorance, confusion, fear.

The voices became low, and Gregoris felt a threat approaching; he moved with noiseless alertness, the muscles of his face trembled, his jaw tightened. A murmur hissed like a snake through the crowd and darted a long forked tongue right and left.

'Retreat! Defeat!'

Numbness. He could hear clearly, distinctly, the cheerful chirping of the crickets, the singing of the birds: a few moments of peace, silence. And then a shriek, which he thought came, in pain, from the roots of a tree.

'To the coast. To the boats.'

'It's the end. There will be nothing left.'

Fear shook the place, panic spread through the woods. Trembling hearts made old trembling feet fly; mothers, like maenads, grabbed their children and ran; children were frightened of their mothers and cried. The men followed behind; then the priests and the chanters, their black robes flowing behind them; the cripples moved with impeded, spasmodic haste.

The place was soon deserted. The candles in the church were still burning, but the icon had gone. A blind man was feeling his way with outstretched arms and stick.

Gregoris ran fast, and calculated faster. He needed the money from the Armenian, and decided to risk going into the town. He found Berberian heaving heavy boxes.

'Money?' He stopped, to wipe the sweat off his eyes and catch his breath. 'Money! The world is on fire and you want money! The knife is on your throat, and you are thinking of money!' He shook his head with astonishment and looked round trying to collect his thoughts. He wiped his hands decisively on his trousers, scribbled something on a piece of paper and handed it to Gregoris. 'Here, a promissory note. It's as good as money.'

Gregoris didn't have time to argue: he put the piece of paper in his pocket and ran. People were running in all directions, calling out to relatives in shrill voices. Children were pushed away from their mothers, a husband and wife, separated by the crowd, were yelling to each other. Doors were locked, windows shuttered. Some people ran towards the seafront, others towards the railway station. Gregoris stood in confusion, not knowing where to go. He ran towards the road that led to his village, and met a new crowd of people, distraught, pushing towards the coast.

'The army is retreating! The Turks are attacking the villages!'

He recognised soldiers: they were emaciated, exhausted, their uniforms in tatters, some very ill. He noticed someone's sleeve hanging empty. Gregoris asked for news, but they looked past him. Life had left their faces and gathered in their feet which were monstrously swollen but continued moving forward as if by their own volition. The civilians looked at them with bewilderment as they went past.

Gregoris made his way with difficulty through the crowd coming against him. 'Is anyone from Mouryes? Does anyone have any news from Mouryes?'

'They are killing and burning everything. The tsettes are attacking the villages!'

'Turn back, turn back, my child!' a woman shrieked to him. 'Save your young life, my boy! Go, for the sake of your poor mother! Turn back, and save your life!'

He felt his insides sink with fear; his legs were trembling from weakness. A soldier lay on the side of the road, his tunic covered with dark blood. Two children, hand in hand, were wandering in the fields. Gregoris approached an old man resting under a tree with his eyes shut.

'Pappou, where do you come from, pappou? Do you come from anywhere near Mouryes by any chance?' He touched the old man to

34

wake him up but the old man keeled over and stayed still, doubled up like a small baby asleep. Gregoris got to his feet, he didn't know which way to go.

An old woman stood in the middle of the road tearing the thin grey strands of her hair. 'Marika! Marikoula mou! Where are you, my heart? Where are you, my soul? Come to your grandma, my angel, my golden one, come to me, my only one left to me.'

She caught hold of people, asking them, 'Have you seen our Marikoula? I have no one left but my Marikoula! They killed everyone else, the dogs: her sisters, her mother, her father – my son. All I've got left is my little Marikoula. Find my baby for me, give her back to me.' She went from person to person, pulled them to her with all her strength, tried to make them stop. She implored, she cried like a small child, 'I've lost my grand-daughter. Have you by any chance seen my grand-daughter?'

Gregoris thought he recognised the woman. He ran to her and embraced her. 'Kyra Pelagia, are you Kyra Pelagia from Palia? Do you remember me? Gregoris, from Mouryes? Gregoriou's son, the mer-chant? Look at me, Kyra Pelagia, tell me – what is happening to our villages, what happened to Mouryes? My brothers, Kyra Pelagia, they are there. My cousin, my uncle and aunt, they're all there. I left them all there. Tell me, look at me, grandmother.'

She paused and looked at him in confusion. 'Our villages!' she murmured: 'They are burning our villages! They are massacring our people! I've lost all of mine. My son – his children – all I've got left is Marikaki, my one and only . . .'

He let go of the woman, she walked away, he was pushed by the crowd. He turned and started running – he ran as fast as he could, pushing everyone out of the way.

The pressure of bodies against him, and the intolerable heat, and the regular thumping of the engine muffled his panic. He felt his body – immobile, impotent – moving fast, forward, while his thoughts dragged him back, to his brothers, his relatives, gathering into a tangle of pain. With difficulty he caught hold of a small hope that his family had escaped, and made their way to Smyrna. He let that thought rock him into a dull forgetfulness, and allowed the rhythm of the moving train to lull the less regular pangs of doubt which, just as they seemed to quieten, startled him at irregular intervals with a spasm of renewed life and ache – like a missing heart-beat that interrupts our sleep with a momentary panicked feeling of falling.

He let his head lean upon a shoulder. The woman next to him freed her arm and placed it round him. He remained, with his head against her, his eyes shut, surrounded by the light weight of her arm, overhearing confused noises, broken histories cutting through each other, voices rising into a high-pitched wail or subsiding into mournful chanting. It sounded like a rare primitive music suspended in the close hot air of the train, resting like balm on everyone's heart. The woman, whose large breast rose regularly under the young man's face, and whose sweat smelled to him like fresh bread, reiterated her own elegy for her son and husband. Like a lullaby from the underworld it put the young man in her arms to sleep.

At Smyrna the train was surrounded by crowds bombarding the newcomers with questions, calling out names at the top of their voices. 'Nicolaos Evangellou, from Panormos! Maria Doxiadou, from Marmara! Soteria Crysostomou! Stamati! Kaliopi! Yiorgo!' Gregoris saw dead bodies unloaded. The top of the train was crowded with people, getting up as if from a long picnic. Two men were trying to hold a woman who was screaming and clutching a child in her lap and would not let go. It was struck by a bridge, someone said, she had travelled with the body in her lap. She was finally taken away, still holding her child, both of them covered in blood.

Gregoris was pushed in all directions. He was grabbed by a man, then let go. Women looking like nurses gave him directions in foreign-sounding Greek. He did not understand. He was lost, the woman of the train who he had thought was with him had disappeared. He looked for her, pushed people out of his way, thought he saw her – no, it was someone else. And he didn't even know her name.

He walked in a daze, overcome by weakness: he was brought to life by the smell of food. His nerves and senses were stretched and tensed. He joined a crowd shoving and shrieking, pushed and worked his way to the front. He held the bowl of soup close and tried hard to keep his hands from shaking as he drank between sobs of hunger. He had lost count of time and didn't know when he had last eaten, but he remembered someone – it must have been the woman on the train – feeding him. He remembered a hand pushing gently one grape after another into his mouth. He remembered the flavour of the crushed grapes and the sound of her voice and the soft pressure of her body in the rocking movement of the train. But he could not remember her face – it would not stay but kept dissolving into his mother's face. He had to find that woman of the train, he resolved, and thank her for saving his life.

36

He was lost in a maze of narrow alleys, looking for lost familiar faces, meeting only unfamiliar lost faces. He walked along treeless streets, between tall aristocratic buildings two and three storeys high; he came upon splendid churches with clusters of domes or spires, large buildings surrounded by Greek columns, decorated mosques, gardens, avenues. Smyrna: the city of his dreams. Endless. Beautiful. A true, Western, Greek city, for all the spiky minarets piercing its sweet summer air.

Turning a corner he arrived at an unearthly sight – a sunlit picnic stretching forever along the sea. People of all ages sat or lay on brightly coloured kilimia and shiny satin quilts, on embroidered cushions or in mothers' laps. What was this gathering – a bazaar? A huge family, an entire village, on holiday? They must be refugees. He walked timidly along its fringes, feeding on the unexpected tranquillity. He saw a woman embroidering, lifting her head every so often and looking musingly towards the open sea. He saw old women knitting with experienced fighting movements while keeping a sharp eye on the comings and goings around them. A boy and a girl were absorbed in a game of jacks; a young mother, screened by a jealous husband, was feeding her baby with private tenderness. An old woman was braiding her grand-daughter's long hair with slow careful love. Small children lay asleep under makeshift tents of white sheets, others were crowded together under brightly coloured parasols. Two men played tavli, clapping the counters triumphantly on the board, surrounded by a keen crowd. Groups of men paced the seafront talking in quiet conspiratorial voices, women looked in their direction questioningly.

Gregoris came closer and tried to share the shade of a tree with a well-to-do couple. They sat surrounded by a heap of suitcases, boxes, bundles of all sizes, which they were guarding with Argus eyes. They sent sharp suspicious glances in Gregoris' direction. The woman, red-lipped and powder-faced, corpulent and hot under layers of fine garments, was worrying the small, sallow-faced man with waxed moustaches. 'Are you sure you locked the door twice, Pelopitha? Did you remember to bolt the basement? Did you cover the trapdoor with the rug?' She snapped at him in whispers. She felt her large bosom to make sure that her hidden treasure was safe; then she poked her hand into a small bundle in her lap, and embraced it securely like a cherished baby.

Gregoris gazed at a slender-waisted, round-hipped girl, kneeling down and looking at herself in a silver-framed mirror: she touched her face lightly, lost in reverie.

A ripple of surprise travelled through the camp. A woman's voice began to sing, languishingly, a sweet, nostalgic melody. All eyes looked round, and rested on something that sparkled in the sun: a brand-new gramophone, all shine and sparkle, standing with pride in the middle of an embroidered quilt, pouring music out of a red-lacquered megaphone that looked like a gigantic open amaryllis. A plump, dark-eyed woman was turning the handle with measured loving attentiveness: her hand, it seemed, made the music, the music guided her hand. Her face was surrendered to secret memories, her eyes narrowed with pleasure.

Her husband was shaking his head in resignation. 'This is not the time for music, wife. We are losing our properties, our lives are at stake, and what do you think of? Music! What is your worry? Saving your gramophone and lugging it around with us from place to place! We don't know whether we'll be dead or alive tomorrow and what does she do? She plays her gramophone! When this turmoil is over, then we'll have all the time in the world for songs and dances. Madness. This is real madness, carrying this gramophone with us. I told her again and again, but when she gets an idea into her head . . .'

She was not listening. Crouched next to her splendid sparkling-mouthed flower, she turned the handle with patience and rhythm, feeding it and feeding on its sounds that healed her heart.

Soon there was no sound in the camp other than the languorous languishing oriental melody. Women with their heads bent to one side hummed to themselves; others were lying back innocently, immodestly, their faces restful and their eyes covered by an arm, a hand – asleep, awake, remembering, wondering, desiring – so desirable, so vulnerable.

Gregoris looked at the dark-eyed woman playing the gramophone, at the girl with the silver-framed mirror, at the women under the parasols, and at all the women of Ionia, lying gracefully in expectation on their hand-woven and hand-embroidered trousseaus. His hands felt small and cold; he thought he felt around them a woman's larger, warm palm. He looked at the women admiringly, looked appraisingly at the beautiful fabrics stretched out in the orange sunlight, and dreamt of Hermes, the quick-witted god of all merchants, unfolding infinite stretches of enticing merchandise for the women's eyes to feast on.

A huge sun descended slowly into the sea embracing all in its last, loveliest light. Rugs, shawls, parasols, copper utensils, icons, the bright red gramophone, all came briefly to a new life in the lingering farewell.

He walked up the brightly lit waterfront through a crowd of people and animals that moved slowly and searchingly in all directions. Out at sea, against the crimson horizon, large dark silhouettes of ships spelt hope and safety. On the land, tall wealthy buildings – foreign consulates, cafés, hotels, theatres – advertised in their bright Western names protection and reassurance: Hotel Palace, Café Paris, Hotel Excelsior. He looked to those large shadowy presences as if to two different divinities, of the sea and of the land, striking across the bay inscrutable bargains over everyone's fate. And between them, a mass of humanity milling around trying to foresee and foretell. Would the Greek fleet intercede, as Hera had once interceded with Zeus for her beloved Greeks?

He approached the fabulous buildings as if they were creatures of a new mythology – Europe, the West, Civilisation! He tried to spell their names, moving his lips with slow, full pleasure. As he formed these strange European sounds, he saw elegant ladies, dressed in superior European clothes, sitting on a verandah holding small cups daintily, while well-dressed, well-behaved children looked doubtfully at the syrupy sweets offered to them, and serious, well-to-do husbands talked confidently and confidentially to each other. Through the open French doors musicians in black evening dress tuned their instruments discreetly. Waiters moved back and forth in courteous servility, sending haughty, menacing looks to a group of refugee children gathered round the verandah. Every now and then, one of the waiters moved towards them and made them disperse, only to gather again after a few minutes. They whispered to each other and giggled, one of them pretended to be an elegant lady drinking tea with her small finger daintily stretched. When the waiters were out of sight they pushed each other with hushed giggles towards the respectable families; and ran away in paroxysms of laughter when they saw the waiters approach.

Gregoris was unable to move away from the picture of wealth and comfortable happiness. He stayed, while the dark gradually exposed the glamorous interiors of the hotels to the vigilant eyes outside. The small orchestra played with civilised restraint. Bottles of wine were brought, smiles were loosened in occasional laughter, a young couple got up and danced with quiet grace. The evening proceeded in noiseless charm; while outside, crowds of uninvited guests sat on the ground in tight groups and passed the time watching, their faces inscrutable witnesses to a vision of grace that didn't touch them. The refugee children still amused themselves play-acting and dancing with each other in exaggerated movements; finally they got tired and one by one nestled into their mothers' laps. The young dancers approached the door, the young woman brought her face near the glass and looked out: she stopped with fright, and covered her eyes, till her escort pulled her gently away from the door.

In the early hours the last guests retired, the orchestra played their last waltz and put their instruments away. The lights went out one by one. Outside, the homeless were temporarily at home, sitting close together, leaning or lying against each other. A few were asleep, their sleep disturbed by the occasional sigh or cry; most of them were awake, their eyes piercing the darkness. But the air was filled with the delicate scent of jasmine that eased the heart.

With the break of day, the Smyrna of people's dreams, gay, glamorous, cosmopolitan, stole away in fear from the army of the homeless arriving all the time and populating a city of nightmares. The bay was crowded with boats of all sizes. Greek and foreign warships stood in the distance, while hundreds of fishing boats loaded with refugees headed slowly towards the nearby Greek islands – Chios, Samos, Mytelene. But more refugees arrived every day: schools, churches, cathedrals were crowded with wounded and sick; the canteens were running short of food and water. With each new rumour of the approaching Turkish army the crowds outside the visa offices became more threatening. But most local Smyrniotes went on with their life and business as if nothing were happening. Some invested their hopes in land, houses, animals, which they bought dirt-cheap from those investing their fears in boat tickets.

Gregoris spent his days wandering round the undecided, divided city: part of her lively, unnoticing, going about today's business with the security of tomorrow – the shops still selling goods, the restaurants serving clients, the theatre crowded every evening; and part of her giving in to the tide of fear, and crumbling silently into the sea.

He searched for faces, asked for news of his village, mistook strangers for friends. He thought he recognised his aunt's neat bun at the back of another woman's head. He startled children as he grabbed them by the shoulder and turned them round to look at their faces. All men had his father's face. The more he searched, the more his eyes deceived him. And such a mass of people! The city was slowly becoming one huge refugee camp. Families, barricaded behind their belongings, set up homes on pavements, against walls, in doorways, under trees. Soldiers were arriving all the time from the front – in ragged uniforms, on crutches, on stretchers, some of them blind and guided by their comrades, others, perhaps deserters, in civilian clothes but betrayed by the defeated indifference on their faces. In each of these faces Gregoris looked for his father, but never received a look of recognition. He spent hours, days, outside visa offices and travel agencies; but he had no money to buy his way on to a boat. He joined crowds at the Red Cross and the Catholic church canteens waiting for food; he walked up and down the waterfront looking at the boats. He walked past the Greek Orthodox churches, the foreign consulates, the Greek High Commission, making sure they were still there, still working, still protecting the Greeks of Smyrna. He walked round the Greek shopping area, looking furtively through the shop windows at the grave owners pacing up and down, glancing suspiciously at the traffic of undesired and undesiring clients on the streets. Depressed shop assistants sat in dark corners, guarding without interest bolts of expensive fabric. Several times he stopped at the door to ask for work – to run errands, to sweep the shop – but he received inhospitable, hostile looks. He made himself imagine his father, in his shop, moving around expertly, touching everything into life, into money; he tried to catch his playful eyes, to smell the scent of women's dresses mixed with the musty smell of cloth; to feel in his pocket the cool slipperiness of a brand-new coin. But his own faint image in the window always interfered and spoiled the vision. He looked at his reflection curiously – how long and thin his nose was, how skinny his face, his shirt soiled and bloodstained – where did the blood come from? he wondered. He didn't look like a child. He did not look like a man either. He combed his hair back with his fingers, and moved away.

He finally mustered enough courage to walk into a dark money-lending shop, and offer his services to the old man behind the counter.

'Do you need a boy to run errands?' he asked hesitantly and, as the man did not hurry with an answer, continued: 'I could sell foreign money for you – drachmas, dollars, francs, sterling. The banks are running short of foreign money, and people will pay anything for it. You could even charge a higher rate.'

The man behind the counter scrutinised Gregoris from behind thick glasses. He had a slender, dark, foxy face with slanted eyes – he didn't look like a Greek or an Armenian. He was not a Turk, Gregoris speculated. He is probably a Jew or a Levantine.

'And what can you do?' the man asked him. That was Gregoris' chance.

'I can sell it for you at the waterfront. People with visas and tickets will not come all the way to this part of the town for foreign exchange, they'd lose their place in the queues for the boats. If they could exchange their money on the quay they would pay any rate. I could do golden business for you – I'd keep a small percentage for myself.' He waited, while his heart took wild, frightened leaps. The man shook his head, looking towards an invisible pair of scales on which Gregoris' proposal, and life, were being carefully weighed.

'Good idea,' the man finally said, 'But why should I trust you? How do I know that you won't run away with the money?'

'Run away where? With what? I don't have a visa. I don't have any papers on me.' He swept his hand across his forehead with a quick decisive movement, as he had seen his father do in an argument with a client. 'I've got a clean forehead. I am an honest man. I come from an honest Greek family. Generations of shopkeepers, well-to-do, respected in the community.'

As he spoke, it came home to him that his father's and his grandfather's shop, and the family name, and the family business and inheritance and honour, did not matter here. They were gone. Lost.

'Keep your money, you . . . Jew . . . you Levantine.'

The man behind the counter was unmoved. He shook his head. 'You Greeks! You should have counted your blessings . . .'

But the young Greek had stormed out of his shop.

Gregoris wandered the prosperous Greek neighbourhoods. Long quiet roads paved with spotless flagstones and shaded by large bay windows projecting over the street. He had never seen such aristocratic houses, so many of them together, in long rows along treeless streets. Elaborate curlicues of wrought iron supported the projecting windows, and plaster decorations crowned the large arched doorways and minutely carved doors. The rows of houses were occasionally interrupted by high garden walls covered with flowering jasmine, clematis, and honeysuckle. The pale yellow of the buildings contained discreetly its own reserve of sunlight; and fine transparent curtains veiled the interior from outside. Through an open window a lace curtain fluttered in the afternoon breeze. He caught a glimpse of a woman – her hair was bunched up in a thick braid, revealing an elegant neck and an animated face, looking and talking to someone in the room whom Gregoris could not see. That face stayed with him, and its memory always filled him with sweet sadness.

He found a flower shop one evening, and gazed at it with amazement: people still bought flowers. He saw a well-dressed man walk into the shop and point with his walking stick to the carnations. He looked Greek but was dressed in modern European clothes. As he paid for the flowers he smiled at the shop-girl and said something that made her lower her head. He offered her one of the carnations, which she accepted after some hesitation; he chose another one, cut its stem short, and passed it through his buttonhole. Then he walked out of the shop with his bunch of flowers in one hand, his walking stick in the other, and a pleased smile on his well-shaved face. Gregoris stayed and looked at the flowers – he had never seen so many different flowers except at funerals – and at the girl in the thin flowered dress. She smelled her carnation, cut its stem, and moved towards the mirror. She pinned it on her dress, rearranged her hair, looked at her face for a few moments, and walked back to her place behind the counter.

Gregoris strolled towards the waterfront. He stopped outside the theatre and listened to the loud foreign singing. A European company was playing *Rigoletto*. After a while he walked towards the noisy and popular Barba Photis which featured the famous sisters from Konstantinopolis, Ta Politakia. He sat at a corner with other refugees, and listened to the women's voices singing rebetika until late at night. Outside the taverna, on a large canvas, the singers' faces, larger than life, red-lipped and dark-eyed, tilted coyly towards each other and smiled brightly at the night air.

That was the last performance of *Rigoletto*; the following night the theatre was shut. Ta Politakia went back to Poli, and Barba Photis was quiet. Some of the prosperous Frankish and Greek houses were shuttered, and the Greek shopping area deserted. Gregoris now spent his day sitting about the waterfront with the other refugees, in despondency. Eyes were habitually directed against the harsh sunlight, towards the bay, where the foreign boats waited and watched, not interfering. The Greek ships, amongst the foreign inscrutable assurances of power, were a legible, compassionate presence; and the occasional flutter of the familiar blue and white flags was read as a kind of greeting by the crowd on the waterfront.

The first day of September arrived with a promise of respite from the August heat. The breeze from the sea reached the land with a flurry. Without consistency or discrimination it flapped flags, ruffled the water, lifted slightly the light summer dress of a sleeping young girl, and touched the face of an old woman, making her suddenly open her eyes. It dispersed the scent of jasmine that had been resting on the

43

still night air, threw the leaves of the poplar trees into silvery confusion and, gathering force, disappeared in the long avenues of the city.

The refugees were starting, wearily, their day. Some men walked to the railway station to meet newly arrived refugees and soldiers, and get news from the interior. Women folded blankets and rugs quietly, not to wake the children. An old woman, who seemed to have occupied her spot for long enough to have made it her home, carefully swept the creases of the night from her rug, and tidied a few strands of thin grey hair under her black scarf. She rearranged her icons against the half-demolished wall she had appropriated, lit the silver oil lamp that had been blown out by the breeze, and knelt with difficulty in front of the icons. Her morning duties and prayers done, she sat against her wall, guarding her few possessions and gazing patiently towards the sea. The early morning cool was welcome.

She screwed her eyes suddenly, leaned forward and peered with concentration and effort towards the horizon.

'A miracle!' she whispered and crossed herself. Gregoris and the people near her turned towards the sea, and in a few minutes everyone on the waterfront was staring at the horizon. All they saw at the start was a crazy sparkle, a conglomeration of cool bluish lights which moved, changed, and dazzled, escaping all shape and definition. It looked like a young, impertinent sun, undecided and fragmented, rising, perversely, in the west, dancing teasingly opposite the real, slow and constant sun which sat in oriental splendour on top of the mountains. The people stared at the sea, until the volatile reflections settled in the shape, wonderful to look at, of a fast approaching ship, more beautiful than any of the ships standing in the bay. Presently they could see a Greek flag waving triumphantly, and in time they made out the word 'Aigaion', in large Greek letters on the bow.

'It's from Athens! My Little Mother of God, let it bring good news!' People were moved, they crossed themselves and prayed, and kissed each other, and repeated the old woman's words: 'It's a miracle – a miracle of God!' They waited eagerly and watched the commotion at the harbour. A launch went out to meet the boat and soon came back with important-looking civilians in dark suits and starched collars, and high-ranking, erect-postured military men. They stepped out of the launch in quick hierarchical order – their eyes avoiding all eyes, their ears deaf to the bombardment of questions and petitions – and made their speedy serpentine way through the confused respectful multitude. People followed them all the way to the High Commission and waited outside patiently. They must be representatives from Athens:

44

they had obviously come with important news. The fate of the three million Greeks of Asia Minor was in their elegant briefcases.

Late in the afternoon, the Athenian politicians reappeared and pushed their way back through the crowd to the quay with the same expression of undeflected, efficient officialdom. They jumped lightly into the boat and sat, straight-backed, on the edge of their seats. As the boat moved rapidly out to sea, one of them raised his hand to his hat, not in greeting but to keep it from blowing away.

The crowd remained outside the High Commissioner's building until, late in the evening, the High Commissioner himself came out on the balcony. He was a small, slight man, in a black suit which blended with the sudden dusk and quickly lost its outline; he had a thin black moustache, accentuated by his pale complexion, and wore gold-rimmed spectacles which, together with a gold tooth in the side of his mouth, gleamed coldly at the people. He spoke in a high-pitched voice and said they should all go back to their homes, they were in no danger, they would not come to harm. They had assurances from the Turkish Government. He announced at the end that no more visas would be issued: there was no need for them. They had assurances. They should go back to their homes. He disappeared quickly into the dark room: someone shut the French doors and drew the heavy dark curtains, while the crowd moved towards the seafront.

The following day the High Commissioner's windows were shut, but there was a lot of coming and going by officials. The order of the day to all refugees along the entire coast was: 'Go back to your homes. The Turkish Government has given assurances that no Christian will be harmed. No more visas will be issued.' But new caravans of refugees arrived constantly, reporting massacres in the interior.

More foreign ships arrived, and discreetly joined the ones already there. They added to the confusion; people took them for a good sign – they had come in order to protect them. Gregoris, like everyone else, was driven by each new tide of fear or hope. They got hold of the American missionaries, the English and French marines, the YMCA ladies, anyone looking foreign, and held them desperately by the arms, begging them to intervene and get them a place on the boats. But all they got were embarrassed, uncommitted consolations in broken Greek: 'You'll be all right, everything will be all right,' and a stream of words in languages they couldn't understand. A few of the refugees dared to say that the boats were there to protect only their own nationals, but they were called traitors and anti-Christs. Caiques to the nearby islands were getting fewer, and the crowds fought, begged, bribed, threatened, sold all their possessions for a place; the islands, they were told, were full, could take no more refugees, and were themselves running short of medicine and food.

The heat was unbearable on the third of September. People crowded under trees and against walls to protect themselves from the sun. Some tried to break into empty buildings. A red-faced, middle-aged woman sprawled next to Gregoris by the locked entrance of the Palace Hotel, complaining of her heart.

'My heart, my little heart, will not survive this heat!'

An aged woman next to her, oblivious of her neighbour's complaints, warned everyone, in a strong ponderous voice, that heat like this was a sure sign of earthquakes. She remembered they had the same kind of heat just before the Great Earthquake. She recognised it. She could already feel the rumblings underneath. 'This stillness, in the air and in the sea, are clear signs . . . wait and see, wait and see.' The people round her said she was crazy, she didn't know what she was saying, but they looked frightened. There was a constant low noise, worried, inquiring, quarrelsome – no one raised his voice, except for the gloomy old prophetess, and no one wanted to keep silent. Another woman's voice rose in exasperated prayer against God, 'Why have you abandoned us, my God? Why? What have we done to you? How have we offended you, our little Virgin, Panayitsa mou?' But higher and stronger than all sounds was the desperate crying of a baby persisting with an inhuman force of anger and unhappiness. Its cries slowly overpowered the frightened young mother who offered in tears her thin darkened breast.

People quietened as the tall figure of Patir Chrysostomos, the Metropolitan of Smyrna, appeared striding down the avenue. He wore his familiar plain grey gown which revealed, as it was pushed back by his long strides, a lean youthful body. Was he a priest? A mountain hero? A saint? The agile body, the keen blue eyes made him look young, but his long wavy hair, tied back, was grey, his face lined and tired.

The crowd attended with passionate devotion. Grown men and women ran to him as small children to a father. Mothers pushed perplexed children forward, made them kneel and touch the edge of his gown and ask blessing. Old women made their way to him slowly and grabbed his hands calling him 'our father, our saviour'. Men waited their turn in childlike obedience. Gregoris stood, paralysed by the moment: the pale skin of his young face was stretched on the bones, the eyes, anxious, restless, deliberated with divinity, striking an unspoken bargain. He knelt with the rest, brought appraisingly the edge of the priest's gown to his lips, whispering to it, 'Save me, save my family, and in exchange . . . in exchange . . .' The baby's cries were tearing the air with concentrated pain.

The Patriarch directed his steps towards the crying infant. He picked it up gently, looking silently at its face, contorted, aged with unhappiness; he said a few words to it, then, unable to console it, returned it to the mother.

He gave the people some encouraging news. He had written to the Archbishop of Canterbury in England, asking him, and the British Government, to intervene with Kemal Ataturk and persuade him to keep the Turkish army out of Smyrna. He had given the letter to the Reverend Dobson, the British chaplain, and he was certain the Archbishop would come to their help. Some took courage, others were caught in sudden terror: the Turkish army, their fear, was real, was near.

At the end of the day, the Metropolitan Chrysostomos was still with the refugees. He moved unhurriedly from family to family as if he had eternity ahead of him. In the evening, news arrived from the English ship, the *Iron Duke*: the English chaplain had come to see him in person with an important message. He took him aside and spoke to him quietly. A few men approached and tried to listen. Gregoris stood at a distance: he couldn't tell what was hiding beneath the genial English face; on the Patriarch's face, a restrained violence at the centre was visible through the layers of other emotions – of anger, pain, tiredness, pity.

The Englishman's words, in good, careful Greek, were that he had given the message to Admiral Brock of the *Iron Duke* and that he wanted to reassure his Holiness that Kemal and his army would undoubtedly behave with the appropriate order and decorum; there was no cause for worry. He repeated the words 'no cause for worry' with genial reassurance, but the Patriarch interrupted him impatiently. 'Is he sending the letter to the Archbishop or not?' The Englishman meandered politely away from a straight answer, and with a perplexed face took his leave.

Fear and confusion grew. The good news that Tricoupis was appointed Commander of the remaining Greek army, and that his battalion was still fighting, arrived together with the news that he and his battalion were in Turkish hands. No news from the rest of the army. Official communications were cut off.

Late in the evening, the news passed through the crowd that the fourth Greek battalion had arrived. Gregoris heard cart wheels on stone; the noise of tramping feet and distant voices continuously passing lasted through the night. Those who had gone out to meet them came back with the news: the carts were loaded with wounded soldiers, many already dead; they were not stopping at Smyrna, they were heading south – no one knew where or why.

A small group of launches were waiting empty at the pier the following morning. They were heavily policed by foreign soldiers, and none of the refugees were allowed in them for all their begging, pushing and threatening: they were reserved for the Greek officers' families, who boarded them with lowered eyes, while English and French soldiers held back the crowds that stood and watched. They were taken to the Greek warship, *Patris*. Then the families of foreign diplomats followed hastily, with mothers and governesses holding tightly children's hands, while the children examined with curiosity the attending crowd. They sped towards the foreign warships. In the secure darkness of the late evening, several civil servants, smart Athenian bureaucrats, were seen slipping discreetly into boats. They were accompanied by suitcases containing, within a mass of documents, a dismantled nation.

There was a continuous traffic of caiques and small fishing boats throughout the night. Gregoris could hear in the dark people fighting, yelling, imploring; he tried to scramble into a boat already loaded with families, but was shoved out of the way. He could not see the boats or the sea, but only compact shadowy masses of people, floating through the darkness. There were sudden shrieks as one of the boats capsized.

At dawn the refugees found amongst them new companions – Turks and Jews – who, like birds of prey, had perched themselves at trestle tables and bought up people's possessions – animals, jewellery, heirlooms – in exchange for badges of Kemal Ataturk, Turkish paper flags, food and water.

Gregoris, the young merchant who had nothing to sell or buy, walked in a daze of hunger and exhaustion round the desperate bazaar witnessing the bargaining for survival. He remembered when he was a young boy and used to run errands for his father, but as he moved from stall to stall he could not remember what the errand was, where his father's shop or his father were. He remembered rich bazaars, abundant with colourful oriental cloths unfolding and stretching endlessly round him, tripping him up: and in the middle of the serpentine dream, his father measuring, with a proud mischievous smile on his face, yards of slippery silk, yards of nightmare, that ensnared his young son in its wavy loops. His father's face was momentarily interrupted by another, hungry face which was also his father's, and by other unknown, devastated faces, so many of them – where had all those faces come from, Gregoris wondered, and then stopped wondering. He felt he was becoming younger and younger, he felt his legs weakening, his knees slowly folding, his body becoming smaller, and, gently, kneeling, then crawling, finally lying, a small heap of a child, on a sea of silk. Someone lifted him, easily, and placed him out of people's way.

He woke to a loud confused noise, and made out jubilant cries: 'The Greek cavalry is coming – the cavalry is entering Smyrna.' People raised icons and crosses high in the air: 'Gloried be her name. She has performed her miracle. She did not forget her children. The Saintly Mother has saved us.' Then a hush, as the Greek cavalry made their appearance at the north end of the waterfront: proud, handsome, immaculate, looking straight ahead with determination. As they approached, people made way for them with reverence. But horses and riders rose through the crowd looking only ahead, their eyes motionless and piercing. They passed, in quick, unfaltering rhythm, and disappeared at the southern end of the quay. But the silence remained, until broken by shrill whispers of panicked ignorance: 'Where are they heading?' And then the shriller whispers of panicked hope: 'They are coming back, together with the army . . .' And the rest of the day passed in bewilderment.

As the day came to a close, in the sweet coolness of the summer evening, a voice made everyone turn towards the sea; and see, after long moments of attention and disbelief – moments in which myriad eyes tried to pierce the gentle, deceiving darkness made up by memories of light which, as they mingle with shadows of approaching night, can create such strange visions to torment our human eyes . . . And as all those eyes followed, with effort, that odd moment of light which is neither day nor night but while masquerading as one runs towards the other, they saw, and did not want to believe they saw, the Greek fleet, noiselessly, sail away. They followed the receding ships for as long as the receding light lasted; and longer. While from one of the foreign ships the sounds of the Greek national anthem – a hymn to Freedom – first with solemn timidity and then brazenly heroical, reached the quay, accompanying the temporary wave that caressed obsequiously, obscenely, the Ionian coast.

The anger was worn out, and then fear, fear of the Turkish army only hours from Smyrna, tightened round them, paralysing voices and limbs, pushing them close to each other in dense suffocating clusters. A large, compact family, made up, overnight, of strangers, and pulsing with an anonymous, desperate, expedient love. Hand in strange hand, arm round a stranger's shoulder, child secure in an unfamiliar lap – rocking back and forth all night to the rhythm of a ceaseless noiseless moan, or prayer. Barrages of shots came from the upper neighbourhoods of the city through the night.

Someone said – 'The Turkish cavalry.' Gregoris saw the crescent on the red flag approach fast in a rising cloud of dust and a loud noise of galloping. The crowd pushed back to make room for the hasty riders. They looked young, strong, proud in their brand-new, decorated uniforms. Some brandished sabres which caught the mid-morning sun and reflected blinding shafts of light. They tore indifferently through the dense mass of people. All sound had stopped, except for the horses' rhythmical easy gallop on the cobblestones. A flock of gulls wheeled overhead. A few faces looked up. Gregoris watched the birds, and waited for the galloping to end.

And then, it did not have to happen, it almost did not happen, but it did happen, in one moment, he couldn't tell how, why, in what order . . . A few shots were heard from the upper part of the city; a woman suddenly threw herself in front of the horses begging for mercy, the horses raised their front legs up in the air in fear; a horseman shot a Greek man dead; then hairy, fierce-looking men, riding on small ponies and dragging their feet on the ground, appeared in haste and disorder. The crowd recognised the Turkish irregulars and started screaming, 'The tsettes, the tsettes, they will massacre us all.' A crowd of people came running down the avenue shrieking, 'They are slaughtering us, they are killing children, it's the end, it's the end . . .' The British and French soldiers had orders not to interfere.

After a time he stopped being startled by the frequent batteries of machine-gun fire and the distant shrieks from the land. His ears became habituated to the stifled moaning. There was a strip of sea between them and the city, now in the hands of the Turkish irregulars. The slow rocking of the crowded lighter gave him a temporary security. He discerned large dark shapes out in the sea, and heard confused noises; he thought they must be other lighters loaded with survivors. Nearby there were noises of people swimming, or drowning, creating on the surface of the sea a phosphorescent ripple; invisible cries for help; people being helped on to the lighter, talking, they never stopped talking – of daughters, raped and then killed in front of their mothers' eyes; of children slaughtered one by one, no sound, no cry; they went from home to home, attics, basements, all; family after family; mass killings in church after church, the sick, the wounded, all. Gregoris felt his cold wet clothes cling on him like the dead on those who survive.

There was commotion at the waterfront. He saw two men, half naked, running like frantic animals towards the sea, goaded by a noisy band of irregulars. The Turks watched the two men jump into the water and try to swim away; then they said something amongst themselves and one of them aimed carefully at the two heads on the surface. The heads soon disappeared, the water went brown, the irregulars slapped their comrade on the back and made their way back to the alleys of the city. Gregoris, still shivering although his clothes had dried and the sun was hot, looked at the open sea to try to forget the incident: the sea was calm and clear and brightly blue. But he noticed dark shadows in it swinging to and fro, to and fro, and slowly saw they were drowned bodies, travelling wherever the current took them, sometimes coming together and almost touching each other, then moving apart. He watched this silent dance until the hot sun and the rocking of the lighter and the stench coming from the land made him ill.

A voice beside him, almost inside his head – he couldn't tell whether it belonged to a man or a woman – spoke in snatches. Underneath the words he heard a drawn painful yelp. It reminded him of the sound their young pup made as it lay run over by an ox-cart, dying and crying at their door.

'He was in the office of Nouredin Pasha for a long time. And the crowd waited outside. And, we saw him come out – we saw him look like Christ Himself. The long hair, the blue eyes, praying, but without a sound, waiting for his martyrdom . . . Then Nouredin, the cursed dog, came out on the balcony and said, "He is yours" to the crowd, "You can do with him what you like."

The yelping now sounded like the thin wail of a baby. The pup panting on the ground and he not daring to touch it.

'Forgive me my words my God, my terrible words, but I saw it and I wish that I were blind! Ah, my God, that I were blind and dumb, my God! They caught him, they caught our Father, our Patriarch, our Saviour, and – God will destroy the murderous hands one day – they caught him and said "You need a shave your holiness." And they took

51

him to the barber's shop and put a barber's gown on him and . . . pulled off his beard, and he gave not a cry. And . . . they cut off his nose and ears, and the cursed dogs blinded him – God blind them and their children for generations and generations . . . They pushed him through the streets – my God, how could you bear to look at your child! And the blasphemers spat on him, and he – not a sound . . . and then . . . '

The wail of the puppy was tearing his heart. The voice was a death-rattle, the words hardly distinguishable.

'They fell upon him like savage dogs, and cut off his legs and arms . . '

The voice was lost under the noise of many, many people dying and many people praying and lamenting. The death-rattle had moved into Gregoris' head and was deafening him.

'Until a Turk, a Turko-Cretan, took pity on him and shot him, in the head. And we lost our lamb, we lost our shepherd, our soul . . .'

The nights were more frightening because the shrieks came sudden and startling out of the dark, and the searchlights from the foreign ships moved along the waterfront all night long discovering snatches of terror.

The bodies of two children, swollen, knocked rhythmically against a nearby ship. They made a soft, plaintive sound. He saw men on the foreign ships with big cameras directed like machine guns against the people on the waterfront and on the lighters. A man next to him stood up and fell into the water, and disappeared.

Gregoris remained still, quiet, with his eyes shut, curled up small, tight – not a sound, not a thought. Only, now and then, he pressed the sides of his head hard, and then went back to his blind gathered posture.

The flames rose high, first in the upper city, the Greek and Armenian neighbourhoods, the Christian churches, all. Then one huge flaming wall came down to the waterfront. It pushed the people, and the people pushed other people into the sea. The sky was on fire. The moon was hidden by the smoke. The war between knife, fire and water was more or less equal. Those who were not killed or burned were drowned. The bay was dark with drowned bodies at dawn.

At dawn Gregoris heard his father's voice, angry and passionate: 'Medea the witch sold the Golden Fleece and betrayed father and brother and ran away with the Greek foreigner. She cut her little brother into pieces, the murderous Medea, and scattered them over the sea, for the heartbroken father to stay and pick up one by one.'

At dawn, Gregoris slipped quietly into the sea. No one stopped him. He stayed suspended in the water, keeping hold of the edge of the lighter. The water felt cool, restful.

He had never learned how to swim properly. But he was not afraid of the water. He remembered how he and his brothers used to play in the sea, in the summer, in the beautiful clear sea of Marmara.

The gentle push of the water made his body light. Then he let go. And started a puppy-like panting swim towards the nearest ship. The sea was covered by drowned bodies, but he remembered the other sea, he remembered his brothers and himself and their young pup, Hector, playing all day in the clear blue sea of Marmara; and he remembered his father throwing sticks for Hector to fetch, and everyone laughing at his funny swim; and his father teaching them how to swim and telling them not to be afraid of the water, and losing his patience and threatening to let them sink but always catching them at the last moment. And he remembered their mother, waving, and calling them from the shore . . . but her voice. . . her voice. . . was always lost, always carried away, by the breeze, and the noise of the sea.

· 3 ·
Cities of Refuge

A WOMAN knelt down, then with difficulty lay down and kissed the stones, crying and praying. She pulled her children to their knees, pushed their heads to the ground and made them kiss it. 'Kiss the sacred soil of Mother Greece! Thank the little Virgin for delivering us! And beg her, beg her with her all-powerful hand to bring us back our father.'

Others knelt and kissed the stones. People coming off the boat had to step over praying bodies, while officials herded them forward. Bodies, wrapped in grey blankets, were carried down the gangplank, their families following in a daze. Trucks and ambulances pressed through the crowd.

Gregoris knelt, like the others, and kissed the sacred soil of his new motherland. 'Your blessing,' he murmured, as he remembered doing when he kissed his grandmother's hand before church on Sunday mornings. But as he bent down and touched with his mouth the grimy stone, the dead animal appeared again in front of his eyes, bleached and swollen on the river bank, feeding a colony of maggots – and feeding by force his eyes. He felt the stench cling on his wet clothes and creep under his nails and through the fine hairs and delicate veins of his nostrils: his stomach, empty, heaved, and he was again taken by the shuddering. When an official asked his name, age, place of birth, any relatives, he answered with difficulty because his teeth chattered and his tongue stuck to the roof of his mouth.

He moved away from the crowd of refugees to get away from the stench, and sat on the steps that led to the sea. He started rubbing his legs to bring them back to life: they were weak from hanging over the side of the boat, so many days and nights, and the woman leaning on them, heavier and heavier, until somebody said, 'She is dead, she stinks, we cannot keep her, we'll get diseases,' and others screamed, 'No, she should have a Christian burial.' The screams, the stench! – Gregoris mused, as he rubbed and scratched his legs and his body – until somebody pushed her off the boat. The relief! They all went quiet and crossed themselves.

He remained crouched on the steps of the wharf, shuddering, scratching his body. The stale smell from his trousers was his own, and made him feel protected, and safe, at home; safe from the other smell around him, of death. He scratched his body, and the more he scratched, the more the itch grew and spread, to his chest and arms, between his legs, to his head and to the roots of his hair; it made him tremble with unsatisfied desire and pain, which he fed as he scratched, furrowing his skin with long, parallel red marks that broke out here and there into blood drops.

The noise! The voices round him! The plague of refugees spread numberless along the coast like a new race of ants, spreading famine and diseases and misery and death. He should stay here, apart, next to the sea. If he moved, he would lose the remains of his life. He only wanted to be left alone to curl up sniffing and clawing on himself, to give in to the shuddering and the chattering of his teeth and the pain and the unbearable itch spreading on the surface and in the inside of his body, reaching his very heart and mind and bringing tears to his eyes.

He sat at the edge of this homeland, this other continent, watching the millions of refugee souls journeying hither and thither, lost and searching: fragments of the common home breaking, drifting. He sat, separated from home by a liquid abyss which applied to his ears waves of gentle comfort, while loss and remorse burrowed like vermin through his mind. He sat, scattered and exiled till the end of his days, shivering with yearning, and tearing with his nails his ailing body into a mysterious mania of survival.

When the sky opened its black cataracts, the crowd of refugees rushed into the customs buildings and warehouses. Some of them watched through the windows a young man, more likely a child, walk unsteadily through the rain down the steps and into the sea: as if he was going to swim all the way back home.

Gregoris' face, distorted by the pain and the relish and the relief, was turned up to the falling sky. In a child's ferocious fight with the element attacking from above and below, he scrubbed his body with noisy violence, grinning and grunting at the sky and the sea with pain and pleasure. He splashed water on his face and with raging noises blew it away with mouth and nose. He splashed water on his head, he dipped it in the water and rubbed as if he wanted to wash away all backward, homeward-looking thoughts. He rubbed his feet, the soles, the ankles, between the toes, with sighs of relief. He washed his mouth and spat out the water with vehemence; his tongue was free and flexible. Then he stood immersed and whole in the water, which came smarting and healing all the way from the Ionian homeland. He stood on the steps of the wharf receiving the cataracts of the divine will: with his arms and hands spread wide, his face turned up to the water-whiplashes in an ecstasy of pain, exposed and abandoned to the Father's wrath.

'Food, they're giving food, and clothes.' Crowds warred round the trucks, officials pulled out a child that had been trampled. Gregoris burrowed his way through while guarding with his eyes the pair of white shoes. His arms stretched out as they were offered to the man in front of him, who looked at them with confused embarrassment and asked if he could have the army boots instead. 'More sturdy,' he mumbled. Gregoris thanked the women profusely, his eyes filling with tears from the pain the elegant shoes caused his swollen injured feet. He spotted a pair of trousers that matched, almost, a jacket with rounded lapels. Elegant cut, he could tell, he had seen it in magazines, the latest thing from America! Ah! and that dark striped shirt! He liked the contrast.

Holding under one arm his parcel of success, he bared the other to the nurses and let them inject him, maternally. The ointment they applied to his skin felt like myrrh from Arabia: the box of food and medicine contained the secret of eternity. He placed his treasures on his blanket – not all the refugees were given blankets yet, he was fortunate – and devised ways of making with it some kind of home. But his best luck was the clothes – different, with a city look, a foreign air about them. He folded them and placed them ceremoniously on the stretched blanket as if they were sacred vestments. He counted carefully his blessings.

He touched with thin light fingers his temples, trying as if through touch to put his thoughts in order. His eyes ran down the long ceiling of the customs house: the sun sparkled in the high windows, but on the floor of the huge, chaotic building, the noise and smell of homelessness and misery was rising to drown him. Remnants of families and villages clung to each other and to whatever memory or loss they had in common; using sheets and blankets for partition walls, they separated into new families and made new homes. A man – he could be his father's age when Gregoris last saw him – was trying to make a table

56

out of a broken crate. His wife was holding a blackened tin can over an oil burner; she kept wiping her eyes as she tried to regulate the flame, which gave out occasional puffs of smoke. Voices complained from behind hanging sheets. A girl of about twelve was rocking in her arms a baby yelling frantically. An old woman and a younger one were lying on the same blanket, looking at the sunlit ceiling.

Men were arguing near the door. 'We told the American – in Greek, of course, what else, in Armenian? He speaks good Greek. "Give us work," we said, "proper honest work. Charities and loans, they go down the drain. We've got skills – Vasilis is a plumber, Spiros is in silkworms, all he needs is mulberries, Greece we were told is full of mulberries. Mr Takis here is educated, he is an engineer, with a diploma and everything. How many such engineers are there in the whole of Greece? Put us to work. So many young men here are in tobacco. They can tell the different grades with their eyes shut. We don't beg, we want work, work according to our skills." We told the American, all the members of the committee spoke their mind to him, and he listened. And the wages – how can you feed a family with fifteen drachmas we asked him. He didn't say anything, he agreed. He said he will talk to the Minister.'

Gregoris' hands rested nervously on his property. He crawled under the blanket and struggled into his new clothes. He emerged a different person. The shoes were elegant, white, and with a modern buckle: they were tight, but they would stretch. The trousers were big, he pulled them up; the shirt just right, the jacket long but a good cut. He touched his face, and combed his hair back with his fingers; then looked round for a window.

'A proper bridegroom!' A woman's voice of mocking admiration. 'A proper American!' A round smiling face appeared from behind a sheet. 'And where to, may I ask? Are you going courting? Or paying a visit to the Mayor?' Other women looked with curiosity at Gregoris walking with quick decision, in spite of the agony of his feet, towards the door, carrying his home and property under his arm.

He walked through a city occupied by refugees. They moved in tight clusters, carrying bundles or pushing wheelbarrows. Crowds were gathered outside public buildings, or camped under elegant arches. Gregoris tried to keep apart from the rest of the refugees, who seemed to him to drag each other down into a common despondency; but wherever he went, streets, squares, buildings – even aristocratic buildings with ornamented windows and balconies – had been turned into refugee camps. He had a glimpse of himself in his different, superior, clothes. He should not be lost in this immobile mass of unhappiness, it would drown him. Smyrna, the massacred Smyrna, was following his steps, stretching long arms, covering his face with bleeding hands, and with her stench and heat taking the very air away from him. He should strike out, away. But he kept peering through the crowds, looking for familiar faces; reading lists of new arrivals posted outside official buildings; and other lists, of people whose whereabouts were unknown; and lists of people looking for this or that relative; and lists of lost children, and lists of children's parents or relatives. He lost himself in the narrow back-streets, arrived again and again at the waterfront, always looking out for Red Cross signs offering aid, of any kind – food, blankets, clothes, tents, jobs, perhaps money, you never know.

His picture of Greece, full of brand-new acropolises, statues of gods and goddesses amongst the oleanders, flags of white and blue flapping in the wind - that ghost of his ideal, distant Mother Greece, was banished into a far corner of his mind, while he stalked with swollen feet through this conglomeration of people and costumes and tongues.

'What kind of Greek do you speak?' he asked a yoghurt seller dressed in embroidered waistcoat and breeches.

'Vlahika – Tourkovlahika.' The seller was amused, he offered him a bowl of his yoghurt. 'You haven't tasted this in your life – cream, pure butter.'

The houses were large, square, with rich stucco ornamentation; he had not seen similar buildings before – they must be European. But he was amazed, disappointed, also moved, to find amongst them wooden Turkish houses, and hamams with domes – even their churches had oriental domes – and mosques! Every corner has a mosque! And the clothes! You thought you were at a bazaar, you thought all the peasants from the Albanian and the Bulgarian mountains, from Serbia and Montenegro, had congregated here: squat faces, fleshy, with low foreheads, small blue eyes. He made an instant comparison with his own lithe and flexible frame. And the Jews! The place was full of Jews, with their long dressing gowns and furs. And the way they stood with their bellies thrust forward, they owned the place. Even the gipsies and the beggars had their own costumes here. Every man a race. Worse than our part of the world. All the wandering Jews and Slavs decided to camp here, in our Greece, and we, true Greeks, have not one centimetre of land to lay our head.

Where is Greece? he mused as he read the Turkish names on fountain and gates; and the Armenian and Jewish names over shops.

58

He hastened his step with the anger of disinheritance. Foreigners own this city – the best and biggest shops are owned by Jews. They do not go for façade much, but they have first-quality stuff, cashmeres and raw silks, and English wool.

He smelled his way to the market place. He sighed with desire: this place had the opulence of East and West, Asia and Europe combined. The spices, the meats, the cheeses, the fish! He lost himself in labyrinths of high-ceilinged courts, each offering its own sweet smells and visions. No wonder they call Saloniki the capital of Vyzantion, the crossroads of continents.

'Panagis Aslanoglou, General Merchant', he read with interest. 'Karamanlis! From our parts of the world.' His heart beat fast as the vision of a well-fed man, the vision, in flesh and blood, of appetite itself, perhaps the god himself of the food market, towered at the entrance of the shop effervescing with smiles.

'Gel burada, patrioti! Come in and choose. Whatever your heart desires, you will find it here!' The voice came full from the belly, deep with large-heartedness and laughter, coarsened by the chuckles and burps: it emitted pungent musty clouds of cayenne. Every feature of the face and every contour of the body betrayed the pleasures of appetite: round, taut cheeks, nostrils alert, healthily dilating with impatience, lips plump and moist, which he was wiping with a large white handkerchief, as large as a napkin. His eyes, brown, the colour of the fertile earth, looked at the world with innocence, interrupted now and then by a surprised look of relish. His legs in huge white trousers stood far apart, his belly protruded with dignity and generosity.

'You must be a Karamanli.' Gregoris needed intimacy. He was ready to reach up and embrace this mountain of flesh from home, although Karaman was a long way from home. He had never met anyone from Karaman – in the depths of Asia Minor, as far as Armenia. His father used to pinch his nose and mimic their Turkish Greek, 'Po po po they stink of paprika, they stink of pastourma sausage!'

'How could you tell?' The fat man laughed with self-pleasure. 'Mana!' he shouted to someone in the shop, 'This patriotaki thinks we are from Karaman!' Gregoris made out the shape of a woman sitting cross-legged on a chair. He had seen Turks sit cross-legged on their carpets and cushions, but never on a chair. The woman inspected him, without taking the hubble-bubble out of her mouth. She said something to her son in Turkish; the son was amused, he gave Gregoris another look up and down. Gregoris blushed and glanced at his shoes and trousers; he stood tall, with self-respecting rectitude, and answered the woman first in Turkish and then in clear correct Greek. 'They are the best I could find. They are of expensive quality and in good condition, and' – he smiled at his over-long sleeves and trousers carefully turned over – 'airy, roomy, and more modern than the garments you have in your shop.'

The woman mumbled something in Turkish and returned her attention to her hubble-bubble; her son was surprised and amused.

'And what do you know of fabrics – of garments as you call them?'

'I come from a family of cloth merchants – five generations at least. My great-grandfather travelled as far as Odessa. He was known even in your part of the world.' Hearing himself utter these words, Gregoris realised with surprise that, yes, he had a family which went back generations: he blushed with self-recognition, and damaged dignity. The atrocity, the violence of loss gathered into a sudden exuberance of desire that filled his head. He desired to possess this shop and other shops, to possess land, shops, merchandise, money, home, family.

'I know a lot about cloth, I can tell the qualities of all your merchandise here, where they come from, what to charge, how to sell. I can bargain, I can sell, I can work hard, sleep little. You don't have to pay me much, just enough for my food.'

'Come closer,' the cross-legged woman ordered him in Turkish. She scrutinised his clothes, body, face; then asked him questions, all in Turkish, in a flat, unemotional voice. Where he came from, his family, how he lost his parents. She wanted to know about Smyrna, what it was like, the boats, was it true about the fire and the massacres, and the Patriarch? He noticed that she was wearing Turkish pantaloons and waistcoat, and pointed slippers. Her eyes were dry, her eyelids, heavy, made them slant downwards; her nose had a strong high arch. He wondered if she was Turkish.

'Sit there,' she said to him, and to her son, 'Give him some food.' And, after a puff from her hubble-bubble, 'Are you hungry?'

Gregoris nodded, while observing the dark interior of the shop: it sold everything from coils of rope and watering cans to satin quilts, from olive oil to Turkish rugs and kilims rolled up in the corner. The familiar smells of a general store – of mothballs, olives, leather, spices – wafted through a tangible, musty cloud of cayenne. General stores are out, he was thinking; they belong to the pre-war world, perhaps to the provinces. In a place like Saloniki, especially in this area, you can't mix fabrics and food and rugs – trust the Karamanlis! But it had potential: it was large, high-ceilinged, it wanted more windows, and more shelves and counters, so that the merchandise showed to advantage. The rugs were wasted, rolled up like that: they should be on show, they should hang on the walls. Karamanlis! he thought patronisingly, in his father's voice.

But they know how to eat! The shop flooded with new, appetising smells. Hunger for the delicacies appearing from behind the counter caught him unawares: it gripped him, he was in tears with sudden total desire. Large green olives swimming in herbs and spices, pickled cabbage fragrant with aniseed, baby aubergines stuffed with dill and basil, pink octopus tenderised in spiced wine, potted prawns as big as lobsters, salted anchovies as big as mackerels and as fresh and sweet-smelling as the sea at dawn, caviar from the Black Sea, each egg as big and juicy as a grape, pastourma – the flower of the Karamanli genius wrapped in layers and layers of cayenne, and underneath, the meat, red and moist and tender, begging to be eaten, ready to melt in the mouth. And home-made raki, scented with Chios masticha, to quench the poisons and fires of this our life. The three sat around the low carved table laden with home. The son offered the first and best of the crop to mother, the mother accepted her due with taciturnity: she chewed hard, with determination, then swigged her raki with an abrupt upward movement. Her eyes, hooded by the perennial frown of her eyelids, sat on distant thoughts. But her son was totally immersed in the delights before him: the skin of his face taut and rosy with expectation, his head tending forward, his large round belly expanding with each breath and extending with love and desire towards his prey. Up the olive and plump anchovy would rise, pinned delicately on the end of the fork, precariously suspended over the mouth gaping with adoration. For each morsel a paean of praise, a sigh to Allah, a whirl of the dervish, a prayer to the Almighty, a eulogy for His blessings, an alleluia. Gregoris was knocked back to life. The pungent strong flavours spread throughout his head, flooding it with a sudden heat, and health, that instantly burned away the deathly visions.

'You'll sleep in the small room at the back. You will start work at seven, and finish at ten at night. Twenty drachmas a week, if you are good it will become twenty-five. We'll give you food and bed.' The mother spoke, and went back to her hubble-bubble. Her eyelids slowly covered her eyes, and her breathing became heavy.

Her son looked shamefacedly at Gregoris, and Gregoris himself knew that she was giving him a poor deal. But it was work: it was a beginning.

'Agreed!' he announced triumphantly, lifting his glass.

Aslanoglou cheered, clinked glasses with him. 'Here's to my new partner! Here's to the union of Karaman and Ionia, the Black Sea and the Aegean!' They both liked the metaphors and drank to them – Aslanoglou the Karamanli and Gregoriou the Ionian. 'With the Karamanli stubbornness and the Ionian cunning! I pity the poor Jews of this city, I pity the rest of the merchants!'

Gregoris was rising in the appetising flames of cayenne and paprika, into Allah's perfumed gardens of herbs and spices, suspended like an angel in clouds of raki, sinking into ambrosia, bathing in his compatriot's benevolence, swimming in homeland, drowning in nostalgia.

'I can start work now,' he announced with spring.

·4·
Ariadne's Thread

THE COUPLE in the balcony sat upright to have a better look at the stranger watering his donkey at the pond.

'Not from our part of the world,' the woman remarked with finality, and sat back in her austere wooden armchair. She was a large woman, dressed in layers of embroidered petticoats in spite of the afternoon heat.

'Anastasia, coffee!' she called indoors, then proceeded to rearrange the thick braid coiling round her head as she examined, from above, the foreigner. Her proud bearing, and handsome features framed by thick brown hair, gave her a regal appearance – softened somewhat by a delicate pink puffiness from her afternoon rest. She undid the top buttons of her shirt and fanned herself with her hand.

'Probably a refugee,' her husband added without obvious interest. He was sitting back, more comfortably than his wife, in a striped grey nightshirt that matched his grey hair. His bright blue eyes, under a low Macedonian forehead, travelled with pleasure over the tobacco fields that spread beyond the village. His fingers were counting the amber beads of his comboloi.

'Hm, another travelling salesman,' she decided, with contempt, but went on studying the young foreigner who was busy rearranging the load on the donkey, glancing occasionally at the three-storey brick house that dominated the flat Macedonian countryside.

'Refugees! Wherever you turn you see refugees. They are taking our villages, our lands, our shops.' She looked with suspicious curiosity at the merchandise overflowing from the baskets which balanced precariously on the donkey. 'Haberdashery,' she murmured, tilting forward to have a better look.

The donkey's liquid noises of relish and the leisurely stomping of its feet on the cobblestones resounded in the empty square. The sun was high and still, and the village was silent, resting. The other houses – one-storey, with their shutters half-closed – seemed to wait in humble attendance for the landowner's home to give the first sign of life.

'They are hard-working people, Maria,' her husband replied quietly. 'They have suffered a lot.'

'I am amazed at you, a tobacco grower, saying that! They brought us all these tobacco strikes; they parade in Saloniki with red flags, they organise unions – you heard what the Mayor was saying last Sunday, you were there – and you feel sorry for them?'

'They are good workers.' Her husband gazed at the distant tobacco fields.

The foreigner washed his face noisily at the fountain, and with pleasure wetted and combed back his hair. He looked openly at the rich house and its owners.

'Good day!' he offered, with emphasised worldly politeness. The man in the nightshirt nodded back, the woman stared at him. She could see from that distance a pale, thin, fine-featured face and distinct brown eyes: he had never worked on the land, he had a city air about him. His movements were quick, spasmodic, elegant: he didn't look like an ordinary travelling salesman, more like one of those dandies sitting at the cafeneion.

'He must come from a city – Konstantinopolis . . . Smyrna probably, he has that Smyrniot womanishness about him and wiliness.' She sat back. 'Anastasia, where's the coffee? Has it got bones?'

'Do you need thread for your embroidery, Anastasia?' The grey-haired man turned to a young girl, hardly sixteen, who had appeared at the balcony door holding a tray. Her round face was already blushing, making her eyes look brighter and greener, under her mother's stern eye. She looked furtively towards the stranger as she lowered the tray in front of her mother.

'Keep your eye on the coffee – you almost spilt it.'

The girl held the tray in front of her father, who took first a glass of water. 'May you have its freshness, my daughter.'

The parents concentrated on their slow sips of the thick, hot liquid as they pursued their thoughts. The young girl stood at the door staring concentratedly at the man in the square – until he lifted his head and returned a smile; she hastened indoors.

In the early evening, as Kyra Paterena set off to visit her cousins with some of her cheese pie, still hot from the oven, and Kyr Pateras strolled down the road towards the cafeneion, and the Patera sons were

64

preparing patiently in front of austere mirrors for their evening promenade, the two daughters settled on the balcony with their embroideries. Anastasia, the elder, talked in low gesticulating whispers, now and then looking cautiously through the balcony door into the dark room, then caressing the sweet basil in the pot beside her and breathing in its scent from the palm of her hand. The younger sister listened and asked questions with a dreamy expression on her face.

'I saw him in my dream. You remember St Phanourios' Eve, when Aunt Penelope brought us some cake and said "Here, put a piece under your pillow and you will dream of the man you will marry?" Do you remember? You don't – you were very young and you slept through it, and the following morning when we asked you, you said what cake, you had eaten it. Well, I didn't eat my cake and I had this dream, but did I dare tell Mother? In the dream, he stood by the pond and looked up at the balcony just as I saw him look up and smile today. I swear by St Phanourios it was him. The same face, fine and pale, and foreign, the same elegant city clothes.' Anastasia let her hand open and touch lightly the round head of the basil; it remained there suspended as she talked. 'As soon as I saw him, my knees bent, and my heart thumped – I was afraid mother and father would hear it – and I knew instantly it was him.'

'Mother said he is a refugee. From Smyrna.' The younger girl's face seemed disappointed. 'You cannot marry a refugee, a foreigner! Mother will kill you first.'

Anastasia pricked the material in her hands with passion. Her face was squat, rosy-cheeked and stubborn. 'You are not beautiful, Anastasia,' her mother would say to her sternly. 'You had better become a good housewife.' 'But she has beautiful olive-green, tobacco-green eyes, and she is the cleverest of all,' her father would add, and wink at her. The deep frown of an angry child passed across her forehead, giving her eyes a bright greenness. It didn't stay long: she started describing to her younger sister the traveller's merchandise in minute detail – the silk ribbons, and the lace collars, and the scarves with the large printed roses, and the embroidered waistcoats, and the linen camisoles. The younger sister, with her mother's handsome face, listened with a faint, vague, dreamy smile in her eyes. She had copied that smile, Anastasia knew, from a postcard on the mantelpiece of a couple, with identical beautiful faces, embracing each other tenderly under a bower of red roses. It was permanently imprinted on Pelagia's face, since that card arrived from America, and Anastasia tried to hide her amusement when Mother startled her out of it and asked her whether she was shortsighted, and said she had better leave off the daydreaming and get on with her housework.

Their brothers came and went with their heads tightly wrapped in hairnets, quarrelling about clean socks and shirts, shouting orders at their sisters – 'Anastasia, where are my shoes? Have you ironed my trousers? My cheese pie, I have to have a piece of cheese pie. Mother made it for me.' The two girls pretended not to hear. They watched them finally walk towards the square – big, square-faced lads, legs slightly apart, arms too long for their sleeves, hands at a loss – and went back to their conversation.

Pelagia's face was suddenly alerted by a small black figure in the distance hurrying towards them with an exaggerated hobble that made her entire body twist and bend to one side. 'What's Kyra Vasiliki doing at the gipsies?' The two girls watched with curiosity the old woman approaching in rhythmical energetic distortions of her body. She was holding a watermelon under her arm and resting it on her protruding hip which with each step rose and made the watermelon rock.

'You are not arranging marriages with the gipsies, Aunt!' Pelagia called out to her, glancing at the same time at her sister. 'They don't honour marriage wreaths, you know! They don't even honour the icons of the saints!'

'Bite your tongue that is getting too long for your brains, brat! Your mother is out and you hang from the balcony looking for mouhabeti. I know you'd pee in your knickers for a bridegroom.'

'I just asked you a question, Aunt!' Pelagia would not let her go: she nudged her sister, conspiratorially, but Anastasia bent over her embroidery with new concentration – sending furtive glances at the old woman.

'She's right, your mother, to be a tartar, to keep you on a short leash!' Anastasia stared, her needle poised: the old woman gave her a furtive look, and continued to Pelagia: 'Dip your tongue in your brain, my pullet, before you wag it! Swooning eyes are not enough! You've got to have bunions on your fingers, if you want marriage: like your sister.'

'Where do you come from then, Aunt, if you are not coming from the gipsies?'

'Oh, you are tiring me,' the old woman said with a bad-moodedness that she enjoyed. She put her watermelon down and prepared herself for further exchanges. 'Where do you think I was? I went to my brother-in-law's patch to cut this watermelon for my supper! Big deal! Why don't you take Anastasia as an example – and let's have more work and less talk.' She looked at Anastasia sharply: Anastasia was counting her stitches. 'Anastasia, where is your mother? I want to exchange a few words with her.' She hardly noticed Anastasia's unwilling answer. 'Wise to hurry with your embroidery, Anastasia – you're at your time, and time flies. At sixteen your mother and I were already up to our elbows in baby-shit.'

Anastasia pricked the material on her lap with determination.

'Gossiping with Pelagia, and daydreaming, and playing jokes on your brother - children's stuff! You are a woman now, time to settle down, many good lads from good families have been dropping hints, but – the walls have ears in this town, so I say no more, o noon noeistho, the understanding will understand. Tell your mother that I stopped by, in respect of preliminary discussions on general matters concerning – but my lips will be sewn for now.' She squeezed her lips together with her fingers, then suddenly let them come apart with an explosion. 'Eh you, Pelagia, get off your lazy soft behind and carry this watermelon for the old and crippled woman.'

'Your mother knows how to deal with you,' the old woman shrieked, as Pelagia took her time getting up. Anastasia's face bloomed with anger. 'What a despot, what a satrap she is!' she murmured with admiration as she lifted her body with difficulty. She watched Pelagia pick up the watermelon. 'Bulgarian blood! Po po po!' She shook the collar of her shirt and spat a thin spray of saliva in the air to exorcise the savagery of her words. 'Bulgarian blood!' she repeated with satisfaction as she put her bad leg forward.

Anastasia watched with a deep frown the old woman hasten away in a quick twist-and-jerk dance followed by the young girl carrying the watermelon. She sighed with relief at the quietness, and freedom. She held her embroidery up and, tilting her head back, studied with pleasure the design and colour combination. It was almost finished: she picked up her needle with sudden impatience. The picture of the marriage broker's twisted figure interfered with her design and made her cheeks blush again with anger, and expectation. She looked at the quiet landscape with hate, at the neighbours' hens and their baby chicks running round the pond making such a racket, and the little ones never learning and always falling into the water and looking so silly and desperate with their beaks up in the air waiting to be rescued, and their owner giving shrieks that made the blood curdle. 'Keeping them on a short leash!' Anastasia bent down to her embroidery to hide the shame and the hate of the memory that burned her eyes. But the mulberry tree stood just below their balcony, a green fruit-bearing reminder. The children laughing and strangers and acquaintances looking away, and friends coming near and asking 'Why, Anastasia? Who has done this to you? What have you done to her?' And going into the house and telling her mother to untie her, 'God doesn't allow people to do this to their children! People tie animals to trees, they tie dogs and donkeys, not their own children!' But she would yell back at them, 'Mind your own business, ante ante apotho, look to your own household!'

Anastasia dwelt with relish on her own cruelty. She chuckled at the memory of the marriage broker heaving into the kitchen with her quick belligerent twist, full of exuberant energy in those days. The look on her face when Anastasia told her, in an innocent little girl's voice – how she managed to keep a straight face! – that her mother was out at the wake for Aunt Eleftheria! The shrieks! The hops and the jerks and the twists! 'Ah you accursed one, do you know what you are saying? What wake, damn you? I was with Eleftheria yesterday and she was as alive and sound as you and I.' And Anastasia with a sad serious face, without looking up, said, 'It happened this morning, at dawn. Colic. My mother ran, found her dying, and she has been there all day keeping vigil with Aunt Vangelio and Aunt Kyriafina. The funeral is this afternoon.' And the marriage broker hopping away and yelling, so everyone could hear her, 'What evil has found us! We have lost our good Eleftheria, our Eleftheritsa! The best of us all! Ach, what evil has fallen on us! Ach, how did you take the good soul away! Ach!' And Anastasia was still folded double with spasms of laughter when the marriage broker appeared, on her way to the church, in her best embroidered apron and scarf holding bunches of flowers and herbs from her garden – and the look on her face when she saw her cousin Maria just out of the tobacco store, in her working clothes and asking 'Where to in all your fineries, cousin? To a·wedding or a christening?' The screaming and crying as she came to Anastasia, still doubled up with laughter and fear, and hit her with the flowers until they were all in tatters, her leg kicking out with uncontrollable spasms of hate, and then left crying. Then her mother caught her and hit her and hit her – 'You've shamed us before the whole village! We won't have a face to show' – but Anastasia gave not one cry. Not even when her mother tied her to the tree and she was there all day, the sun travelling slowly down, and almost the whole village came by and saw her, and near the end of the day her brothers came home and saw her and laughed and made a big matter of it. She looked down, not a sound, not a tear, keeping her face composed and still, a deep young frown, while she watched the fat black mulberries fall from the tree and lie in the dust, and she didn't stretch a hand to take one, although she was hungry, until her father came home and saw her, with such horror, and only then, under his horrified eye, she let her body collapse into a small heap of unhappy child, as she saw his body over her untying her, and his face ravaged by pity and sorrow. 'How could you do this, Maria? How? And only a child!'

She looked up, taking into her frown of hate the tobacco fields and the melon patches. Remembering: running through the tobacco fields to her father, crushing the young plants as she ran and pulling him pulling him by the hand, his sleeve, his jacket, her voice and words lost in her tears, shaking his arm up and down because the words would not come to her mouth, and finally 'She – she is stopping me from school! Come and tell her. Tell her. Tell her to let me go back to school.' And then listening to her father talking to her mother in the parlour. 'Maria, let her stay at school. She is clever and loves reading and learning!' But her mother was unbending. 'I need her in the house. Time to do housework. I am tired of washing floors all day. It's her turn. And if she does not become a good housewife what will she be? She is no great beauty, and without a good dowry and good strong hands, who is going to look at her twice?' The school teacher came, and tried to talk sense into her. 'Maria, this is a sin. Such a clever child, and quick in learning, and full of curiosity and dedication! The best pupil I ever had, the cleverest of all your children, Maria! She catches birds in the air, while your sons, Maria, they swallow flies.' And the priest came and talked to her, quietly, about the parent's duty to the child and to the community, and scolded her, but her mother sent them all packing and yelled after them, 'A daughter's place is in her home. She's had enough letters, more than I had. Now it's time for housework. And the other one, as soon as she is twelve, home. Work. The boys will finish school, whether they like it or not, because they are boys. But daughters, I have no daughters for the streets.' And that was the end of it.

Anastasia thought with pleasure and rage that she would never, never forgive her mother. She looked at the mulberry tree with triumph: and the stranger's face, almost one with her father's face, smiled down at her as he untied the rope that surrounded, like the serpent of pleasure, her body. She passed her thread through the eye of the needle, pulled, and tied the knot. Unaware of the failing light she continued embroidering, bent down to the weave of colour spread on her knees and embroidering her hate and life, pushing into the fabric her needle, with all her girlhood's vengeance and despair and love gathering in her blushing fingertips, concentrating in each of her prickings and scattering in countless, counted stitches. But the thread connected them, and made subtle, intricate, original designs of unreal trees and flowers, and rich subtle marriages of autumnal russets with blue from the heart of an April day and the yellow of the wallflower startled by specks of gold and black. She sat there making her labyrinths of thread, losing herself in them, always holding in her fingers Ariadne's thread.

Her sister came back and the two girls sat and talked into the evening. Old women crossed the square on their way to the church, carrying bunches of stock and carnations. Kyra Persefoni came and sat in her minute garden suffocated with dahlias. She sat all evening saying nothing, doing nothing, watching her dahlias, watching her hens and their babies. Now and then she gave a shrill, long yell at her hens which echoed through the tobacco fields and along the ravine and river beds; it stirred the town square and startled the two girls into fits of laughter, but caused hardly a flutter in the birds, which continued their dangerous acrobatics round the pond.

'How are your daughters, Kyra Persefoni?' Pelagia called across the square.

'Daughters? What daughters? I have no daughters! I gave birth to dogs, bitches.' She yelled shrilly for the entire village to hear and then sank back into her silence.

The two girls stayed on the balcony, watching the occasional acquaintance go by – 'Good evening, how are your parents?' – until it was too dark to embroider, then with wide open loving arms they embraced and leaned on the rail, gazing at the fields in the twilight, and talking, talking into the night, their voices tender and pleasing, mixing in the still air with the sweet smell of basil and of green tobacco.

Kapnohori was filled with women in the tobacco season. Anatolian women from refugee villages made homes out of rugs and blankets under the plane trees. Itinerant Turkish women, wrapped in their dark scarves, made their homes across the river, that lay dry and stony in the summer. Greeks and Turks, both refugees in this country, shared the spring patiently, exchanging greetings as they waited to fill their jugs.

The Patera household became the centre of the world during the tobacco months. Kyra Paterena, with her sleeves rolled up and her scarf wound tightly round her head, flush-cheeked, bridal and hoar-frosted with a fine layer of flour, supervised the bakery.

'How can I feed so many mouths!' she complained as she pushed with satisfaction into the white dough. She was hoarse from giving orders. 'Wake up, Sotiri, we need more flour from the mill – and yeast. Pelagia, water. We need more jugs. And stop swinging your hips, you're not at the fair. Don't pack the leaves so tight, Zeynep. How will they breathe? Turks. Anastasia, come and show her.'

She strode between the women in the long, cool tobacco stores, examining their work with a sharp eye and tongue. She stopped by the refugee girls: on their faces lingered an interrupted pleasure, curiosity, a hint of defiance. They lacked shame, those foreign faces – the eye that looked back, the lifted head, the stockinged leg – but she restrained her righteousness because they had quick hands and a good head for sums. She kept an eye on them, though, because they came with new ideas every year and talked about conditions and wages. She took out her indignation on the local girls, most of them nieces, and naive. 'More work and fewer words,' she murmured, took the skewer from Euridiki's hands, stacked the leaves neatly for her, then walked past the Turkish girls, in their grey homespun pantaloons, their heads and faces hidden. She did not say anything to them, because they were not Greek.

As soon as she left, voices would rise, interspersed with the occasional laugh, or the beginning of a tune that might spread or stop short, or a yell at someone at the other end of the shed. The local girls, whose world was made up of near and distant cousins, stared with suspicion and admiration at this foreign breed of Greek women with the quick tongues and ready smiles. Their arms and hands danced in the air, as if for independence. They filled the room, breathed all its air. They talked to men without lowering their eyes. They danced not in a circle holding hands, in step, in modesty and grace: but shamelessly, shaking hips and bellies and shoulders at each other, rolling their eyes and crying 'Aman, aman manoula mou' as if they were Turks. But when they sang their songs, laments for their homeland, their voices soared into a high-pitched, sustained wail, that was Turkish and was Greek, now in Turkish now in Greek, obliterating the differences. Then the room hushed. And all hearts, Greek and Turkish, ached with homesickness.

These refugee women came to the village like a gusty sea breeze to a valley deep in the lap of mountains, that had not felt the smell of salt and storm, the sudden tingle on the skin. The Macedonian girls listened to them talk about love, and about men. 'Don't let those foreigners, those unleashed Smyrniotisses, give you ideas,' mothers warned their daughters. But the women from Smyrna had a way of talking about love: they brought in the sun that scorched the air of love; and the endless blood-red poppies of love, and the anemones hanging on the crags of love, and the saltiness of its tears and its icy north winds. And the way they talked about men! Suave men, subtle men, who wore brilliantine on their hair and eau de Cologne on their wrists, who had long elegant fingernails and always a carnation on their lapel, who gave you flowers, and looked at you from above with eyes as deep as oceans, who opened the door for you, who held you tenderly, lightly, with the tips of their fingers! Men who freed you and wrapped you round in your sweet female immobility. Men, ideal men, men of the carte-postale who inhabited only the worlds of young women. The smell of tobacco, cured by women and forbidden to women, carried the pure essence of men gazing at them through the mysterious veil of smoke and romance. And the women let themselves be drawn deep into the heavy-scented mystery, enticed by what felt like its heart, yet still unsure whether there was a heart.

'He sells everything your heart desires. "And only for women, young beautiful women," he says. "Come to my shop to buy your dowry, and you will leave with a husband in your pocket." Oh, he does have a way with words!' A dark refugee woman was gesticulating her enthusiasm, and even the Turkish girls had stopped to listen to her.

'She thinks she owns him and his shop,' Pelagia murmured to Anastasia, wanting to share her feelings.

'And he is ready to bargain; the more you buy the better the price. A queue of girls at his shop already!'

'We all know what they are queueing for – not just dowries! Ah, he is free and open with the compliments and the smiles!'

'He is known even up at the borders. I visited my in-laws in Bariachtari at Easter – my mother-in-law's navel got untied again, that woman goes from one illness to another! – anyway, Meropi, my sister-in-law, was there, and she was wearing for the old man's nameday this very elegant suit, in European style and all, and of course in that shepherds' village they don't know what Europe means, let alone wear European clothes. Still, that suit was very nice material, and a good cut, and the finishings – very nice. And naturally I asked my sister-in-law: "Well, sister-in-law, have you been visiting the city, Serras or Saloniki? Such modernities we don't find so easily in these parts of the world!" Of course, as you know, I was referring to the sad fact known to everyone that she and her husband have been milking the old man regularly, and of course she perceived my meaning, and pretended to be the innocent dove, nothing but mother's milk had touched her lips. "Who? Us?" she exclaimed, as if you had killed her father, "Where would we find the money to go to Serras and Saloniki?

As a matter of fact, if you want to know, I bought this suit in your own village – in Kapnohori!" "In my village?" I said. She said, "In your village, as I see you and you see me. At the refugee's." "What refugee?" said I, "We don't have any refugees in our village!" "Don't you know the refugee?" she said, "Well, I am surprised!" And then I realised! She meant that dandy-looking man, you know, with the suit, who bought Avramides' shop. Well, I always thought he was from Saloniki! Because to me, and I have been to Serras, to Kavala, he has that look, you know, of a man of the city. So: I take the decision – to go to his shop. I thought I should give it just a look. Why should Meropi from Bariachtari, if you please, know about this shop, and not us? So I went! And I was right! I spoke to the man, and he impressed me very well. It's true, he comes originally from – somewhere, I don't know – but his first shop was in Saloniki. And you can tell that the man is refined, progressive, liberal. A European!'

'European! A refugee from Turkey. What do we know about the man? His roots. His family name. His history. Tabula rasa, as they say.'

'But his shop has everything! It's the best in the province! And he is so suave with the girls, and makes us feel so like ladies. He is so complimentathoros – a true galantomo, a true man of the world. He could have the beauty of the village!'

Silently, with concentration, Anastasia stacked the tobacco leaves on the long skewer. She and Pelagia had passed outside his shop, and Pelagia saw – Anastasia, of course, gave not a glance – that it was full of women. And he left them all and came to the door and said, in his flattering Anatolian way, 'Won't you do us the honour?' And Anastasia felt her cheeks go red, and to hide them and because she didn't know what to say, she turned away, but fortunately Pelagia had the readiness to say 'Another time.' And when later they passed outside the shop, tightly arm in arm and pretending to be absorbed in their own conversation, the shop was still full of women and he in the centre making jokes and paying compliments.

A passing pleasure softened her brow and made her mouth round and plump. She thought of the smile he had given her at their first meeting, the lift of his head, just as in her dream, but in her dream he loved her, he was her bridegroom. She knew it and he knew it, he did not need to say it, it was fated, written by Destiny's hand, ordered by St Phanourios. But out of the dream, a different man. He loved all women. Her eyes filled with tears: she thought of her mother in sudden rage – then of him, sweetly. She imagined his face over hers under the

73

mulberry tree bending down to untie her, and tie her in his arms, and all those ripe black mulberries in the dust, but she would not stretch her hand to touch them, although so hungry, and the memory of those mulberries and the face of her father over her, and the pain and the sorrow, made her body limp and her head hot with a pleasure.

'He doesn't keep his dignity,' a voice said loudly. 'The way he smiles to all the girls, and kisses their hands! What does he think he is? An Italian? Ah! He has known women – a lot of women.' The woman held up her skewer like Goddess Athena raising her spear to protect her city.

Anastasia's fragile pleasure flowered in angry clusters of images: of him with women, red-haired, brunette, raven – the looks, the kisses, the kissing of hands, knitting of arms, all real and tangible as this needle she held in her hands and this leaf she tore and crumpled, whose lovely smell she could not bear because of the tenderness and yearning clinging on the green leaf-shreds in her lap.

Gregoris Gregoriou wished his father was there to see his first shop. Women's dowries were the secret of his success. Merchandise to please women – to feed their womanhood, vanity, coquetry. To feed their dreams of marriage and motherhood. Sell dowries, and you sell a future to the daughter, and the past, once again, to the mother, and to the father who pays – you sell the pride of ownership of mother and daughter and past and future.

Gregoris Gregoriou liked selling to women, because women liked buying. They instantly bloomed in his shop as if in an enchanted garden. Like birds of paradise, they preened themselves, and fluffed their plumage and spread and fluttered their wings ready to fly, but stayed – as he effortlessly unfurled with elegant, large gestures and sweet words stretches of fabric negligently billowing in mountains of colour. With quick artfulness and inexhaustible largesse he unfolded pleasure itself in front of startled young eyes. Every item promised moments of untried love: and young Anastasia's eyes looked guiltily down as he rapidly spread the snow-white marriage sheets in front of her.

'The best quality, for my best client.'

'My best' – that night she shut her eyes and the words glowed separately like beads of amber.

Without waiting he scattered several embroidery-designs in front of her: traditional Macedonian designs – she probably knew them by heart – a rather uncommon one from Epiros, perhaps not delicate enough, a rare one from Trapezous brought by a wealthy refugee family: truly aristocratic this one, he insisted it was for her. It needed the hand and eye of an artist. The curtains - gossamer! Even as they hung from the shelf they seemed to tremble in a strange light breeze, raising ghostly pleasures of intimacy. Satin quilts in deep blushing peach, for the wedding night, half enveloped by white lace that formed a little transparent paradise of flowers, birds and plump cherubs. Pillow cases to match. Macedonian silk for nightdresses, pure white – of course. But she turned away, as proper, and he put the material aside. She asked about the Kilimia hanging on the walls: she had never seen such a beautiful weave, such colours, sienna red and brown together! Ah, they were Anatolian, he explained with pride, from his part of the world. They were brought by the refugees. Heirlooms. Treasures. But the women had brought their art with them, and he explained to her how they made the dyes, all natural, from plants: only they knew the secret. It went from mother to daughter, it was an old art, from home! She admired them and was moved by them, and asked him about his family. She listened with tears in her eyes.

'I can't see tears in your beautiful eyes!' he said, while the gratification of those tears, meant for him, was bearing its instant fruit of love. 'Green like emeralds are your eyes! With golden lights, oh!'

Oh, such words! No one had spoken such words to her before!

No one has shed tears for me, not since my mother died, he thought in the night, and mused lovingly about the motherly daughter possessing all the things he did not possess: a family, a large rich home, acres of land, enough possessions and blessings to be able to spare tears for him and his terrible adventures. He thought of the young Macedonian girl, sturdy and quiet and constant like the roots of a tree.

'But stay, don't go yet. I have the loveliest georgette, specially ordered for you, from Saloniki, green, the colour of your eyes.' She had to go, but promised – and the promise made her cheeks bloom with colour – to visit his shop again, with her mother, who chose and decided. She looked wistfully at the sea of colour she was leaving behind, while his arms moved gracefully about her. 'Our honour, our pleasure,' he repeated.

What gallantry! she thought.

She went back to have another look at the embroideries. And finally in sailed Kyra Paterena, filling the shop with motherhood, examining, judging, demanding, while her daughter said little but spoke intricately with her eyes. The mother had the shop turned upside down, while the shopkeeper proudly showed her his superior merchandise, explaining with gusto and finesse about textures, and weaves, and processes of printing and colouring. She showed austere appreciation, approval, then bought half of the shop, as if she already owned it. And the young shopkeeper danced round her flamboyantly, like King David in his tent, measuring and cutting and counting and dividing, unwrapping and wrapping and parcelling up – offering all at such an irresistible price! With gusto the bargain was struck and the unspoken agreement made; with pleasure, and some pain, he had given in, and given this Macedonian girl, who looked at him as if she already possessed him, his finest fabrics and strongest threads and sharpest needles, for her lively enduring designs.

For a moment, of pleasure and loss, the moment of the bargain and the sale, he was back in his father's shop, at once the father and the son, wrapped in feminine smells and silky surfaces and women's laughter; carried by a woman's plaintive song suspended in the tendrils of the vines, unfolding out of a flower-like gramophone. Carried to a refugee camp where the women of his homeland had spread their brightest cloths in the sun and lay waiting for the boats. The sparkle of a mirror with a young girl's face in it looking at itself brought tears to the eyes.

Like a mother, he folded up his merchandise and put his household in order. The sale agreed, the gain calculated – and the incalculable moment of loss, of home and mother, brought to him home and mother in a fleeting feeling of exhilarated possession.

He paced up and down the shop looking at the empty shelves, thinking of his merchandise, divided and scattered in his calculations, pursuing, pursued, the delicate muscles of his face dancing with worry, his hands clutching each other protectively. He pushed a door at the back of the shop, and came into a small bare room, more like a cell, with a bed and above it an icon of the Virgin Mother – a dark young Panayia with her baby son in her arms. He looked round his secret home for reassurance. He lifted the corner of the mattress and pushed his hand underneath, examined a thick wad of money and folded documents, counted the notes, and put everything back in its place. He touched the small window high in the wall, making sure it was safe from thieves and enemies. He uttered a few words to the icon, then examined his face in a small mirror, scrupulously. He smoothed his hair back with delicate fingers, looked at himself again with some pleasure, and was ready for his next client.

The Patera family were crossing themselves with drowsy satisfaction, and murmuring in different degrees of devotion and digestion their thanks for God's blessings on their table, when they recognised the marriage broker's uneven tread on the stairs. From her heavy sighing at each step they knew she was coming on serious business. The father wiped his mouth and sat back in his chair; the mother sat up with dignity, and ordered the two daughters to clear the table. The sons were engaged in picking their teeth – mouths stretched and contorted by intruding hands, eyes turned inwards, all feeling dwelling on the intruded intimacy and all thought absorbed by the imagined cavity of their mouth, harbouring, well wedged between strong teeth, remnants of food exaggerated by the annoyed imagination and exasperated finger. Their used-up ammunition lay in small heaps of broken match-sticks – witnesses to long efforts and doubtful victories.

'Coffee, Kyra Vasiliki?' mother offered tolerantly.

'I won't say no.' The marriage broker sighed as she arranged her body on a chair offered by the youngest son.

'Coffees for everyone,' mother shouted towards the kitchen.

'How's life, Kyra Vasiliki?' father inquired.

'Life!' she complained. 'Ach, it torments me, this body, it punishes me!' She rearranged herself on the chair. 'But I am here for a specific reason.' She looked suspiciously towards the boys, who had resumed their intimate operations, screening them with their free hands, and then with meaningful intensity at the father. He nodded, while mother, with a hardly perceptible move of her head, signalled her sons to leave the room.

'As you hypothesise . . .' The marriage broker straightened her upper body – stretching her left hip and leg twistedly under the table – into a posture suitable to her office. 'The purpose of my visit concerns your elder daughter.' Her voice became low, conspiratorial. 'The interested party – to come to the heart of the matter – is a man of growing property and prosperity, and respect in our community.' With some discomfort she leaned forward over the table towards father, meaning business. Anastasia entered the room quietly, holding a tray with small, delicately ornate coffee-cups. The marriage broker stopped, but her eyes were full of words and meanings as she looked at the father, and measuringly at the daughter, resuming impatiently as soon as the girl left the room.

'He owns the best shop in town, specialising in dowries, and is negotiating another one in Serras. A man with a future, and foresight. A man with the demon of commerce in him!'

'The refugee. My daughter to a foreigner, an upstart, a refugee! Never.' Kyra Patera stood up.

'You mean Mr Gregoriou?' father said thoughtfully.

Anastasia heard her mother's voice, and stood behind the kitchen door clutching her apron. Then her father's quiet voice, reasonable, reassuring. Then her mother's angry steps down the stairs and into the bakery; but the marriage broker stayed some time. Their voices were low, Anastasia and her sister could not make out the words. Finally they heard her slow uneven steps. 'I have done my duty, acted with the best intentions. Now it is for you to decide.'

There was commotion in the Patera household: secret discussions between husband and wife, between father and the two older sons, between father and his three brothers, and his wife's brother, and the brother's wife. The marriage broker would pay short sudden visits. Finally father said to Anastasia, kindly, 'I want to talk to you,' and at dinner he announced that Mr Gregorios Gregoriou was going to pay them a visit on Sunday evening. The younger daughter looked at Anastasia with an expectant, questioning smile, but Anastasia had buried her face in her lap. The sons looked questioningly at their mother, who kept a silent, defiant composure. Father turned to his accounts at the end of the meal with a quiet finality, and the unhurried scratching of his pen on the paper was the only sound disrupting the respectful mysterious quietness of the room.

Anastasia danced through the house buffing old furniture into new life, setting out embroideries, rubbing soft, honey-coloured wax into splintery old boards until she saw her reflection in their warmth, spreading and arranging thick slippery rugs of all patterns and colours, watering the plants, wishing them instant full bloom, wishing the red geraniums redder, caressing their lacy leaves for the lemony perfume. As if not she but they, her mother's household, were to be the bride. The mother allowed Anastasia to display her own dowry when she was her daughter's age, and younger, not to receive the bridegroom but to show him how unacceptable he was.

Early on a Sunday evening, when the inhabitants of Kapnohori were fresh from their nap, and vegetable gardens and backyards had just been watered and the smell of the earth eased troubled spirits, a company of three approached with slow ceremoniousness the Patera household. The marriage broker, in a new scarf and apron, walked ahead, with energetic elaboration of movement, occasioned by the importance of the visit. Gregoris followed, impeccably groomed in a slender off-white suit, a carnation in his lapel, an impatient spring in his step. A very fat man came behind with slow negligence, gazing up and down the houses and wiping the sweat from his forehead and chin.

Gregoris touched his jacket, feeling his pockets to make sure everything was in order. He adjusted his handkerchief so its snowy peak protruded from his top pocket with artful precision. His fingernails were neatly filed, the nail of the small finger longer than the rest, as was the fashion in Saloniki, to show he was not a manual worker. He looked back at his friend with impatience, and examined his clothes which were already too small on him. The way he was sweating, he would stink out the house with paprika and cayenne.

As they entered the Patera house, Gregoris was overcome with timidity, almost devotion, as if he were entering a church. The Patera parents were standing at the top of the stairs. The three visitors ascended for what seemed to Gregoris centuries – the marriage broker, cruelly, at the front, the fat friend huffing and puffing, innocently, behind her, and Gregoris, whose temples were by now throbbing with impatience, politely, last. The large sombre house was quiet, except for a clink of china from the kitchen – he heard a feminine welcoming note in it.

They were led into the reception room, austere, airless, smelling of mothballs. The necessary introductions were made.

'I have known Gregoris from the day, the very moment he got off the boat.' Aslanoglou brightly gave his credentials, as his arm stretched to embrace his friend, but was stopped in the air by Gregoris' intense look.

'Mr Aslanoglou is a colleague – one of the best-established merchants in Thessaloniki. We have engaged in trade for many years.'

Aslanoglou looked impressed by his friend's educated Greek. The night school, he thought, I should have gone to night school. 'Excellent man, Gregoriou here. A diamond. Twenty-four carat.' He repaid his friend's compliment, as he sat down on the hard settee.

'Mr Aslanoglou specialises in silks and wools. He also has a collection of Persian rugs, and some rare Bokharas.'

The Macedonians shook their heads seriously, the marriage broker smiled broadly round the room as if Aslanoglou were her son and she were responsible for his successes.

'Specialise! You are exaggerating, Gregori! You would like me to have only the expensive fabrics, but me, I am a simple man! I like to have a bit of everything in my shop – the odd rug, the odd dress, a bit of haberdashery, my few cans of oil, my olives, my halva. A bit of everything, to please the housewife.'

The marriage broker smiled emphatically in utter agreement; but there was predatory preoccupation in her eyes. Gregoris touched his temples lightly, the throbbing was stronger. He took in the narrow, pew-like furniture; the harmonium in the corner, which they were told father played on Sundays. Everything in the room portrayed moral rectitude: Gregoris sat up. His friend Aslanoglou spread his legs with relief. The embroideries, softly draping the hard furniture, took Gregoris' eye: they were crowded with colour and richness, hiding great patience and a confined female flamboyance and passion that hovered like a ghost in the room. He expressed his admiration and asked whose artistic hand had produced these masterpieces; to his surprise, they were done not by the daughter but by the mother. In her youth: they were her dowry. She sat erect in judgement.

'Anastasia's embroidery is almost as good,' the father added, and the mentioning of the girl's name brought a blush to Gregoris' face; he cleared his throat. The marriage broker sighed with relief, things were taking their proper course. The sofa creaked under Aslanoglou, who looked brightly round the room expecting the girl to appear on a platter. A fragile gap in the conversation was filled with the noises of Aslanoglou's body. Gregoris could hear his friend's breathing, digesting, sweating, he could even hear his growing appetite as the evening progressed.

Aslanoglou asked about the crops, the local medicinal water – extremely light and digestive, he had heard. The father answered politely, the mother looked towards the kitchen as the girls' voices were briefly raised. Aslanoglou mentioned the tobacco strike. Gregoris shifted the conversation to local trade, then fell silent. The mother watched and waited. The marriage broker looked at Gregoris expectantly, he in response sat up in his chair, right at the edge as if the chair were not for sitting and resting on but for stopping him from falling to the floor. He attempted to cross his legs, but stopped in time – he was not at the café. He looked half-threateningly, half-pleadingly round the room. The girl walked in holding a tray full of sweets and drinks, her eyes glued on it. Aslanoglou sat up; his smile travelled sweetly between the girl and the parents, indicating – you have a sweet girl.

'This is our eldest daughter, Anastasia,' her father said, looking at her with kindly appraisal and pride. Gregoris moved his head slightly, affirmatively, not daring to look. The marriage broker smiled with coy pride, as if she had raised and owned the girl, and also Gregoris, and even Aslanoglou, the best man, as if she had conceived them all especially for this match. She moved her leg to a more comfortable position; its pain and discomfort were one of the necessary sacrifices. Anastasia held the tray in the middle of the room, not knowing to whom to go first, made a step towards her father then looked at her mother who raised her brows curtly towards the guests. Perhaps out of shyness, or perhaps drawn by the fat man's appetite, she approached him first. Her mother and the marriage broker simultaneously made a coughing noise, Anastasia paused in confusion, then, as if she just remembered, she directed her steps towards Gregoris. She held the tray to him. Gregoris looked at the elegant, thimble-sized cup and followed with his eyes the unstable tray and the trembling small plump hands holding it. He did not raise his head to look at her face, but the warmth and movement of her body feeling large over him, and he, curiously, small, moved him with quick familiarity. An immediate recognition, a memory of a moment, a return . . . a recovery. He drank his brandy in one gulp, as he believed to be the fashion, and felt tears in his eyes.

Anastasia stood in front of Aslanoglou, and the room was soon filled with his noises of relish. 'May you have its sweetness,' he wished her with feeling, his mouth the garden of Allah as his taste-buds blossomed instantly. The girl then offered the tray to the marriage broker who accepted her hard-won portion with smiles and sighs, indicating the labour of love that was required for this happy, but difficult, event to come about. As a reminder, she rearranged her leg so that it protruded straight into the middle of the room; the Patera mother looked at it with distaste. Anastasia left the room and left Gregoris pale and fragile.

'I too come from a good home, with a large property – vineyards and olives, and a shop that went from father to son . . .' Gregoris glanced quickly at the surprised faces suspended bodiless in the room. His words gave him courage, and justified complaint. 'I was to take the shop over from my father, but I lost him, young, and lost everything – land, property, family, home.' He faltered, overcome by the rush of words and feelings, which were lost, and lost, and all that remained was a gathered war with the world.

'True, very true!' Aslanoglou confirmed, like the chanter's assistant accompanying the chanter. 'Only I can tell you in what shape he appeared at our shop. Skin and bone. Famished. Diseased. Only I can tell you what adventures this boy has gone through!' He looked upwards in recollection of the past, opening his palms to indicate, or weigh, what was so hard to describe in words.

'Our homeland was God's paradise,' Gregoris said.

'A paradise!' Aslanoglou nodded in agreement.

'Blest with riches!'

Aslanoglou gave a long deep 'Ach!'

'It had everything a man's heart could desire.' A heart could, what could a heart desire – his own words distracted Gregoris, and robbed him of their meaning and memory. 'Look at us now, our homes made of cardboard and oilcans.'

'Ach! you should see how they live!' Aslanoglou assisted mournfully.

Gregoris looked straight into the faces of the girl's parents. Kyra Paterena was frowning at her apron, and the marriage broker was looking at the others apologetically. The father was listening, shaking his head in agreement and even sympathy. Gregoris took courage. If he could only explain to this wise and kind man, as if to a father, and make him understand.

'I lost my brothers and my other relatives in the Katastrophe. I am still looking for them.' He looked at the mother's embroidered lap. 'I visited the refugee towns in Athens and Saloniki, the refugee villages. Nothing. I listen to "Refugee Hour" on the radio, lists and lists of names of those lost – nothing. I send messages: Gregoris Gregoriou looking for brothers lost in the Katastrophe at the age of seven and nine in Mouryes in the province of Marmara. Nothing.' The silence in the room left a huge gap which he felt he ought to fill; he couldn't stop talking. 'Someone told me they burned the whole village. It can't be true – not the children. They may have gone to America, like so many other Greeks. I couldn't go back to save them. Our army retreating and the Turks after them massacring everyone in sight, I couldn't go back.' He waited for another's voice to fill the emptiness in the room.

'You have suffered terribly,' the father said plainly. 'But you are brave and good people. And one day you will have a proper home in this country.'

'He has suffered,' Aslanoglou nodded, 'but I can tell you, there has not been a more hard-working boy in the whole of Macedonia. Don't call me Aslan Aslanoglou if this boy does not own your whole town one day' – he got a fierce look from Kyra Paterena – 'He came to my shop a mere child. Famished, ill, looking like a skeleton. And it is true my mother and I took him in as if he were my younger brother – for I too have no brothers, only a mother! We have our own long story of sufferings. Ah, who from Asia Minor does not have his tales of woe! – but of that another time. We took him in as one of our own, and he honoured us as though we were his family. He loved the shop as if it were his father's. And the change! You wouldn't believe the change. He made it a true cosmopolitan shop – he wanted us to call it "Cosmopolit", he said it was French. Imagine up there "Aslan Aslanoglou, Cosmopolit". Eh? Impressive! But I said, no, Gregori, we are only poor Karamanlis, from the Black Sea, this is not Paris. But Gregoris is very progressive, as you can see. He worked during the day, and then went to night school – and he even learned English, on his own. You see, he wanted to go to America then, to find his brothers, and make a fortune. Eh, Gregori, you remember? Your dreams about America? But he has made his fortune in Greece. Eh, Gregori?'

Aslanoglou became confident and exuberant, he found it easy to talk, and felt he was helping his friend. He was thinking, Gregoris gets emotional easily – people do not want to know about sufferings, they want to know about success, prospects. He should build himself up, throw his weight around more. But Gregoris is a nervous character, restless, a worrier – and when he loses his temper! Aman, they had better not know about his temper, not before the wedding!

Gregoris had listened, moved, to his friend. 'Eh, with the help of the Virgin Mother I have built a good business, with the honest sweat of my hands.' He spread his palms open as if for inspection. 'I don't drink, I don't smoke, I don't play cards, I don't waste my time in the cafeneion, discussing politics and getting into fights. I don't believe in rest days, because I have to produce, to create – a name, a reputation, a proper home while I am still young and strong. I believe I have gained a good name, and a good reputation in your town.'

'No question! No doubt!' Aslanoglou was giving his friend his vote of confidence with exaggerated gestures and sounds.

'I believe you know the purpose of this visit. I would be honoured to ask for the hand of your daughter, Anastasia, in marriage.' As he uttered the words, he felt he loved her. The room was silent with doubt. Just as Anastasia's father was going to speak, Gregoris continued: 'You may have a big property, a big house full of wealth. But I am not asking for a dowry. I want only her. And I will be able to give her everything she had at her parents' home and more. Everything her heart desires.'

Aslanoglou was briefly surprised, then murmured, 'An honourable act!'

The marriage broker was stunned – a marriage without bargaining! Bargaining was her forte, she had her reputation, she had taken him for a shrewd young man, like all those immigrants. What had come over him? Perhaps he loved the girl.

The mother drew herself up to return the insult, but the father, looking the young man straight in the eyes, said, 'Shall we ask my daughter what she thinks?' The mother's eyes hardened – ask the daughter? Not the mother? But obediently she got up, filling the room with wounded dignity, and went to fetch her daughter.

83

The marriage broker felt the pain of such irreverence – cutting the Gordian knot of marriage bargaining which she had fastened with such art and patience and experience. With a fatigued face she shifted her lame leg slowly across the floor through the debris of intricate coils, tendrils and wreaths.

'Whatever she touches becomes gold.' The women of the town paraded through the Patera household inspecting Anastasia's trousseau, laid out for admiring and envious eyes. They praised the mother's, they praised the daughter's art, they confirmed their approval of the daughters' upbringing – 'girls from a good home, with principles'.

The mother ran the prolonged marriage ceremonies with vindictive efficiency; Anastasia watched with bewilderment, trying to remember the face of the bridegroom whom she was not now allowed to see. She secretly touched his presents for her, placed with the other gifts on the sideboard in the reception room. In the church she gazed spellbound at the rich garments of the priest chanting to her the mysterious bonds of marriage. The incense and the noise made her feel weak. She did not dare turn and look at the bridegroom, but felt the pull of the silk ribbon that connected the lemon-blossom wreaths on their heads. Once, as they followed the priest in the dance of Isaiah, showered with rice and wishes, their heads accidentally came close and the ribbon rested lightly on her shoulders.

For their honeymoon he took her to Saloniki, the Bride of Thermai-kos Bay, and promised to take her to Athens one day to show her the Acropolis and Lykavittos. They had a room with a sea view at the Méditerranée Hotel, where only foreigners and rich Athenians stayed and the waiters said 'merci beaucoup' and 'thank you', 'très bien' and 'please' and 'avec plaisir'.

From the battlements of the White Tower they admired the sunset behind Olympus that made the city sparkle like mythical jewels, stirring and blinding in the restless palm of an avaricious god.

He showed her round the famous monastery of Vlatathon on the heights over the city, where beautiful peacocks strolled with leisurely self-pleasure in the yard. They would hop on the marble benches, look with indifference at the city lying at their feet, and with a sudden thrill of self-assertion display their glorious plumage to the dazed gaze of the visitors. The young couple drank cold water from the marble fountain, and the Abbot of the monastery explained to them with great pride and pleasure the ancient palindrome carved on the marble: *Nipson anomimata mi monan opsin* – Wash your sins not only your face. He read it for them from beginning to end and then read it from end to beginning, spelling out the syllables, and they all admired the wisdom of their ancestors. The Abbot told them that St Paul had preached to the Thessalonians on that very spot: the couple were moved with true holy sentiments. They sat on a marble bench, enjoying the view and the flurries of the peacocks, and spelled to themselves the beautiful palindrome like a magic spell repeating itself back to front: they thought about the things the Abbot had told them, and vowed they would have their children christened and one day married at that very spot. They realised, with awe, that they were married to each other.

A boatman took them out into the bay, where they looked back at the city, leaning back on embroidered cushions and rugs. Like Venice, he told her, and decided to take her to Venice one day. In the evening they promenaded on the waterfront, and ate ice cream at the Astoria Palace. The orchestra played waltzes with flair and feeling: a few people danced, the rest watched. Gregoris pulled his young bride, but she held herself tight on her seat, almost in tears. Children danced with each other while frantic waiters pirouetted round them with elegant agility. Late in the evening the waiters stood at a discreet distance, while children leaned drowsily on their chairs like unsupported plants, finally landing on the nearest convenient lap.

Gregoris took his bride to the open-air theatre, a real theatre, with stage and scenery and lights, not like *Golfo*, that peasant pantomime in Kapnohori. This was European theatre, with foreign names like Pierre and Louise. Anastasia had never seen such elegance – men who flourished tall hats and canes, and women who played with fans and held glasses of champagne or long cigarette holders. It turned out to be a comedy, which disappointed her because she did not find it funny, and when the wife came back suddenly from holiday, filling the stage with suitcases, and found the maid, giggling in the husband's arms, she thought this shameless. She was disappointed at her husband for being so amused, and putting his arm round her in front of everyone. She preferred serious melodramas, which moved you and taught you something about life. On the way back to the hotel, he was animated and flirtatious, and teased her about her blushes, and when he pulled her towards him, in public, she said disapprovingly, 'You behave like a drunk,' in a voice like her mother's.

Then it was time for business: he should look at the autum fashions, take the pulse of the market, and, most important, establish connections. It was important to break into the Jewish network; they ran the market, he had to be on good terms with them – and they were good merchants, he could not deny it, with acumen, taste, foresight. He must break into the local ring – his hands re-enacted with frantic vividness this ring made by hundreds of merchants squeezing all business from him, starving him of success. He had to make up for the time he had lost. 'No, of course not lost!' he comforted quickly his young bride on the verge of tears.

'But, my love, it's for you I want to create, to create. These are the most productive years of my life: I must grab them by the scruff of the neck, my father always said if you don't grab life by the scruff of the neck it will grab you. The crab, my little wife, my little love: my father said a true merchant has the crab in here, it eats you all the time, the more you work the more you feed it, and if you stop it eats your innards!' And with a crab-like movement he clawed his shirt with both hands. The young wife, overwhelmed, agreed.

He swept through the city like a sudden gust from the north, racing down alleys and avenues, eyes on the alert, quick and curious, lean and agile as a mountain goat. She followed him in her high heels and delicate honeymoon dresses, rosy-cheeked from the exertion but not complaining. They went from shop to shop, examined samples, admired well-dressed windows and clients, heard strange Greek in Jewish accents and Armenian accents and accents from the Black Sea and the quick clever tones of Smyrna. This was not a Greek city, she thought, missing her Macedonian village.

'We have to move to Saloniki. Do you see the wealth, Anastasia mou? The crystal candelabras! The mahogany shelves! The windows – a proper theatre! And the mannequins – you could take them for real women!'

'But Gregori, you have the best shop in Kapnohori – large, new, with clients from the whole province.'

'Kapnohori! My love! We cannot stay in Kapnohori all our lives! The people are still asleep in Kapnohori! They haven't even got wind that we are in the twentieth century – that we are in the age of the radio, and the cinema, and the motorcar, and the airplane. Your compatriots, Anastasia mou, still play the lyra, and dress like Albanian brigands, and ride on a donkey. The shops smell of oil and soap and salted sardines; and the merchants sit all day sipping coffee and treating you to turkish delight: and they call themselves businessmen!'

She looked at him, puzzled, unhappy, and he tried to cheer her. 'I'll make you a real city lady. You will have your hair cut short like the women in Saloniki, and you will wear sleeveless dresses, like the mannequins in the windows, and dressing gowns at home. You will

have a telephone, and live in a modern flat, and you can watch cars go
by from your balcony, not animals.'

Anastasia blushed. Her clear light green eyes – Macedonian eyes,
Gregoris thought – remained unconvinced.

True Slav stubbornness, he thought, not untenderly, and smiled
with the confidence that he would persuade her in the end.

The Anatolian merchants were different. In a constant turmoil of
love and pain. They made you sit down and take coffee or sugared
fruit, they philosophised, recollected, and did their bargaining with so
much heart. 'Aman Gregori mou, my son, my compatriot, you are
wounding my heart if you say this is expensive. I am making a special
price for you for the soul and the blessed memories of our mothers,
whom we both lost young – for the memories of our homeland, because
we are both compatriots and refugees, Gregori mou – have another
ouzo and let all the venom of our refugee life go down. There, let's clink
glasses and drink together like brothers as we are, and make the
agreement. And because I love you, Gregori mou, and because your
bride is lovely, although Macedonian, and because you look like an
honest and hard-working young man – although I met you only a few
minutes ago – I want you to come and meet my family and taste my
wife's smyrniotika soutzoukakia and her imam baildi that will make you
lick your fingers and bring tears to your eyes and make you sigh for the
homeland. And you'll tell your young bride here what paradise, what
blessings we had and lost, and we'll remember some of the old stories
from home and be nostalgic together, and cry and laugh together.' At
every refugee shop they visited and every refugee restaurant where
they sat down, they would start the stories from home, the good days,
the massacres, the miraculous escapes: stories of relatives finding each
other after so many years – by chance, by a miracle – only by a miracle
can such things happen, Gregori! Or receiving a letter from Australia
from older brothers or sisters who had made fortunes.

'Our life is a miracle, Gregori.'

He took her to the home of their best man, Aslanoglou, covered with
oriental tapestries and rugs, and smelling of hot spices. She was
introduced to Aslanoglou's mother, who sat cross-legged in her
Turkish pantaloons, smoking her hubble-bubble. She gave a nod and
said something in Turkish. To Anastasia's surprise, her husband
understood and spoke back in Turkish – his face had a playful
tenderness that she had not seen before.

He took her to Anatolian restaurants where he made her eat
tripe soup reeking of garlic. He got addresses of compatriots, and

wandered through the petrol-can and hardboard homes of Neon Vyzantion, looking for his godmother Kyveli from Marmara. They made their way through barbed-wire yards, amongst an army of chickens and barefoot children, asking for Mrs Kyveli, finding people who knew her but didn't know where she lived: Kyra Thalia knew her well, but Thalia is dead, she died last year, she couldn't take any more of this black exile, ti mavri xenitia. They found people from villages near Mouryes, each of whom gave a different story: they burned them all, alive, in the middle of the cornfield; no one survived. No, some children escaped, I don't know names. No, it was not Mouryes they burned, it was the other village behind the hill. The Red Cross will tell you. Kyr Yiassemis here has a radio and his son, who is a good mechanic, has made a big megaphone and every afternoon, when it's 'Refugee Hour' on the radio and they play songs from the homeland and the Red Cross announces names of lost relatives, we all listen to the radio together, and we cry and remember together. Sometimes we sing, Kyra Vangelio will dance . . . and now and then someone will hear the name of a sister or brother, whom they had thought dead: and then, Gregori mou, the yelling and the crying and the laughing! The heavens quake! They open their gates! You would think it's the Apocalypse! You would think it's the Epiphany! Very moving. Very emotional. Very tragic, my son.

This foreign world, this sea of bereavement and homelessness, these floods of emotion and vivacity and pleasure – it all frightened her, spent her. She was homesick and tired, she missed her brothers and sister and her embroidery, and some days she preferred to stay and wait for Gregoris at the hotel. She sat on the balcony, resting her head on her folded arms, embracing the railings, and gazing at the sea and the pleasure boats travelling back and forth, filling the bay through their loudspeakers with sweet nostalgic melodies that made her skin tingle. Songs about love and love-sickness.

Some nights she woke up startled by the dark quietness in the room which seemed to her to hide a noise or a movement she couldn't hear or see, perhaps an imperceptible presence to which she attended with eyes wide open and a disturbed heart. She would discover, always with new bewilderment, that she was married to a foreigner, who lay next to her, and had strange ways. She would stay quiet and listen to his uneven breathing, and feel a tightening in the air, a contained fear, or anger, a curtailed movement, that stopped her heart.

'Anastasia, are you awake?' he would ask untenderly, and she would say yes, and nothing more. She drew the light summer blanket over her as she heard him get up suddenly and go to the window, open it, then come back to bed as if after a long painful journey. She imagined him surrounded by a company of nightmares that related to him horrors, and he hearkened after them: but she did not want to hear or know. When he came close to her, for all his sweet words, she feared his body was not with his heart, his heart not with her: he came surrounded by his ghosts and ghostly voices. She feared him. When his body came close to her, her thoughts scattered bewildered, and always came against the large dark body of her mother, standing sometimes outside the room, or at the door or near the window or over the bed, scarring her with her condemning eyes and words. 'The shame of it, the shame and the pain of it!' a voice in her would murmur and a hand would press her eyes shut.

She thought only of the pain and the betrayal as she lay in bed alone, seeing her childhood vanish in the face of all that pain, under the dark shadow of her mother, presiding. As she lay alone, hearing the whispers of the women at the other end of the room – 'There's still time, it's still early, but they are getting stronger': but when she yelled for help, for someone to take the pain away, the women were deaf and dumb; then she contemplated in the brief intervals their betrayal. She realised they were the guests at her marriage, the blessed mystery of marriage, and now the blessed mystery of birth, and now the Easter feast, swallowing her right into their heart but their heart was pain, and she, like their Easter lamb Haido lying dead and still bleeding in the backyard, her mother wiping her hands on her apron. When she cried 'Mother save me', her mother over her said, 'You have to suffer it, my child – all women do. If I could take the pain from you and suffer myself I would, but I cannot. I cannot help you, my child.' They were heartless words, coming from a mother, but the mother's face bent over her daughter looked tired and pained and old, and Anastasia felt for the first time that this woman who was unable to help her was, truly, her mother and herself a child dying. Small, she became very small like the rat that she and her brother watched through the barred window running back and forth in the cellar trying to climb up the walls but always sliding down – and trying to remember why they locked her in the cellar. She became even smaller, like the noisy horsefly she and her brothers had shut in a match-box and listened to making such a desperate racket. All the small creatures she had mothered and tormented in her games came back now to play their cruel games, saying, 'You wanted to be a mother, now be a mother.' And as she got smaller and smaller her belly got bigger and bigger, like a mountain that stirred and breathed, whose life was pain. The blessed mystery of marriage and the blessed mystery of birth: growing and swallowing her right into their heart, but that heart lived only by fear and pain, and the blood that made it beat was, she realised, her own blood. The mystery of marriage and the mystery of birth made her die bit by bit. The priests and midwives and mothers and husbands, best men and bridesmaids, the crowds of guests whispering at the other end of the room – not time yet, still a long way to go – were all killing her bit by bit. And she only a rat, a horsefly, a baby lying on wet sheets yelling and yelling for help, compassion; yet it was not only herself crying, another baby was crying, taking, mysteriously, all her pain away from her and yelling it to the world. Her mother placed on her, in flesh and blood, that yell of pain.

'A girl!'

'To my girl, and to my new shop in Saloniki,' Gregoris announced triumphantly at the cafeneion and ordered a round of ouzo for everyone.

· PART 2 ·

· 5 ·

The Pantocrator of
the Backyard

ELENI BECAME worried whenever there was mention of the war ending: what grown-ups thought of as war she – having grown up in war – thought of as life, having had no other life. But the war was not ending, and she lived in its security. The heavy iron bar across the door, the oil lamp gathering and stifling the family in its smoky dimness, the worried faces looking reassuringly at each other.

War was a frequent word in people's mouths, and a daily dull ache of hunger in the middle of her being that made her want to cry, or quarrel. It had its familiar voices: the woman's long, crawling wail that started low, lower than any voice she had ever heard before, slowly going up and up and on and on to a shrill wail which lasted intolerably long and sent everyone into hiding. Eleni blocked her ears to keep the woman's wail out, but the siren with the long snaky hair went round the streets of the city sweeping everything and everyone into her long wail, like an endless tongue licking clean the streets and alleys of Saloniki, from the seafront to the city walls on the hill, winding down as it went uphill until it came, with a subterranean long-drawn satisfaction, to a halt. No one could tell why that woman wailed: from her sound Eleni guessed her to be the forlorn mother, or daughter, or wife, of the war. She possessed the streets of the city while he possessed the skies. He would come from the mountains in the north with a low quiet drone at the start, but as her wail became shriller his drone became louder, shaking tables and beds and homes over people's heads. Man and woman then devastated each other, while children all over the world held their heads between their hands not to hear the fearful voices that could creep in under doors and through shutters, and linger.

They lingered, and with time might possess the faces and voices of

93

her father and mother, and no shutting of ears and eyes could keep them out of her head. But hiding her head in her mother's lap, seeking its familiar smell – warm, sweet – salty – stale, forbidden – drove the ghosts out. Father paced up and down in his pyjamas as if he had a long distance to cover; he paused only to lift the corner of the dark grey blanket at the window and then resumed his race. His eyes were elsewhere, on a place that sometimes filled him, it seemed, with fatherly pleasures and at other times with a rage that made everyone, even Mother, tremble.

When the fight between the war and his wife was over, mother lifted the corner of the curtain carefully to see who had been swept away. The family saw a young man once, lying as if asleep in the middle of the street, and no one went near him. They waited for him to get up and go. An old woman came and talked to him, and kissed his hands and arms, and shook him and cried. Until others came and carried them both away.

Eleni was seldom allowed out, because of the war. But when the weather was good she could go out on the balcony, where she sat on tiles warm from the sun, and looked through the railings at the street. The iron railings made the world look sliced, but if she rested her head between the bars so that she felt them, cool and hard, on the sides of her face, she could see without interruptions. She knew all the bumps and holes in the road, the pattern of the cobblestones and slippery patches, and knew when someone might stumble. She noticed people going by quietly, arm in arm – *engagé*, as her sisters called it – in conspiratorial affection. She recognised the soldiers even before they appeared, from the loud foreign voices and purposeful synchronised steps. She followed the activity in the other balconies, and tried to see into other people's homes. A lady in a bright flowery kimono made a lot of fuss over her curly-haired, hare-lipped boy, whom she called Bouli or Bebi, and who kicked and punched when she tried to kiss him or pinch him on his plump cheek. Then she sat on the balcony and sulkily painted first her fingernails then her toenails bright red like her lips and the flowers of her kimono. In the flat above, two grown-up boys spent their day fighting with each other; they were separated briefly by their mother, who wore a grey suit and high heels as if ready to go out, but Eleni had never seen her go out. Further down the road a serious young man in glasses and striped pyjamas sat out on the balcony reading and writing all day, while his mother, who always wore black, brought him cups of tea: mountain tea it must be, Mother thought, because where could she find all that tea – did she have a

German general for a lover or what? Eleni once saw her pushing her son in a wheelchair.

From the kitchen balcony Eleni could see the back of the German building, full of soldiers sitting behind desks, or taking papers from one room to another. Between the two buildings were two courtyards: the German yard, full of wooden boxes and surrounded by barbed wire, and 'our yard', or the 'Greek yard' as the children called it, which was a square piece of earth without grass or flowers, with one tree in the centre. Her sisters, in their black school uniforms, would meet other schoolgirls in the courtyard, to play hopscotch and exchange transfers. Eleni watched with awe the older girls who wore with such confidence their school uniform, the mark of privilege and age and power – washed and ironed every evening by their mothers – separating them and putting them on a higher rank than everyone younger. They wore those privileged clothes with such ease! With what speed they did up the bow at the back if it came undone, with what enviable negligence they slipped their hands into big pockets containing secret possessions! For Eleni, those black-clad superior creatures transformed the courtyard into a paradise.

She spent her days watching the Germans in the building opposite. In most windows, soldiers sat behind desks, tapping on machines as if they played the piano. They walked with a straight back, and spoke and moved without fear; they had yellow hair and bright faces, different from the thin bodies and old-looking faces that appeared in the street. One of the soldiers, very blond and young, would interrupt his writing every so often and come to the window: he looked at the sky, then stretched his back with pleasure, whistled for a while and went back to his desk. Through another window she saw someone who looked very important, because the other soldiers stood to attention in front of him, and got up from their seats whenever he entered a room. He was older and more serious than the others, and wore thick-rimmed glasses which he took off now and then to rub his eyes; he stayed with his eyes covered for a few moments as if trying to remember something. Sometimes he looked in Eleni's direction, his eyes dwelling on her: he did not smile but she saw a recognition in the way he tilted his head. One day he approached the window and stood there with his hands resting on the window-sill, looking at her and almost smiling; she smiled back. She listened to the music coming through the window; many voices and many instruments together rising, only tentatively, and then falling, and again falling – and the sadness and peace in that fall held her.

95

Someone pulled her back, Kaliopi's voice shrieked, 'Mother, she's looking at the Germans! I caught her looking at the enemy – smiling and waving to them.' Mother took her indoors and told her about the war and the enemy, but Eleni could not listen, her head was buzzing with what seemed torrents of tears that swung in circles in her head but could not reach her eyes. She moved slowly, almost lifelessly, round the table; then faster, round and round the room, with purpose, pretending she was the siren woman, the wife, the daughter of war, starting a child's warlike cry which went up and up as the bare feet ran, until, as she increased her orbit and increased her speed, it became a woman's wail – and down she swooped on her sister, down on the floor, while she heard her voice sweeping with fear and devastation the streets of the city from the waterfront to the walls.

'The menace, the maenad!' her mother cried in tears of exasperation. 'It's the Orient in her! The Asiatic blood! Her father's daughter!'

Boots, foreign voices stopped outside the door. A heavy knock, demanding. Mother stood in the middle of the room, her hands protecting each other. Another knock, she pushed her daughters into her bedroom and went to the door. Through the half-opened door, Eleni saw her mother standing back near the wall, confronted by three men in uniform. She recognised the important man with the thick-rimmed glasses who had looked at her through his window. Mother looked small, clenching her apron in a knot, and Eleni ran to put her arms round her leg in mutual fear and protection. And curiosity: wondering whether the man would remember her, whether he had come for her. She was overcome by the guilty and pleasing certainty that she had brought the enemy home.

The men in uniform walked round the house inspecting rooms and furniture. A young man with thin straight hair asked mother a chain of questions, in Greek: 'How big is the house, how many rooms, how many people live in it, who are they, how old are the children?' The man with the thick-rimmed glasses was examining with curiosity the massive carved dining furniture that seemed to have rooted into the floor by sheer will and weight and long-enduring immobility: a preternatural petrified forest that had withstood wars, occupations, floods and fires; a ponderous reminder of outlandish feasts not to be had. He lifted the corner of a white sheet covering the velvet armchairs in the reception room, which were used only on namedays. He said something to the interpreter, who said to Mother in Greek, the house is too big for one family; they might take one or two of the rooms for officers, they would let them know. The man with the glasses asked Eleni her name, in Greek; Eleni looked at her sisters standing now at the opened door of the parents' bedroom disapproving of her for having been spoken to by the enemy. Eleni covered her eyes coquettishly.

'Eleni.'

'Eleni of Troy?' the man asked smiling, and Eleni, not knowing who Eleni of Troy was, smiled back.

'Eleni of Troy,' she murmured to herself in front of the mirror. She imagined the German officer pacing back and forth in their apartment, humming or whistling the foreign music, but was instantly ashamed of her imagination, and was made to feel its full horror by Kaliopi's condemning eye and tongue.

'You brought them here! You brought the enemy into your home and family! You attracted them with your evil eye! You are responsible for all the disasters that may fall upon us! And the smiles, the blandishments! As if they are our relatives!'

For the rest of the day Kaliopi foretold the horrors that would befall the family if the enemy moved in. They might kill them any time, in the night, just because they happened to be drunk, or suffer from insomnia. They would certainly take everything they liked, furniture, clothes, china, jewellery: they did that with other families, who could stop them? They might put Father in prison, and Mother, they might – she whispered something in Sophia's ear, what a terrible disgrace! Sophia was slow to believe Kaliopi's apocalyptic stories, but Eleni was already trembling with fear and remorse for even looking at those monsters. Telling them her name! She knew she was the cause they had come to their home; they had stamped her family, they would persecute them till they destroyed them. And she was the cause!

With trepidation Eleni settled in the balcony waiting for her father to appear and erase instantly Kaliopi's words.

A man appeared at the corner, she sat up: it was not her father, it was Mr Kostas from the first floor. 'A civil servant,' she could hear her father mumble to mother, especially if Mr Kostas happened to have won at the card game: 'He has the heart of the civil servant – that's why he can concentrate on cards! The last to roll up his shutters, the first to roll them down. No crab.' Mr Kostas smiled at Eleni as always, and as always asked her, 'Are you still spying on us?' She smiled back, pleased with the greeting.

Then the landlord appeared, at his usual time. Eleni was dejected. He was ugly: big, shaved head, big droopy nose, small eyes, thin mouth which said, as it drooped so far downwards that its ends almost touched his chin, 'I have never smiled and shall never smile.' Eleni imagined God's hand giving that face life with a final, fed-up, unloving caress downwards, stamping on it lovelessness for ever, and saying to it, 'Thou wilt not smile.'

She watched and waited for her father to appear round the corner, and as time went by and he did not appear she erected nightmares. He was taken by the soldiers, was absorbed into the darkness of the curfew, swept down by the siren. She stood on her toes to look over the railings, now on this now on that leg, in a quick dance of expectation and fear; or sat, or knelt on the tiles and peered through the railings which she held tight wishing them to materialise her father instantly – and materialise, instantly, the outside world that he brought back with him: full of noise and exchanges, shops, perhaps food, and pleasure – and also, sometimes, inexplicable black fear, and war.

She would recognise him at once, from his walk – quick and unprotected, scattering looks and attention in all directions. When he brought food, although Mother had told him always to hide it under his coat or in his pockets, he never did, but carried it openly, moving his burdened arms with the rest of his body in great, constricted excitement. At some point, always at the same point, he would stop. He would look up: and would make a great show of surprise and joy to see her, raising his arms to her with ohs and ahs, and saying 'Is that my daughter? Is that my Benjamin? Is that my last and best?' And before Eleni had time to answer back, he would vanish into the doorway. She would run and wait for him at the door, and he, promisingly, temptingly, might put his hand in his breast pocket, on a good day, and quickly raise a parcel up in the air out of her reach. Her sisters would join the contest, leaping up round him trying to catch the parcelled token of love being raised as the bids were raised: 'Who loves me most? How much do you love me? To the ceiling? To the roof? To the sky?' And tokens and promises and assurances of love would fly up like long-imprisoned birds from the lips of the merchant's daughters. The youngest would promise, and be given, the best. 'You wily Ionia, you sweet Mikrasia.' Her father would shake his head with pleasure while dusky Sophia observed him with serious unforgiving eyes, and Kaliopi urged mother for her favours.

When Father was in good spirits, he held in his hands the key to the pleasures of life: when he said 'my girl', there was no question that she was – a girl! And when he said 'my girl is beautiful', she wanted no other beauty in life.

Eleni leaned over the railing to him and to the world's promised pleasures – but retreated: she knew instantly he was angry from the way he kept both hands deep in his pockets, his head thrust forward with purpose, his eyes darting about looking for a target.

'Not a soul! Not even a black-marketeer!' She heard him through the shut doors. 'It's not a shop, it's a gravestone! It sits right here, on top of my chest. My shop, my home, my innards – do you understand what I am saying, Anastasia? My being is withering, dying, in this war. What am I? Am I a shopkeeper? Without customers! Without new merchandise!'

'Gregori, stop. Listen to me. The Germans may requisition rooms – they came round today. Do you understand what I am saying? What are we to do?'

'Eleni is friendly with one of them! You should have seen her how she fluttered her eyelids at him when he talked to her.' Kaliopi described the visit in all its horrific detail.

'Stop tormenting me! All of you! You are crucifying me! And you – what kind of a wife are you? Always the bad news when I come home, as if I don't have enough.'

Eleni listened to her father unleashing his fury against her mother as if she was responsible for the Germans and the war, and the want, and the bad business. He paced up and down, slammed doors, stormed into rooms wanting something and not knowing or not remembering what he wanted. He coughed with rage, and panic.

His daughters stayed out of his way, divided even in their alliance of fear. Sophia looked at him with gathered vengeance. Kaliopi sided with Mother, but Mother was consumed by his rage. Eleni sat still and small in a corner wishing she was a worm, in a cocoon, till the anger went away. But the anger, blind and deaf to her wishes, devastated her games and the world: it gathered into a lump and lodged somewhere below her throat. While he raged blindly, helplessly, looking about for enemies, or allies, she kept her eyes down, out of fear and dislike – and the knowledge of a betrayal. She played house, and mothered her toy soldiers, perennially pointing their weapons at her, as the war moved into the home drowning her in dark heaviness.

'Go to him. See what treats he will give you now.' Kaliopi heaped her own fear on Eleni, and Eleni found nothing to say, because she knew she was paying now for her accumulated guilt, and for the open favours and the secret alliance with her father. Now, when he couldn't protect her, and she could do nothing to appease him, the rest of the world pushed them together. She knew that he was betraying her and that she was betraying him, as she had betrayed her whole family and home to the Germans: mesmerised, her eyes pursued his well-polished shoes pacing up and down.

The family sat at the evening table as if the entire German army had already invaded them. The food was not enough, Father and Mother, the providers, were empty-handed and silent. Mother shut doors and windows and with secretive ceremony distributed the corn bread amongst her children, who had developed a special faculty in measuring and comparing portions instantly, meticulously. They crossed themselves and prayed silently as their eyes travelled from plate to plate.

'You gave Eleni more,' Kaliopi whispered.

'Eat your food. I gave you all the same.'

'You always favour her! Your baby, your spoiled brat! And after what she has done!' Kaliopi was encouraged by the parents' silence. 'I wish she was never born. I wish I was never born.' She was overcome by the stupendous injustice done to her by the world. 'You give Sophia favours because she is the eldest, and you give Eleni favours because she is the youngest, and me? Where am I? Nowhere.'

'Children! Ungrateful children!' Mother broke into tears. 'You struggle for them, you go through agonies to find the next slice of bread, and all you get from them is ungratefulness! You see what you do spoiling her like that?' She passed on the burden to Father. And when, at other times, Father happened to be in a good mood, he would take his wife's scolding as if he were a son – 'Me! Poor me! What have I done now?' He would coax and tease, but appeased no one when, at the end, he drew his youngest one to him in sibling solidarity. 'Come, we are out of favour! Who says I spoil my poor little baby? If I catch anyone giving her a hard time, she will tell her daddy and he will show you . . .' Mother would leave the table and grab her embroidery in exasperation.

But now Father was no one's brother or friend or ally.

'I should have more because I am the oldest,' Sophia said, to heap coals of fire on Kaliopi's head. 'I am bigger – a bigger body to feed – with bigger responsibilities. Don't you always tell me to be the good example? Don't you always blame me if they do something wrong? I should be given more. I was here first.' With level voice and dark looks and subterranean motives, Sophia presented Kaliopi with locks and chains of logic that left her dumbfounded.

'So what?' Kaliopi broke the deadlock. Eleni felt secure while those two were at war.

But then Sophia decided to follow different tactics and take Kaliopi

100

into her confidence: Eleni saw the whispers and looks between them. Without Father's all-powerful friendship, she was exposed to her enemies. They would get her: they would crush her. Something, she was certain, had disappeared from her plate – then injustice, blind-folded, held its sword over the table, and fear and rage filled her head. The words, they would not come one by one, but altogether in a big heap, and out of her mouth they would all tumble in a clutter, or they would all stop, somewhere in her throat, and only half-words and pieces of words and yells could come out, or as if the words had moved through legs and arms, which lashed out at them and hit and broke and destroyed – bringing upon herself in the end the blame and just punishment.

At the end of the day, time to wash: the kitchen was the warmest room. The daughters took turns sitting on the stool between Mother's legs: with her fine comb dipped in paraffin she combed through their hair thoroughly and strongly. Eleni liked to feel her mother's hands hold her head firmly, move it in this or that direction, and search the surface curiously, separating the hair into different patterns and sensations. Then the slow dull scratch of the comb's fine, crowded teeth, the slight pull at the roots. One by one, the daughters stood in the tin basin that looked like a boat, covering their bodies trembling from the cold, and the shame. Mother washed and scrubbed them with quick assurance, with the combative efficiency, and hope, with which she kneaded her bread-dough. Eleni secretly looked at her reflection in the steamed-up glass door, scarred by newly formed tears sliding down the glass.

When her mother took the scissors in her hands to cut her hair – 'Easier to keep clean' – Eleni panicked, and ran, wet and trembling, from room to room and round the furniture, her mother behind her, threatening and losing her patience, while Eleni leaped right and left, trapped in a forest of massive black furniture, with treacherous carvings of fruit and flower feasts leaving their bruises on her as she ran round for her life. She knew she could escape Mother for a time, but in the end she was hers.

The hair was cut short, and it was only as she was losing her hair that it crossed Eleni's mind that girls have long hair and that she is a girl. Of course I am a girl, she thought, and was again struck by the thought, as she saw her girlhood cut away from her. 'It will grow,' she vowed, 'I am a girl' – and had a purpose in life.

'Go and lie with your father,' her mother said unlovingly, 'I will sleep here.' And Eleni had to go and lie next to him: cold and motionless with unhappiness, she hoped he wouldn't feel her presence. He tossed right and left, and coughed, and sat up holding his head between his hands, while she lay still as a statue, holding her breath and squeezing her eyes shut, pretending to be asleep, or forgotten, but betrayed by the playful tremulousness of her eyelids.

When she next opened her eyes he had already gone to his shop, and through the day she was given his guilty part to play. Their alliance of the night made her his substitute in guilt, and she waited loyally for him as if for a long-lost brother, or son, or father.

'Is that my boy?' he exclaimed with irrepressible gaiety at Eleni's short hair. 'Ach!' – he scolded himself with great drama – 'Did I say boy?' and with even greater astonishment, 'It's growing! It's already grown since yesterday!' He caressed her head, filled with admiration at this new miracle.

'And a surprise for my little wife! Write home and tell your mother to come. We'll see whether there is any room for the Germans.' The daughters rejoiced at the solution.

'One more mouth to feed, Gregori.'

'Haven't I told you not to upset your little mind about such things? What am I here for? I will feed you all! The shop will feed us! Look!'

As a final triumph, and to everyone's admiration and desire, he produced a large plump white loaf of bread. Eleni was persuaded there was no miracle on earth her father could not perform. He could please each one of her heart's desires.

'I gave wool for this, Anastasia! A hundred per cent wool – yards of it! And that big-arsed black-marketeer, that pimp, would give me only half a loaf of bread. "Take it or leave it" he said. I said, "a whole loaf". "Done," he said. I took the bread – and what bread, eh, Anastasoula! – and gave him the wool. But wait' – he couldn't hide his glee; he pulled Eleni close to him. 'He took it, but did he look at it? The great big pumpkin? Does he know the first thing about materials? The peasant! The Vlach! The Albanian! The material was all moth-eaten, Anastasia mou! Covered with tiny little holes! You have to hold it in the light to see them. A sieve, my little wife, a sieve!' The daughters joined in the triumph; Mother almost smiled, but remaining sulking. 'I had it from the shop in Kapnohori, a whole crate, crawling in moths! I almost threw it away – but divine providence stopped me, and now it will bring the odd egg, the odd little sardine for my Lenaki here – eh, Lenaki mou?' Eleni was chewing the full sweetness and pleasure of the bread.

'I'll take him more, Anastasia. I'll say, there, patrioti, have some more wool, first-quality wool, cashmere from England. He'll swallow it, the Vlach! He will buy it! I tell you, Anastasia, I'll fill the whole black market of this city with moth-eaten wool.' The daughters were impressed, and amused, as they chewed with slow, full relish the triumph of Father's shrewdness. And Mother tucked in her smile under her frown.

Father talked while Mother kept her eyes down on her embroidery. He made plans about the shop, how he would open it properly after the war, and knock out another door and window, for more air and more light; he worried in case the Germans got wind of his warehouse – without the materials hidden there they would all starve. But it was a good thing their money was in merchandise; it would keep them from starving. 'And after the war, Anastasia, that merchandise will shoot up in value! It will be gold, Anastasia mou, gold! The drachma – people wipe their arses with drachmas. I was wise not to touch it. Yesterday, you gave a thousand drachmas for an egg, today you give a million! For one egg! One egg! Currency! Shit-paper! Those golden coins' – he would whisper – 'that I put aside when the war broke, that was divine providence, Anastasia mou. They will give us a bite to eat if things get really black.'

Mother still sulked, but Eleni basked in Father's new mood and in the shared exile from Mother's love. She crept to his bed in the mornings to mother and console him, and made him yearn for Mother and home. In a perplexity of love he reminisced.

The market place of Mouryes, with the old Turk and his hubble-bubble, and the sweet hanoums that smelled like rose gardens. His father's shop decked in the silks of the Orient, light as a spider's web, crisp as the winter air. His mother in her European dress, the first in dancing and singing. Rows of mulberry trees, their juicy black berries feeding the children, their leaves feeding the silkworms that spun out of their entrails their endless silk thread. Thousands of yards of silk thread which they wrapped about themselves, until they were shut in their cocoons, warm and protected. 'Just like my little Elenaki here' – her father squeezed her tight – 'Till, after many days of waiting, out they jump! But what a miracle! They're not worms at all any longer! But – you wouldn't believe this, psyche mou – they're beautiful butterflies!'

'Those mounds of cocoons – pure gold, my daughter! One day you'll learn about the Golden Fleece. A great, a legendary treasure, kept in my homeland – until foreign interests and foreign capital set eyes on it. Their belly gurgled. And they came, like Jason in his boat, and stole it. They stole, and destroyed and ravaged and wrecked and killed. Cut us to pieces. Scattered us to the four winds! You will learn one day, Lenaki mou, about Jason, and Medea the witch, the whore of Babylon!'

He told her of the god Dionysos, from the depths of Anatolia, who brought madness to the women of Greece! 'You want to know about Eleni of Troy, eh! Don't you know who Eleni of Troy was?' He was shocked with pleasure at her ignorance. 'Ah, she was a compatriot of ours! The most beautiful and famous woman of Greece. Wars were fought for her! Why do you think I called you Eleni? Just by accident? I named you after our ancestor and compatriot! Troy was down the valley from us, the Trojan War was fought just outside our village, only for her beautiful face. Just like yours. My land was full of Elenis. My grandmother was Eleni. My little cousin whom I lost was Eleni. And all of them beautiful.' He told her about the Greek fleet, and General Agamemnon who had to sacrifice his little daughter Iphigeneia, to release the wind so the ships could sail to Troy and start the war: he brought tears to her eyes.

Eleni drank his words telling her who she was, where her true home was, to what terrible stories she owed her name and life. She thought of those lost homelands, but as she thought and yearned for them, the pain of their loss brought, almost, the sweet finding of them. She saw the poppies that colonised the fields and the wild anemones that appeared rare and alone on the cliff, carpets of camomile that brought sweet sleep and blessed dreams to disturbed hearts, oregano that gave flavour to everything, and laudanum that cured the bellyache and the stone in the bladder. The scent of wisteria in the late afternoon.

Ionia! The land of blessings and histories, of golden fleeces and witches and the sacking of cities, of unheeded prophecies and terrible mysteries that made men and women not know what they did. One day, when the good winds blew, she and her father would sail back, back to Ionia. Lying next to him, she was filled with the bitter-sweet music of nostalgia. 'Ach, Ionia mou! Me troi i nostalgia, Ionia mou. It wounds and eats me, here in my heart, and kills me every day.'

But time to go to the shop: he would take her to the shop one day – full of home! It was a promise. But now, Eleni stayed in the warmth of his bed, dreaming.

The air is heavy with stories, and with the scent of roses in the walled garden; and the honey-eyed hanoum is humming melodies of love. The barefoot Greek boy climbs up the wall to steal a glance, perhaps a word. In the distance the officers of Kemal Ataturk ride their Arab stallions on the empty shores of the Black Sea. At the top of

Mount Ida, where Zeus and Hera had played their loves and wars, Allah is sitting surrounded by mounds of pilaf sprinkled with sugar and cinnamon. He listens with drowsy pleasure to the muezzin's passionate prayer that echoes through valleys and ravines: his eyelids are raised to his cavalry riding on handsome large-haunched stallions on the beautiful shores of the Black Sea. Under his gaze the riders gain speed and power and number, and branch like red rivers of fire through the land. To forge a new map of the lands of Allah. Through lemon and orange groves, through pine forests and fields of delicate young wheat, down terraces of vines and olives, along endless avenues of mulberry trees. Wherever they go the land dries and burns, and the scent of burning young sap is incense to the powerful nostrils of Allah. The coasts of Allah crumble into the sea, taking with them cities, and myriad Greeks who appear in Allah's eyes like small ants: till the sea loses its blueness and darkens and thickens with the drowned bodies. The sun hides his face in guilt. But in the dark confusion a young boy has escaped from Allah's sated eye and is swimming, still swimming, towards her, calling out to her as she listens, and tries like a mother to make out his words. He could be taken for a seagull bobbing up and down, waiting for his fish. The tide brings to her fragments of his homeland. She watches in wonder the fine feather-light specks of ash settle noiselessly on the parents' white sheets.

Grandmother arrived from Kapnohori as if from the underworld – in black for Grandfather, pale, lifeless. But she had food hidden in her basket – corn bread, and flour, sesame-seed oil, kouskous, eggs.

'I thought we would never arrive!' Awesome in her layers of skirts, she lay back in one of the ebony thrones in the dining room as her daughter brought her water, and cologne to smell.

'You will uproot our souls, my Christian man, we said to the driver, but would he listen? He raced as if he was driven by demons. He took those turns on the mountains as if he wanted to kill us all. We prayed and retched, prayed and retched. People were going green and yellow, moaning and groaning, and would he stop? He went on, deaf to our misery, possessed. The smell! The noise! You thought it was the Day of Judgement. He could have gone through the valley – he said no, the Germans are guarding that route, we'll go through the mountains. We said the guerillas are guarding the mountains, he said so much the better, we'll give some food and courage to our brothers. So we crossed all the mountains of Macedonia, and Epirus, we came via Albania from the look of it. Fortunately he stopped at the chapel of Prophet Elias

105

where we lit a candle to the saint, and sprinkled holy water on the bus when the driver went for his physical needs, and we all washed our faces in the water of the spring, which is miraculous they say – miraculous! We saw two lorries turned over only a few metres away – and we recovered our souls before we got back into the accursed bus. Here. Here it is. My soul has come up to my mouth. We arrived just in time.'

When Grandmother recovered a little, she sat back with dignity, tied her silk scarf behind her head, and extended, like an exhausted queen, her hand: her grand-daughters kissed it respectfully, and then compared the coins she had slipped into their hands. When the family were sitting round her quietly, she told Anastasia to shut the doors and windows and started the stories of true outrage.

'It's gone, our village – gone. A battlefield! A refugee camp! The Germans come – they plunder, burn, kill, take hostages. The Bulgarians come – the same and worse. They dishonour our girls, and bring diseases. Then the guerillas come, take our boys and girls to their army, take what little food we have left, any old gun, even the antiquities from '21, even forks and axes, and disappear in the mountains. They come through our houses as if they are thoroughfares, our walls and doors are sieves from the bullet-holes. An inferno! Thank God both my daughters are married and out of the village!'

Anastasia asked after Pelagia and her husband: at least they were far from trouble in Serras. She asked after relatives, and friends, and shed fresh tears at each tragic incident. Her daughters followed her example. Grandmother sighed with the satisfaction of catharsis at the universal woe and wonder she had produced, and continued.

'Women – women wear the trousers nowadays and give the orders! Christ and the Virgin, what has the world come to! God protect us! Do you know who is the captain of the guerillas? You won't believe it! Olga, Baxivanis' daughter! And Aunt Marigoutha's. You remember Olga – a third cousin of yours, younger, much younger than you?' She was getting impatient with her daughter's puzzled face. 'That ugly, dark little fox, she played with the boys, with your brothers, and her mother was telling her she would grow a – you know what, if she were not careful.'

'Olga! Little Olgaki!' Anastasia exclaimed with astonishment, excitement. 'She ran messages for Gregoris – and never any shoes on her feet!'

'Kapetanissa Olga, if you please,' her mother corrected her. 'She is

106

the leader of the guerillas in our area! Trousers, cigarettes – paf-pouf, just like a man. The gun on her shoulder, the bandolier across her chest. And what happens on those mountains? God knows! Men and women together, comrade they go, comrade they come, God protect us!' She crossed herself looking upwards, while her grand-daughters hung from her lips.

'But she has devastated the Germans!' she continued with pride. 'She blows up bridges, she steals their ammunition from under their noses, she even takes hostages . . .'

Eleni and her sisters listened with awe. The world and war, in all their excitement, had finally come to them.

'Your brother Sotiris is with them, one of them,' Grandmother mourned. 'He hasn't gone to the mountains yet, but he works for them body and soul. Body and soul,' she repeated as if he were irretrievably – in body and soul – dead. 'But I lost Sotiris a long time ago – since he married that woman!'

'So the family has grown bigger!' the German translator said; the harshness with which he emphasised the vowels made his Greek sound like a foreign language. 'Who is this lady? Does she live here? Since when?' But he slowly lost fire before the towering black figure of Grandmother, standing solid and erect on the broad base of her petticoats, her eyes level, her hands resting with dignity on her apron – the family gathered behind her.

The Germans left and Grandmother settled in her daughter's home like a household goddess, black, stern, larger than life, giving orders to her grand-daughters, politely tolerating her son-in-law. Seated volumin-ously on her throne near the window, knitting socks and scarves for sons and grandsons, she established moral and religious order in the home, in which father became a generous and obliging guest.

The winter arrived overnight. A mad Vardaris got up suddenly and created havoc: it broke a window, overturned two of mother's gera-niums, and banged the shutters with such rage you thought the war had finally moved right into their homes.

'Kyrie Eleison!' Grandmother crossed herself with vehement indig-nation. 'Listen to him, the god-mad, the demonised Vardaris! You'd think it's the end of the world, the way he goes on.' She howled indignant prayers to the elements, while the elements howled back their fury and destruction.

In the morning, the tree in the backyard stood with bare arms raised

107

in anguish, savaged, still struggling against the wind. Eleni gazed at the empty backyard and the diminishing days through shut windows, and at the evenings prolonged by the shadows of the oil lamp.

While the droning of aeroplanes and the wailing of the sirens ruled the city, she gazed at a green world of mountains and gardens in pictures. If she put the pictures behind glass and half shut her eyes, they became brighter and more real, and mixed her reflection with their green and coloured landscapes. As she moved her face she had now a mountain slope for a cheek, now a tree on the tip of her nose, spreading its roots in her mouth, its branches through her hair, her eyes blinded and peering through flowers. Smiling cherubs rested round chins on plump hands in infinite comfort, while cats cried all night like babies in infinite sorrow.

A battery of guns at dawn. Dishevelled people with overcoats thrown hastily over nightgowns and pyjamas shivered on their balconies: startled, goose-pimpled faces questioned each other.

'Executions,' someone said. 'Reprisals. They've turned the White Tower into a prison.' Another battery of guns – crisp, clear, shattering the air people breathed to pieces. Sighs of resignation condensed in small warm clouds, disappearing in the cold morning. Shivering prayers, batteries of Kyrie Eleisons – hastily crossing themselves, they disappeared behind locked shutters.

The executions in the early dawn, the cart at any hour trundling up the cobbles to the cemetery. As by a sinister compulsion, Eleni and her sisters peeped at the nightmare, ready to fall to pieces as it jolted on the stones, carrying skeletal bodies thrown haphazardly on top of each other at different angles of intimacy that changed all the time as they jumped and danced to their destination. The swollen bellies oddly belied the spectre of hunger. To Eleni it brought tearfulness and belligerence in the middle of her being. Gnawed by hunger and by the fear of hunger she and her sisters fought perpetually over food, which they measured, weighed, counted, compared, in impassioned short-lived appeals to an ideal justice – which sooner or later let them down.

One hundred and sixty-five people! Burned alive in the public bakery for the killing of one German soldier. Justice, blindfolded and crazy, threw down her sword and abandoned the city.

The night noises. The cats. Eleni shut her ears not to hear the infuriated shrill miaulings and mournful wailings of the army of crippled starving desperate animals attacking empty dustbins and each other. It was worse when they disappeared and the nights became quiet: she listened for them. She knew they had killed each other, had died from hunger.

'People cook and eat them, that's what happens to the cats.' Kaliopi broke the peace of the room one evening.

'How do you know?' Sophia asked hesitantly, wanting and fearing to hear Kaliopi's tale of horror, which was already filling the room with shadows.

'What do you mean, how do I know?' Kaliopi shrieked with indignation. 'The whole world knows. Didn't you hear the piano teacher, Miss Euterpi, yelling at Mrs Mary in the basement and threatening to take her to the Red Cross? Pandemonium, doomsday, and you dozing! "She was my baby, my one and only, my Psipsina. I starved to keep my Psipsina fed and happy. I would give my life for my Psipsina, and you, you murderess, you cannibal, you Medea, you cooked and ate her!" She was pulling her hair, such as it is, and tearing her clothes, and do you know what Mrs Mary said? She said, "I had nothing to do with your Psipsina. Your baby, if you want to know the truth, has been rubbing her you know what with all the tomcats in Saloniki. You see, you feed her with chocolates, which you find who knows where, and how, and then our poor little Psipsina is on heat and rages and froths at the mouth night and day with all the stray cats. That's what happened to your little Psipsina – she's probably still having it away in someone's dustbin! Pity the pink ribbon round her neck!"

'"Liar, blasphemer, harlot," the piano teacher screamed. "They saw you talking to her with your poisonous sweetness – 'psi psi psi Psipsina – come to me, Psipsina, come and see what I've got for you.' And the whole street smelled of cooked meat, the very day my little angel disappeared."

'And then Kyra Katina next door said to the piano teacher, "I don't take sides, you are a good woman, and an excellent piano teacher, but, truth and justice should out, when the rest of us are starving, and could sell our soul for a slice of bread, it's a sin to feed your cat with chocolates."

'"Lies, all lies!" the piano teacher screamed.

'Then Kyria Eirini chipped in, "What do you expect, Miss Euterpi? Having that plump cat of yours strut around while our children waste with hunger."

'Well, I smelled the meat cooking.' Kaliopi gave her verdict. 'Everyone did, and it smelled different, like cat meat cooking. But the story doesn't end there, because Kyria Eirini's son, who reads all day long and knows about those things, he said that Mrs Mary will probably die from diseases that you catch from eating cat meat. She will get thinner and thinner and paler and paler and she will waste away. She is already showing the signs.

'That's what I call divine justice,' Kaliopi concluded with resolution, and let the other two wrestle in the dark with the hunger and the horrors she had unloaded on them.

'I saw the landlord's hoard the other day.' Kaliopi could not stop. 'He keeps it under his bed. Tins and tins, of jams and marmalades and corned beef, and ready-made soups, English chocolates, German cookies, hams and salamis.'

Eleni wanted to cry, she had no strength to block her ears, Kaliopi knew it and continued.

'His son brings them the food. Black market. He works for the Germans, and, as everyone knows' – she waited before she spat out the most damning accusation – 'he lives with a woman, in sin.'

'Lives with a woman in sin!' Hunger, food, sin, black market, living with a woman in sin. Eleni swallowed the clear and the dark meanings with greed. Achingly, relishingly she crawled, as Kaliopi meant her to, under the landlord's bed bearing unknown black acts of shame, and drowned in lakes of honey and mountains of pilaf, and rivers of milk – aching with emptiness.

Kaliopi was so thrilled by her stories that she started squirming in bed. Eleni knew her moment of power had come. Her tyrant and tormentor, the prophet of disasters, the perennial messenger of evil tidings, God's instrument of punishments and distributor of supernatural fears, had a human weakness: she was afraid to go to the toilet after dark. The corridors were full of ghosts, she was convinced, and was convincing everyone around her; and Eleni was forced, or threatened, or persuaded to go with her. She accompanied her sister on those visits to the underworld gladly, for the satisfaction they gave her of being the braver of the two, and to appease the demon of vengeance and condemnation in her.

As the air-raids became more frequent, the families in the apartment building gathered in Mrs Mary's basement flat. It was dark and dingy by day, you felt the damp in your bones; but at night, in the light of the oil lamp, the furnishings glowed with warmth and elegance. The pink lace curtains, the crimson velvet cushions, the satin spreads and lampshades, and the artful satin flowers, made the reception room look like a picture, a stage. Large frilly dolls posed in corners or rested on cushions, thick-legged porcelain ballerinas tip-toed on the sideboard. And in the midst, Mrs Mary's svelte, hungry-looking figure, always in the same black dress with the faint green sheen, moved stealthily, hospitable to everyone. The visitors always brought a contribution for the evening.

The cards were brought out. The children, securely sinking in the heap of overcoats, watched in a daze the mysterious preparations of the grown-ups as they distributed chips of various colours. They opened and closed fans of cards in private rituals of hope and reassurance, and studied secretively each other's faces. Nearby, Eleni's sisters, and Mr Kostas' and Mrs Lefkothea's daughter Electra, sat round a smaller table playing their own noisier, more light-hearted games. Sophia and Kaliopi sent furtive, envious glances towards Electra's bosom, which, thanks to her new soutien, seemed as if it had grown overnight; aware of the attention, Electra could not decide whether to hide it under the table or rest it on top. Soon the two sisters, despite maternal supervision, were listening with blushes and giggles to their friend's hushed accounts.

Through the night, the children's sleep was interrupted by the ghostly apparitions of the card players, whom they stared at with startled eyes. The self-absorbed circle of players was permanent, but the faces appeared full of shifts and changes. Mr Kostas' eyebrows danced with enigmatic signals to his wife; Mr Harilaos from the top floor pondered his cards – a smile passed over his face; Mrs Mary talked and played and teased; Gregoris, next to her, was excitable, reckless, optimistic, lucky, glancing for reassurance at Anastasia who sat quietly behind him.

Anastasia bent over her embroidery, absorbed in the luxurious landscape she perpetually conjured with her needle. Her motherly body, with its large, gentle curves, that seemed to Eleni now near and now distant, was a vigilant guardian over daughters and husband and the entire confused gathering in Mrs Mary's basement. Her stitches arranged everyone's moments according to her own secure designs. But her face was the face of a child: the angry knitting of her brows perennially reminding the world of a violence done to her. Her own mother concentrated on her knitting, pulling her wool with quick, determined tugs.

In one of her awakenings, Eleni saw her mother's body crouching over the copper coal burner in the corner of the room, rearranging the hot embers – her face flushed, her eyes bright olive green, her auburn hair neatly brushed in a bun. Eleni sighed with recognition and fell asleep. The next time she opened her eyes, the slim dark figure of Mrs Mary, bent over the coal burner, her face hidden by her black hair, frightened her. She remembered the cat, sniffed for cooked cat meat.

111

Perhaps there was not going to be an air-raid that night. The card players' voices were lullabies to the children. They gave them dreams of such magnificence: the Queen of Hearts, the King of Spades, the Knave of Diamonds, the mischievous Jester – fascinating couplings, intriguing triangles, powerfull alliances and original enmities – all dwelling in the familiar faces of fathers and mothers and neighbours.

The familiar voices muffled the fears, and the children stayed suspended in seas of warm drowsiness, interrupted perhaps by the sudden touch of creatures of the deep or icy currents chilling the backbone: weird yet familiar territories, where thoughts wander breezily, freely, aimlessly, sinking momentarily into dream; and dreams stay near the surface for a few fragile moments and, with each new wave of wakefulness, break – with relief or unutterable pain – into a thin white spray of images.

The quiet hum of voices was interrupted by an air-raid. The oil lamp was put out. A few moments of silence, vigilance in the dark, you heard people's different, uneven breathing warming and devouring the air, you felt the tightening of the heart, the children's sleep broken – then the raid stopped. The oil lamp was lit, the card game continued, everything was back to normal. Mr Kostas' turn – he played quickly and decisively; his wife decided after some deliberation and coyness to pass. Mr Harilaos' turn – he took his time. Father got impatient. But Mr Harilaos remained pensive, his head resting thoughtfully on his hands, his face bent downwards, his cards on the table. Mr Harilaos always took his time; the other card players waited. Father coughed with annoyance. Mrs Lefkothea teased him – 'Are you asleep, Mr Harilaos? It's your turn.' 'It's your turn, Harilae,' his wife repeated gently – she was always gentle and quiet – and stretched her arm round his shoulder as if to wake him up. 'Sweet dreams, sweet and sinless dreams, Mr Harilae,' Mrs Mary hummed in playful sing-song, while Mr Harilaos, under his wife's tender touch, keeled over and slid into her lap. Where he remained. It took her some time before she could utter in meek wonder: 'He is dead.'

Imitating the adults, the children clutched each other in mutual ignorance, and mutual knowledge of a horror hovering in the words – 'He is dead. He died from fear. Mr Harilaos died from fear.'

Mr Harilaos' death lingered in the neighbourhood as a person's smell lingers on one's clothes.

Like an epidemic, another man died from fear that winter. The seamstress's father – not old, not even retired yet. He was sitting on the toilet during an air-raid, he was taking ages. His wife and daughter knocked on the door. No answer. 'The blessed man, I always told him not to lock the door, we are humans, something might happen to us.' They got Mr Takis who works at the harbour and has muscles like overfed hamsters to break the door down, and what do they find – forgive me, my little Virgin, for laughing – there was Mr Menelaos, with his trousers down, sitting comfortably on the toilet seat, with your sympathy and all respect, leaning back on the wall as if he was resting in an armchair, God rest his soul, and dead. Dead. What a way to die! He always was a strange man, Mr Menelaos.

Mrs Mary was not the same after Mr Harilaos' death. She heard noises at night, things disappeared from her home, she felt someone hovering close, breathing her air, asphyxiating her. 'Right here' – she placed her hand between her breasts – 'He puts his hand here, while I am asleep, and presses and presses.' Kaliopi had seen Mr Harilaos' ghost disappearing down the basement stairs. Eleni listened to her stories, even giving new evidence herself. But when she was with her older sister, Sophia, who remained aloof, she put on an indifferent, sceptical front, and behind Kaliopi's back she even joined Sophia's sarcasms. Kaliopi was disgusted. 'You are either with me or against me. Traitor! I'll tell you no more of my stories!' Kaliopi's reign was the night: her whole being was so soaked through with the 'extrasensory phenomena', as she called them, that even the rationalist Sophia joined her younger sisters on their nightly journeys to the toilet. Eleni said that Mr Harilaos' ghost was hiding in the toilet bowl, what if a hand came up? 'Obscenities, smut!' Kaliopi could not allow jokes to undermine her fabric. But one more fear was added to the ghostly edifice, and for a long time all three would look well into the bowl before they half-sat on it.

The taste for ghosts was spreading. Mr Kostas began explaining to people about ectoplasm, and when doubted by Sophia, he brought out a massive volume of the *Encyclopaedia Pyrsos*, and showed them the photographs. 'This is the first encyclopaedia of Greece, written by scientists and learned people; it is no hocus-pocus. Ectoplasm is one of the latest discoveries. You cannot come here, a mere schoolgirl, and tell us that ectoplasm is fairytales.'

In the meantime, a séance was organised. Kaliopi had persuaded mother to hold it in their apartment, and to make a sweet loaf especially for the occasion. Mr Kostas came early with the medium – a distant cousin of his – carrying a small round table, which he placed with care in the middle of the room. The medium, a strong-looking, black-eyed woman with a scarf round her head, sat importantly near the table and kept a mysterious silence. The Gregoriou daughters asked her about the table – 'Does it really have no nails in it?' The woman answered in tired monosyllables; she took deep breaths frequently and raised her eyes towards the ceiling. Everyone spoke in whispers in her presence. Eleni brought the kitchen stool, and secured a privileged position near her. When the woman rolled her eyes upwards so only the whites showed, Eleni softly touched her to make sure she was alive. Kaliopi, who felt this was her field of power, kept telling Eleni to sit further away – otherwise it would not work. The medium was given the largest portion of Mother's sweet loaf because it was important for her to be fed and strong: the communications took it out of her.

When Gregoris came home, the atmosphere became fragile. Who was this woman doing hocus-pocus in the middle of his home? He threatened to throw everyone out, he had his accounts to do. The medium said she sensed there was someone in the house who doubted; he should be taken as far from the room as possible, because otherwise the spirits would not come. Mr Kostas began explaining to Gregoris about ectoplasm, but Gregoris effervesced with contempt. 'Ectoplasm! Pumpkins! As if we don't have enough worries, we want to communicate with the dead! And what dead? Harilaos! Harilaos was dead when he was alive, imagine what he is now!'

'Don't blaspheme, Gregori,' Mother pleaded.

In the meantime, dark blankets were hung round the window. The medium was mumbling unstoppably. Mr Kostas gave directions: once the communication started, no one was allowed to leave the room; whoever was weak should go now. Sophia got up and left the room. Kaliopi looked at her with contempt, then glared ferociously at Eleni, watching for the slightest blasphemous grimace. Under her eyes Eleni agonised to stop her father's word 'pumpkins' echoing in her head: she felt an uncontrollable need to laugh until she exploded with laughter into thousands of pumpkin seeds.

'Shouldn't we ask the bereaved to be here? He is after all her husband,' Mrs Mary remembered suddenly. A look of 'How could we have forgotten!' dawned on everyone's face.

'She will be upset,' Mr Kostas decided, 'and will disturb the spirits.' Heads nodded in agreement.

Fingers, all sense and perception, caressed the table into movement and life with featherlike delicacy, faces were absorbed in the desire for a sign. The mumbling of the medium became faster, her breathing heavier, her thighs further apart: drops of sweat appeared on her

114

forehead, a stench came from her crotch, heavy thuds shook everyone, the table moved in all directions. 'He is with us! Harilae, talk to us, Harilae, how are you? Are you well? Do you have any messages for your poor wife? Ah, she is melting with sorrow, Harilae!' they all shrieked at once.

'Harilae, are you there?' The medium tried to restore order. 'Speak to me, Harilae, don't go away, don't be frightened. Tell me what you want from Mrs Mary. Is there something you want to tell us about Mrs Mary? Are you with us, Harilae, or not? One movement for yes, two movements for no.'

The thuds were stronger this time. 'It's the door,' Mr Kostas announced.

Instantly, the oil lamp was lowered and Eleni found herself thrown on the couch under heavy blankets. Enemas, hot-water bottles, thermometers, glass-cups, alcohol were dumped on top of her; Mother sat nearby applying alcohol compresses on her forehead, Grandmother raised threateningly the enema. Eleni became the centre of attention and hope, but hardly had time to exult in this new role before she found herself surrounded by a group of soldiers staring at her with intense interest. They looked round the room, measuring furniture and people as if intending them for liquidation, then examined the curious medical instruments. One of them took the enema from Grandmother's hands, said something in a foreign language and they all laughed. Eleni felt a hot wave of shame go through her body; her face was breaking out in fever; her mouth was dry, her lips chapped, ready to tear and bleed. She lay immobilised, embalmed in her own sweat; her eyes burning with fever were seeing things – the medium staring up with no eyes, Grandmother raising the enema full of hot garlic water over her, Mother pushing the thermometer into her mouth. She realised then, and was petrified by the thought, that she was dying from fear. 'This is what dying from fear is like': she thought of Mr Harilaos and Mr Menelaos with camaraderie. Mother's cool compresses gave her relief; and the smell of urine reminded her with endless sweetness and pleasure that she still lived.

'Piccolo malato,' cried Mr Kostas, who was good at foreign languages. 'Piccolo malato,' he repeated triumphantly when he saw some response in the soldiers' faces. 'Piccolo malato' – her father repeated the words confidently, looking at Mr Kostas for confirmation. The soldiers were looking at each other in some confusion. Mr Kostas poked a finger in Eleni's chest, repeating with slow emphasis 'pic-co-lo ma-la-to'. The soldiers looked at him, looked at Eleni, looked at each other, puzzled:

115

finally one of them cried with great triumph of discovery, 'Piccolo malato!' The rest of the people in the room took heart and repeated with relief the magic formula. 'Piccolo malato,' mother repeated politely, and 'piccolo malato' said father obligingly. And 'piccolo malato' the soldiers sang, amused, winking at Eleni as they left the room.

'What is piccolo malato?' Father asked.

'Don't you know what piccolo malato is?' Mr Kostas was amused by his friend's ignorance. 'It means the child is ill.' He repeated the words slowly and emphatically, letting the sound reveal their meaning. Everyone was impressed.

'But this is Italian,' Sophia announced, and her words fell in the room like a bomb. 'Piccolo malato is Italian. What good is Italian with German soldiers?'

'What Italians, what Germans?' Mr Kostas said with largesse. 'They are all enemies.' And the others accepted the truth and wisdom of his words.

'Nea Ionia,' he read out to her with pride. 'Gregorios Gregoriou. Clothes Merchant.' She looked at the dark hieroglyphics over the entrance and repeated to herself the words. He pushed up the corrugated shutters with one confident agile movement, unlocked the glass doors and stood on the threshold:

'Our shop. It will be yours one day.' He bent down to her, his face looked serious. She stretched up to him and to the seriousness of the occasion.

The dark lingered even after the light came in, and the furniture remained still, still paralysed by the night's inertia. The long wooden counters showed a surface smoothed down and polished by years of touching and caressing with fabrics; even the corners were soft and rounded, and Eleni's first move was to run her fingers up and down the worn, warm wood. The bolts of fabric, neatly stacked, kept their colour locked in themselves. She looked round the shop for something with more animation. Slender yard-sticks leant neatly in a corner; stacks of wrapping paper hung from a string. A row of scissors, slender, elegant, lay neatly next to each other on a shelf. The shop was not splendid enough; it was smaller, darker than she had expected.

She studied a picture on the wall: it looked old but it told, animatedly, a story. On the right-hand side a fat man with a rosy smiling face sat back in a deep armchair, his hand resting on his round belly which bulged out of his clothes; on the left, in a dark, empty shop a scrawny, unhappy man crouched on a stool. Her father read to her

116

the words under the pictures – 'Dealing in cash' under the fat man, 'Dealing in credit' under the thin man.

He paced up and down the shop looking impatiently at the shelves where his fabrics lay. He examined the half-opened entrance to the shop, trying to decide whether to open it wide to the world, or to shut and double-lock it to keep the enemy out.

Eleni sat at the cashier's desk, trying to avoid his angry eye, but feeling it concentrate and deposit on her the melancholy of the empty, unused shop. It was like a home without a heart: and the shared melancholy of homelessness imprinted in her their unwritten alliance and partnership.

The shop assistants arrived one by one. Thick-built Phrosyni, the cashier, came first. Eleni's mood was deepened by the woman's austerity, the opaque stockings round her large-ankled legs, the tight-braided hair at the back of her head. Everyone knew that Phrosyni was a woman of God, a Sunday-school teacher, who never revealed her arms or legs to anyone.

'Poor orphan, poor refugee orphan,' Father liked to say, relating to his family the sufferings of Phrosyni and her mother. 'A young woman at the Katastrophe, her husband lost at Aivali and Phrosyni only a baby. But she and her baby managed to cross to Thrace. What adventures, what sufferings, looking for her husband all over Greece – and not a sign, the earth had swallowed him! And with what heroism she raised that child! What a life of chastity and good works, and prayers for his return.'

And when his feelings of pity and sympathy were satisfied he would vehemently apply the moral of the story to his own family: 'Sunday school – all of you to Sunday school! Anastasia, I hold you responsible. That will put an end to their wasting time with— novels. Because where would you all be without the intervention of the holy Virgin? To whom do we owe our shop and our business, in these days of starvation? Eh? To whom do we owe my miraculous salvation in the Katastrophe? A young, innocent boy! She took me by the hand, and gave me food, and led me to the boats. And one day who knows, she may bring me to my long-lost family.'

Eleni sat next to the embodiment of her father's religious fervour, oppressed by sanctimony. She leafed through a stack of thin grey books that Phrosyni produced from a secret cupboard, concentrating on the small grey pictures of Jesus on the Cross and the saints in different postures of torture.

Shortly afterwards, Mr Argyrios arrived: a small, elderly man, in a

117

threadbare but elegant suit. He stood behind the counter in silent dignity: Father treated him with respect. Chubby-cheeked young Steryos came last. 'Time for siesta,' grumbled Gregoris, as Steryos gave a furtive twinkle-eyed wink to Eleni and grabbed the broom and dustpan.

'They do nothing – there is nothing to do,' Father would complain in the evening to Mother. 'But I keep them. I pay them. Do I let them starve? They are my people. My compatriots.' He rapped his forehead with his knuckles in exasperated charity.

Phrosyne pored over yesterday's account books; Mr Argyrios stood motionless, as if he were the owner. Gregoris walked to the entrance decisively and raised the shutter higher. The street, quiet and grey, crawled into the shop bringing not customers but fear of foreign armies.

Steryos was placed at the entrance: 'Come and see our new cottons,' he mumbled to the occasional passer-by. Gregoris paced up and down behind him: 'Put more feeling into it, my boy. More heart.'

Mr Aslanoglou walked into the shop like a memory and promise of plenty – a generous voice, ample laughter, sagging folds of flesh, loose, tamed, recalling poignantly past satisfactions. He smelled of cinnamon and nutmeg, as if he had just been feasting on steamy, buttery semolina halva; and carried with him the flavours of Karaman and Capadocia, and of the lands of the Black Sea. Mr Aslanoglou, the Karamanli, brought into the shop the land of herbs and spices.

He sat abundantly on a chair which suddenly became small and flimsy under his volume, and gave a deep sigh that contained the sweetness of lost homelands – and an 'Ach' of premeditated pleased surprise when Eleni landed proprietorially in his large motherly lap.

'Ah, Gregori! Don't eat your heart out, Gregori! When the war is over, you will make business again, you will make bargains, you will make money. Now come and sit here with your friend Aslanoglou. Come. For a good mouhabet, a good lacridi, as in the old home.' He spoke now Greek now Turkish with a lilt that sounded like the plaintive music of the lyra. 'You remember the sausages at home with all the spices of Arabia, Gregori? And a swig of raki to punish, to quench the bitterness! Eh, what fire! Ah, Gregori! Gone. And what are we left with?'

Eleni, at home in his lap, followed her father: his jawline moved up and down; his eyebrows came together in hard concentration on his friend's words. 'It's all right for you, Aslan. You have sons. You can sit back and let them run the shop. You may die, but the shop will be there, in your name. I've got three daughters, and three dowries to provide. I've got responsibilities, duties. And if I don't produce now while I'm still young, when will I do it? And who will look after the shop in my old age, when I die? Dowries! We can't buy a loaf of bread!'

'Gregori, we can't take our shops with us. Saltiel's shop is shut. Molho's has been shut for a week now. Kounio's, the same. All the Jewish shops are locked up. And the people? Gone, disappeared! Their families, the same. Things could be worse, Gregori, much worse. Yesterday it was our turn to feel the knife, today it seems it's someone else's. And no one knows about tomorrow. All we can do is have patience. Come now, Gregori. Come and sit here with your old friend, your compatriot, your brother, and let's remember the good old days, the good old homeland. I've got such longing, Gregori, for that tearful amane that only the Turk knows how to sing.'

They talked about the war, the enemies and the allies, the victories. The Greeks were now fighting amongst themselves on the mountains, Grivas on one side, Captain Markos on the other. The Greeks! Always fighting between themselves! What a history! They remembered old wars and histories: 1922; Pontos; Smyrna; Ayia Sofia; the Patriarch. Familiar, mysterious names of unknown significance, splinters of worlds, half-recognised feelings. As Mr Aslanoglou wandered the shores of the Black Sea and came to rest in his village, his voice in an unstable sing-song glided along stretches of sweet-sounding, mournful-sounding Turkish. Eleni listened to their outlandish lullaby, nestled in the lap of a world-large loss – the land and the sea about her perpetually falling. Mr Argyrios joined them, and spoke, in archaic Greek, about a Sunday morning, in a summer home in Koutsabasi, just out of Smyrna, where his wife and daughters were massacred. In Eleni's ears the unmelodic note of despair struck, in measured, pure Greek, like a lucid, evil thought.

Father wanted the talk to stop. He got up and walked decisively to the door as if to go; stopped and examined the street, cautiously, to the left and to the right, then came back and with sudden exuberance, and love, pulled Eleni to him.

'Come, Lenaki mou, now I'll show you where I keep my real shop – where I hide my treasures.'

Eleni left Mr Aslanoglou's comfortable lap with misgiving, but curiosity and her father's wish won. She took his hand and followed him to the back of the shop, where he tried his keys on the two padlocks of a small cupboard door. He guided her in the dark: a few steps down, a bitter smell of mothballs, and – click – she found herself in a large room, much larger than the shop itself. It was crammed with boxes of all sizes, crates, chests, rolls of fabric, suitcases, furniture. Wax dolls with ideal faces and figures, bigger than herself, leaned with inflexible rectitude against the wall.

'Sh! Not a word! Not a whisper! If the Germans get a whiff of this, we are lost. Come! Have you seen such velvet, Lenaki mou? Touch it – soft like a peach!'

Eleni's admiration and the soft pleasure on her fingers gathered in her mouth and made it water with imaginations of gigantic paradisal fruit, which she had not tasted.

'Fit for queens! You don't find this stuff any longer, my child. This is pre-war work, *veritable*, by honest good hands, made with patience, with art, my child, with art. Look at these cottons – woven in Naoussa and Edessa, where big waterfalls make the machines.move, and create this beauty. Look at these prints. True gardens! Imagine what lovely dresses you will wear when the war is over! And these kilimia – from home! Let Vardaris blow, let the sea freeze – Lenaki mou has nothing to worry about, wrapped in these soft kilimia. She will think she is hidden in a silk cocoon, in the heart of summer itself. They're made by refugees like me, like us. Only they know the art.' He shook his head in contemplation of all the blessings and graces his compatriots had brought to this country. 'The locals?' he murmured with conspiratorial contempt. 'Albanians! Bulgarians! Thick-headed! Your mother excepted, of course, and don't you tell her this. But without us Ionians where would they be? They would still be in the Middle Ages!' He held his finger to his lips, his eyes dancing with conspiracy: 'Not a word!'

'Not a word,' she agreed, proud at this new confirmation of their alliance, their partnership. She wanted to be a true Ionian, like her father. He made plans for her: he would take her to the shop, she would start as a messenger-boy, then be an assistant – she would travel with him to learn the trade. It didn't matter that she was a girl, no one would know. They would go to big cities with splendid restaurants and cafés to choose and buy, they would go to villages in Macedonia to sell, they would travel all over Greece, they would see the sunset from the rock of the Acropolis one day. They would have fresh mullet in the harbour of Piraeus.

'Now this is what I call silk, Lenaki mou. No thinness, no flimsiness here. Feel the weight, my soul, see how it slips through your fingers! A waterfall! This is art, psychi mou, this is beauty, this is pleasure, and Father will dress you in such silk from head to toe when you become a bride, when you grow up – what am I saying? I forgot! We won't let you marry! We won't let you grow up – you'll stay with us and look after us in our old age!'

He led her to further schemes and wonders. He unrolled oriental gardens woven in rugs, he unfolded Allah's paradise in tapestries. And Eleni – perennial daughter, doubtful bride – instantly blooming and instantly wilting from the worm in his words, followed: the illusive beauties of womanhood.

Aslanoglou was calling from the shop. 'You stay and play house here like a good girl.' And without waiting for an answer he hurried back to the shop.

She opened the first box hesitantly. Soon, taken by a hunger for possession, she was opening chests and suitcases, pulling out curious, new, old, exquisite, priceless merchandise which she left strewn behind her. Transparent, slippery, ideal stockings for ideal legs; white, tender gloves to fit the most delicate of hands; scarves scattered with bright red roses or strewn with forget-me-nots, or blue like the Aegean, dotted with small and big islands. Lacy curtains, shimmering in the electric light. Towels with an embossed Acropolis flanked by two large angels; ladies' lace-frilled combinations, tight-waisted big-bosomed corsets, tiny ladies' hats with large coy buckles, ties and bow-ties striped or dotted, and stretches of fabrics in colours and textures to her heart's desire.

She wore the most ethereal stockings, the highest-heeled shoes, the most shapely corset, a nightie with the most delicate scalloping round neck and shoulders – long, white, perfect. She stood precariously in her instantaneous womanhood. A lace curtain, all airiness, fastened on her head under a hat, trailed several yards behind her, investing her with bridal magnificence. She built her seraglio out of silk rugs and satin quilts, and velvet tablecloths; she spread round her bright cushion-cases portraying sad Pierrots and coy Columbines. She hung tapestries of oriental gardens glowing in unearthly light, with secretive kiosks and lakes reflecting a moonlight you could drink: ferocious-looking, black-bearded sultans abducted beautiful hanoums – their torn veils revealing black terrified eyes. She reclined, in accomplished feminine beauty, bridal incandescence, letting her eyes rest and play on the delicious scene, letting the day roll past in royal leisure.

When she entered the shop, her father threw up his arms in wonder at the apparition. 'Are my eyes deceiving me? Where has this beautiful bride come from? From Smyrna! The bride of Smyrna! No, she is not my daughter! Not little Eleni! What a transformation!' And Eleni, transformed, gazed from her pedestal with amused pleasure at her eternal admirer.

'Such a beautiful bride should have a beautiful trousseau – the freshest, whitest linens, and the shiniest satins. And an entire wardrobe: greens, to match her eyes, and her warm complexion. Bright prints to suit her Ionian temperament. This light blue, the colour of the sea, the colour of an April dawn.'

Eleni watches the sunlight catch her father as he moves – his white shirt, his agile fingers, the taut forehead, the finely lined skin. He pulls bolts of fabric from the shelves, makes them turn and dance in the air, unfolds a profusion of colour which falls on the counter in large generous waves. Instant waterfalls lie billowing on the wooden surface like a multi-coloured sea flooding pastures and gardens. He picks up the supple landscape and lets it fall and drape from his hands and arms so that it catches the light, and eye.

Eleni, the daughter and bride, still as a statue, is trapped in the scene congealing about her: her father moving, talking, smiling, caught in the perpetual fall of an outlandish landscape of fabric and word; tangled in the perplexity of the word, drawn into its watery mazes like a young, inexperienced swimmer. 'The water will carry you' – a woman's familiar voice comes with the sea breeze that blows through the shop. Eleni wonders what all those drowned bodies are doing suspended in the underwater haze of the shop; then she imagines she has caused them to drown, all, except her father walking to the doorway holding a mass of fabric to examine in the sunlight. 'Look how the greens and blues come to life in the sunlight!'

A young fly watched, dazed, the busy spider weave round her his exquisite ethereal web; watched and measured the liquid silken thread as it spun out of the father's entrails to enthral a daughter in unsuspected timelessness.

To pass the time, Eleni pretended to herself she could read. She stared at the black labyrinths of print, each curve and line a riddle. She concentrated on the figures, trying, by sheer wish, to hook their meaning which, like a shoal of young fish, fearfully and gracefully evaded her insistent eye. Occasionally she recognised a letter, or a word, like a familiar, remote face in a crowded street, the end of Ariadne's thread. She looked at her father doing his accounts, filling sheets of paper with numbers in confident extravagant lines. She saw her mother pricking with her needle the fabrics from Father's shop, conjuring with her thread her own flower labyrinths that imprisoned her eyes in their intricate patterns. Her sisters, perplexed in prehensile tendrils of girlhood, that left her out. Each attended to their

122

own private world. Like a silkworm she wove her own riddle, wrapping herself with the liquid thread that came from her entrails – as the lamplight condensed into drowsy darkness.

With scissors and staple-gun, she made her own book out of wrapping paper from Father's shop. She held the book with pride, and to seal her possession she asked him to write his name on it and the name of his shop in big clear letters. She studied the intriguing figures on the blankness of the paper, trying to pair them with the familiar sounds. But his name, exposed to her eyes and forming itself on her lips, still remained secret – no, not secret, but open and simple and clear like the daylight: letter paired with sound, figure with movement of tongue and lips, the words became large, legible, magnificent, and she small, strolling in the early hours of a summer morning in a strange, still unawakened city.

'I can read,' she whispered to herself. 'Gregorios Gregoriou. Clothes merchant. Nea Ionia. I can read.' Her words hardly disturbed the gathered family silence.

'Mother, I can read,' she said in a firm, clear, imploring voice, and with agonising eyes she read, and heard her voice rise up in her like a wail, like a war wail, which as it reached her mouth formed into words – Gregorios Gregoriou . . . Good, loud, clear words, familiar words, loved words, which shattered the surprised silence of the room.

The war ended spectacularly. Bombs exploded with triumphant finality, and the siren gave her longest, most desperate, last wail that shook the city and the hills to their foundations. The fire began at the warehouses near the waterfront, and was pushed by the sea breeze towards the market place.

'The shop! The fire is near the shop!' Mother and Father threw their overcoats over their nightwear and ran into the night. Grandmother shot a battery of prayers to the Almighty. 'Theouli mou sose mas. Eftase to telos!' The daughters wandered round the house in a somnabulist alarm. Eleni climbed up the forbidden stairs to the roof terrace. She stood on tiptoe, a head taller than the parapet, and saw the city illuminated by a thick cloud of orange smoke travelling fast towards her. Beyond it, where the sea was, and beyond the sea where Olympus should be, darkness. She saw flashes of light followed by deafening sounds; the glowing smoke carried small pieces of fire with it. She wondered where her father's shop was, where her parents were. She was lost in the light and noise. And as she stood there and watched, the flames became so large and bright that they lit the entire city and

123

bay: Turkish minarets rose erect through the flames, she saw multitudes of people pushed by the fire into the sea, till the bay was thick with drowned bodies, floating on the luminous surface, pushed by the tide back and forth. She ran down and saw her mother and father climbing up the stairs, their faces and hair covered in soot, their eyes sparkling with alarm, and holding in their arms, with such secret tenderness, their babies!

'Babies!' she mused, sinking into a fathomless question. 'They saved the babies!' She wanted to lie down and die, but ran up the stairs to the terrace and watched with rage and desire the flames raging through the city. At dawn she saw her parents, ravaged by the night's holocaust, unwrap smudged bolts of fabric. 'We'll start another shop with these,' Father comforted Mother.

A large crowd had waited at the German building since early morning. Soldiers heaved crates into trucks, the crowd at the gate quarrelled, shoved each other out of the way. Eleni was separated from her mother and sisters; neighbours didn't recognise her. When the German soldiers appeared at the windows, the crowd pushed forward, their arms stretching upwards for the packages that came flying down. Eleni was overcome by desire, agonising need, for her parcelled-up portion of salvation; she thought of her father holding up in the air his parcel of love, bartering with her, and she jumping as high as she could, raising the price, 'I love you – as high as the ceiling – as high as the sky!' She fought on all fours through the feet and legs about her until she finally held her trophy – a squeezed, broken tube. She automatically put its nozzle in her mouth, and with distaste swallowed the minty soapy substance.

Someone's hand guided her out of the crowd. She looked up and recognised the German officer with the thick-rimmed glasses. His hair looked lighter than she remembered, his face serious, private. 'Come with me,' he said in foreign Greek. They entered the building, climbed dark flights of stairs, walked along corridors lined with crates: through open doors she saw large empty rooms. He led her into one of them, where the darkness was razored by shafts of sunlight through the shutters. She discerned a few pieces of office furniture: a desk, with a disturbed layer of dust on it, caught the light interruptedly, a cupboard opposite it, a chair in the middle of the room. There were faded patches on the wall surrounded by square, dark, dusty haloes. The brown linoleum had marks and worn areas. He pointed to a heap in the corner of the room, and she saw as she came nearer, in petrified ecstasy, treasures: dolls, blue-eyed, pink-faced babies, in pink organdie dresses, toy prams, cookers, trains, merry-go-rounds, tiny trees and animals, village houses with bright red roofs.

'Take them – you can have them,' he said in his foreign Greek. His face remained passive. She stood still, silent, matching his silence. The same window that had breathed out the foreign music now let in the piercing shafts of Greek sunlight. She could almost reach the music, she stretched her thoughts to it, but its melodies still evaded her. Still evaded her, as the blades of light and the voices from outside rushed in, reminders of war and the enemy, and changed that sweetness to fear. She rushed out of the room, along corridors, down flights of stairs, into the stabbing sunlight.

At the end of the day, the family sat round the table in the room reserved for Christmas and Easter, and Mother distributed evenly and justly the loot: soap, chocolates, toothpaste, biscuits, cigarettes. Kaliopi said, 'We cannot have this soap, it's made of Jewish flesh.' Eleni did not understand. She allowed her mother to put into her mouth, with religious solemnity, her first ever piece of chocolate, but as the brown cloying sweetness filled her mouth, recollections, recollections kicked their way out in a small dirty river on her mother's starched, white tablecloth.

At the end of the war, Father took the family to the seafront. They promenaded past the cafés: he and Mother in front, arm in arm – Eleni holding now his hand, now her mother's; Grandmother, flanked by her elder grand-daughters, following behind, huffing and puffing under her voluminous skirts.

The daughters paused opposite a café where a group of officers – English, they thought – sat drinking beer, laughing noisily; two well-dressed ladies sat with them, their legs crossed, smoking, sipping granita and speaking in Greek to each other. Mother herded the family to the opposite pavement, pulling Eleni by the hand while she stole backward glances at the scene of pleasure. A beautiful woman walked past in a thin flowery dress, unstable on her high heels but moving legs and arms with free grace; her hair tied back in a ribbon, revealing a graceful neck; she looked like spring in person.

Father announced he would take them on a boat ride. Amidst a flock of voices of shock, joy, thrill, he haggled with the laconic boatman. Small boats rocked sensuously on the wave: their white canopies fluttered in the breeze, plump white cushions with seagulls embroidered on them waited for bodies to lean upon them. Brief idylls, fragments of paradise, impermanent, swaying in a light-hearted unstable dance.

'He wants to drown us all! Children – wife – and me in my old age!' Grandmother, who had never been in a boat, crossed herself endlessly, delivering her last prayers of anger and resignation at the blue sky. Sky and sea remained silent and amazed at the large black-clad figure at the edge of the wharf quarrelling with the peaceful elements.

'Gregori, this is madness,' his wife scolded him tenderly. 'Think of your children! What if the boat turns over – none of us can swim!' Her voice was young, her eyes danced with the boat, and as her husband took an exuberant, triumphant leap into the boat, making it break into a wild unrhythmical dance while he kept his balance with spirited acrobatics, she sang excited appeals – 'My little mother! My little Virgin! Gregori! Don't!' But when he stretched his arm and pulled her, she leapt as lightly as the wind into the boat and into his arms. She glanced a blush at her mother, standing upright on the quay in her dignity and defeat.

The daughters, seeing the spirit of childhood win, jumped in a frenzy of excitement and impatience round the black-clad solid figure. The boatman fluffed up a cushion and helped Mother to a seat, while Gregoris lightly and irreverently urged his mother-in-law. She shrieked and moaned and threatened and pleaded as the two men coaxed and guided her weight with big noises of effort into the boat, which was thrown into a whirlwind of alarm and bewilderment. They seated her in the prow, surrounding her with tiny embroidered cushions: she could be taken for a gigantic mermaid courted by a flock of plump doves or round-cheeked cherubs. The daughters now took high arching leaps into their father's arms – 'Oppa! Hoppla! Bravo!' Father made a great show of losing his balance to frighten the women and amuse his daughters; the boat, at the mercy of the different movements and tempers and whims, had lost all sense of order. Amongst the great confusion of fright and gaiety, the boatman rowed firmly and rhythmically out to sea.

Grandmother sat quietly reminiscing, perhaps missing the tobacco fields; Father had one arm round Mother, the other hung outside the boat, leaving a watery path behind it. 'Is my little woman happy? Is my girl pleased now?' he teased his wife, and she leaned her head on his shoulder. Kaliopi, the nightingale of the family, was humming a tune. Her voice was balm to the heart, her face moved with sweet melancholy dreaminess as she sang 'I wish I were taken by the waves, by the winds, by the clouds.' Everyone listened in reverie. Eleni said she could see their house. Their eyes followed the edges of the city as it embraced the bay. The afternoon sun was reflected in the numberless windows, and to those rocked by the waves the city appeared in an inconstant dazzle. Other boats in the bay rocked each to its own rhythm; voices sometimes came with the breeze and sometimes were lost. Mother's face was soft, and Grandmother's thoughts were distant; Father rested his head on Mother's bosom. He looked asleep. Mother passed round handfuls of roasted pumpkin seeds, and Eleni admired her sisters cracking the seeds between their teeth with such quick deft movements of tongue and lips, keeping the kernel and spitting out the shell – tsik, tsik, tsik, like busy happy cicadas.

When the sun was about to set, the boatman stopped rowing and everyone turned to look at the shore. He started singing a monotonous Turkish melody that sounded like a persistent high-pitched moan. Father followed the boatman's dirge in a language no one else on the boat could understand. His daughters had never heard their father sing. The city was ablaze for a few moments, like a haunting spectacle conjured by the song. Then, Mother said, it was getting chilly, they should be thinking of home.

· 6 ·
Civil War

NOW THAT the war was over, Gregoris Gregoriou decided to take the market by storm. He strode down Ionos Dragoumi Street, his face quick with changeable emotion, his hand in his pocket clutching a large bunch of keys. He shook his head disdainfully at the locked corrugated shutters of the shops.

'Sweet dreams! Sweet, sinless dreams! The markets are open and free, full of opportunities, the world is racing to make up for lost time, Europe is rebuilding, reconstructing, and now that Greece needs active hands and shrewd minds, our merchants here are having their siesta! Lolling in the arms of Morpheus! And then we complain that we are backward, underdeveloped!'

He crossed himself several times with energy and determination as he passed the church of Agios Minas, the local protector of good merchants. Then he went back to his bright speculations: his new shop was three times larger than the old one, embracing the entire corner, with façades both on Ionos Dragoumi and Ermou, a good central position, ideal orientation, plenty of space and light, possibilities of a large second floor. He would need to increase his stock, of course, make connections with European markets, America perhaps. He should be well stocked with the expensive, the classical stuff, georgettes and brocades, but the real business is in the new, inexpensive fabrics: something light and fresh and cheerful and cheap, especially cheap, like cottons, rayons, not just for wealthy ladies but for all women, the peasant women and the factory girls. This is my new clientele: women of all denominations, all places, all purses. Women. They had enough of war, and mourning, and rags, and hunger. Now they want – new clothes, modern, fashionable. And I will dress them, I will dress these women of Saloniki, with the latest European fashions. I will bring

Europe to the refugee towns and to the tobacco factories, and to the smallest mountain village of Macedonia.

'Gregori, what boat are you running to catch? Have you forgotten us?'

He stopped to wait for his wife and daughters, shifting his weight with the impetus of a runner from one leg to another, searching his pockets distractedly, making sure he had not lost anything: his keys, in his trouser pocket, front, back, no, here they were in his jacket; his wallet, safe in his breast pocket; the golden sovereigns which he liked carrying with him, just in case, one never knows, were all there in the secret pocket; his handkerchief – did his wife forget to give him a clean handkerchief, on such an occasion? He found his handkerchief, starched white, and blew his nose impatiently at his women approaching, flushed from the haste and the effort to keep the heaped covered trays they were holding balanced. His eyes played at them brightly, busily, his thoughts skipped about and away from them. They were a good advertisement for his new stock in their bright billowing dresses! That parachute silk from the English! What a bargain that was! Shrewd, shrewd; Aslanoglou's eyes popped out when he heard the price: by the kilo, my friend! He looked at his daughters with pleasure, he would fill the entire city with English parachute – silky, slippery, billowing parachute!

He patted his wife exuberantly on her corseted behind to make up for his unhusbandly thoughts, but was given a girlish, prim, not-in-front-of-the-children look; to see how far he could go he planted a quick kiss on her cheek, and triumphant over her enraged helplessness he gave her a hug that almost overturned the tray. Eleni caught the excitement of the moment and went into a crazy precarious skip with her tray balancing on her head: to match her father's mischief and draw him into her game; and also to assert her defiance of her mother and elder sisters who were exchanging mutual eyebrow-raising glances of sane adult forbearance. Mother made impeded impatient attempts to restore moral order, with indignant, disapproving looks at her husband and threatening head-shakings at Eleni – 'How he brings out the worst in her!' But the afternoon heat and the long walk and the weight of the tray and the importance of the occasion – ah! it was all too much.

Gregoris soon resumed his quick strides and speculations. They had fleshed out, the elder ones. Suddenly they looked like proper young women, one dark, Anatolian, the other fair and plump and Macedonian. And they both have a playful eye, they'll soon be asking for husbands, and dowries and trousseaus! Husbands! Sons-in-law! He looked up at the passers-by with distaste, alarm. I should have sons! My own sons! He looked at his wife's plump body. A shop wants a son, sons – for whom am I working? For what? For strangers? My shop – which I have built with my own hands! He quickened his step in panic. Sons-in-law! They'll come into my shop, my home, and plunder. Let them have my daughters since they must marry one day: and from the way they spend hours in front of the mirror and over cheap romances they can't wait. The delicate muscles of his face jumped at the thought of those husbands. He took Eleni's hand and found reassurance in its smallness. She is still little. Still mine. She may come into the shop one day, why not in these modern times? She can bargain all right, the Smyrnia, she can do sums, she likes the shop the way she rummages about.

He remembered his young cousin Eleni; not much older than this Eleni. He thought of her in the village celebrations, smiling and waving to him. She must be a grown-up woman now, it occurred to him with astonishment, and sadness, if she is alive, somewhere. He tried to imagine his young cousin grown up, but her small face peered through the adult features he tried to give her.

He held tight the small hand. The concrete pavement broke and crumbled into fine warm earth and the naked, red-stained feet made a soft feathery sound that brought back to him the taste and craziness of crushed grapes and a woman's voice singing 'My son, my cherished son' – her distinct syllables falling about him like clear water-drops.

Her small hand in his gave a tug and a swing forward – 'Hurry up, run' – and he looked at the daughter that was his, the woman following that was his wife, his daughters, all dressed up and walking down the foreign streets of this foreign city, he saw that the shutters of the shops were not wooden but corrugated iron, and he in a European navy blue suit, and white leather shoes. Elegant. A stranger.

'Where does all this come from, Gregori?'

They had all stopped together on the threshold, gazing round at the freshly painted walls, the polished furniture, the new till, the ethereal mannequins supporting with such effortless elegance cascades of landscape. Opposite the entrance was a large picture of an oriental city next to the sea sprinkled with domes and minarets.

'Buying, my little wife! When property was cheap – those who kept their drachmas are papering their walls with million-drach notes, to keep warm! But have you seen the ready-mades, Anastasia mou? That is where the future is. The department store – where a woman can dress from top to toe. She won't have to trudge from one little shop to another in the cold and rain. She will come to me, naked, so to speak, with your sympathy, Anastasia mou, and will leave – dressed!'

Anastasia looked embarrassed, sceptical, moved, impressed.

Eleni touched her father, lightly, with admiration. With a quick gesture of self-pleasure he combed back his hair; and the familiar gesture made his daughter pull him down and give him a loud strong kiss on his clean-shaven face: he had a lemony smell of geranium. With exaggerations of surprise and pleasure he rearranged his hair.

The guests arrived: shopkeepers, compatriots from Asia Minor, business acquaintances. Aslanoglou the Karamanli filled the shop with satisfied flesh and kind-heartedness, with spicy smells and sing-song accents from his home in Karaman. He was followed by his sons, Timoleon and Diomedes, who had inherited their father's bulk and their mother's taciturnity. Whenever Gregoris saw their large faces and ox-like eyes, he shook his head with pity for his friend – 'Poor Aslanoglou! He will never make merchants out of them. Sons! I should count my blessings for having daughters, rather than such sons.'

Timoleon and Diomedes stood aside, close to each other, and stared at the elder Gregoriou girls, who, excited by the attention, dissolved into giggles every time they caught their eyes. Mother sent them sharp looks.

'And where have you left Mrs Hariclia?' she scolded Aslanoglou.

'Ah! You know Hariclia! She doesn't go out.' The shop reverberated with Aslanoglou's efforts and difficulties catching his breath. 'She decided she had washing to do! Kouroufexala! She just won't go out. She won't talk to anybody. If I tell her one day "I'll take you back to your village" then you will see – how she will run, how she will hop!'

His attention was drawn by Eleni's new parachute dress. 'Beautiful, straight out of a fairytale! But I bet your mother still makes you wear thick cotton pants, for babies!'

Up went the parachute dress, for everyone to see the new nylon undies, shiny, delicate, grown-up. 'American,' Eleni boasted, as she turned round for Aslanoglou to have a good look, but catching her sisters rolling their eyes in fits of mockery she recovered herself instantly and covered her legs, holding her dress tight between her knees, while rivers of blushfulness rushed through her face.

The moment of shame was interrupted by the arrival of Mr Tombakides, tall and important, followed by his short, plump, sweet-spoken wife, Mrs Kyriakoula, and their plump, pampered son Konstantinos, or Dinos, or Dinoulis, affectionately. The proud parents pushed their one and only into the gathering: 'He is learning English! Come, Dinouli, say a few English words – "Hello, how are you!" – show the people here we are not wasting our money!' But Dinos had retreated behind his mother, embarrassed by his short trousers, cutting into his well-fleshed and mature-looking thighs.

'We are preparing him for America! Where my brother is, in Virginia. He will study – tell us, Dinouli, what you are going to study!'

Dinoulis mumbled something in her ear.

'Bu-si-ness a-dmi-ni-stra-tion,' she said slowly and clearly. The rest looked puzzled.

'Don't you know what it is? Ah! it's the latest word in America and Europe: you learn to do – business. My brother says that's where the money is these days. In America, without business administration, you are nothing!' The gathering looked at Dinos pensively, indecisively; Aslanoglou snorted dismissively – and the important, well-dressed guest just entering the shop looked offended.

'Mr Sarafis, the Mr Tax Inspector!' Gregoris introduced him to the other guests flamboyantly, as if the visitor were a new acquisition. The tax inspector, elegant in his dark striped suit, responded to the merchants' deference with measured dignity. He proceeded to offer his carefully considered opinions on the Greek economy, the world economy, the state of the drachma, the Greek countryside, the communist guerillas, the English Empire, American interests, Soviet interests – while touching lightly his black brilliantined moustache and hair, and measuring with small, olive-black eyes the Gregoriou shop.

'Watch out with this new tax inspector,' Aslanoglou teased his friend Gregoris in loud whispers. 'Old Peloponnesian breed! Royalists! Fascists! Dark souls! They hate refugees and Venizelists.'

'Large, handsome woman, the Mrs Tax Inspector!' Gregoris evaded.

Aslanoglou agreed with a deep, appreciative sigh. 'Loud, immodest, but what breasts! Like honey-dew melons!' he confirmed in liquid gutturals. 'And what hips! What buttocks! What a sway, back and forth, up and down, like the Sultan's frigate! And the arms? Fresh Easter breads!'

Gregoris' eyes dilated with a child's awe at the large goddess of the pleasures of the land and sea, that materialised out of his friend's mouth. He sought his wife for reassurance.

With the volume of an opera singer and the stature of a warrior queen, the Mrs Tax Inspector was examining the Gregoriou girls with brusque military efficiency – dresses, hairstyles, shoes, bearing – down to the fingernails. She asked about their education:

132

private or state? Extra tuition? Languages? Music? The piano! Excellent.

'The American College! Now that is a school! Strict. Classy. For girls of the best, the wealthiest families. That's where we'll send our little Koula here, to make a lady of her.' Koula directed a murderous frown at the world.

'She doesn't love the letters,' her mother continued, 'but at least she will be given a polish, a *patina*' – she pronounced the word with the appropriate emphasis, separating the syllables in order to communicate its foreignness. 'At this sort of school she will make the right acquaintances, enter the social circles appropriate to her father's position, become a *comme il faut* young lady.' The merchants' wives agreed, socially.

'She is not a great beauty, of course,' the Mrs Tax Inspector explained, 'oh no, she is not that. Nor is she a great genius. A great genius she is not, by God.' Koula was tugging at her arm with the intention of pulling it off her body. 'Unfortunately she has her father's sour snout and temper.' There was a quick flash of cruelty in the Mr Tax Inspector's small black eyes, a slight, sharp movement of the head. 'But a few accomplishments, a few merci beaucoups and avec plaisirs, the Blue Danube on the piano – Eh! Willy-nilly she will find a suitable husband. Perhaps an established businessman – ' She looked contemptuously at Aslanoglou's sons trying to start a conversation with the Gregoriou girls, and at the unhappy Dinos furtively pulling his trousers to ease the pressure on his tormented flesh. 'But preferably someone from the professional classes – a doctor, a lawyer, or even better a tax inspector, like her father. Perhaps even a judge, or police inspector, an army man – what better position in our society than keeping an eye on law and order, with all these communists infesting our villages and cities.' Everyone in the shop quickly re-examined his secret mental files, relatives, friends, contacts. She means my wife's relatives, Gregoris concluded. I am undone. I'll lose it all in taxes.

'Glory be to God,' the Mrs Tax Inspector continued, without pointing an accusing finger at anyone, and everyone sighed with relief and agreement. 'Glory be to God, her father has offered me a secure, respectable life, not that I want to boast, but a life of a certain class and style. And of course, let's not hide behind our little finger, there are certain privileges attached to his position, certain tokens of respect' – the merchants looked at each other – 'and gratitude, from the wealthiest members of our society. Ah, I cannot complain, God would burn me for my ingratitude. My dear Inspector here hasn't deprived me of

133

anything. He has set me up like a queen! Except for his foul temper, my life with him has been milk and honey, milk and honey!' And out of sheer joy at the thought of her good fortune she gave her husband a good affectionate pinch on the cheek, which brought tears to his eyes. But he soon recovered from the sudden attack of cordiality, and with his hand on his throbbing cheek, he tried to recover his central place in the gathering.

Anastasia directed at her husband a look of accusation. His glances now played innocent, now admitted mischief – 'What's done is done. Don't scold me - how could I not invite him? Be good to me now, give us a smile!'

'We'll arrange something for Koulitsa – but for our minister here, no need to worry. He will govern Greece one day, mark my words!' she prophesied triumphantly, while her young Minister, like a sleeping prince, woke up at the sound of his mother's prophecies.

'We knew he was a Minister from the day he was born, bless him – from the way he tightened his fists and hollered, may the Lord give him life! What am I saying – even before he was born! The way he kicked my belly, I thought – What have we here! A proper little dictator, bless his liveliness! Ah! We'll slaughter the golden calf for him one day! Eh, Inspector?'

The five-year-old Minister, in confirmation, rampaged: guns, revolvers, machine guns, bazookas, hand-grenades, anti-aircraft guns, atomic bombs were all conjured up by a whirlwind of arms hands legs mouth throat lungs with which the frantic young war-god devastated the world. 'Ch-ch-ch-ch---m-m-m-bm-bm-bm-bang-bang-chstzpong-chr-chr-chr-sbm-ch-fffff – halt – stickemup – bang! Dead!' The air was shattered by war-shrieks, blasts, rumblings, hummings and dronings and buzzings. The battleground was littered with myriad broken bodies, the walls vomited fire, death, destruction. The foul breath of war had crept into the shop.

'Lively, lively boy,' Mrs Tombakidou agreed as she rubbed her bruised shins.

'May the Saints protect him from the evil eye!' his mother concluded.

'It's in our blood!' She started with new energy. 'Generations of military men and politicians – Ah! Look who is here! The Church!'

A devout silence at the entrance of Patir Athenagoras, the priest from nearby Agios Minas. He ceremoniously wiped the sweat from his face and neck with a silk handkerchief which gave out a heavy sweet scent. He greeted gravely the host and hostess, and proceeded to rearrange his purple vestments and the jewelled crosses round his neck, while a burly young assistant – through his open-necked shirt a coy little crucifix nestled in his thick glistening black hair – prepared the sacred utensils for the ceremony.

'He will send you to hell if you are not a good boy! Go, go and kiss his hand!' The Mrs Tax Inspector pushed forward the young Minister who watched, petrified with agony, the preparation of the instruments of torture. The priest stretched a soft, perfumed hand towards the boy, who jumped back as if he had seen a snake, while his mother pushed him forward. 'Go, kiss the holy hand and ask for his blessing to become a minister, even a prime minister one day!' The boy's lips touched the priestly flesh as if they were tasting venom, the priest pulled his hand away as if from fire, and extended it to the rest of the congregation.

'Patir, forgive me for the interruption, unforgivable as I am!' A woman full of gaiety and beauty sailed into the shop with a scent of roses, knelt gracefully before the priest, touched his hand with her lips leaving a red heart-shaped mark on it, and rose airily, with a smile for everyone. The priest remained with his hand in the air, in offended astonishment; the burly assistant interrupted his preparations and stood mesmerised by the new presence, Kyria Marika from Smyrna, who with extended hands and arms greeted and embraced the congregation, filling the shop with laughter, scent, sparkle, colour.

Gregoris felt the shop now had meaning, purpose. Here was womanhood, gaiety, fashion. He repaid the compliment to his beautiful compatriot, the *alegra* Smyrnia! The women of Smyrna! Ah! Famous for their feminine coyness and modernity! Anastasia was flustered, but remained polite, hospitable. Sophia and Kaliopi interrupted their secrets to study her: Kaliopi was copying her expressions – the pouts, the smiles, the slanted glances. The Aslanoglou boys blushed. The Mr Tax Inspector remained austere, but was distracted. Eleni decided she wanted to be like Kyria Marika when she grew up, then she remembered Kapetanissa Olga, the mountain guerilla – she postponed the decision, gazing at the woman from Smyrna. Her dress – a garden, with large deep red roses; a skirt that swung wide whenever she turned; high-heeled shoes that made the rest of the women look like dwarfs. Her hair a jungle of black ringlets piled above her forehead; her eyelashes curled up coyly like a delicate curtain over her eyes that were all sweetness, all coquetry and promise.

'Divorced!' the Mrs Tax Inspector murmured in her husband's ear. 'Where does she find the money for this get-up, I would like to know.' He nodded, like a judge taking note of new important evidence.

The priest had reasserted his dignity; he ordered the shutters to be lowered to keep out the sunlight and curious eyes, looked austerely at the congregation, and, accompanied by his assistant, started a languorous chant, which slowly rose, and fell and further fell.

'He is cheating, he is cutting out passages,' the Mrs Tax Inspector whispered to Anastasia. 'You should pay him less.'

Anastasia smiled politely. She was attending to the blessing of the new shop with serious emotion, mixed with a resigned motherly tenderness for the difficult man standing next to her. Gregoris was moved. When he heard the priest mention his name, Your son Gregoris, and then his new shop: 'May it be blessed and may it bear fruit and wealth and happiness to Your son and to his family,' he had tears in his eyes. Once before God had saved His child Gregoris from the slaughter. He must have special plans for him. He felt the secure, protective presence of his family – the good wife, the beautiful daughters, the loyal employees, the worthy business acquaintances, the glamorous clients.

He must not disappoint the father, who watched – and might even appear any moment from under the lowered shutters. A moment's alarm: they were good, these shutters, they kept out the blinding sunlight, and the noise and the enemies. It was good, the darkness of the shop: it soothed the mind and quietened the worries and fears. He had dreamed last night, he remembered, of a young boy sitting on a kitchen sofa, where his mother and father should be sitting, with his face covered and rocking back and forth like an old woman. The boy's sorrow had touched him to the quick.

Eleni, stationed next to her father, held the long, ornamented candle with pride. She was hoping Kyria Marika had noticed her; she wondered what she thought of her parachute-silk dress. Her eyes moved from the beautiful woman to her city – of course! The picture on the wall was Smyrna! She travelled through the exotic city with the domes and minarets and the elegant arched windows, searching for the woman's home. Her father's home. But the city remained undisclosed, suspended in a territory behind a mirror which she could see but not touch: like the motes of dust in the air illumined by the blades of light but eluding her curious fingers, or like the candle flame involved in its own constant inconstant life, enticing the eye and offering no resistance to the hand except for the sudden pain of heat. With the sprigs of basil the priest sprinkled holy water around the shop, and Eleni felt the cool drops on her face.

Renewed by the baptism, Gregoris kissed the priest's hand with filial, passionate, obedience – 'Your blessing, Father' – while slipping into it a wad of money – 'For the church, Father, and for the poor.' He ordered the mounds of Anastasia's kourabiethes, buried under layers of fine snow-white sugar, to be passed round. The priest brought the exquisite pastry to his mouth with ceremonial dignity and felt its sweet crumb melt like holy communion; a fine white cloud of sugar settled on his sacred vestments. Then he signalled his leave-taking by extending once again the plump hand to children and grown-ups.

With his departure spirits relaxed, the special pre-war liqueur from Corfu was opened, the guests wished their hosts well in new puffs of sugar. Gregoris celebrated his good fortune with a generous proprietorial embrace of his wife and his embarrassed daughters. But his largesse and excitement could not be contained, he ordered his assistants to cut from the new parachute silk dress-lengths for each of the ladies, first and foremost for his compatriot. The women effervesced with pleasure, the shop overflowed with good spirits, and the blessing of Gregoris' new shop came to a slow close with leave-takings, heartfelt good wishes, greetings to relatives and last-minute eager inquiries about everyone's health. Kyria Marika waved farewell, pleased with the blessing she had bestowed on the shop.

The young minister came back to life and spread a last departing wave of death and destruction – ch-ch-ch-ch-ch, br-br-br-br-br-br, bang-bang, bang, bmmmmmmmmmm – before he was let loose in the darkening streets of the city.

The blessing of the shop produced instantly its sweet fruits. Curious women, beguiled by the immobilised cataracts of colour in the windows advertising instant beauty at half price, flocked into the shop like moths into a brightly lit room on a summer night. Women of all ages, and faces, and moods. Low-browed, fair-haired Macedonians, and dark, olive-skinned Peloponnesians, plump Turko-Bulgarians and proud Vlachs from Epirus; women with thin aquiline noses from Caucasus or with rippling Etruscan profiles, or with high Balkan cheek-bones, or with stubborn square jawlines. Wealthy Jewesses and elegant women of Thessaloniki with padded shoulders and cork-heeled shoes. Peasant women hidden under scarves, and layers of pinafores. Small-waisted, small-ankled women, women with large breasts and women with broad hips. Women born to be mothers and women perennial virgins. Women from Smyrna known for their quick eyes and slippery tongue, and from the depths of Anatolia with their almond eyes and heart-shaped lips. Women with accents and voices and tongues from the old home, and from the new home, and from other, lost, homes. Women who bought and women who liked to bargain; women who just looked, or could not decide, or wanted the lot. Inscrutable women or women flirtatious and coy. Women who shopped alone and women who loved shopping with friends, with sisters, or mothers, or daughters, or husbands: or with the entire family – aunts and uncles and grandmothers included.

Gregoris Gregoriou pleased and obliged them all. A compliment, an appreciative look, a telling smile, a sympathetic question, a recognition, a face from the old country, a personal interest, a moment of moved reminiscence, and – a special, a very special price, almost a present for the sake of the old lost home. He was everywhere at once. He knew what each customer wanted and needed, what was her secret desire, what her favourite colour, which shade favoured her complexion, which brought light to her eyes, what style suited her figure. He knew what was especially made for each woman, just and only for her, and offered it to her as a tribute. And as if he and only he possessed the secret key to her hidden, undiscovered beauty.

Now that the war was over, children played freely on the streets during the long cool summer evenings. Their improvised games of war spread to include entire streets and neighbourhoods, doorways, cellars and abandoned derelict buildings; armies of children were recruited to play, with untold thrill, their part in daily battles, imprisonments, guerilla warfare, hostage bartering, survival, death. New techniques of war were invented daily, new allies and enemies were added to play old, ancient parts. Where before you had Germans and English and Greeks now you had security police, fascists, communist guerillas.

Names did not matter in a world made up of enemies and allies. What mattered were the exquisite moments of hiding, a band of guerillas bonded in soul and body, while the enemy death prowled around. What stayed for ever was the sweet protracting of that moment, the moment of life and death, of fear and of love, when the inevitable steps become distant and it seems death will miss you out, for now, and fear relaxes its grip just enough for you to feel the comradely body at war loosening into separate boys' and girls' bodies, young, hiding and hugging, inevitably: the boy's cheek as smooth as a girl's next to yours, unavoidable; his arm closing slowly round you, inescapable; the hand crawling under your skirt up your leg – and the moment of crisis: do you close your eyes and surrender to pleasure, with pleasure, for the sake of the game of war and of love, or do you unravel the mysteries of war and love and the pleasures of pretence and run out of hiding to fall straight into the hands of the security battalions and scream 'Truce! Peace! I'm not playing! I want to go home!' And in the midst of 'Coward, traitor!' you run home – and tell mother? While the sisters are listening – are they sniggering? Eleni said nothing.

When the war was over the German building was occupied by English soldiers, who came and went in flared shorts down to their sun-burned knees. From morning to evening Miss Loula sat or stood on high heels at her first-floor balcony, dressed up in low-cut, small-waisted, hip-hugging, breast-uplifting dresses, the lips red and round, the eyebrows fine and arched, the hair in perfectly regimented curls. Miss Loula was always prepared for an important social event, a splendid outing, a fated encounter. You thought the moment had come when the lips pouted expectantly, the brows were raised in recognition of the destined moment, the curls trembled, the breasts heaved towards the English soldiers who raised timid heads and dispatched stealthy smiles. They tossed with manly bravado the odd chocolate – hard, bitter, the best – to bands of children following them singing, 'Yupi yaya yupi yupi yaya.' Children loved Miss Loula because she brought to the neighbourhood a world of cinema, glamour, and intrigue. Chocolates and corned beef.

The English allies settled in with ease, and Eleni liked to sit on the shady kitchen balcony during the sun-blazed deserted afternoons and gaze at this new occupation army. She recognised the furniture the Germans had left behind, the large square desks with typing machines on them, the metal drawers. The uniforms were different, and the walk and posture; the flag at the top of the building. But she saw the same young, well-fed, uncrinkled faces, the same blond hair and blue eyes: angel-faced messengers from the West, but Eleni could not decipher their message.

She gazed at the building with no feeling, perhaps with a half-remembered feeling. The wide-open shutters stared unblinking as if they had no guilty secrets to hide, and the present uniformed inhabitants seemed to continue where the previous ones had stopped. She gazed at the uniformed men, from window to window, while the shadow of a memory travelled through the dark corridors, which she could not see but knew were there. Something hardly remembered dwelt in the building, moving towards the windows, then retreating unseen. And an expectation she could not divine or foresee played hide and seek with her eyes, while the windows of the building remained forever innocent. While her eyes strayed, her ears held a music: which came from a window near the centre where a man's face used to appear. She waited and wished to hear again that music, of many voices together, that contained, in its falls – ach, the pity in those falls of sound – she did not know what it contained. Her eyes looked for the face, tired, of a man at the window, wiping his glasses and looking at the clear sky. For a moment she had thought he looked at her – only a glance – and smiled. She wondered then whether he had a daughter her age, whom he missed, who might have been killed in the war – such stories happen in wars – and for whom the toys were intended. She remembered her journey holding the stranger's hand through the German building, along interminable dark corridors, the silence she could not decipher, and the heap in the corner of the room which always changed definition, and now seemed like accumulated treasure and now like broken miniatures of cities. She remembered the room, and tried to locate its window, through which had come in – it seemed now a long time ago – a razor light that revealed to her not offerings but war and damage.

She spent long afternoons gazing at the building lodging enemies or allies, her memory scavenging through an abandoned room at the verge of a promised land or an atrocity; her imagination gnawing at the edges of the secret intention and meaning of the man in the uniform. She heard the music. She knew her wishes with quick simplicity: she wanted the German man not to be an enemy; to have nothing to do with men and women burning in an oven in the village square; nothing to do with gun-shots, executions in the early dawn; nothing to do with the pain of hunger. A heap of skeletal bodies stacked high in carts danced before her eyes in ever-changing postures of indifference or mockery – to no music. But she heard the music coming through the window near the centre: its melodies tracing a palpable pain, spelling a sorrow and sweet devotion to which like an unseeing tendril she reached out. She wondered how such music could be heard within such war. She wondered whether, if she could only touch it – whether it had a large enough pity in it to scatter the nightmares.

A man stood naked in front of an open window, smiling. She stared, first disbelieving then believing, uniquely guilty, damned, at the sight of the man, standing within the frame of the window, naked and real, uninvented, smiling a grimace of shared obscenity. She stared, and saw, now she knew and was appalled: sin personified. She went indoors carrying, she felt for ever, the secret unredeemable damage. She closed doors and windows, but the image of the naked enemy man in his sinful anatomy had already invaded: on his body she saw the geography of wars that had been and wars to come, the massacres, the drownings, the fires, the hunger, the fear, the unaccountable deaths. She saw a landscape burning with civil wars, familiar wars. Her heart contracted, lost a beat, perhaps a measure of life. But the music, would it play for her? Would it play now its sacred melodies of pity and wonder?

The children's games were disrupted by new army lorries delivering more armies to unknown destinations. They became part of the game, and gave ammunition to young imaginations. When long, luxurious foreign cars, armed with friends or enemies, stopped, and watched, and a man was pushed inside by three men in raincoats and trilbies – these were new and unforeseen sophistications, they had glamour, they had cinema. They made games of war grow and spread through the city, and across the bay where the newly arrived American fleet stood in a sea thick with garbage. But when dark came the children stayed at home, because it seemed a civil war, which some foresaw might never end, had long ago come home.

Father was taking his rest in the bedroom. The shutters were half-closed, and the off-white linen bedspread and gauze-like curtains gave the room a cool quiet brightness. His breathing was erratic, disturbed. In the reception room, Sophia was teaching Kaliopi in irritated whispers a new French song. Eleni hovered around them, restlessly. She went through Sophia's few valuable books looking for something easy, with action and dialogue. When she saw the evenly dark page, uh! she knew – philology! Sunsets and philology!

The knocks on the door were abrupt. 'Kyrie Eleison! At this time of day!' Grandmother wiped her hands on her large, homespun apron, ready for action. Anastasia went to the door, and opened cautiously the small iron shutter. The face behind the glass was very young it seemed to her, an eighteen-, nineteen-year-old boy; a good-looking face, the fierceness of the dark stubble was only momentary, the eyes looked innocent under the gathering strong eyebrows.

'We want to see Mr Gregoriou,' he said. 'We are doing business with him, could you please open the door.' Quietly, insistently. And Anastasia took the heavy iron bar down and opened the door to them. 'He looked so young, a child, he could be my son, only a few years older than my Sophia,' she said afterwards, disconsolate. Two other men, almost boys, moved in fast, shut the door behind them and with their guns signalled the women and girls to stand all together – 'There against the wall – where is Mr Gregoriou?'

'Away on business. He had to go to Volos to collect a shipment.'

The thinness in mother's voice made the gun directed at them more real.

'Here I am! What can I do for you, my young men?' Father came forward, before the family's dazed eyes, all energy, all exuberance, all camaraderie and friendliness. Ah! it's all right, a misunderstanding, thought Eleni. Father will put things right: she wanted to get out of the scene and join her father who obviously saw things differently, much more happily, but father was walking straight into the scene, taking it in rapidly: 'What can I do to help you?' The voice was less exuberant, less stable, still conciliatory. Eleni was frightened. 'There's no need for guns! We haven't got any differences! Anastasia, coffee for the young men! I didn't catch your names? Please sit down.' The mention of coffee steadied Eleni: this was a world where people sat around sipping coffee – the gun became unreal.

'Tell me, my young man, where do you come from? Where are your origins?'

'What does that have to do with it?' The man was nonplussed. 'From Adana, my father is from Adana, my mother from Proussa.'

'Refugees! Anatolians! I knew it immediately! Mouryes was my village, I don't know what they call it now, near Marmara. As soon as I walked into this room I knew we were compatriots – the spark in the eye, the shrewdness.'

Eleni sighed with relief: the scene was turning into a friendly visit, between acquaintances, business associates, they might find themselves relatives. At any moment out would come the silks and cottons, the laces and the ribbons, things of peace and beauty; at any moment he would strike the bargain of his life. But she saw Father's eyes run about the room looking for escape and the muscles of his face make their small rapid movements, and happy bargains fell to shreds as two of the men took him into the bedroom.

Through the open door Eleni saw her father sitting on a stool at her mother's dressing table. His back was turned to her, but she saw his face in the mirror: the men on either side were resting their gun-barrels on his temples. The sight was so odd and impossible, she did not know what to feel. But small details about him moved her to tears: his head was hardly able to move between the gun-barrels, his eyes raced round the mirror like panicked rabbits, avoiding their own reflection. His neck was slender, sinewy, his hair ruffled, his nose thin and elegant in profile. In front of him, at his disposal, stood bottles of cologne, a crystal bowl of powder with a fluffy puff resting lightly on it, a jewellery box of alabaster, a silver-backed mirror and brush, his present to mother from Yannena – she hardly used it, it was so nice. His eyes moved from item to item in his wife's narrow territory as if preparing for an odd, desperate toilette. The men talked to him, and he nodded. To see him nod, and nod again made her cry. To see her father without his fatherly power, and beauty. And her beauty – that she had secretly contemplated it locked away in all those bottles and bowls and jars! The pale powdered complexion, the evenly lined, heart-shaped lips, the painted almond eyes. One day, she had thought, the scattered beautiful features might come together and to life. Eleni had touched with reverence those mysterious guardians and weapons of her beauty, that he was now examining with agony.

He bent down, the guns still pointing at him, and took from the bottom drawer an old handbag of mother's made of red and black beads. He emptied a handful of gold coins on to the wooden surface: she would remember their distinct noise. One of the men put them in his pocket; the other tipped out the contents of the alabaster jewellery case. The empty handbag remained on the dressing table. A few more words were exchanged, the bartering concluded, the bargain struck.

He came out of the room looking feverish, tired. 'The young men are not our enemies! They are our own people, compatriots!' He was the gracious host making the appropriate social gestures and introductions. 'We have to support their movement in any way we can. They mean no harm to quiet citizens like us.' The man who had been pointing the gun at the family said something to mother, and she slipped off her rings and bracelets and gave them to him. Eleni could not remember her mother's hands without the warm yellow bands with the small sparkles round her fingers and wrists; without the jingling sound that indicated her presence, and the light scratching that went with her caresses and fondlings. She had gathered her daughters round her once and showed them her jewellery – the almond-shaped ring from their father, the round one with the large stone in the centre surrounded, like a mother, by the little ones, that had come from her mother. The Venetian ducat had been in the family for generations; a mystery how it had travelled all the way from Venice to Macedonia. And the bracelets: she had danced on Father's nameday waving her arms in the air and making them jingle with the music. Eleni had not seen her mother so happy as on that day.

The man put the jewellery in his pocket, they said something to Father and left. Grandmother put the iron bar back across the door, and Mother fell on a chair, touching and rubbing and caressing her naked hands and crying like a baby. Father knelt by her and promised to buy her more jewellery, to jingle to the tune of Yerakina, but he could not console her. Eleni noticed a ring of tender white thinness on her mother's finger, that filled her with pity.

The men came back one evening and told Father he must come with them. They did not say where, for how long, why. There was just enough time for mother to prepare his pyjamas, a few shirts, a towel, soap, an icon. At the door he said brightly to Mother, 'Don't cry, my heart. I'll be back in a few days. We'll clear up matters, and they'll let me come back – in a few days.' He sounded as if he was going out with friends for an evening's entertainment. There was a negligence – an exuberance and nonchalance about him. But he kept hold of his wife, as if they were his tears she was shedding. 'Don't cry, don't be a child! I haven't harmed anyone, remember that!' He turned towards the men with the guns. 'I have been looking after my family and my shop, like a good citizen. I haven't got mixed up in politics. I'm a foreigner, a refugee in this country – like you, like your parents, you should know. I don't know its politics or politicians, I don't belong to a party, I voted for Venizelos who supported and helped us refugees. Ask your parents how he helped us – when he died, I voted for his party – middle of the road, neither with the Russians, the communists, nor with the German king. Is that a crime? Tell me. I work hard – is that a crime? And what I've created – my shop, my home – I created with my own hands and the honest sweat of my brow. Like all refugees. If your parents could see you now, with the gun, a man my age! An innocent man! I didn't steal, I didn't kill, I didn't commit an injustice.' A light pinkness spread around his eyebrows; his face was angry, his eyes imploring. 'They can have all I possess – although it's my life!' He got his arms free suddenly and started beating his chest in an indignant outburst of assertion. 'I will make it all over again! I will start from zero, once again, and as many times as I have to, as I did when I was a mere child, and I'll double it and triple it. Because I'm not afraid of work.' Mother was crying. 'What they cannot take away from me is this' – he knocked his head with his knuckles hard, painfully.

'Don't, don't, Gregori!'

'And these – my hands – they are honest, industrious hands!' He stretched hands and arms out to the world in bitter exasperation.

Mother took Eleni to church to pray for father. She held Eleni's hand tight throughout the service and looked at the congregation suspiciously. Eleni was oppressed by the serious angels and dark saints and the all-seeing concave Pantocrator on the dome. The thought that He might be looking at that very moment at her father and yet kept so mysteriously silent brought tears of rage. Her eyes were drawn to the dark-skinned blinded Mary on the wall holding a blinded Jesus in her arms; their faces and bodies were covered with holes, and the sight gave her a strange consolation. That, and the small flames of the candles, always moving and always disappearing upwards, while the candles stood still and quiet, never changing and always diminishing. Eleni waited with fear and thrill for the brief moment when there was no candle but only flame which finding itself all on its own and free gave a sudden happy leap, big and bright, before, with a quiet whisper cry, it disappeared, leaving a thin trail of smoke. The candles went out one by one leaving behind them frozen waterfalls of wax.

The chanting was like a flame that one could hear, always the same and never the same, steady but tremulous, at rare moments swelling with a harmony that felt like love. The words were few, but lasted for a long time – Kyrie Eleison, Christe Eleison – and each syllable spread through the ever-changing sounds that travelled together with the clouds of incense.

Everyone pushed when the priest appeared with the Holy Communion; the women first, dragging and pushing their children – 'The child, make some room for the child! You'll kill it, asphyxiate it! Are you Christians, or wild beasts of the jungle?'

Hats were thrown on the floor and trampled; handbags burst, their contents scattered; dresses unbuttoned, unzipped, ripped; heels and toenails broken, bunions and corns – a torment.

'My ribs! You've broken my ribs!'

'Your elbow is in my mouth!'

'I'm strangled! Air! Air!'

'You should be ashamed of yourself! You pervert! And in church! Waiting to take Holy Communion! What has our society come to, my God and my Holy Virgin!'

'I am going in,' the priest shouted. 'That's it. No one will get Communion until you stop pushing. If you start pushing again I'll go in and have you wait till tomorrow. What do you think you are doing, my woman? Where do you think you are? In the cafeneion? You will eat my finger, my child! Just one sip! One sip and only one piece of bread. This is not a restaurant!'

They sighed with relief when they came out, their faces cooled by the breeze.

The congregation stayed outside the church in small indeterminate groups. Family gatherings, meetings of friends, light-hearted conversations. The crowd moved slowly, groups skirting other groups, then splitting into threes and twos; couples arm in arm, acquaintances walking next to each other without touching, an unexpected arm round the shoulders, a sudden pause face to face. The law which determines meetings and separations left a few individuals apart, unmet and unkissed, like sobering punctuation marks in the movement and variation of human sympathy.

Mother sought out friends and acquaintances, tried to find things to say, made small talk with lips white and parched while her eyes leapt about in fright.

'They let me see Gregoris once. Bitter times, these. Brother turning against brother, neighbour betraying neighbour, civil war. Yes, they are rounding up the businessmen. I go to the shop. It's difficult.'

Soon the churchyard is empty; a child is in tears watching his balloon fly up and away; the balloon man is strolling towards the waterfront. Eleni thinks the seafront is probably full of people, the children sipping their iced granitas, the small boats dancing on the waves, their white embroidered cushions waiting to be pressed by loving lovers' bodies.

Mother and Eleni stood in the churchyard in the bright sunlight, the lively April breeze made their thin dresses flutter around their legs. A man appeared in the distance: lean, brown-haired, in a white shirt and dark glasses. Eleni thought she saw a smile on his face, thought somehow he was her father – later she was thinking, how could I have thought it was Father! – and took a step forward, but her mother's hand held her back tightly and the pain spread along her arm and body.

'Have you brought it?' the man said to Mother. 'Act naturally. Not a word. I'm pointing a gun at her.' He put the money in his pocket, then, 'Go home now. Slowly, naturally. You won't talk to anyone. You won't run. You are being watched.'

They walked back through the Sunday quietness. Eleni watched a lace curtain flutter in the breeze in an open balcony door: the thought of the family inside, the lightness and beauty of the movement, and the pain from mother's grip, made her weep.

Eleni observed the irregular surface of a stone covered by a fine film of dust: the aimless stillness, the accidental sharp edge. She looked at other stones nearby. Some all edginess, some flat on their backs, some half-buried in the ground. Two of them leaned lightly against each other. She touched them, and the small one fell over while the other stayed. Like a giant, Eleni crouched over their separation. A large finger pushed the stone that had rolled away near the one that had stayed, till they touched. They might be alive! she thought with horror, and thought, with unbearable unhappiness, of tender small stones locked in their stoniness. They might think and feel – she tormented herself with further speculations – and miss each other, or miss other backyards, or the rock, the mother-rock from which they were broken off! She pushed some of the stones together, in pairs, in families of threes and fours.

The following day they were still there. She carried them, in threes and fours, to different parts of the backyard: sunny spots or hidden corners of shade, under the tree, next to the wall, for a change of air and view, she thought. For several days she moved the stones around the backyard, with gentleness and attention, looking for a sign, a movement, a change.

In the end, she looked at them with a dull eye and decided, bluntly, that stones perhaps have no life, and perhaps are a waste of time. She walked upstairs to her mother and sisters, wondering, her legs so tired and heavy she thought she was carrying the weight of all the stones of the backyard.

'He was pacing up and down, dishevelled, wild.' Mother's voice came through the kitchen door. 'He didn't sit for a moment, he roared at me as if it was all my fault. He waved his arms, I thought he would hit me. But as soon as the guard walked in he was quiet as a lamb.'

'Ah, he was always like that.' Grandmother's unperturbed voice. 'Refugee blood, I thought the day I saw him. Unsteady – his nerves come out of his head!'

Mother lowered her voice. 'I don't even know who these people are. Gregoris doesn't think they are ELAS – just a band calling themselves what they like, and going around terrorising people. I have to find Sotiris -'

'Sotiris!' Grandmother remembered her own worries over her son. 'Sotiris is getting deeper and deeper into ELAS, and if the battalions catch him, or Grivas' men, God protect him – him and his wife. Wife, marriage! These people recognise neither marriage nor family nor religion! Olga – you have to find Olga. She is your only hope. She wheels and deals in the mountains, and even the big names here in the city respect her. They say "Kapetanissa Olga" and stand to attention!' Grandmother was lost in superior perplexity. 'Why, how, God knows! Who would have thought the world would turn upside down like that! Kapetanissa Olga!'

'I'll go and see her. Gregoris helped them when her brother and sister were ill, and the older one in prison. She was a small girl then, but she should remember. Her mother should remember.' Mother sounded heartened. 'At least he is not alone. They've rounded up the entire market. Ioannides is there, Savaides, Stamoulis, Aslanoglou – it's good he has Aslanoglou with him. Poor Aslanoglou! How is he going to feed all that flesh!'

'That Karamanli – he will stink them out with his garlic and paprika,' Grandmother murmured.

'As long as they keep them here, and don't take them to the mountains.' Her voice weakened. 'They kill them, on the mountains.'

'At least he's got the right sort of company.' Her mother tried to distract her. 'He can talk business with his friends from morning to evening.'

'The others play cards – at least they let them do that. But Gregoris, Aslanoglou told me, won't sit down, won't lie down, won't sleep.'

'I told you – go and find Olga. She will put them in order.' There was pride in grandmother's voice.

'I will. You know, mother, he didn't ask about the children once. Nor me. Nothing. All he talked about was the shop. I told him, don't worry, the shop is all right – I go to the shop every day – and I take Eleni with me, because they keep making threats. I told him about last Sunday, after church. That shook him. He kept saying – you had to take Eleni with you? I told him yes, they watch us all, especially the little one. I wanted to give him a jolt. You know, mother, sometimes I wonder whether he loves any of us – his children, his wife – as he loves that shop.'

'Difficult man, difficult! Uprooted! Homeless! Once a refugee always a refugee. I warned you.'

'I asked him straight out, "Tell me, Gregori, have you missed us? Your children, me? Do you think about us? Or is it only the shop?" He became wild again. Beating his chest and shouting "Don't you understand that shop is my soul? You take my shop away, and you kill me." And he pulled his clothes, he almost tore them, as if he were uprooting his own heart. "Where would you and your daughters be without that shop? Tell me." "Why my daughters, Gregori? Aren't they also your daughters? Did I have them with another man?" "My daughters! My daughters!" he was shouting. "What will I see from my daughters? They would throw me out on the street if it was left to my daughters!"'

Mother was crying. The kitchen sofa creaked. Grandmother gave a sigh as she made an effort to get up.

Eleni walked away.

Two men and a woman walked into the shop and said, 'We're taking over. The shop belongs to the party and to the people.' Anastasia's face crumpled in pain and outrage; she pulled Eleni to her.

'You can't do this to us.' She pushed Eleni down behind the counter as she got up. 'This is our livelihood. My husband and I have worked all our lives for this shop. You have taken our savings, you have taken my jewellery, you have taken my husband. What more do you want? What more?' The visitors stood perplexed, the shop assistants made a few frightened, sympathetic steps towards her, the cashier was crying. Eleni crouched behind the desk wanting to stand up with her mother, and saying to herself she was a coward.

One of the men took the keys from Anastasia and walked through the shop unlocking chests and cupboards. The other two paced near the door nervously. Women of all ages started arriving, and formed a small crowd. The woman, now installed at the door, distributed pink tickets to them and told them to keep in order. She would let them in one by one. The first woman ran in, then stopped and looked round, bewildered. Abruptly she shouted, 'This one – and this – and that one,' pointing at different shelves. The man who had taken the keys directed the shop assistants. The woman grabbed the pieces, looked round her. 'No more, go,' the man said drily. She went out unwillingly while two more women were allowed in. The crowd was increasing: three, four women showed their tickets to the woman at the door and pushed in. They all had the same look of confused greed on their faces. The two men and the woman were shouting at them, 'Wait for your turn. One piece each.' The woman tried to shut the door: the crowd pushed back, wedging her between the door and the desk, and burst in. The shop was full of female bodies: powerful breasts and hips, fighting shoulders, mobile elbows, hungry faces, eyes looking for prey. Mother, her arm gripped around Eleni's shoulder, retreated against the wall. The men were shouting, 'Wait your turn! Don't push! We'll turn you all out! You'll get nothing!' Two women grabbed at a curtain and pulled at it, shrieking till it tore. Another heaved behind the counter and took under her arm a whole bolt of material. Another hugged a bundle of dresses. The men shouted at the crowd, the woman at the door screamed, the shop assistants stood together in a corner. Women were climbing on the counters, bolts rolled down on the floor, they crawled and grabbed and pulled and stampeded, tripping on stretches of dirty, torn fabric.

'Tasia, I found the blankets! Over here, you moron! Get your sister to come and help! Wake up! Stir! Move!' A mother, by sheer breadth, had cleared enough space to possess the blankets. Another moved through the crowd like a bulldozer, driving her powerful haunches right and left into other women's bellies and breasts. An old woman, her black scarf on the floor and her thin grey hair flying loose, was hopping with impotent rage giving sudden shrill shrieks. Another was blindly shoving materials under her long black skirts and into her unbuttoned shirt.

'My teeth! They've stepped on my teeth!' another lisped in baby-moans as she crawled on the floor with her hand on the empty, bewildered mouth.

A few latecomers sent disappointed glances around the empty shop. They loitered by a grieving woman with a child: she sat on a chair with her face turned to the wall, rocking back and forth – 'Why have they done this, my God? What have we done to deserve this?' The child stood by her, impotently.

The thin cloud of dust went pink from the setting sun, as if something in the shop were bleeding. Tatters of fabric hung here and there from the empty shelves, its last shreds of life and colour. The rest turned cold grey. Distant sounds of crumbling walls and cities, bleeding dust that bruised the sight and clogged the breath. Eleni gasped, as if drowning.

Mother stood up, and then Eleni noticed the regular, familiar tick-tock of a clock, and took heart. She let her breathing follow the movement that measured time so evenly and justly.

'Let's go home.' Mother took her hand.

That night, just as she closed her eyes, the room, alert with its own square empty presence, startled her. It made her look at it, at its symmetry, the right angles, the sharp corners. The emptiness, sharp, crisp and clear, hurt. Not like a room, but like a box looking like a room, or a picture of a room drawn by a remorseless hand, which allowed her into this work of art and hate, to cause her pain.

The empty room and the guessed-at empty piece of corridor beyond brought her a deep melancholy – the knowledge of a loss, an absence. Someone had walked out of the room for good. Someone was standing outside the room, not intending to enter. That room she realised took its horrid life from someone's absence. She stretched her arm, and her fingers felt the error, the betrayal, the sadness inhabiting the room from beginning to end.

For days and nights she prayed for her father to return. 'Our Father, which art in heaven . . .' She prayed, and waited for a sign. At night, in front of the icon; at noon, when the street was deserted and the sun blazed overhead. Night after night. Not a sign: not a word.

She offered silence for silence; stood in front of the icon uttering not a word. The days closed with the wordless meeting of eye with divine eye, while she lived in frightened wonder at the precarious balance of mutual mute gazing.

Silence put down roots that spread through mouth and throat and throttled the words. It became an animal with a shadowy, insubstantial body that turned back and devoured all sounds at birth.

She broke the silence one night. She waited until her sisters' breathing had been absorbed by the darkness of the room, and with eyes and ears wide open, and attending to what might lie on the other side of the silent darkness, she spelled out with deliberate voice a blasphemy, a string of dirty words at God, that she knew would send her to perdition. She waited, to be shown how the loving tender palm of God the Father turns into the roaring mouth of hell. In unspeakable loneliness she waited. And waited.

Through the nausea and light-headedness of the early awakening, Eleni saw the empty, grey street stretch away before them. A man walked by himself on the opposite pavement; a taxi disappeared at the end of the street. Mother pulled her into a room crowded with impatient men and women pressing to the till. The clerk, unshaven, glum, was arguing with the luggage man. A fat woman who arrived just after them pushed her way to the front calling loudly to the clerk, 'Koumbare, herete, how is the family? We hope you might pay some attention to us?' She glanced at the rest of the passengers with the superior confidence of the well-connected. She was answered with hostile looks.

'Go back to the end, woman, where you belong, and forget the koumbarlikia.'

'I'm a sick woman, just out of hospital! Post operational! My heart is still weak! Don't you have any compassion?' With a fragile smile she sought the clerk's eyes, and working her hip, pressed closer to the till.

'Sell those stories elsewhere, Kyria Evlalia!' an older woman shrieked at her. 'You had that operation three years ago, and you serve it up at your convenience: "A seat, a seat, my good people, just out of hospital!"' – the old woman squeaked in mockery – 'Three years you play this tune, and you are stronger than any man in the village. With one blow you could kill an ox!' The others joined in; Kyra Evlalia didn't budge, she gave small sounds of weakness and pain and started relating her ailments to a polite young man at the front. 'Heartless, heartless!' she whimpered to the clerk. 'They could see a poor woman die in front of them and they wouldn't give her a helping hand!' The clerk nodded, but continued serving tickets to the queue in his tardy solemn way. She took off her scarf, undid the top button of her blouse, and fanned herself with her hand, taking noisy, difficult breaths – while resisting with her broad buttocks the advancing body of passengers. The clerk gave her her ticket last of all, exchanging a few tired sympathetic remarks with her as if he had nothing to do with the way things had turned out.

Getting into the bus, when it came, was a matter of life and death – they all pushed, in a congealed mass. Getting good seats was also a matter of life and death. Heart-rending separations, last-minute admonitions. A man gave directions to a woman through the window. 'Send me the power of attorney – and the contract. She must sign that power of attorney. Our hands are tied without it. And the birth certificate.' Another man was haranguing a woman who had taken his seat: she would not talk, she would not budge, she just looked straight in front of her pretending he was not there. He appealed with emotion to the rest of the passengers, who eagerly took sides. At the back of the bus, on top of a mountain of boxes and old suitcases, a pair of chickens tied by their legs made furious attempts to fly. The doors slammed heavily, and at the loud underground moan of the engine the passengers all crossed themselves, and with sighs of submission to the Divine Will wished each other a safe journey. 'With the protection of the Virgin, and the Saints, and Christ – a traveller Himself!' Small crosses and evil eyes were brought to lips; lemons and bottles of cologne were brought to noses to guard against sickness, food appeared in laps to guard against hunger.

Mother and Eleni kept quiet and to themselves: they had done well, although not as well as Kyra Evlalia who pushed Mother against the door at the last minute and grabbed the first seat, behind the driver, with the best view, on the shady side, next to the priest. 'Let us thank our good fortune for having an officer of God with us.' With public righteousness Kyra Evlalia lived up to her privileged seat. 'God would not let anything happen to His own minister! Would He, Father?' Gurgles of coy ingratiation. 'Meatballs, Father? Fried this morning! Choked in mint! Or spinach pie? Home-made! Not fasting, Father! Travellers do not need to fast! Neither travellers, nor women in their unclean days of the month. The Church has said. You should know that, Father!'

Eleni asked Mother for food. 'Not at six o'clock in the morning,'

Mother said. She asked for cologne, she thought she felt sick; they had no evil eye with them like the other people. Mother's answers were short, negative, grim. Eleni did not know how to deal with the fear and excitement of the trip. She looked through the window and was soon sleepily absorbed in the perpetual disappearance of the appearing landscape. An endless conglomeration of tin-roofed shacks, junkyards, windowless buildings with huge chimneys, overgrown fields, occasionally a home with a balcony full of geraniums and dahlias. The plain, then a sudden swelling of the land, which the bus met with bad-humoured coughs and splutters. The land, in blissful negligence of the clumsy, sulking creature climbing it, continued its green roundness which became, in the distance, mountains.

Eleni dwelt on the familiar peaks of Olympus. A god of what anger must have pushed those mountains to such heights. What war within, suddenly petrified as it reached up for escape, or frozen at the moment of supplication. What monument of punishment, this many-bodied, many-faced mountain. Oppressed by the swelling volume, she leaned her head on her mother's breast; a sweet musty smell came in through the window.

'Tobacco! Smell the fresh tobacco!' Mother stretched her neck to look at the women in their front yards threading the large oval leaves on long needles.

The next village looked deserted. Clusters of bullet-holes in doors and shutters; blackened, ruined houses fallen within themselves. Eleni turned to her mother, who seemed locked again in her own desolation. Eleni returned her attention to the abundance of emotion and sensation in the front seat.

'Eh, Father, we should all thank God and say – things could be worse! Ke mi hirotera!' A deep sigh. 'We all have a cross to bear, and I have mine, Father! But then I say illnesses are for humans! Genithito to thelima tou! His will be done!' The priest nodded.

'I'm not the same woman since I had this operation. Simple appendicitis they said! Simple! I haven't recovered since. Ah, you should have seen me, Father – I was like a frothy Easter bread.' She accommodated her thighs, the priest made room. 'But what with the war and this operation, I am a shadow of my old self! I pine daily! I have these flutters here, here! I get short of breath, I get tired with the slightest exertion, drowsy after meals – a general weakness of the organism. I ask my doctor for vitamins, a tonic for anaemia, and you know what he says, Father? He says I should lose weight! When they operated on me, the butchers, they cut off – they told me later, didn't even ask for permission – they cut off several layers of fat from the abdominal area, with your pardon, Father. Otherwise, they said, the charlatans, they couldn't operate, they couldn't find the spot. Ah, they wanted it for their experiments! Of course! And they left me weak and fragile ever since!'

Eleni felt car-sick, and hurt and disappointed that Mother did not have cologne or lemon with her. But the generous lady from the front immediately obliged. 'Smell the lemon, my golden one, and look out of the window towards the horizon.' Eleni felt comforted, and flattered by the look of interest on the priest's face.

The chickens at the back were fighting, and losing, another battle for freedom. A few agonised, unsynchronised attempts to fly in several directions at once with squawks of quick, hysterical enthusiasm followed by angry exasperation, and dejected silence.

A cluster of children sitting on a mound of rubble waved at the bus. Further on, a pair of old men sitting at the roadside followed the bus with small slow eyes. Large families, entire villages, were on the road, burdened with bundles and suitcases. Men in military clothes, with rifles, stood confidently at the edge of the road.

Kyra Evlalia leaned over the priest – who suddenly remembered nostalgically his mother's freshly baked Easter bread – and waved triumphantly at the armed men, who did not bother to wave back. She noticed she was the only one in the bus to greet them, and sat down in defiance, and suspicious worry. 'We have to encourage our vigilantes. With the country torn to pieces, and the army busy clearing our mountains of the Soviets, we can only rely on our local heroes to protect us.'

'What Soviets, my woman?' a man shouted across the bus. 'The men you call Soviets are your brothers – who fought the Italians in the Albanian war, and fought the Germans, and now are fighting the fascists and the collaborators.'

'I don't call them Greeks! They are Soviets, Slavs, communists!'

'They're more Greek than you are.'

'I am pure Greek – my mother from Thessaly and my father from Naoussa, well-known family. Ask anyone. And most of these guerillas are from the borders, Serbs, Slavs, or riff-raff from the refugee estates and the tobacco factories.'

Eleni froze with fear, and self-doubt. If the lady knew, she would not have given her the lemon. If anyone knew where they were going – Mother held her hand tightly, signalling her to keep quiet. Eleni looked round in alarm, suspecting everyone of suspecting them. Her eyes caught another pair of eyes in the mirror of the bus, serious, purpose-ful, concentrating on something that escaped her.

'How dare you speak of refugees?' A woman at the back of the bus stood up. 'Your government's let us live in shacks, for decades now. Worse than gipsies. No jobs. No homes. What happened to all their promises? The communists are the only ones who did something for us. The Venizelists, just words, and the King, that German fascist – he doesn't give a fart.'

'The communists! The communist party is made of refugees. We had no communism before you came to this country.'

'And if it were not for you, and your crazy ideas, to take Konstanti-nopolis and Asia Minor and the Black Sea, we wouldn't have lost our families and homes and lands, we would be landlords in our own rich fields and vineyards. Hm! They wanted a Byzantine Empire, the Vlachs! They didn't know how to use the tractor before we came here, they didn't know how to wipe their arses, and they wanted an empire!'

Men in uniform stood decisively in the middle of the road with their guns raised. The passengers were thrown forward as the bus braked suddenly. 'Identification cards – papers – purpose of travel – open your suitcases. We want the chickens for the army. Driver – your papers, your licence, army certificate, vehicle documents. No, you don't have to inconvenience yourself, Father.' Eleni sought her mother's hand. She was impressed by her readiness when she said calmly and confidently, and somewhat harshly, 'We are visiting our aunt who is ill, nearly dying.'

The men ordered the driver to continue – they would accompany them to the next village. 'Cheese pie?' Kyra Evlalia offered, with shrill pleasantry. They distributed it amongst themselves. A long stretch of heart-beating quietness, heavy with the smell of cheese and sweat and stale tobacco and vomit. To escape, Eleni gazed at the decorations over the windscreen: postcards, icons, evil eyes, plastic flowers, photo-graphs. A soldier's face leaning and touching a girl's face, both contained in the red outline of a heart. A football team, broad smiles and hairy legs, arm in arm in close-knit camaraderie. The soldier, now in a dark suit and tie, standing solemnly next to a serious bride – both of them staring with startled eyes. A larger, tinted picture, the bride-groom in the same dark suit, the bride stouter, in a dress with padded shoulders – a small boy between them rode a tricycle with a determina-tion that seemed to carry him out of the photograph.

The men stopped the driver at the beginning of the village and took him to their offices; one of them took the chickens, which gave their most heart-rending cries as they were dragged away from the blanket where, having accepted their fate, they had nestled. The passengers were left to wait. They sat under the plane tree and opened food bundles and baskets; they asked each other in whispers what was happening, and offered with pride their own home-baked bread. Mother kept Eleni near her; their picnic was solemn, quiet. The men smoked; Kyra Evlalia lay in the densest shade for a rest.

Two of the men came back, one of them sat in the driver's seat. They ordered the passengers to their places, the journey was resumed. They had gone past the village and past the ravine when they heard distant shots; the passengers looked at each other but kept quiet. 'He looked suspicious to me from the start!' Kyra Evlalia whispered to the priest.

The cover felt harsh and smelt of sheep. Eleni tried to disentangle the smells in the dark, but all she recognised was the cold smell of earth, which made her think of the chrysanthemums her mother brought home in the first autumn days.

The old woman was moving about in the room next door. Eleni tried to keep her body from slipping into the middle of the bed, where her mother's body was, large, warm, silent, awake. The iron bedstead creaked every time she stirred. Eleni tried to think of the mountains with the lambs lolling on their slopes – green in the sunlight, and dark, massive when the sun went.

'What did they do to the man?'

'What man?'

'The man – you know, the bus-driver.'

'I don't know. Be quiet.'

'They killed him. I heard the shots. Why did they kill him?' She nagged, insisted. She wanted to heap all the blame on her mother.

'Leave me alone,' her mother's voice threatened, implored. She rested her arm over her eyes, as she did when she was unhappy or wanted to be left alone. But Eleni knew she was awake from her irregular shallow breathing which sometimes paused and became a deep sigh.

'Why did they kill him?' She stretched her arm and pressed her mother's shoulder. 'Why did they kill him?'

'He was a communist.'

'He was a football player. I saw the photograph.'

'I said leave me alone.' Mother's voice was angry, and weak. Eleni thought perhaps she was crying.

156

'Olga, your cousin, is a communist. And your brother.'

Mother held her arm tight, till it hurt. 'Be quiet.'

Next door the old woman was talking to someone who never answered. She must be talking to herself, Eleni thought, as she concentrated on the shadows in the room moving and changing and bringing to her all the tiredness and fright of the day – and the accumulated desolation of that summer without Father. She could not sleep and did not understand and did not even know what to ask: she looked at the large body in the sagging middle of the bed and thought it contained all the answers and all the blame.

'I want my father, where is my father?' she insisted, cruelly, and she heard her mother crying. It was some comfort.

She dreamed that she was wandering through a dark city looking for home, although she knew there was no home – and the desolation of the knowledge, and also a feeling of falling, woke her up as her mother's body was disentangling itself from hers, leaving her limbs exposed and aimless. And leaving her in a pool of still certainty, her arms trailing blindly in space, that her father, the joy of her eyes, was dead. And she was daughter no longer.

She heard voices, and tiptoed to the door. In the shadowy light of the oil lamp she saw a man and a woman embracing, and felt a quick pain of jealousy at the sight of love. The man was no man, but the Andartissa, the Kapetanissa Olga – oddly, her aunt, who governed the mountains, and her Father's fate. Eleni looked with awe at the tall unwomanly woman standing flat and secure in her thick dirty boots, her hand on Mother's shoulder, who looked like an unhappy child, barefoot in her long nightgown, and wiping her eyes with her sleeve. Olga wore large army trousers and an old army jacket. Her hair hung down plainly in short strands. Her face was thin, brown, not beautiful, not like a woman's face, or like a man's either, but it made you want to look at it because it had a way of measuring quickly and confidently everything in the room, perhaps smelling everything out with her long aquiline nose, or piercing everything with her dark-centred eyes.

The old woman was stationed at the window, lifting a corner of the blanket in front of it, and peering out. The two women sat at the table opposite each other. Olga was devouring soup from a big earthenware bowl and talking at the same time with interrupted vehemence at mother, who looked unhappy, in the wrong. Eleni caught fragments – and the smell of lentil soup that made her hungry.

'They hung them upside down over a pit of shit, Anastasia.' Mother buried her face in her hands. Olga was moving her head and body back and forth as if she were trying to remember or understand something. 'They ate and drank with the Nazis,' she shouted. 'Now they call themselves Nationalists and hang our young heroes over their shit.' The old woman rushed to her in alarm and blocked her mouth: 'They'll kill us all.' Olga pulled her mother's hand from her mouth and tossed her head with sudden feminine pride. 'They pay one golden sovereign for each head. They decorate the village squares with them.' Another toss of her head. 'What do you think, Anastasia? Is it beautiful? Will it do?'

The old woman was holding her shoulders. 'Stop, Olga, stop! If they find you here they'll butcher us all.' To Anastasia, as if appealing for help, 'She never stops. She has no fear of God in her any longer.' Olga freed herself from her mother's hold, and turned to her, cool and collected. 'I won't stop. Because my brother died in Metaxas' prison. Your son, the apple of your eye. He was twenty-five when he died and looked like an old man, dead from the tortures before he died.' She shook her head for a while. 'You are old, Mother.'

Eleni noticed, as the old woman turned her head, that one of her eyes was covered with a white film, giving her face a sinister wink.

Anastasia reached over the table and gripped Olga's wrist. With tight teeth she said, 'Olga, give me your word about Gregoris. He is well, he is safe, they will release them.'

Olga turned her hand and caught Anastasia's. 'He is all right, Anastasia. He is. He is all right. They will release them. The merchants are not important. They could have helped us. But they are not the enemy.' Suddenly she was very tired. 'I don't even know who these people are who arrested them. The cities, they do their politicking, and we pay with our blood. They haven't been harmed, Anastasia.' Anastasia's tears were free now, relieved.

Olga turned to her mother. 'Are the provisions ready? They should be here – have a look.' She inspected the sacks near the door, then picked up a bandolier from a chair and slung it across her chest.

'Have you seen our fields, Anastasia?' She came near her and kept pulling her sleeve as she talked to her. 'They are destroying them with chemicals. Our villages, our mountains, our Greece, they are burning it with napalm. It's different in the cities.'

'They are here.' Her mother went to the door. Olga counted the sacks.

'Gregoris – you promised,' Anastasia said.

'Kali Antamosi.' The two women embraced.

Eleni surfaced, from no dream, under the inspection of a bird-like figure looking like her father. She sank briefly, grasped a fragment, drifting – of thousands, millions of migrant birds populating the shore across the sea, darkening land and sky.

'Home!' Her mother's voice. 'Your father is home, Eleni!' She stared startled at the two shadows overhead. Her father pointed at the shore black with birds, saying 'Home'. Eleni saw them swooping down on the land eating, devouring –

'Eleni!' her mother said.

Me, they are eating me! Eleni thought.

'Your father, Eleni! He has come home!'

Eleni stared at the man and woman standing over her, losing from her eyes the sanctuary, now sunlit, of birds, and the flock of beautiful, pink-bellied flamingoes hovering over her. The woman was opaque, the man a migrant bird looking for refuge, a bird of bad omen perched, hungry, over her fate. His long blade-like beak and eyes red and tearful concentrated their aim. She lay quiet with fear of this man looking like her father: the woman's motherly round silent shape gave her no refuge. Unwillingly she recognised her father – witness and reminder of atrocities, and refugee messenger from lands of pain and sorrow. He carried them in his visage, the black stubble on his hollowed cheeks remnant of fires, his worn clothes hanging on him hiding damage!

The man, who could be taken for a beggar, stretched out empty arms in a universal offering embrace: his eyes, bewildered, still hooked on painful visions, played with the surprise and triumph of his appearance. His daughter gazed at him, seeing it all, recovering: like a bird she swooped on him as on to a mother, and held, with fear and pity and untold love, her father, her damaged love.

'Help! She is strangling me!' Gregoris became the willing victim of her games, weakly.

She remained, his only daughter, on his tired body, taking if possible the air he breathed, with avaricious fingers testing and feeling him thin and tired, not the same, not all hers. She released him from her embrace only to have another look at the face consumed in its fleshlessness by a voracious surprise.

'Eleni, stop savaging your father.' Mother's firm grasp held her back while her sisters gave him their bewildered welcomes.

His daughters made him lie back on his favourite sofa, tired and ill-looking, distracted, and played on him, competing in fervour and virtuosity, their tunes of womanly tenderness and devotion. Who would take his shoes off, who would wash his feet, who loved him most – offerings, proofs! Through their noise he sought his wife's hand.

Gregoris and Anastasia talked until late, while Eleni leaned against him. Her mother asked him questions, cried at his sufferings – but he was back alive and hers, she loved him. He asked her about the shop and mother timidly, with difficulty, told him. Eleni felt his body come to life, a life that allowed no love: he pushed her away and got to his feet.

'The keys.' He grabbed the keys from Anastasia's hands, as if they were unworthy, as if they had betrayed him, and ran out.

Anastasia ran after him – 'In the middle of the night, Gregori?' – followed by Eleni, Kaliopi, Sophia.

The sisters, left behind by their parents, ran holding hands in the dark deserted streets. They saw – and ran faster in terror – an American sailor holding a woman against a wall, pushing her with rhythmical hate. They ran past another sailor sitting on the pavement, his head between his hands, retching his heart out.

When they arrived, panicked by the violence of the night, their father was standing in the middle of his shop. Their mother remained near the entrance in fear and respect for his bereavement. The emptiness of the shop timidly took flesh and blood. They couldn't see their father's face clearly, would probably never know his thoughts. But they could guess from the movements of his head and body that he was busy talking to someone; no sound escaped from his lips. He was examining his hands, as if wanting to prove to the world that he was all there and whole. He touched his sides lightly as if to feel his pockets, then his temples as if trying to ease a terrible headache but then quickly changed his mind and stroked his hair back in place. He walked to the light-switch, and at once the destroyed shop jumped at him. He stood with his hand on the switch contemplating the ruin: he was the carrion bird inspecting his territory of death and destruction. He turned his beak towards the picture on the wall: the fat man of the picture still looked sated, the thin man sorrowful. His eyes, owlish, blinked spasmodically, perhaps ignored the wisdom. With a few strides he was at the small door of the warehouse: still locked.

'And the clock.' He went to the deaf and dumb clock on the wall – he had bought it in the war dirt cheap. 'Someone come and wind the clock.' The landlord blackbird had reclaimed his territory.

Anastasia approached, reached up with difficulty, and patiently wound the clock and set it at an approximate time. Tick-tock, tick-tock: the sound brought some equanimity to the place and to the family. To

160

Gregoris it steadied, perhaps measured, his step, as he possessed dwellingly his shop.

Who would have imagined so many people could go in the back of a lorry! A compact, intricate mass of families, relatives, friends, business partners, padded round with rugs and cushions; children and picnic baskets wedged between bigger bodies and surrounded securely by legs and arms. The women wore bold-patterned scarves to protect their perms from the wind, the girls held large straw hats between their knees, enjoying their hair flying in all directions; the children, held tight in parents' laps, played violent games with arms and faces. Mrs Tombakidou solicitously asked her Dinoulis whether he was ready for his boiled egg. The men were arguing vehemently which was the best way to Neos Marmaras.

'We are taking ages! We cannot waste our day here! As if we have all the time in the world!' Gregoris was muttering irritably to himself, and to the world, as if the world, like the loaded lorry, could not go fast enough for him.

'We are not going to our shops, Gregori,' his friend Aslanoglou teased him. 'This is a holiday! No one works on May Day! Not even you, so sit there quietly, and be thankful you are back with your family – your lovely daughters and your excellent Kyra Anastasia. And with your friends, so many good friends here. Be thankful for this lovely air and sun, and that we are alive! It's not worth it, Gregori, quarrelling with your clothes like that! Shops come and go! Enjoy the sun, the air!'

Anastasia nodded in confirmation and patience; and Gregoris nodded with impatience. 'Yes, yes, you can talk, you can talk,' searching round for a quicker way, a busier world, an instant aim and success.

Eleni, in her father's lap, felt his arms round her distracted, not quite knowing they were holding her: his head restlessly turning right and left, his legs ready to get up and go if it were not for her weight on him.

With a jolt and a crunch the lorry changed gear, a sudden wind stung their eyes, they were surrounded by countryside, careering down the empty road. Gregoris jumped with impetus: the ferocious movement of the lorry was his, he was the motivating power. 'He is mad! He will kill us all!' They slid to the back, then slipped to the left, and shortly, in the midst of triumphant yells from the children and shrieks from the women, were flung to the right. Eleni clawed on to Father's clothes and he, as if just realising she was there, grabbed her tight in tremendous exuberance. The children were told to sing May Day songs; one of them tried to stand up but was pulled down by a

161

screaming mother. A few jerky voices were raised, but couldn't agree about the words, then all were drowned in the deep droning of aeroplanes.

'Americanika,' one of the men declared, with personal pride in the country's powerful alliance.

'Englezika,' someone corrected him.

'They are ours,' the tax inspector said conclusively.

'Whatever they are, they're cleaning the country of communists,' the Mrs Tax Inspector shouted triumphantly.

'They are killing our brothers. And our heroes in Albania and the Resistance.' The voice of Mrs Marika, the Smyrnia, tore through the engine. Then she paused, looking at Gregoris and Aslanoglou; but Gregoris, with an energetic hand, scooped his troubles out of the way – 'That's past, gone. We have to move on.' He paused contemplatively. 'They were children – some of them children of refugees.' He shrugged. 'That's past history! We are used to ups and downs, eh, Aslanoglou? Now we must get on our feet.'

'And start running, eh, Gregori?'

Gregoris laughed with pleasure.

'Look at all the packages they send us from America – the clothes and the dollars and the aeroplanes.' The Mrs Tax Inspector wanted to argue with Mrs Marika the Smyrnia. Her husband was right about this woman – suspect, very suspect!

'And napalm to burn our countryside, and us alive,' said a tall young man sitting against the back-flap. The others were taken by surprise.

The children renewed their own deaf-and-dumb war with gesticulating arms and distorted mouths.

The women spread their rugs on a thick layer of pine-needles: the bright oriental geometry moved and changed in the dappled light. The children ran to the sea. Surprised feet hopped on the burning sand, soon strewn with clothes: screams and splashes from the shallows. The men were arguing about the Marshall Plan, while the women prepared the food. Gregoris walked along the shore examining the landscape.

'We'll find an escape route, patriotaki,' Aslanoglou called with affection, while lodging the large demijohn of wine in the shade. He told his sons to set up the barbecue. The Mrs Tax Inspector was inspecting the lamb: 'Young! New-born!' she was exclaiming to herself. 'It will go down like turkish delight. It will melt in the mouth!' Anastasia gave directions to her daughters – 'You will stay in the shallows, Eleni, there's nothing wrong with your petticoat, you've nothing to put in a grown-up bathing suit. And you, Sophia, Kaliopi, not too far, stay where I can see you.' She kept an eye also on her husband – restless, so restless again – while she unfolded her latest embroidery to the other women's admiring eyes. The lorry-driver sat in the shade of a tree; he played his comboloi and studied the horizon.

Mrs Aslanoglou, kind and timid, was preparing a comfortable throne for her mother-in-law, the Karamanlou, who sat back in sullen dignity, surrounded by the mounds of her black pantaloons. She looked at the people round her with dry suspicion, and said something in Turkish – to no one in particular, but the youngest of her grandsons fetched and lit her hubble-bubble. She inhaled deeply and resumed her inspection of the world. From a distance, her face looked part of the trunk of the tree.

Sophia and Kaliopi, in their new identical 'lastex' swimsuits, were standing in the water up to the waist, deep in conversation. 'He is a communist!' Sophia was saying with dark excitement. 'He reads Kazantzakis!' Her dark almond eyes followed softly the tall young man walking barefoot at the edge of the sea. Her serious face, usually pinched by a vigilance against the world, now looked peaceful, tender, her mouth rested satisfied in its young fullness. Eleni, circling aimlessly around the older girls, thought her sister looked beautiful at that moment – her neck so delicate, her hair rich, her breasts round, her waist under the lastex so small: at that moment she loved her.

'Who is Kazantzakis?' Kaliopi asked with shaky superiority.

'He is the greatest Greek writer alive,' Sophia snapped back. 'His books are forbidden. He is excommunicated, because he is a communist and an atheist. Everyone knows Kazantzakis.'

Kaliopi looked puzzled, discontented; Sophia wetted her shoulders caressingly. Then they walked together in the water, moving hands and arms in unfinished circles, letting the water run through their fingers, gazing wistfully at Cousin Nikos' tall handsome figure becoming smaller and smaller.

They joined cousin Steryos, from father's shop, busy mending his accordion; the Aslanoglou boys, having helped their father dress and fasten the lamb, had persuaded the tax inspector's son, the warlike Minister, to turn the spit. He undertook the job with hot-cheeked dignity, while the Aslanoglou lads tried to decide whether to join the girls. Dinos – Dinoulis as his mother liked to call him – sat dejected and hot on the sand a good distance from the sea. He inspected with regret his new long trousers: the first day he gets to wear his long trousers, it's so hot all the rest of them have taken their clothes off and are splashing in the sea. Large stains of sweat were already forming on the inside of the leg. His mother shouted one-word commands to him, accompanied by animated, impatient gestures. 'Off. Take them off.' She pretended she was taking off an imaginary pair of trousers. 'To the sea.' She pointed to the sea. 'Dirty!' She touched the sand squeamishly. Dinos sent back vehement constrained signals of intense embarrassment and hate. Eleni and Koula, the tax inspector's daughter, were making unsuccessful attempts at swimming, by falling with spread legs and arms into the shallow water and making frantic swimming gestures as they sank. They soon began to quarrel about who sank slower: the petticoat helped Eleni float, Koula sulked, they splashed water at each other. The Minister, hot and bored with the enemy carcass, ran to join the more sprightly, sprayful violence in the sea.

The men, hot in political discussion, were taking off shoes and socks and rolling up trousers and sleeves. Some said the Civil War had ended, some not; some wanted the Americans, some not. Gregoris thought if it is not the Americans, it will be the Russians, what's the difference! He did not seem interested, he had other cares. Aslanoglou had taken his shirt off and was slapping happily his enormous white belly. He dipped the sprig of thyme into a thick marinade – a secret recipe from Karaman – and caressed with a feathery touch, with motherly tenderness, the revolving animal, whose young flesh returned intimate delights to his nostrils. He rearranged his mother's cushions, checked her hubble-bubble, said something to her in Turkish. She nodded back.

Gregoris had gone back to his own battles, which he was conducting with a silent movement of lips and eyes. He gave an occasional nod, of confirmation or agreement with someone. His eyes, restless, measured, searched the promontory that sharply cut the sea. Eleni stood in the water studying him, the coldness of the water touched her to the bone. She ran, and landed in her wet cotton petticoat right in his lap. He jumped with alarm which he turned instantly to exuberance. 'I caught my dolphin, my little mullet, my sweet sardine!' He rummaged in his pocket, then a tremendous show of surprise – 'Ah! What have we got here! A chewing-gum. A real American chewing-gum!' He raised it high up, and she jumped for it with playful, belligerent greed. Then he was suddenly tired, and looked at the people as if they were strangers, and pensively at the sea. Eleni was content to sit by him, chewing the cumbersome syrupy rubber. She wondered whether he loved her; she wondered where he was, how she could grab him back to her. She went behind him and embraced him, vengefully, kissed him on his cheeks hard, while he gave alarmed cries of help – 'Help! She is attacking me!'

'Will you tell Mother to buy me a proper bathing-suit like my sisters? Lastex, American, without straps?'

'A whole shopful of them!' he promised with ease. Then with mock-innocent bewilderment – 'How will you keep it up, without straps?' She, predictably, attacked him again with red-cheeked anger: he felt good. So did she. She pulled out a graceful thin strand of gum, studied it, then gathered it quickly in a tangle and pushed it back into her mouth. She did not have his heart.

'Will you tell her to buy me a bicycle?'

'Anything you like,' he promised, absent-mindedly. Mrs Marika had taken off the tiny waistcoat and revealed with coy defiance her naked shoulders. Father complimented her on her modern style of dress; she repaid the compliment by reminding him she had bought the material in his shop – and at what a price!

'I'll have two or three such shops within the year,' he bragged with new animation, 'and you can have as many dresses as you like.' Mother concentrated on counting her stitches. Eleni went and sat next to her, wanting to be allies, and wanting to blame her for not having a proper swimsuit. Her attention was soon absorbed by the glamour of Kyria Marika.

'Ah, the Smyrna blood is hot in your veins, Kyria Marika.' Aslano-glou sat back like a pasha relishing the sight. 'In Smyrna, women went bathing, even with men, "bagne mixe" they called it – didn't they, Kyria Marika? They were liberated, progressive, not like us in Karaman! Eh, Mother?' His mother was falling into a drowse. His wife pulled his sleeve, whispering to him to stop. Mr Tax Inspector was looking away, disapprovingly, and the Mrs was ready for open war. But Mrs Marika arched her back with coquetry, impudently protruded her small delicate chin, arched her fine eyebrows. With a slight tilt of her head she brought her shiny black hair forward so it covered half of her face, an inviting smile flickered at the corner of her eye. The girls, young and old, watched her with fascination. Eleni, who had devoured the photographs posted outside the Dionysia and Titania cinemas, was enthralled. She had never seen anyone looking so much like a film star: the cinema had come to her, in flesh and blood, for real.

The shot of Kyra Marika the film star suddenly burnt from the centre, as the young war-god stormed into the scene of womanly beauty, spreading fear and devastation: 'Take cover! Take cover! I am holding a hand-grenade! Run for your lives!' People ran in all directions, to the forest, to the sea, to the fields, as the Minister zoomed about the picnic in crazy circles and zig-zags and spirals, holding up in triumph his trophy of death.

'Throw it away!'

'No, don't throw it away!'

'Put it down, gently!'

'Throw it into the sea, stupid! The sea! Yes, the sea!'

'Run into the sea!'

'No, don't run! Walk!'

'No, not the sea!'

Only the young lamb remained silent and defenceless. The Minister stood tangled in violence, then dropped the grenade on the ground: his father grabbed him as the object rolled towards the barbecue, and stopped. Moments, ages of horror: except for the happy chirping of the cicadas. The lorry-driver walked calmly towards the grenade and picked it up. 'It's dead, useless,' he said flatly and went back to his rock. The gathering returned, exchanging accounts and responses and arguments, tears and condemnations. The Minister's parents were pulling him, one arm each, towards the trees. But Kyra Kyveli, large and beautiful and kind like a goddess, intervened.

'Go and cut some flowers for your May Day wreaths.' She took the young Minister's hand and walked through the trees. The younger girls, and then the older ones, and soon the boys, followed behind. Godmother Kyveli walked with difficulty because her legs were swollen with varicose veins, her body was massive; but children and adults obeyed her and loved her. She seemed to have come from a different land: her calm, even features, the sky-blue eyes, the gentleness of her face, wreathed with a braid of pure white hair, made her seem like a goddess whose beauty was not touched by age, whose peacefulness could dumbfound war. She presided over the gathering like a large protecting angel.

She went part of the way with the children, then tired, and sat on a stone waiting for her husband. He was a small, slight man, but with the same blue eyes, white hair, gentle features. Since they left their old homeland of Marmara, Kyra Kyveli and Kyr Yiannis could never be apart. Eleni went to her with a grazed elbow and felt Godmother Kyveli's hands heal her skin. She grew the sweetest-smelling roses in Neon Vyzantion; and her backyard was full of young chicks. In the midst of the tin-can refugee estate, Kyra Kyveli's garden was paradise.

The children hesitated on the edge of the blood-red field. The young Minister rushed in first, stampeding and rampaging through the secretive vegetation. The spell broken, the rest of them followed, cutting the tallest and reddest poppies, crushing accidentally the hidden camomile that gave such sweet scent. They emerged triumphant, holding bouquets of elegant, already dying poppies, and set about making their May Day wreaths – while an entire bewildered population of rabbits and hares, moles, field-mice, hid in their holes with fast-beating hearts.

The young war-heroes returned wearing wreaths of red, dead, poppies, and fell on to the feast spread on white tablecloths.

The Anatolian delicacies were passed around first. Mrs Marika offered her native speciality – Soutzoukakia à la Smyrna. Hot, spicy, delicious! She accepted the compliments with girlish coyness. God-mother Kyveli had prepared the Imam Baildi that she had learned when a girl in Marmara. The Imam truly swooned, everyone confirmed; Aslanoglou praised her in Turkish. Mother defiantly presented her huge Macedonian cheese pie – layers and layers of paper-thin pastry that she had rolled out with exquisite art.

Then the crown of the feast: young and old fell on the lamb. With professional solemnity, Aslanoglou and the Mrs Tax Inspector were tearing the young animal into manageable pieces which disappeared as soon as they were placed on the platter. Delicate limbs were wrenched off, tender ribs were pulled apart, mothers took priority over children but fathers had the lion's share: the scent of the torn young flesh moved even the stones.

'It melts in the mouth! It's mother's milk! Manna! Ambrosia! God's blessing!'

Mr Aslanoglou filled everyone's glass, promising eternal youth to young and old. 'Nectar! The elixir of youth and beauty! It gives rosy cheeks to children and bright eyes to our women, and supple joints and tongues to our mothers.' He filled his mother's glass regularly, and she downed it with serious promptness.

Soon, only the head of the young lamb remained on the platter, hollow-cheeked and dim-eyed. The Mrs Tax Inspector gouged one eye and gave it to her husband, sucking the other herself. 'Great delicacies,' she exclaimed with full-mouthed relish. She pulled the tongue out and forced it on young Koula, then scooped the tender brain from the skull and pushed it into the surprised mouth of her Minister. 'It will make you grow into a real minister.'

Tongues were loosened, voices raised, memories wandered free. Mrs Marika took out her brand-new camera, a present from relatives in America. It was passed round and admired, then the snapshots.

The older girls posed in their bathing-suits at the edge of the sea, turned to show breasts and leg to advantage. Mr Aslanoglou exhibited rolls of solid white flesh through his unbuttoned shirt, and raised his glass of wine – a happy Dionysos surrounded by children still wearing their wilted poppy wreaths. Father lying close to Mother, his head resting on her lap – Eleni is pulled into the photograph, at the last minute, in a pose that stays permanent. Mother arranges her three daughters, 'The big ones on either side, the little one in the middle – closer, no, not so close. Eleni, be still.' Eleni agitates within the sisterly parenthesis closing in; feels the two heads uniting above her – Angels of the Apocalypse, the Pillars of Hercules, Scylla and Charybdis – as the lastex curves incline threateningly towards her. 'Don't frown, Eleni,' mother shouts; too late: click!

'Now be quiet everybody!' The Mrs Tax Inspector pushed her little Minister to the centre of the gathering. 'Our Minister here will recite a poem he learned at school.' The Minister stands at attention, right arm bent to an imaginary gun, chin disappearing into his chest, his voice shrill: 'I will become a soldier, A brave evzone I will become.'

While everyone still applauded, the Mr and Mrs Tax Inspector anxiously urged their Koula to sing. 'Sing something, say something, all this money we pay to a private school.' Her mother in exasperation gave her a pinch, her father pulled her away to try to persuade her – and Gregoris, mischievously, seized the chance. 'Eleni, my child,' he ordered confidently, 'recite a poem for us!'

'In her turn,' Mother corrected him austerely. 'The older ones first, Gregori! Sophia, perhaps something in French? English?' Sophia looked insulted. 'I am not a child, Mother!' But the rest of the gathering insisted. 'You read all these books, Sophia – you are literate, intellectual!' Father was not pleased by the words, they smelled of immorality, but his pride was at stake. 'Sophia, my child, perhaps something Christian, something moral.' The tall young man looked interested, Sophia walked slowly – impudently slowly – towards the trunk of a tree, and half leaning against it, with a long meaningful look towards the young man, she announced, '"If" by the English poet, Kipling.' The young man's face was lit by the secret communication, the rest were deep in blank meditation. She explained to them the meaning and they shook their heads in bewilderment.

'Good, good,' the Mr Tax Inspector irritably opined, 'but it doesn't come up to the little finger of our poets – our Solomos, our Palamas! The patriotism, the sentiment! And as for our great Ancients, eh, everyone, but everyone, takes their hat off and kneels in front of them.

Incomparable! Superhuman! Our Homer! Our Euripides! Our Plato! What genius! What a race!' They all contemplated the glorious past – and shaky destiny of the nation.

Emotions were aroused, they wanted more emotion, they wanted music: Kaliopi's moment had come. She stood, now in her flowery dress, looked towards the sea, entered the appropriate mood and expression, and announced '*Madame Butterfly*'. People sighed with recognition; it was Mrs Marika's favourite, she hummed with Kaliopi.

'Let the girl sing!' Anastasia smiled at her intensely. Nothing could stop Kaliopi now: with hands clasped under breasts heaving with emotion, eyes on the horizon as in a trance, she poured her heart into the song. Her voice, clear, young, tender, moved all hearts. Her father's eyes were homesick. Her mother's full of quiet pleasure. She had heaped education on her daughters, now she was reaping the fruits. Her own mother had stopped her, had stopped everything for her – 'You are plain, Anastasia. You will stop school and become a good housewife.' This was her answer.

'A nightingale!' they all exclaimed in chorus. 'Bravo, Encore!'

'*La Bohème*,' Kaliopi announced readily. More sighs of recognition, intimacy.

'Very tragic,' Mrs Marika informed the other women. 'I know,' said Mother, 'Sh!'

Eleni was transported, she knew the words by heart, had seen herself sing them so many times in the mirror, synchronising the movements of her lips with her sister's voice. 'They call me Mimi, but Lucia is my name,' Kaliopi was singing, with such feeling that she was Lucia, she was Madame Butterfly; and so was Eleni.

'A beautiful sight.' Gregoris caressed Eleni's back absent-mindedly. His daughter by the sea singing arias! He had not done badly considering they were girls. Comely faces, curvy bodies. 'Beautiful voice, beautiful sight – but not like my mother's voice, not her beauty.'

'And now our little actress, our great little actress.' Father pushed Eleni forward before someone else took her turn. 'Eleni will do Red Riding Hood.' He had seen her play the part at school: so pretty, so convincing, his heart was tightened when she was grabbed by the wolf. He saw contempt in her face, and tried again. 'A serious poem then.'

Eleni took her place by the edge of the sea, stood tall, raised one eyebrow to look like Greta Garbo – her idol. For emphasis, she raised the other eyebrow also, felt the sea breeze blow back her hair, and announced, '*Iphigeneia in Aulis*. I am Iphigeneia. And Agamemnon, and Clytemnestra. And also Calchas, the priest.'

When she started, she felt she was also the boats that stood still in the harbour, she was the stillness itself. And the wish and bitterness of the voyage to Troy.

'You voyage far, father, leaving me behind!'

She felt exquisite pleasure to her last nerve: kneeling, the bride to be, and embracing her father's knees, pleading.

'Suppliant will I twine my body round your knees, my body which this mother bare to thee.'

She felt the daughter's, and she felt the father's grief. And the pain of the bride that would not be a bride. She saw her body stretched out instead on the marble altar, the cold piercing her to the bone, the knife's blade pressing on her skin. The vengeful virgin Artemis waited; Zeus and Hera watched. She shuddered at the sharp point of her happiness when she announced she would willingly be sacrificed, so the breeze would blow and carry the boats to Troy.

'Prosper, father, so far as rests with me! Find victory, and return to the fatherland!'

Her father's face floated amongst the spectators pursuing her, Eleni moved from role to role to avoid it.

She shuddered, a daughter of Troy, as the sea breeze arrived from the other shore, touching her spectators' faces with tragic voyages.

She sought her parents' faces, and saw with happiness that they had tears in their eyes. Her sisters studied her with surprise. 'What emotion, what drama!' people said. 'Sarah Bernhardt, Kotopouli,' Mrs Marika exclaimed. 'She will be a great actress. She must become an actress.'

'No daughter of mine becomes an actress,' Father flared up. 'Girls from honest families don't become actresses – making up like whores and taking their clothes off on the stage, and jumping up and down showing their knickers.'

'She already does!' Sophia whispered in Kaliopi's ear, and both burst into uncontrollable giggles. Eleni wished she had the evil eye.

'We are not serious, Gregori, she is only a child,' Mother intervened.

'That's what you teach them, all the education and immoral ideas you fill their heads with. All the erotic novels, and the melodramas. Sunday school. Sunday school and shop from now on. Finished. Settled. No more talk.' He looked at the people round him with anger and suspicion; he was pale with violence.

Eleni almost fell to her knees, but did not. She watched his long nose, his rapacious eyes, that made him look like a bird of prey.

The sea breeze was welcome. 'Ti oraia avra!'

'Niko, play the flute – something from home,' Godmother Kyveli said to the tall young man, her son. He tried some notes on his flute, the lorry-driver picked up his guitar: a few clear strums on the guitar, the flute climbed in a sustained plaintive love song. The guitar followed with patient rhythm, vibrating expectation: the flute slid from note to note, sank in dejection but quickly rose to young high-pitched trills and tendrils of delicate sadness. Godmother Kyveli sang the Anatolian words, men and women joined her, the bay of Neo Marmara reverberated with nostalgic oriental melodies, from the old and lost Marmara, from Smyrna and Panormos, from Redestos and Aivali and Troy. Land and sea were populated with sighs and ghosts and legends. The dead were resurrected.

The old Karamanlou had fallen asleep; the hubble-bubble had fallen from her mouth, her head leaned to one side, her hands rested on her lap, her half-opened palms looking upwards faintly questioning, accepting: ke mi hirotera! Her son covered her with a blanket.

Ach, what sweet-smelling oleanders, wild rhododendrons, ripe pomegranates; orange groves whose fruit glowed like lanterns; the bells of Ayia Sofia, and Smyrna in flames. The old Karamanlou sighed, dreaming of her young husband wearing round his waist his bright silk sash – the pride of Karaman.

The sea, so warm at the end of the day! One last swim. Father holds Eleni under the chin, teaching her to swim, while she beats the water with arms and legs fighting for life, her petticoat trailing. The feast on the beach has disappeared, and Gregoris gazes from a distance at the bright oriental rugs in full display; he looks for a sparkling red gramophone. Steryos is playing on his accordion the new American crazy dance, rock-and-roll, and girls and boys are flinging their limbs in the wild foreign rhythm. The Karamanlou has woken up and is staring at the sea while her son buries the young animal's bones in the sand. Mother is beckoning Gregoris and Eleni to come out, it's getting late. But Eleni's ears are filled with the humming pleasures of the sea, while fear sprawled on the seabed stretches towards her his enticing tentacles. Her limbs move in the water like lazy seaweed, always travelling and always rooted in one place.

·7·
Miracles

'**A** MIRACLE! Wake up, Christians! The Virgin has shown us her sign again! She is telling us something! She is talking to us!'

Eleni and Kaliopi ran to the balcony. From other balconies housewives were staring at a crowd of people running down the street, led by a short fat woman in her slippers and apron, her hair dishevelled and hanging down in long strands. With her short round legs almost tripping each other, she kept up a good speed that left the others behind. Her large buttocks danced with excitement as she negotiated the holes and bumps in the unpaved street: ripples of religious enthusiasm ran through her compact body as she called to the people on the balconies to come to the miracle.

Her face taut with passion, Kaliopi stood like an avenging angel over Sophia, pointedly concentrating on her book. 'The Virgin has appeared! God is talking to us! And you sit and read?' Sophia gave her a look of contempt that seared what it touched. 'Phantasioplecti!' she murmured through her teeth, and bent down to her reading. Kaliopi instantly heaped her humiliation on to Eleni, who stood witnessing the scene with open satisfaction.

'And you,' she snapped, 'you'll be as faithless and blasphemous as her!' Eleni stood undecided, divided between curiosity, and the wish to frustrate Kaliopi even more. Curiosity won and Eleni tumbled down the stairs ahead of Kaliopi.

The crowd had stopped in front of a three-storey building with rain-stained walls. A large woman in a dressing gown with big crimson flowers, balancing on tiny high-heeled shoes, her hair in tight perm-curls, talked to the onlookers with emotion, crossing herself and pointing now to a window, and now towards the sky, clasping her

172

hands as if imploring or bewailing. The crowd examined the window attentively, exchanging views in reverent voices.

'Look! As clear as daylight! What do you mean you can't see her?' A man in striped pyjamas was explaining impatiently between puffs of his cigarette to a younger man. 'Don't you see her head? Jesus' head is next to hers, a bit lower down, and her arms – do you see her arms? What do you mean you can't see her arms? Are you blind? Can't you see the blue stain coming down towards the centre, there, near the window catch? That's her sleeve. And that grey area is the baby's body.'

'I don't see a thing.' The younger man, with his hands resting nonchalantly on his hips, looked at the window. 'Not a thing,' he repeated calmly, shaking his head in disbelief. The man in the striped pyjamas made harder efforts to explain; with exasperation he pointed out the lines and spots on the window, until suddenly his cigarette burned his finger. He threw it away in fury as the young man walked off shrugging his shoulders and muttering 'I don't understand what all the noise is about. I can't see a thing.'

'Because you are an infidel. That's why you can't see. Because you are not God-fearing! Because you are a communist!' Having expended his anger, the man in the striped pyjamas turned back to the crowd. They were more sympathetic: some shook their heads up and down in agreement.

'Of course you can see it,' the large woman urged. 'As I see you and you see me. There's her head, her face, and little Jesus in her lap, and the halo round His head! You see? You see with what sweetness she is looking at Jesus? The sweetness in her eyes?'

'Now just a minute, Kyra Persephone. What eyes? What sweetness in her eyes? All right, perhaps there are some lines, some shapes. Perhaps they look like heads. But not eyes, not the sweetness in her eyes, manoula mou, my sweet Kyra Persephone mou!' The man from the kiosk was protesting loudly and jovially. 'I've never crossed words with you, Kyra Persephone. You and I starved together in the Occupation, but truth should be told: there are no eyes in that window, and no sweetness in the eyes. Ah!'

'Oust, palioskylo, you infidel dog!' the woman in the dressing gown shouted back, and continued her story for the sake of the newcomers.

'Well, we had no idea. Until Kyra Katina knocked on our door – we were having our morning coffee, still undressed. "What Christian could it be at this time of the morning!" I said to Euripides – and in rushed Kyra Katina screaming her head off. I thought her house was on fire or her husband who suffers from his heart – years now – had an attack.

Before I could ask her, she yelled "God bless you, Kyra Persephone! There is a miracle in your house! The Virgin herself has visited you, in body and in mind, and holding her little baby Jesus in her arms – and you sit drinking coffee!" Her exact words. "What Virgin, what Jesus are you talking about, Kyra Katina?" I said. "Has God taken your mind? Has He confused your tongue? The Virgin and Jesus haven't visited our home since my Euripides lost his shop and all his fortune. Don't play with our misfortune, Kyra Katina!" "Play with your misfortune?" she screamed. "Ach, Kyra Persephone! If you saw what is on the front window of your house you wouldn't utter such blasphemous words." She dragged me, just as I was, outside the house, and we saw all these people praying and crying. And there was the picture, as clear as day – the Virgin in blue, with baby Jesus in her arms, still naked, the poor little baby, and the purple halos round their heads.' She was overcome.

'The bad days are over, my Euripides,' she said to the man in the striped pyjamas. 'The Virgin has visited us, you will start another shop and you will thrive. And make everyone burst with envy.' The man in the striped pyjamas shook his head in solemn agreement and muttered between deep puffs of his cigarette, 'I'll show those bastards, those cuckolds, those pimps, who the real Euripides Eustathiades is!' He beat his chest with self-recognition, starting a cough that stopped with the first puff of another cigarette. The short fat woman who had led the crowd to the scene of the miracle was so moved that she started chanting the canticle of Kassiani; a few other women joined her. Kaliopi was moved by the occasion, and by the opportunity to exhibit her voice, and sang louder and clearer than everyone else. 'I en polles amarties peripesoussa gyni, the woman who fell into many sins . . .' Even the children were moved by the melody that meant for them the expectation of Easter; everyone was transported.

'What do you mean, singing the canticle of Kassiani outside my house? What is the implication, if you please? Singing about the woman who fell into many sins, months before Easter! Are you, by any chance, making allusions?'

'Me? Allusions? The Virgin and Christ and all the Saints be my witnesses, I had no such thing in mind. It just came to me, because – it's such a sweet melody, such moving words! I loved it since I was a child.' The short fat woman was wiping her tears with her apron. But when a taxi slowed near them and the driver shouted that there was another miracle on Skoufa street, at the barber's shop, she decisively marched up the road, taking with her most of the crowd. Kaliopi, now second in command, shouted at Eleni to hurry up – didn't she realise these were rare, apocalyptic times, and God would punish those of weak faith and slothful disposition! Eleni looked back in a last effort to make out the picture on the window, but all she could see was a confusion of blues and purples. The woman in the dressing gown and the man in the striped pyjamas watched contemptuously as the crowd moved off, and took up with new vigour their discussion with the kiosk-man.

Outside the barber's shop the customers gazed at the large window, which reflected all the colours of the rainbow: with the white bibs round their necks and soft white foam on their cheeks, they looked like mature corpulent children.

'The Garden of Eden,' the short fat woman announced decisively. 'I can see the Tree of Life.' 'And the Tree of Knowledge,' another woman added. 'And the serpent,' someone joked. 'Watch out that the serpent doesn't get into your knickers.'

'Iconoclast,' she hissed at him.

'And angels, I can see angels!' Kaliopi was transported.

'You are always seeing angels!' Eleni said quietly.

'Blasphemer!' Kaliopi shrieked. 'I'll tell your Sunday-school teacher.'

'I can see the rainbow of peace,' another woman remarked, and others agreed.

'The rainbow of peace, and death to the war criminals!' one of the customers cried as he pulled off his bib and wiped the foam from his face.

'Have you no shame, Kyr Yianni, to utter such words in the presence of the Miracle? And who are you calling war criminals? Do you mean us, who fought the enemy while you filled your belly from the black market?'

'Collaborator!' someone murmured. Kyr Yiannis bunched his bib, ready to defend himself.

'It moved. The picture moved! My little Virgin, forgive us, forgive our wrangling in your divine presence! Kneel, infidels, kneel!'

Kaliopi was on her knees at once, pulling Eleni's dress.

'Send for a priest,' an elderly woman advised. 'You should sprinkle your shop with holy water, Kyr Panteli, and have a trisagion done.'

An old woman in black appeared at the corner of the street, pulling her hair and beating her breasts. 'She came to us too, she visited our home!' she screamed. 'Ah my little Virgin, my mute little Virgin, what are you trying to say to us, Panagoula mou? Tell us that we are sinful! Tell us that you are angry, bitter! Whisper to me, little Mother of God.

Ach, we are all killers! We are all murderers! Brother kills brother! Come and see her face, so pained! So sad! For us, for our crimes! Come and repent, infidels! Come and wash your filth! Herods! Judases! Mary Magdalens! Jezebels! Fratricides! Patricides! Ah! The sins! The miasma!'

Some people followed the old woman in trepidation; others waited for the priest, who appeared, slow and dignified, at the end of the street, followed by a small crowd of women.

The newcomers said the city was full of miracles: the churches were crowded with people chanting, the priests were running from house to house sprinkling holy water, and the Virgin's image was imprinted in so many windows! Someone saw Saint Demetrius standing on the city walls at dawn, gazing at the sea; his shield and sword sparkled in the sun. Others said that the Virgin appeared in a young girl's dream and said to her, 'Tell them to stop the wars. It brings me such sorrow. Look at my tears.' She had true tears, big and sparkling like pearls. 'Tomorrow I will fill this city with miracles. My image will be imprinted on your homes, as it should be imprinted on your hearts.' Her very words, it makes my skin tingle. People crossed themselves, and agreed the Virgin had come to expiate the atrocities of the Civil War.

Kaliopi and Eleni wandered round the city from miracle to miracle.

Suddenly it all went. The faces, the haloes, the saintly figures, disappeared. All that remained was glass. People walked desolate from street to street looking for miracles, but the miracles had ceased. The Holy Mother and her baby, the Garden of Eden and the Garden of Gethsemane, the Company of Saints, and the Bands of Angels, and the Tree of Life – where had they gone? Even the sun had hidden, behind Mount Olympus.

A man in a suit was insisting to a handful of passers-by, 'These are no miracles! This is pollution. The air is polluted. It's from the factory. Can't you smell the fumes? You should go to the railway station to smell the foulness!'

'It's DDT. They're spraying the marshes,' another said.

'Uh! It's those chemicals they chuck in the bay. Why do you think they've forbidden fishing and swimming?'

Some of the men nodded, others said those were blaspheming words. It was getting chilly, and people were reluctantly and sadly preparing to go home.

A gipsy decided it was time for his performance. The children gathered round him and his monkey; and the monkey knew his moment had come. He climbed up the pole the gipsy held, and perched at the top with self-satisfaction, looking alertly and suspiciously at the crowd about him.

'Show us how the old man and the old woman sleep together on a winter's evening!' the gipsy ordered him. The monkey leaned his head on one side, placed both paws under it, and shut his eyes. The gathering laughed.

'And now show us how the young miss puts lipstick on her lips and rouge on her cheeks while waiting for her fiancé.'

The monkey was excited. He settled securely on the pole, grabbed a hand mirror from the man's pocket, and with one paw held the mirror while with the other he slapped his face, screwing up his eyes and preening himself. People laughed – what a clever monkey! The children wanted more, but the gipsy passed his hat round for drachmas. Time to go home.

· 8 ·
Prospering Designs

'I'M GOING back home, Gregori.' Anastasia stopped in the middle of the promenade and shouted to Gregoris who, as always, raced ahead. And as she caught up with him she had her say: 'You are not alone, Gregori! We are one family! Look at the other families strolling together in the afternoon sun. It was your idea to take us for a stroll.'

'Home? I'll take you home! How could I leave my little wife, my plump little wife, who has become so plump lately that she needs us to help her along!' He pulled her to him and embraced her tightly, pleased with her exasperation. 'I'll give you such a home, my little wife, you'll be a queen. I'll buy you the most expensive, the most modern apartment in Salonica! Apartment – a block of apartments! In the best location, with the best views, the best prospects – of the mountains, of the sea, whatever your plump little heart desires.' And, in immediate manifestation of largesse, 'Eleni, what does my child want her father to buy her? Peanuts, ice cream, chocolate? A word – and your father will buy the world.'

Sophia and Kaliopi turned watchful faces towards their father; they exchanged ironic smiles. Eleni noticed the quick conspiracy, alert and divided in her wishes and alliances.

'I'm too old for sweets,' she mumbled with embarrassment, without conviction.

'Her pockets are full of treats, anyway,' Mother scolded.

Eleni balanced her forbidding mother against the father that gave. 'I would like roasted chickpeas.' She sent the three women glances of guilt and victory.

Every few steps they met friends and acquaintances. 'How your daughters have grown, Mrs Anastasia! What beautiful girls! And yourself – what a fashionable suit! From the shop of course – nothing but the best, but you have to tell me who your seamstress is, or do you keep her a secret? And your latest window arrangement, Mr Gregori – so tasteful! Such style! Tell me, is it true that the Kyriazis brothers are facing difficulties? We've heard the bank is coming in. Such an old firm! We must come to your spring collection, Mr Gregori!'

How well-groomed and pleasing and pleased with themselves parents became on Sunday afternoons! How generous to their children – and their children how satisfied with temporary delights! Passa tempo, passa tempo, the street sellers cried – and the promenade lay in the glance of the gods. The light made things jump with tangible clarity, the breeze went where it pleased – 'ti orea aura' everyone exclaimed. Even Father Zeus put down his instruments of fear and war and listened with astonishment to this new music of love pouring from the pleasure boats; he remembered with nostalgia and pride the women of his youth.

Eleni observed her father walk with his hands partly raised, as if he were exhibiting merchandise, or granting superior favours. He turned his head occasionally to inspect the bay, or to inspect the houses in their privileged position, exhibiting to the world his fine long nose and keen face, his alert jaws, involved in perpetual silent bartering – at which, to judge from his light step and the agile movement of the shoulders within his smart suit, he was winning. He moved next to his wife's corseted, steady body with a child's impetuousness, restrained only by a child's unforthcoming obedience to the laws of the world.

Popping roasted chickpeas into her mouth, Eleni watched her sisters' rounded hips rock rhythmically, making their tight-waisted, full-bodied skirts, with layers of starched petticoat underneath, sway coquettishly in one assertive mutual fling of feminine defiance. As they turned round she saw the round lipsticked lips complimented by round breasts and round hair-dos. She crunched her chickpeas as she contemplated the hermaphroditic pinafore hanging on her body.

They were smiling with conspiratorial pleasure as companies of young men stared at them provocatively, making, Eleni knew, inane, obscene comments.

'Aman Manoli mou, hold me, I feel faint. Do you see what I see, Manoli? Oh, how they shake them. And I don't know which one to choose. Do I want the dark one, sweet like treacle, like black molasses, or do I choose the white one like milk and honey? Ah, Manoli mou, look how I swoon, look how I dribble.'

'What a piece, Lefteri, what a syrupy piece of baklava! Samali manoula mou!'

Mother turned back furtively and sent her daughters mute war signals.

'You're asking for it, you're provoking them,' Father shouted at them.

'Walk in front of us so we can keep an eye on you,' Mother ordered.

With lowered eyes and serious faces, they hurried forward.

'Virgin Marys,' Eleni thought.

Father turned round and stopped in the middle of the promenade, stretching out his arms and blocking everyone's way, his eyes wide open with unruly triumph.

'There it is. You can move in tomorrow. The best in Salonica.'

At some distance, a modern four-storey building stood by itself, surrounded by balconies that overlooked the city and the bay. The family looked incredulously at the building which, as it opened up in so many balconies, seemed to be all smiles. The ochre yellow of its walls gave it a perennial sunniness.

'The best location in Salonica! The best views! Does my little wife want to admire the White Tower? She stands on her balcony and admires the White Tower. Does she feel romantic and want to gaze at the sea? She sits at her balcony and gazes at the sea. Does she feel nostalgic for her Macedonian mountains? She sits on her northern balcony and looks at Mount Hortiatis. Does she want to look at the city? Wherever she turns she sees the city and its people and its traffic. Like a queen.'

'Don't mock me, Gregori,' Mother complained, but was pleased, and asked 'Is it true?' with her eyes – but still wanted blandishments and confirmations.

'And does my little wife want to go to the theatre? The Royal Theatre is at her feet – indoors for the winter, open-air for the summer. The afternoon band? She listens while sipping her coffee. She sits back and sees the world promenading for her pleasure!'

Mother was red with pleasure and confusion, she made angry, whimpering noises. 'What is all this, Gregori? Has God taken your mind from you? Blessed man, eylogimene andra!'

'One flat, the largest and the best, for my wife and myself, and our daughters while they are still with us. One flat for Sophia, when she gets married. One flat for Kaliopi – and one for Eleni, although Eleni is not going to marry -' The daughters drew close to their father, looking at mother for permission to believe. Mother effervesced with fury at this prankishness, and kept telling Eleni to behave herself.

Like an exasperated martyr, Mother appealed to all the saints for help and explanation: 'The blessed man! Full of surprises, full of adventures! Life for him is one long adventure. Mia peripeteia! What a tasteless joke! No sense of propriety, no decorum!' But her green eyes were big with questions and satisfied wishes. The daughters started quarrelling who would have which flat. Kaliopi said I'll have the top one, I said it first; Sophia said the eldest should have first choice; whoever will marry first, Kaliopi snapped; Eleni flared up at this outrage – and me, an old maid, on the ground floor? Secretly she believed her father would give her all. They all talked at the same time, to different purposes and tunes, but the sound was sweet to their ears.

'Stay still! Don't move! You have to have your photographs taken on such a sunny day!' A man in a white tunic, with waxed pitch-black moustaches, stood in front of the amazed family, exhibiting a three-legged black-hooded box.

'You can have it in black and white, or you can have it *retouché*. With the White Tower for a background, or the Royal Theatre, or the bay with the boats in the distance.' While a barrage of words poured from his mouth his hand and arm and finally his head slowly disappeared into the ominous black hood.

'In front of our house! Just what the occasion wanted! A photograph – to immortalise the moment.' Father stood in the centre of a photograph that had already been snapped in his mind, owner of this best of houses, and satisfied owner of his women that surrounded him.

And another one: Father and Mother, he with his arm round her shoulder, she with her head leaning on his shoulder, just like the photograph that Eleni would gaze at, trying to retain the faces that slowly disappeared with time. And one of the three daughters – closer, not too close – smile please, the hand crawled like a snake into the black bag, the sisters still sustaining their precarious triangle, the head appeared again behind its waxed moustaches: click – and all three were gobbled by eternity. The house was without its sunniness in the photographs; the balconies, empty of people, made it look open and deserted and exposed to the sun and the sea winds.

An ugly roar swept along the promenade and made parents push their children on to the pavement, the photographer with his tripod jumped several steps back, as an army jeep like those used by the Germans and the English shot past like a hundred machine guns, unmindful of the crowd it was tearing in half.

'The cursed one! The demonised one!' People crossed themselves as they threw themselves right and left. A man with a drooping ginger moustache, a cigarette hanging from his mouth, sat nonchalantly at the wheel, gazing at the crowd with superior, amused contempt through dark polaroid glasses.

'The playboy,' someone murmured. 'Who does he think he is – a king, a general?' 'Uh!' another announced. 'His father got money from the Americans – the Marshall Plan – and the son is spending it on cars and women.'

The jeep slowed in front of the Gregoriou family, and the man in the polaroid glasses sent a slow look of superior, appreciative interest to the elder sisters. He brought his hand to his glasses, as if to take them off, rearranged them, and with an unearthly roar he disappeared from sight, leaving behind him dust and exasperation. Kaliopi's face twitched with eros.

The new apartment soon overflowed with bric-à-brac and objets d'art, celebrating the new prosperity of the Gregoriou household. The balconies were filled with flowers, thriving in the sunlight and the sea breezes that travelled round the house all day. At noon the air was smothered with the spicy scent of pinks and carnations. The geraniums with their large scarlet umbrellas released a subtle lemoniness if you happened to brush by them. The fuchsia gave no smell as the elegant acrobat dancers hung precariously from its branches. And the sweet peas, eternally young, spread with such demureness their evanescent delicate sweetness wherever they climbed, or hung, or trailed.

Eleni would stand with her mother on the kitchen balcony which caught the morning sun, and look at the Old City climbing up Mount Hortiatis. Mother would take deep breaths and say to Eleni, 'Breathe the mountain air. Can you feel it in your lungs?' Then together they would try to find their old home, which somehow always vanished in the remote labyrinths, where their homesick eyes remained tangled.

'My village is behind the mountain,' Mother would say and then remain silent; while they separately tried to imagine, or remember, a different life, made up of cries of animals and distinct smells of plants and the dappled shade of trees. They would talk of father's village: the distance threaded painfully through her eyes, and through her memories of their backyard and children's violent games in the dark. The yearning for those lost homes crept like a parental hand into her belly and held it.

From the front balcony that faced the sea and the afternoon sun, they watched lovers in small rowing boats with embroidered cushions being taken by the silent boatman for endless love-rounds and love zig-zags. Suspended fingers would tear, with momentary vows, the sea. At the far end of the bay, Mount Olympus, that had seen eternal and ephemeral lovers, and their perennial games and pleasures and deaths, gave his blessing. On the promenade well-fed parents who had forgotten love attended to the discipline and good nutrition of their unruly children. The White Tower rose sinister and grey, dwarfing the trees round it, and the white-clad photographers lying in wait. On Sunday morning the Greek flag was raised on its mast by a brass band that played patriotic tunes; their instruments gleamed and sparkled in the Sunday sun, and well-dressed families paused with reverence on their way to the church.

On summer evenings the open-air theatre – the Royal Theatre – came to magnificent life, and filled the air with warm-coloured electric lights, and music, and voices that spoke as if they sang. With other children Eleni stood near the entrance and passed the time gazing at the theatre-goers. Slowly the ladies in their high heels and soft summer dresses, and the gentlemen in light jackets vanished behind the gate, the lights beyond the wall went out, and the children sat and listened to the accentuated voices. They mouthed the words, invented gestures, recreated the drama with exuberance and gusto until, drunk with the pleasures of exaggeration, they subsided against each other.

One evening she watched a couple that seemed pleasant, the woman with bare arms, smooth and round, the man like her father in his hasty movements. She walked near them, as close as she could without their realising. She went near enough to touch lightly her dress, catch her scent; she looked at the expression on their faces and assumed the same expression, imagined she was their daughter, their one and only, cherished, child, entering with them the courtyard of miracles. The ticket clerk, convinced she was with them, returned her smile; the couple, unaware that they had become a family, walked towards their seats.

Eleni, abandoned by her brief adopted parents, slipped through companies of people, looking amongst that plentifulness of men and women for other plausible parents. She approached good-looking and gentle-looking people and stood by them or sat not far from them, just so she gave the impression that she was part of a family. She looked for resemblances with her parents, she thought she found them and felt at home. She tried to hear what they said to each other. They all looked round with great animation, searching for friends or better seats; they greeted their acquaintances with enthusiasm, the women admired each other, the men asked after each other's business and promised to meet at the café later for a granita, but afterwards they would remark to each other heartlessly that the friend's business was not doing well, and they hoped he would not ask them for a loan, and not only that but their marriage was going through a crisis. A man nearby was reading the programme and the names of the actors slowly and loudly to his wife; people behind told him to keep quiet. People sat up nervously on their chairs, stretching left and right to make sure they had a good view of the stage. No one looked at Eleni. A woman pushed her by mistake but said nothing, as if it were a chair she had pushed. Eleni moved quietly to the dark edge of the theatre, protected by the honeysuckle on the wall that stretched its thousand tendrils into empty space - which suddenly became dim. Three heavy knocks: people grew quiet, then became noisy again as they shushed and hushed each other.

'Sh! Please be quiet, my dear madam. Nag, nag, nag – don't you have a home where you can solve your domestic problems?'

'Impudent! Telling me what to do! You think we couldn't hear you smooching away with your – Miss. A man of your age – and in public! Shame!'

'Be quiet for God's name!'

'You be quiet!'

'Sh . . . Quiet! Silence!'

Three louder knocks from behind the red, heavy curtain. The noise subsided. Eleni could hear her heart thump.

As the curtain slowly swept across the stage with a sweetly promising rustling noise it revealed a scene of such splendid illumination that you thought it was the heart of a sunrise or a sunset. A village, hardly real in its beauty, appeared on the stage. Eleni had never seen such splendid Turkish palaces, such brilliantly whitewashed Greek houses, such a clean and neat and perfectly round well – and the bucket next to it, brand-new. Everything was washed in a warm supernatural glow that did not seem to come from a real sun. There was no breeze because it was not necessary, the air was immobile, ideal.

The young heroine, the beautiful Kyra Vasiliki of Yannena, had raven hair and eyebrows, red lips and a skin as white as marble; she wore skirts of white raw silk, a waistcoat embroidered with golden thread, and coyly pointed slippers. The young Greek in love with her had long brown hair and no beard, a small waist and slender legs; he was beautiful like a girl and when he played the flute the birds fell into a trance. But the old and ferocious Ali Pasha, with a long white beard, and soldiers all round him naked to the waist holding long sharp scimitars, kept Kyra Vasiliki locked in his arms day and night. She loved the young Greek, and swooned when he played his flute for her, and also loved the old Turk, whose prisoner she was. But he was her prisoner as much as she was his, and he liked to lay his head on her lap and dream of empires.

Surrounded by the honeysuckle, Eleni watched, transported, the love, and pain, and anger, and the horrible deaths. The young Greek's love was like the music of his flute – clear and distinct, full of the sweet swooning and complaint of love. And the music that Ali Pasha played was of the powerful war-drum that made one's blood freeze. The audience made not a sound, except for the occasional sob, and at the end, when the lights came on, most of the women had red eyes, and the men looked serious, chastened: 'A true tragedy.' Eleni slipped through the crowd and ran back home preparing to face her father's anger.

The play the following week was, the advertisements said, the classic French comedy, from Paris. Such elegance and wealth, the European manners! The men kissed the women's hands with such grace they hardly touched them with their lips, and called them *madame*; the women would hide their faces behind their fans or play with a glove and laugh playfully, or play with the fresh flowers in a vase with a feathery seriousness, and say, 'My dear Count, you are exaggerating.' Madame would appear suddenly at the French doors and drop the suitcase on the floor and cry 'Ah! You have betrayed me! And with the maid! Mon Dieu!' And would faint on one of the elegant armchairs while her husband fanned her and the maid ran for water. It was so refined, so European; people trod lightly, moved as if they danced, quarrelled with elegance, fell and reclined on couches or chairs as if they had no weight. It was as if they had no bodies; they were naughty, charming, coy, amusing, *chic* – that was the word they used – never crude, gross, primitive, loud, fat, sweaty, as Greeks could be; she was ashamed of her mother's village, whose streets and backyards smelt of animal manure, and of her mother's Macedonian accent, and her father's rages, the way he sipped his soup noisily. Ashamed of her country and longing for the civilised West, and ashamed of the shame and the longing: the betrayal.

The season at the Royal Theatre ended with a repertory of Greek tragedies; they made her forget all shame. *Iphigeneia in Aulis* was hers. The father's sea-voyage, and the sacking of Troy, and thousands of years later the burning of another Troy and another father's sea-voyage from the fatal shores back to Greece, made up for her one story, beginning and ending with the prayer for good wind and the killing of a young girl. She shivered again at the sharp edge of the knife and of the parental mystery, and felt its flames consume her.

The massacred shores of Ionia appeared to her again as she watched with fear Medea, the witch, the foreigner and exile, the beautiful refugee from the Asiatic coast, the woman of nightmares, the daughter who betrayed her father, the sister who cut her brother into pieces, the mother who now holds the knife over her own children, consumed by the flames of jealousy. As she watched the raging woman, a pain came back to her from a half-forgotten darkness of herself asleep with mother and father, and waking at the edge of the bed, in the dark, with the knowledge that a terrible event had exiled her. But Medea the beautiful witch took Eleni into the exhilarating rages of womanhood, without shame. Without shame, with secret love, she thought of Olga, the other woman now in exile, accused of betraying sisters and brothers. Sons and daughters and brothers and parents. Medea's words washed off the shame of love.

What word and what reason, when the soft-spoken, soft-fleshed god Dionysus, with the long curls, wily, libidinous, ruthless, arrived with his manic women followers, refugees from Asia, bringing to the women of Greece the dark and merry mysteries of the grape and love and madness. Transfiguring the forested mountains of Greece with miracles of beauty and plenty and terror. Young mothers suckled gazelles and baby wolves, while writhing snakes licked their cheeks. Their hair, loose on their shoulders, was crowned with ivy and oak and young bryony. A woman struck the rock and a fountain of cool water bubbled up; another struck the soil and a spring of wine flowed; another scratched the soil with her bare hands until warm white milk swelled up: pure honey streamed from their wands. But when they made of their wands weapons and attacked men and animals and tore them to pieces, and the aged mother tore her son, not knowing it was her son, Eleni felt the ache of a torn body, and the pleasure of the young suckling and the pleasure of the young mother with the breast full of sweetness, and the violence of the manic dancer. Her body was pulled by the different imaginations. She saw in the face of the Asiatic god the face of her father.

'Where is the young one, Anastasia? Who gave her permission to be out at this time of the evening?'

Father paced through the new apartment, crammed with furniture that overflowed with carved ebony feasts and flowers in celebration of his wealth. He searched through the furniture for causes of anger.

'What kind of a mother are you? They need a short leash – look at the middle one, hanging on the balcony all day long, making a spectacle of herself! No shame! And the elder one, where is the elder one? Reading those foreign books - those love-romances.'

He stumbled absent-mindedly, unlovingly, against the unrelenting bulges and corners of the massive proof of his success.

'They need watching, day and night. There is no decency left in this country, with all these dowry-hunters and playboys. Boarding school – convent - that's what they need.'

His wife shook her head with resignation. 'God forgive the man, he gets worse every day. Eaten with suspicion, quarrelling with his own clothes. What's eating you, Gregori? The big ones are here. Since when are we not allowed to sit on the balcony, in the midst of summer, when even the cricket is dying from the heat? As for the young one, she is your daughter – you deal with her. The apple will fall under the apple tree. Like father, like daughter.' She approached the balcony prepared to let her anger fall upon her elder daughters.

'Enough fresh air, you two,' she said harshly, 'get down to your reading.' She heard the demonic noise of a jeep and saw the man with dark glasses take the corner fast, making everyone in the street leap on to the pavement. She saw her daughter Kaliopi look at the disappearing vehicle entranced.

'Under lock and key! That's what they need – and shortening of the rope. School, home and the shop – where I can keep an eye on them. And they can learn the business, and keep away from the dowry-hunters.' Gregoris heard the soft metallic sound of a door shutting and rushed towards it, his arm raised. But he was stopped by the sight of his younger daughter waiting for the blow with her eyes shut, pressing against the wall, trying to disappear into it.

'Come here, Eleni! Where have you been? Tell your father where you've been, or -'

Eleni looked at her mother, but Mother stared at her sternly; her sisters watched from a safe distance.

'I was helping Nicholas with his homework.'

'She was at the theatre!' Kaliopi screamed triumphantly. 'She's been going to the theatre all summer, every evening, behind everyone's back, and watching all the dirty goings-on on the stage. I've been keeping an eye on her.'

'Anastasia! Is this true? What kind of a mother are you, not to keep an eye on the child? She is only a child!'

'Your child. You made her, now you unmake her.'

'Judas Iscariot!' Eleni shot at Kaliopi.

'Come here, Eleni, how did you get into the theatre? With what

187

money?' Mother sat down for the interrogation. Father approached with threat and alarm; the sisters were all ears.

'I walked in. On my two legs.'

'Sell the smartness somewhere else. How do you get in? You need money to get into the theatre. Does someone give you the money, Eleni?' Mother's voice was becoming conciliatory. 'Come and sit here and tell us.'

Father paced up and down, pushed furniture out of his way, looked at objects and people as if a new enemy had appeared in the room.

'It's not a crime, going to the theatre, mother,' Sophia intervened. 'They are showing plays of quality. They are literature.'

'Literature!' Father growled. 'Immoralities! Erotics! I'll burn all that rubbish you hide under your beds. Don't think I don't know.' Sophia kept quiet, her face radiated contempt and sarcasm.

'Where do you find the money, Eleni?' Mother wouldn't be distracted.

'Children under twelve don't pay money.' Eleni took courage from Sophia's unexpected support. Now she would not be stopped. 'I look young, because I am small – because you starved me in the war – and because of the hair-cut you give me, all short and straight as if I came from an orphanage, and these baby clothes you make me wear take years off me.' She heard Kaliopi murmuring, 'What other clothes can you wear, flat-chested as you are?' But she continued the attack. 'I go in free.'

'Free!' A gasp of astonishment. Eleni took courage: perhaps they were impressed.

'Children have to be accompanied,' Mother cut in.

'I walk near couples, nice, pleasant-looking couples, and pretend I am with them. Their daughter.' Eleni, confident in her triumph, continued with the details. 'I choose a new couple every evening: well-dressed, pleasant. No one knows.'

Sophia smiled sympathetically, Father came and sat near, looking at her with new interest; a near smile wandered through his face, but Mother brought the room back to order. 'At home. After sunset, you stay at home from now on.'

'Under lock and key,' Father added, not to be accused of giving her special treatment. 'Home and Sunday school. Homework. Otherwise – the convent.'

Eleni looked at Sophia for sympathy, and allied condemnation of the oppressors.

'And you, Anastasia, keep your daughters in order. Not just

embroideries and trousseaus, and gossiping with your cousins. Teach them housework, and Christian morals.'

Mother looked at Father with inarticulate indignation.

'Kaliopi looks at this man in the jeep,' Eleni announced in a clear loud voice. 'Every evening. He drives round our house all night and she looks at him and dribbles.' Father turned to Kaliopi and Mother with renewed anger.

'Lies! All lies! She is mad!' Kaliopi shrieked. 'She is jealous, that's what she is, she is mad with jealousy.'

She stood panting, looking at Eleni with unspeakable hate, and at Father with alarm. Mother covered her face in despondency. 'Take them away from me, all of them.' Eleni sat down, tired and depressed, feeling the heat of Sophia's disappointment and contempt: but she waited obstinately, heavy with triumph, while Kaliopi in her turn tasted Father's temper.

When it was over and the sisters were alone – 'Judas!' Kaliopi spat.

'Judas Iscariot yourself!'

They pounced on each other and rolled on the floor, fastened in equal blind hate, hitting, strangling, kicking, till they both, having caught a strong fistful of each other's hair, were held immobile. Eleni felt the roots of her hair pull and break and bring tears to her eyes; she tightened her grip. Sophia left the room with superior indifference. And the parents, having bequeathed so much war to their children, retreated into their bedroom to continue their own.

They followed the naked woman across the empty marble hall. Shafts of sunlight came from small windows round the dome and made wreaths of watery glow that hung in the air. The woman's large wet haunches danced and bulged and rippled as the flesh came together into baby fists which tightened and loosened rhythmically as she walked. Elegant blue veins ran up the muscles of her legs. Her hair was cut short and she seemed to Eleni to be now a woman and now a man as she walked with manly confidence on her wooden clogs – clop clop, clop clop – on the wet marble floor. Fleeces of underwater luminescence sailed round them as they walked towards the sound of running water and women's voices.

Eleni walked precariously on her wooden clogs, crossing her arms in front of her to hide her body. She wanted not to look at the naked bodies of her mother and sisters: her mother's, ample, round, white, painfully familiar; Kaliopi's, full and confident; Sophia's, delicate, dark, silent. Eleni studied her sister's feminine walk. She gasped for air as they entered a hot white cloud populated by voices and moving silhouettes of women. Their guide showed them to a small cluster of marble seats, and – clop clop – she disappeared into the steam. Eleni thought she was at the bottom of a strange sea echoing with women's voices and water and myriad wooden clogs – clop clop, clop clop.

Mother and daughters sat facing each other round a marble sea-shell constantly overflowing with warm water that ran in rivulets between their feet. A deep gurgle of supply and satisfaction came from its hidden centre. Mother distributed soap, pumice stone, loofah, and a silver bowl each for the elder daughters – Eleni would use hers. She ran her fingers, with enjoyment, through her long, greying hair.

Eleni looked drowsily through the watery mist: the room was pouring out to her water and steam through invisible mouths and eyes set in its walls. Women's bodies sat or bent, splashing themselves with water, or moved unhurriedly through the hall, depositing their full, exposed weight at each step. Unashamed of their nakedness! Eleni's eyes negotiated through the mist the unabashed womanhood. Parading, exhibiting themselves! she thought, and sat upright in judgement, clasping her arms in front of her. But soon she was absorbed by the moving forms. The gentle curve of someone's hips, a scooped-in waist, the slender agile bone-pattern along a girl's back, gave her unadmitted pleasure, and atoned for the affronting mass of flesh.

She bit her lip with discomfort as Mother turned her large body towards her. 'Are you napping, Eleni? Here's the soap, here's the loofah, get on with it.' Eleni sat back as her mother's breasts, resting comfortably on her body, almost touched her; dark nipples stood out, her daughter concentrated on the soap. Her eyes travelled towards her sisters who were rubbing their legs with the pumice stone. Eleni noticed with dislike Kaliopi's sturdy ankles, her skin reddened and roughened by the stone. She observed her sitting comfortably, strong in her nakedness, pouring water on her face and body from her new silver bowl, while her free hand caressed her breasts and belly. Her face was ready to break into song. Dark Sophia, her body small and delicate, her face hard and secretive, stirred with the studied art of the *femme fatale*. Eleni admired her, at times loved her, feared her. Her sisters, she noticed, sat and moved with a new confidence; in a mysterious alliance with each other and with their mother, and with the rest of the naked women. Her sisters were now studying and comparing their naked bodies in the minutest details – who has the smallest waist, the roundest breasts, the longest legs? They asked Eleni to be judge. She gazed at them coldly. She was perplexed and appalled by all this womanhood: she concentrated on washing with vigour her own undecided body.

Sophia turned to her suddenly. 'What happened to your breasts, Eleni? Has the wolf eaten them?'

'Perhaps she won't grow any breasts!' Kaliopi beamed with her inspiration.

'Perhaps our Eleni is a boy!'

'Get on with the washing.' Mother scolded them, lightly – too lightly, Eleni thought, as she traced with a cruel eye the stretch-marks on her mother's belly, which she had caused. Her sisters had forgotten her, and were whispering to each other: Eleni knew what they were whispering about – she was overcome by the desire to get clean. She rubbed herself with the loofah until her skin hurt. About love. And about boys, and about what boys say to girls on the street – obscenities and smut – and what they do to them in dark stairs and basements. That's all they think about, all the time, you can see it on their faces. She picked up the pumice stone and rubbed her legs, until the skin looked flayed.

She was startled by what she saw through the arch in the next hall. An old woman looking like a man, with dark empty breasts hanging down in front of her, was bending over a body lying headless on a marble slab, pounding it with all her strength. The old woman's face had a serious, tired frown as she pressed her hands into the young girl's body and rolled and kneaded it as if the body had no life, or as if she were trying to give it life, and a new and different shape. Eleni was reminded of her grandmother making dough for Easter bread – hitting, stretching, rolling it, playing with it and tormenting it until she transformed it into a delight. The old woman stopped and wiped the sweat and steam running into her eyes, then attacked the body in front of her with new vigour.

Eleni felt the humid heat press down on her like a gigantic, white, plump hand. She moved, trying to free her face, and saw the young woman's head resting at the edge of the slab – eyes shut, features calm, perhaps satisfied, the wet hair spread on the marble.

She thought she was looking at Iphigeneia lying on the altar, waiting for the priest's knife, while the virgin goddess Artemis watched and waited. She thought of the war, of the bodies lying on the cart at odd angles and postures. She was overcome by the volume of flesh filling the room and filling her mouth with nausea; she put her hand to her mouth to contain the disgusting sweetness of her first chocolate at the end of the war. Her eye caught a woman's head suspended over a marble tub, she remembered Olga shaking her head coyly, defiantly. 'They decorate the squares with our heads! Will it do? Will it do?' Olga was behind the Iron Curtain now: she couldn't imagine what an iron curtain looked like. The head moved, she saw it had neck and shoulders.

'I want to go home. I cannot breathe.' She turned towards her mother, who was rubbing her thighs with the loofah with professional enjoyment.

'You cannot stay still, Eleni. Just like your father. You nagged and nagged to come to the hamam, now you want to leave.'

She looked at her sisters' chased silver bowls and was filled with envy. 'I want a bowl like theirs.'

'When you grow up,' Mother promised. 'Here, have mine.'

'I don't want yours. I want my own bowl. Like they have.'

Mother took the soap from her hands. 'Come, Eleni, don't be difficult, sit here between my legs, I'll wash your hair.' Eleni leaned back and rested her head on her mother's leg, and shut her eyes to keep the soap out. She gave herself up to her mother's soothing, comforting hands. She remembered her mother washing her, in the kitchen, her bracelets jingling, her ring scratching her skin ever so lightly – then the memory went, and she wondered if it were true. Warm rivers poured down her head and body, she looked through the watery fringe at the women moving back and forth, on their wooden clogs – clop clop, clop clop – talking and laughing and looking appraisingly at each other. And Eleni was taken into the movement and the noise of those bodies. The young girl through the arch sat up on the marble slab and stretched her arms and her repaired body with pleasure. The woman rose from the tub with slow graceful motions. Eleni leaned against her mother, gazing, an unsure male or female spirit that had stolen into a foreign female universe, gazing interrogatively, possessively, as it appeared now like an underwater garden travelling with the tides, and now like a school of gentle amphibia.

The women talked and washed each other's hair and scrubbed each other's backs, and sprinkled water on themselves and on each other with their silver bowls. Their faces and bodies were pink from the heat, and the scrubbing. They sat back and looked at other women coming and going on their wooden clogs; they made comparisons, their eyes stopped at oddities, or beauties. The dome overhead was light green; no Pantocrator's eye watched from above. The sunlight coming in through the portholes changed hue and direction as time went by: when it fell on a stream of water or a silver bowl it gleamed and sparkled. The women's talk continued, sometimes quick and lively, at other times slow, pensive; light-hearted laughter gurgled with the water; moments of watery silence – the day did not want to end, and the world was all water and women.

Eleni sold her soul to the forbidden world of books, Sophia's books, as if they held the secret of salvation or damnation. In the day, like a miser, she fingered and studied her half-understood treasures; in the night, she dwelt in their exotic landscapes of sin.

She searched in the cellar amongst damp newspapers and magazines, bundles of million-drachma bills from the war, torn suitcases, broken furniture, a violin without strings. The damp crept into her bones while scavenging eyes and nose and hands, accustomed to the darkness, felt their way through other people's discarded memories. She knew there was long pleasure hidden in the book when she felt its extraordinary thickness: it was damp but complete, and, judging from the uncut pages, unread. The title read *The Accursed Daughter:* the purified, archaic Greek gave authority to the condemnation. Like a sister she suffered with the heroine her trials and tribulations – betrayed love, heroic chastity, paternal anger, disgrace, poverty, wasting illness, and finally the sweet erotic embrace of death. The beautiful chaste Clarissa, who had lived and died in the dank rooms of England, united with Eleni's other heroines: young Cosette walking alone in the forest of Nancy, growing into a young woman behind the walls of a convent in Paris – Paris, with its dark river and labyrinthine sewers underneath, at every street corner the long shadow of Javert. The gay frivolous Nana scattering her quick life in the avenues of Paris. Passionate Anna Karenina covered in furs at the busy station of Petersburg listening with fear to an old man's tap tap, tap tap on the train-wheels. With her heroines, Eleni lost herself in the dark northern cities of Europe, following coaches with mysterious passengers and secret destinations, looking for lost lovers in the fog, feeling damp fear cling to her skin, and listening for different rhythms and echoes of horses' hooves on ancient cobblestones.

Or an unforeseen sun would blaze an ancient unnatural landscape into existence, touched with mysterious, oriental mania. Again, the Anatolian god Dionysus led a manic dance through the vines, bestowing on women his violent grace. 'The grace of the God touches you with violence,' an even older chorus sang. Knife-sharp rocks bleached by the salt and sun delivered rare flowers through their crevices; women, their naked breasts swollen with milk, nursed newborn jackals and wolves; honey oozed from tortured trunks of olive trees. In the quiet dapple of the olive grove an old mother, her long white hair loose, rapt with enthusiasm, was tearing her son to pieces: the crickets never stopped their song.

Eleni took from Sophia's drawer a book with a new, slim spine and gazed at the title, printed in plain black letters – *Flowers of Evil*. She leafed through the book, and at the sight of the picture guilt and accusation made her blush to the roots of her being. A man and woman lay naked, their bodies made of dark wood-grain, his hand resting on her breast under a dark lustreless moon. Eleni covered them hastily with the next page, and the next, which revealed other women and men. Their proximity to each other, their posture, the identical wood-grain and the surrounding darkness, fastened those bodies together, leaving Eleni out, enthralled, anguished, young. She read the poems paired with the pictures and dwelt on lines and shadows, looking for the secret links that made up this world of sin and pleasure.

When she raised her head the room had gone dark. Someone switched on the electric light, and she was faced by furniture with a multitude of corners and by her mother's snapping eyes and voice.

'What is that book, Eleni? Give it to me.'

Eleni crouched in the corner of her bed clutching the book. 'No.' She shut her eyes so as not to face her mother's body and face and arm approaching. She wanted to hit back, kick back, but could not, so she waited for the blow. The book was torn from her hands, torn in half; her mother stared at the picture of a woman's dark naked body: her head – the eyes shut in secret reverie – was still in Eleni's hands.

'Where did you find this, Eleni?' Her mother inspected the torn pictures and poems scattered on the floor, her voice tore the words of the poem from her daughter's mind, her blow left on Eleni's cheek the imprint of shame, which swelled up into a strange, purple, flesh-eating flower.

'To my beloved Sophia, Tryphon' her mother read out with disbelief. She sat on the end of the bed. She gazed at the dedication shaking her head and muttering 'My daughter! With her upbringing! Her education!'

Her sister's shame dawned on Eleni. The inscription in the book consigned her amongst the damned, she pitied her sister and contemplated her guilt and her own borrowed guilt. She shut her eyes not to see the torn leaves strewn on the floor, but the beautiful long dark-grained bodies were stretched out, voluptuously performing unholy dances.

'Her father will deal with her. And you.' Mother walked out of the room threateningly, leaving behind the evidence of shame scattered on the floor.

When Kaliopi came in, she looked with interest at Eleni crouching in the corner with her hand on her cheek, brooding on her newly hatched hates and pleasures: with a quick smile of recognition Kaliopi picked up pages from the floor, and pored over them with a growing fervour of disapprobation.

'Dirty pictures, eh! So they caught their "baby" reading dirty poems! Ha! What smut! What filth!' She dwelt on a poem; then on another and another; then with an outburst of contempt she got up. She stood in front of the mirror. Absent-mindedly, she smoothed the creases of her school uniform with tender hands, then she rested her hands round her waist and tightened them until it looked small and her breasts large and prominent: she examined her figure with approval. She saw Eleni looking at her and left the room in irritation.

'So you finally found out. You've all been so proud of her reading. Well that's what she's been reading, night after night. Filth. Books about prostitutes, books about daughters who took the wrong way. They're all hidden under her mattress.' Her voice was becoming loud and shrill. Mother's responses were brief and gruff; Eleni could not make out the words, but her voice sounded tired. Kaliopi was gaining in strength, she sounded like an angry prima donna – 'All my life you've called me blockhead. Blockhead I come, blockhead I go. "The middle one won't take the letters – they won't fit into her head. But the youngest one – a spark!" Let's see now what sort of fire your "spark" has started for you.' 'Get out of here. Let me be, let me be.' Mother raised her voice – but still sounded tired, hoarse – 'Scylla the one, Charybdis the other. Dogs for one and bears for the other.' 'I don't like books. I don't read books. At least I don't read dirty books.' Her voice was going up and up, you thought at any moment she would break into song. Instead, she stormed into the room, lifted Eleni's mattress, and grabbed the hidden books. She read aloud: *The Accursed Daughter; The Tavern: the Story of a Poor Prostitute; Nana, the Story of a Rich and Gay Prostitute.* She held them in a crumpled heap, preparing to take them to her mother, when Eleni gave a long shriek and darted at her, grabbing the books. She retreated to her bed with the books in her lap; she placed her arms round them protectively, as she had seen mothers hold their babies, and measured the enemy world closing in upon her.

'Give them to me or I'll call Mother.'

Eleni, petrified, stared back; she scanned the small territory around her looking for weapons. As Kaliopi took a step towards her, Eleni took off her shoe and threw it at her sister; it missed Kaliopi but made her pause. Eleni pulled off her other shoe and held it up; Kaliopi lurched forward but caught the shoe on her shoulder and stopped.

'You will pay for this.' She took a step forward. Eleni, against the wall, watched the large womanly figure move towards her: her hands groped for a weapon – she got hold of the paper-knife and threw it at her sister.

'She's killed me! She's murdered me! Mother! Help!'

Eleni covered her face and waited, surrounded by her mother's steps, her voice, the running back and forth, her sister's high-pitched moans.

'You could have killed her!'

'Your sister's murderer! Everyone will know you as your sister's murderer. The name and the shame will haunt you for the rest of your life.' Kaliopi sounded comforted by the thought and the rhetoric. Eleni lifted her head and looked round her: her sister's firm white belly occupied the room. Mother was bent over her, tending the wound. Eleni gazed through narrow eyes at her mother nursing her other daughter: she felt a deep stab in her own belly, as if it was torn by a maternal hand.

Eleni sat on the corner of her bed nursing her belly tearing at her, in punishment. She wished she became invisible, as Kaliopi rehearsed with tragic enthusiasm the story of near fratricide. The choric cry 'her sister's murderer' distilled the terror and the pity.

'Is Father back?' Sophia walked brightly into the room: she was out of breath, her plump, well-shaped lips kept a smile, her eyes were toying with a pleasure outside the room. Eleni noticed a resemblance between her sister and the naked woman in the book: the dark skin, the lips, the thick long hair, the secret sight that touched them.

'My books!' Her face looked as if all the pleasure had been scratched out of it.

She knelt to the torn pages and picked them up one by one with reverent tenderness; she raised her face menacingly at her sisters. It occurred to Eleni that 'her' books were not hers after all? Her pleasures, her shame, the pain – not her own! Bereft, she watched Sophia pick up the pages and hold them to her breast, bereft. She wanted to come near her sister and say something about the books, but was afraid of her.

Kaliopi, convalescing against piles of cushions with her hand protectively on her own wound, attended the scene with expectant curiosity: she knew her lines and Mother's lines soon to follow.

Mother tore the pages from Sophia's hands. 'What is this, Sophia! Is

196

that why we educate you? And send you to the best schools, and pay the best tutors? To read pornography? Is that an example for the younger ones? Corrupting their minds!'

'Eleni was born with a corrupt mind!' Kaliopi was impatient for her part.

But Mother was just starting: she pushed the page with the dedication in Sophia's face. 'What is this? Who is he? What kind of a man is he, giving you – this to read! If your father found out he would kill you, he would kill us all.'

'I love him.'

'You what? You haven't finished school and you talk of love! What do you know about love? Who is he, Sophia?'

Sophia turned to her a silent face.

'It's not that student from across the street! Not that barefoot gipsy!'

'He is intelligent. He works hard. And I love him.'

'Love him! And what do you love him for? His patched elbows, his hungry face, his consumptive looks? Is it for such as him that your parents have been preparing one of the best dowries in Saloniki? Is it for that I have been wasting my eyes embroidering the finest trous-seaus? Children! Ungrateful children! I have no child for this tramp.'

'He loves me. He doesn't want me for my dowry and trousseau. He wants me for myself. You can keep your money.'

'He wants you for yourself! For your beautiful eyes!' Her mother shook her head with worldly wisdom. 'You can tell he's a dowry-hunter a mile off: from his rapacious eyes, his wide nostrils. He goes around smelling for money like a hungry dog in the Occupation. I have seen them around.'

Her daughter set her face – hard, contemptuous – against her mother's unloving words. 'I will marry him, nothing will stop me. Let him want me for my dowry, as my father wanted my mother for hers.' She walked out of the room and the apartment. Mother shook her head in hurt, bitter resignation – 'Children! Better give birth to dogs.'

'Blood is coming out of me,' Eleni mumbled. Mother gave her a quick puzzled frown, as if she had misheard. But Kaliopi sat up and looked at Eleni with astonishment, indignation, suspicion.

'Blood is coming out of me,' Eleni said again.

'Liar!' Kaliopi wailed.

'Where is the blood?' Mother asked incredulously. Eleni got up shamefacedly from her bed. She pointed at the light red stain: the ultimate proof of all the accumulated shame. She covered with both hands the wet warmth on the back of her dress and waited for the maternal verdict. Kaliopi stood up in outrage: her own murderer, playing the poignant victim of this much larger and richer wound – a tragic fountain of blood – that made her own look like an accidental graze! Eleni watched her bloodstained guilt and shame run down her legs, and spread throughout her body.

Mother took her away and helped her wash. 'You are a woman now,' she said sombrely.

'I don't want to see my father. Don't tell my father.' She stood there, a sudden unwilling woman, clutching on to her childhood. She washed herself, with nostalgia for the maternal hand, perhaps rough and hasty, perhaps soft and tender, if only she could remember.

Through the balcony door, Kaliopi and Eleni watched the scene. They stood side by side amongst their mother's geraniums, hating each other. Their bare feet felt the day-long sunlight in the tiles, and as their legs rubbed against the geranium leaves the air was filled with a lemony scent; but the balmy autumn air softened no hearts. Father, in his grey suit, sat in one of the black stately carvers, his small, mobile body hardly contained by the powerful proliferating volume of the chair. Mother sat in the other carver, her corseted round body framed snugly by the black squareness of the chair. She cast dagger looks, her frown – young, set – condemned the universe. It cast on Eleni its perennial shadow, although now it was meant for the eldest sister, Sophia, who stood at the far end of the room, dark, serious, persistent. In the middle of the room stood the student, Tryphon – Tryphon Tryphonithes: tall, thin, stooping, in a worn suit that hung loose around his shoulders and legs. His face was swarthy, with a thin black moustache over fleshy dark lips, and slanted, puffy-lidded eyes, black like olives.

The student, Tryphon – Mr Tryphon to Eleni – listened to Father with a patient, obsequious, ironic grin that crawled out of his face on the look-out for prey. He grinned persistently at Father, who questioned him in a loud voice, asking how he made his living, how he expected to provide for a wife, who his father was. Father disregarded the answers, harangued him; the student remained patient, his grin slowly gnawing at the other man, who began to look overwhelmed by his powerful armchair, stretching hard, dark arms round him like a heartless mother – his eyes were running about the room like young hares caught unawares in the middle of a field. Mother snapped angry blinks at her eldest daughter, who stood erect and defiant, her face dark and womanly, her thick hair covering her shoulders. There was no love in her eyes – only a long-dwelling memory and threat.

The student talked of his plans to work in the office of this important political person, very big in the machinery of the Right; he would make his way, and one day – who knows, he had aims, ambitions. He wanted to see a secure military democracy restored, clean of communism. As he talked about the Civil War, his lips pulled back tightly, revealing a row of faultless, white teeth; the puffed flesh around his eyes separated. Eleni shut her eyes not to look at his face. He was an idealist: he believed and dreamed of a powerful Greek kingdom; he wrote poems about it – oh yes, he did have his poetic side, he was not ashamed of that! He looked meaningfully at Sophia, she looked back with admiration. Father, unmoved by the poetry, glanced nervously at his wife; she glanced back in secret communication. Eleni could read her parents' fear – what did he know about Mother's communist brother, Uncle Sotiris, just out of prison, and about Olga, in Romania? Perhaps the whole family were 'coloured', and in the police files, and this man was telling them that he knew, and had them in his hand, and he only had to say a word – but no, whenever Mother talked like that, Father made light of it. Would they let me become so rich, own half of Saloniki, if we were in their files?

The student knew he had made an impression, and without asking permission sat down on a chair.

'They took your shop, the communists,' he reminded Father, and without waiting for confirmation continued, 'Your family suffered from them, but of course not as badly as other families.'

Father gave quick nods of acknowledgement. He feared this man; he feared politics; he feared the police, armies, uniforms. Refugees should stay out of this. 'All this is past history. We merchants keep clear. We look after our business. With God's help I have recovered what I lost, and doubled it and tripled it.' Gregoris had regained his confidence. 'Hm,' he smiled, 'this whole building is mine, I have two shops in Saloniki, smaller branches already in the provinces – and what I am preparing, that is something quite unique for this city.' He needed the security of his words, sat deeper in his relentless seat, at home: but caught warning glances from his wife signifying, No talk of property, so he stopped. But his shops and his property were his strength and if he could not exhibit those, he was weak, naked. He didn't like this barefoot student, this gipsy sitting on his chair without his permission, telling him what was what as if he owned Greece; but he found it difficult to tell him to get up, and get out of his house.

'You were lucky, of course. Others were killed.'

Father was taken by surprise. What did he mean? He felt his wife's eyes on him.

Tryphon sat back. With a politeness that stretched his words into slow liquid nasal sounds, he said, 'You would agree with me, Mr Gregoriou, you refugees make good merchants – it is well known. We of the Old Greece have different securities: the King, the army, national unity, the law and the old order, the forces of the Right. The merchant, the entrepreneur, they are our friends. They can help us in our task of educating the mob – liberals, so-called democrats, strikers, communists.' Tryphon paused weightily. 'My roots, Mr Gregoriou, go deep. I come from an old family of the Old Greece. A military family.' He paused again and allowed time for the meaning of his words to reverberate.

Sophia looked at her man of power with admiration and pride. Out in the dark, Kaliopi and Eleni stared through the glass with fright and astonishment at the invasion. Separately, they imagined their sister loving this man and separately they were repelled by their imaginations.

Eleni narrowed her eyes with dislike, and fatigue; and the room became small and distant, the human faces and forms indistinct, except for the dark young man in the middle of the room, who took the shape and visage of an animal: a predatory being, perhaps a bird of prey, perhaps a legendary mammal with anthropomorphic features, who had perched in the middle of her home sniffing round with distended black nostrils and eyes hidden in pockets of purple flesh. He smiled at his prey, as he reduced them to small live morsels. His female, who was once her sister, moved close to her malign lover, drawn by his appetite and preparing to have her share in the family feast.

Agreements were made, tentatively, unwillingly. 'Wait and see,' Mother suggested. 'When you finish your studies and are making your living, and she has finished school, and is ready to become a wife, and if you still love each other, then we can think about an engagement.'

'I have planned generous dowries for them – for all three,' Father said impatiently. 'For whom am I toiling but for them? Everything I make is for them.' He hit his fist against the hard, senseless paw of his armchair with indignation. 'But I am not giving them to the first passer-by.' His power was returning to him; both fists were resting on the arms of his chair and feeling round his body its dark, silent support. 'I want guarantees that your prospects can match her dowry. Till then, you will keep your distance.' He jumped from his chair in sudden violence. 'And I want an end to the hanky-panky in the streets.' He had raised his voice; he walked up and down the room, his face animated with secret battles. There was silence in the room, Mother gave a deep sigh, of relief; and the young lovers looked at each other conspiringly. 'You can go,' Father interrupted. He observed with dislike the young man walking confidently towards the door, and his daughter following behind.

Mr Tryphon soon made the Gregoriou home his home. He would call at dinner time, and as soon as he walked in, he would dilate his large dark nostrils and roll his eyes upwards with swooning pleasure, and let those exuberant organs of sense guide him directly to the kitchen. There his nostrils would tremble and his eyes would close with pleasure as he inhaled with deep sighs the aroma of Mrs Anastasia's cooking.

'Po po po – what rare delights! What oriental spices! What art you have in your hands, Mrs Anastasia! Now let me guess, what is this wonderful smell – is it mousaka? Is it youvarlakia? Is it papoutsakia? It is out of this world! I have to see it, my curiosity is so moved, my nose so tickled, my appetite – ah, my appetite is so spurred by this divine smell, it could swallow the whole world. I just have to lift this lid, or I'll faint – Imam Baildi! The Imam has fainted! Po po po – of course he fainted; Mahomet fainted, and even Allah fainted, and I am going to faint too from the beauty of this aroma.'

Mrs Anastasia, unused to such compliments, demurred. 'Please have a taste. No trouble at all.'

'Mmmmm! Ambrosia! It melts in the mouth! I haven't tasted anything like this since the Sunday dinners my mother prepared for us – may her soul be blessed!'

Mrs Anastasia was moved. 'Please stay and eat with us, Mr Tryphon.'

'How could I refuse! How could anyone refuse such an invitation! To such a paradisal feast!' In anticipation he would squeeze the back of Eleni's neck till he brought tears to her eyes, saying, 'Ah, you, I'll eat you up, you little devil!' filling her with nausea.

'Poor orphaned youth! Poor starved boy, and in the years of his development!' Mrs Anastasia was filled with pity. 'If I had a son, I would like a tender-hearted mother to give him a bite of food. Of course I was not blessed with a son, the little soul of a boy that God granted me died even before it saw the light of day – thanks to the kicks on my belly of that "lively" little Eleni.' She wiped her tears with her apron.

But now it seemed that mother might yet find her lost son. Mr Tryphon soon called her 'Mother' and called Father 'Father', and Mother called him 'my child'. Father didn't call him anything.

In time, he joined the family for all their meals, always with the same exuberance of compliment, and pleasure, and appetite, and impatience, until all the different sentiments gathered in one and made him choke. The family stared with fear, but Father with contempt, and Sophia with embarrassment, as her fiancé, his mouth filled to the brim, his eyes popping, his face red, his body writhing, gasped – 'Water'. Father moved his head pensively over his plate.

Eleni watched this new 'brother', elated with dislike. She watched his face grow fat, his stomach round, his shoulders narrow; she watched him pull his fiancée to him and touch his wet lips on hers making a sound which condemned for her all kisses. She saw his clothes become small on him, and with sublime displeasure she saw him appear in his new suit given to him, for Christmas, by Mother. She noticed that he stopped giving books to his fiancée and she stopped reading; now she could have all the books to herself. The love poems became rare, and instead they talked and conspired about their future. Mother was busy embroidering her daughter's trousseau; the topic of the dowry was touched on, with Mother first, then with Father at dinner, but Father was non-committal. When the time came, she would have her dowry, but the time had not come yet, and at this particular time, with his business taking such leaps, everything else would have to wait. Sophia worried and complained, her fiancé seemed angry at times; Kaliopi was jealous of the elder sister's engagement, she wanted her own trousseau and dowry. When Mother said, 'But you don't have a fiancé yet, you haven't even finished school,' she said, 'I can find a fiancé and I don't need to finish school.'

One afternoon, when their parents were sitting on the balcony absorbed in talk, and Sophia was busy whispering sweet words to her fiancé, Kaliopi approached Eleni with a tantalising fat envelope. 'Mine is much more handsome than hers. I can show you his photographs.' Eleni, overwhelmed by the confidence, leaped into womanhood. 'Look!' Kaliopi handed her the photographs one by one, with reverence. 'Clark Gable himself.'

With fascination and revulsion Eleni peered into the heart of Manhood: the man with the polaroid glasses and the ginger moustache posed for her in front of his jeep, or driving it, or together with other young men, all with moustaches and polaroid glasses, and all looking like Clark Gable. He posed looking straight at her with a knowing, heavy-lidded look and ironic worldly smile, a pipe between his teeth. He posed on the beach in a safari hat and stretch bathing trunks, looking down at the ripply muscles of his shoulders, and at the world, with proud superiority. He and Kaliopi posed together, she happy, vulnerable, he, with his arm tenderly round her shoulders, the proud proprietor. Kaliopi needed to talk about him: how much money he had, how much in demand he was, how he could have any girl he liked – they all died for him – but he preferred her, and only her. He had been to Paris, and his mother spoke French, and had French nicknames for him. Kaliopi considered herself the luckiest girl in Saloniki, she swam in seas of happiness.

When she had gone through the photographs, Kaliopi felt the urge to re-read his letters; she locked herself in the bathroom. Eleni was left contemplating with pleasure and displeasure and fascination and disgust these couples kissing and embracing and loving each other. She approached the balcony and looked at her parents through the glass door. They talked in animated whispers. Her father was gesticulating with enthusiasm – 'What a revolution! The first in Saloniki! Equal to the American ones!' Mother looked patient, sympathetic, admonishing. 'We have to be cautious, Gregori. You are taking big risks, it's a lot of money, you are leaving yourself open from all sides.' Her hands never stopped pushing the needle into the fabric, making the beautiful patterns on the bridal sheet grow and flourish.

In the room, the prospective son-in-law was lying on the sofa digesting his mother-in-law's meal and reading *Romantzo*. He had his arm around his fiancée, who sat at the edge of the sofa looking at him cherishingly; slowly she was drawn into inspecting his face, till she located a fat blackhead on her beloved's chin which she squeezed with passion.

The building rose with a certain self-esteem to five high-ceilinged storeys, and ruled over the crossroads like a modern Acropolis.

'A building with history,' Gregoris thought. He was impressed by the Greek pilasters, straight, refined, hugging the building at regular intervals and giving it dignity, antiquity. 'But' – he sighed with pleasure as his eyes dwelt on the stucco vignettes crowning doors and windows – 'not without a feminine touch.' His eyes threaded the perplexity of curls and tendrils. The building married – the estate agent had said it like a poet – the respectability of hellenism with the elegance of Europe. 'Nice turn of phrase but' – he now calculates irritably – 'it's costing me heaven and earth, heaven and earth.' His mind spiralled through the astronomical costs and gains, his soul hooked on the perplexities of speculation.

He worked through a heavy bunch of keys while his lips recited numbers. The right key and the right, studied turn finally opened the door. He calculated as he climbed the fire escape – so many thousands he was owed, he could not collect all of it at once; so many thousands he could borrow from the National Bank, and so many thousands from the Commercial Bank. If you add the interest – the muscles of his jaw jumped. He paused, and stroked his hair back; he held his temples, to keep his thoughts in place and in order as he calculated the vertiginous sums of debts. For reassurance he computed instantly his monthly turnover, the clear profits from each of the other shops, the total sum: substantial, good, but not enough. He might have to sell one of them – but not the wholesale shop, that was the foundation, the heart of his trade. The one on Egnatia Street, perhaps – though, only five minutes from the railway station, it caught the peasants still with their pockets full. He pushed absent-mindedly through a fire escape door and followed a corridor. But the Egnatia Street shop was retail, with a slower turnover; he might have to let it go.

He pushed another door and entered a bright, sunlit gallery surrounding a large stairwell. He glanced with appetite around the serpentine room, his speculations brightened: what shop in Salonica could compete with this, with a department store! He would sublease the Egnatia Street shop for the time being, until the new shop started working, and giving profits. And then payments and interests and expenses would be toys, would be dwarfs compared to the daily, hourly turnover of this shop. Incalculable – but still he worried. He looked up, blinded by the sunlight pouring in through the huge rhomboid stained-glass window in the ceiling. Then he walked around the gallery touching reassuringly the polished mahogany balustrade, ready to catch fire where the sunlight fell on it. He would have the rugs up here, Anatolian, Persian, Greek rugs from Ouranopolis, Turkish kilimia. He saw them hanging round the walls, or spread sunlit on the floor: images and smells breezed through the room and made his face tingle.

He stood at the top of the stairs. He liked the height, it made him quick with decisions. He ran down a flight. This floor was for the ready-mades: to satisfy all a woman's desires – dresses, scarves, underwear, stockings, fine like a spider's web. Instantly he was wrapped in visions. Jewellery and perfumes would be in the mezzanine, intimate, romantic, he already had his contacts in Rhodes and Kastoria. The ground floor would be fabrics, his speciality, his kingdom. But still he was worried: he walked round the large hall, examining walls, clothing them, enlarging windows, calculating the light, measuring spaces, risks, successes. He could always sublease the shoes, Anastasia's cousins had already made an offer, they had capital, they were old hands in the trade, sly – but none too smart, Macedonians.

No, he could not start subleasing right and left, before he knew it they would all move in, taking bits and pieces. I should have sons, he thought, who would ache for their own property as I do. Women, daughters, wives, they do not understand property, possessions; they do not have the crab, the crab. He felt the anger of the man without heirs, and without inheritance. He walked round distractedly: his worry at last surfaced, and possessed him: how could he, how could he have agreed to buy the building in Anastasia's name? It would cripple him. How could any businessman in Salonica respect him – when his property was owned by a woman? It was for her and for their daughters that he was working so hard, so hard. Had she given him sons, he could reach far, he would be secure in his possessions, there would be a line, roots, home. No, he could not write this building in her name. The very thought left him desolate. He was angry at the lawyers and accountants for suggesting it. 'For security, in case something went wrong!' – nothing would go wrong. But she herself liked the idea: her face was bright with pleasure. He stretched his arms, testing their reach. All my efforts, he thought, all my work – how can Anastasia want to take it away from me! Even Aslanoglou, his best and oldest friend, had said, 'No question, Gregori, it should not be in your name. We are going through difficult times, the drachma is tumbling.' Even Aslan!

He was possessed by his isolation; and by a fear, constantly, of losses; and by blind desire – for earthly, material, for heavenly goods? The pain of an anonymous need kept him on the rack: the fate of the dispossessed. Possessed, he was possessed by possessions never adequate, in the end expendable. So immaterial!

But he had the building. He ran down the stairs into the large main hall, and walked round touching the walls. In a dark corner, an elevator looking like a gilded cage waited to carry him. He stood in the centre, the heart of the building, and followed the spiral upward sweep of the staircase, flooded by sunlight from the enormous, blinding window. That central fountain of light and warmth that dispersed through the building in blue and pink rhomboids filled his spirit with earthly delights. Instantly the place was populated with women – where had all these women come from? – bartering, preferring, doubting, lightly stepping out of a garment, or raising arms as they pulled it off, revealing soft round bodies. He followed their forbidden perfume in the warm airlessness, listened behind closed doors for their voices, was distracted by a song. He saw small feet hide in elegant shoes, delicate hands slip into soft gloves, golden chains surround fine white necks, earrings pull on tender earlobes. He speculated, guided and distracted by desires that eluded him, things evanescent, a world or a love that was scattering and coming together into faces or voices of women. He saw the women of Ionia lying on their rugs and waiting to die, those women who always populated his shop, their voices making it so echo with desire. The corseted body of Anastasia embraced him protectively and repossessed him.

Mother, all dressed up and fresh from the hairdresser's, sat on the balcony making conversation with Eleni, touching absent-mindedly her plants; she kept glancing at the street and every now and then at her golden watch. She looked appealing in her new dress – green, the colour of her eyes, with a fine azure embroidery in the front. Her hair, piled up high, gave her a queenly air; her hands indolently exhibited her rings and bracelets. Father was still at the shop, Sophia and her fiancé with Kaliopi, their permanent chaperone, had gone to the cinema. Eleni was pleased to have mother all to herself, looking at her best, and in a good, easy mood. Eleni asked her to tell her again her stories from Kapnohori – what a dragon Grandmother was, the goings-on in the tobacco stores, the secret courtings, what a dandy Father was, all the girls queuing at his shop! Eleni wanted to hear again how her mother hid her brother's hairnet when he was preparing for the Sunday promenade, and the trick she played on the marriage broker – the rage! The fury from her mother! Po po po!

But Mother became restless as time went by: she looked at the corner of the street and looked at her watch, her mind wandered, she was not getting much pleasure from her stories. The dusk became dark, quickly, it caught them by surprise. Mother got up and with a sigh turned the electric light on in the living room, which made the balcony even darker. But both of them stayed on the balcony, saying little and watching the lights in the bay. Mother asked Eleni to bring her her shawl, it was getting chilly, and told her to wear something warmer herself. They were both silent for a long time. Eleni knew that her mother hardly knew she was there now, and was weighed by a melancholy that often visited her at dusk.

She tried to bring her mother back to her: 'Do you ever hear any news from your cousin Olga, Mother?'

206

'No. Her younger brother receives letters from her, but not often. She lives in Romania. She married someone.'

The melancholy deepened.

Abruptly Mother got up, peered at her watch and walked indoors. She made a telephone call from her bedroom. She reappeared after a long time, in her dressing gown.

'Have you done your homework? It's time for bed.'

She was woken up by her father's voice, exuberant, uncontrollably exuberant, triumphant. 'Come, my little wife, just one glass, the best champagne in Greece, imported! You must drink – I insist. To celebrate the new shop.'

'But Gregori, hadn't we agreed that you would come back at six – that was six hours ago – and that we would go to the solicitors together? Wasn't our appointment with them at six thirty, and didn't you say be ready, I'll be there with the taxi, we cannot delay not even a minute? And not even a telephone call. No, don't come near me. You are drunk. Get away. There's nothing to celebrate.'

'Nothing to celebrate?' He was loud, jovial, peremptory, he filled the house with harsh triumph. 'I bought the biggest, the best property in Saloniki. An entire block – so many floors, shops, offices, at the heart of the city. Mine. Ours. It's all for you, my little wife. Everything for you –'

'I don't want it. I don't want any more shops, and business and money. Enough. We have enough. Don't you have enough, Gregori? Tell me.' She was crying. Eleni covered herself with her blanket while the dark, silent shadow travelled through the house. She tried to get a hold on her father's exhilaration but she couldn't find purchase.

'You've been holding me back all my life,' he shouted at her. 'What kind of a wife are you? Instead of encouraging your husband, supporting him, celebrating with him! I will not let you hold me back any longer. I'll tell you now. This is only the beginning. This is the first, the only department store in Saloniki: there will be more. I am negotiating for one in Kavala. I am going to start a chain of them. Do you understand, Anastasia? No. You have a small spirit. You have no vision. And there's more. I will buy land on Neos Marmaras. They don't know yet the beauty of Neos Marmaras, the most beautiful spot on earth. I've got my people there, my compatriots, I trust them. I'll build them hotels, I'll bring them visitors, who will be amazed at its beauty. No one will stop me.'

He stopped. Eleni listened to the heavy silence. She made out her mother's quiet crying. 'You are running to the edge of the cliff, Gregori.'

'You are driving me crazy, do you understand? Crazy!' A crack ran through his voice, as it appealed.

Eleni was woken up by her mother's steps up and down the verandah. She was watering her plants. Then it was quiet. Eleni saw her through the balcony door sitting on one of the folding armchairs in her flowery dressing gown. In the moonlight, the printed flowers covering her breasts looked large. Her head was resting against her hand which hid her eyes, casting a dark shadow over them; it was protecting them from the moonlight or keeping something out of her sight. She stayed in that posture for a long time. Eleni wasn't sure whether she was awake or asleep: then she moved and Eleni saw a face cold with unhappiness. From the bedroom she heard her father's footsteps.

She hadn't heard her mother get up or move, and was startled by the outline of her body, opaque and large, at the balcony door. Framing her, the fine lawn curtain looked delicate and transparent.

'Go and sleep with your father.'

Eleni got up and walked heavily towards her parents' bedroom. Her feet felt large and thick, her legs bending under a disproportionate weight. She opened the door and lay down noiselessly on her mother's bed. Her father lay on his bed with his arm resting on his brow, covering his eyes; he lifted his arm and turned his head towards her momentarily, took a sip of water from the glass on the table between the two beds, then lay back and with a sigh rested his arm over his eyes. He lay quiet, his breathing hardly audible, but Eleni knew he was awake from the small sudden movements of his limbs, and of his mouth, as if he were carrying on a voiceless discussion with somebody, or tasting unsurely of something. Eleni lay still, holding her breath, wishing he forgot her existence. He moved his fingers as if counting or calculating, or simply exercising them. Eleni lay paralysed, convinced that she was causing his agitation. She remembered those endless nights lying between her parents, awake with discomfort and unhappiness, being told not to fidget, not to move, to go to sleep. The startled waking and finding herself at the hard edge of the bed and the knowledge that something too terrible for words had happened, preyed on her memory. She tightened in the same paralysis and fear, and felt the same pain run through her left leg as she lay in that foreign, unloving bed. The furniture of the room was so concrete, and the corners of the wardrobe protruded so into the air, which felt thick. She was hurt by so much solidity. Except for the polished sides of the wardrobe, which reflected the dancing light of the oil lamp in front of the family icons. On the dressing table, her mother's possessions, her powder-puff, her jewellery-box, her brush and comb, her perfumes, lay in waiting, duplicated by the mirror.

She moved her arm and hid her hand under the pillow; she felt one of Mother's hairpins. She thought of her mother's wavy hair gathered up; her lips red and shapely; she thought of her looking pleased in her new green dress, attending with absent-minded tenderness to her plants. Those pieces and moments of her mother she thought of with tenderness, even longing: but the opaque silhouette at the balcony door – she didn't want to think of that mother.

She heard her father get up; his feet looked for his slippers, he walked to the door in quick irregular steps. The light in the hall came on and her parents' bedroom stepped towards her. Her mother's dress hung empty behind the door; the flowery pastures on it, which Eleni had studied on her mother's body, were barely visible but brought to Eleni a recollection of pleasure. Her father's clothes lay abandoned on a chair, a few gold coins were scattered underneath. Eleni wanted to crawl under the chair and steal them. For consolation, she thought of all the money her father had given her behind Mother's back, holding it up in the air and asking 'How much do you love me – tell me how much you love me, first.' She heard him opening and shutting doors, switching lights on and off, clearing his throat. He stopped in the hall, then took a few steps and stopped again; he opened a door slowly. 'Come back. Come back to your bed, Anastasia.' His voice sounded young in the silence of the apartment. A slight creaking on the floor, his steps approached the bedroom, his bed. Eleni closed her eyes but could not stop them running right and left under their soft lids. He cleared his throat persistently, then lay down. Someone in another room got up – she recognised her mother's steps – and switched off the lights in the hall that he had left on. The flowery pastures of her mother's dress vanished, the mirror went opaque. The folds of the curtains were filled with shadow, crawling with nightmare. Eleni lay still, the pain travelled quickly up her leg, watching with absorption the flame that could not stay still.

Her eyes stared startled at the darkness, her body floating in utter blank ignorance, her mind clawing onto a vacuum. Her body, she realised, rested on a surface, which she touched for reassurance; but she did not know where that surface was. She did not know where she was, what her name was, or how old, or who she was. She was lost within a vast loss and there was no foothold in the universe. And no identity, no identifying, nothing to identify: only poised at the brink of the inevitable fall. She heard someone breathing out there in the dark, and she hung her being on those breaths. She clung blindly on each individual breath as her fingers felt her body, her limbs, the sheets covering her, her mind trying to draw from them the self-made silk thread of memory which would slowly identify her, and all. It all started returning with the pain in her limb, familiar, which led to her steps slow and unwilling to the parents' bedroom; the image of her mother standing at the balcony door, in her flowery dressing gown – her breasts looking large and powerful – her father's cough: this was her father's breathing, she realised, then she knew and remembered all, the universe was there again and she in it with a face and a name. But the flame in front of the family icons was out and the room in darkness.

The next minute, the room emerged shrouded in a cold light; and things looked like their own ghosts. Grey shadows of shapes were suspended inanimate in the air; her mother's dress was hanging in the same position, but the printed meadows were devoid of colour; and the mirror reflected the bloodless room back on to itself, unredeemed. Someone had just left, the door was still open and she could hear again her father's steps outside the room. She counted his footfalls, tracing his presence. His steps stopped in front of the room where her mother lay, in Eleni's own bed: she recognised the creaking of the door, the pleading tones – 'Forgive me, my love. Come back to me, my wife, my life.' She didn't hear her mother's voice, but she heard their steps out in the hall. Eleni waited, watching now the delicate light of the dawn discover in every nook and cranny, with cruel clarity, an absence; absence and solitude. She wanted to cry, but her parents now stood over her holding their fingers to their mouths, signalling to her to be quiet and to go back to her own room, quietly. He in his striped pyjamas, dishevelled, tired, she in her crumpled flowery dressing gown, revealing her deep cleavage, her face red and swollen with sleep and tears. In that beautiful dawn light they looked ugly. Eleni got up and walked – the pain in her legs reached up through her body – back to her room.

She stood in the silence of the dawn, surrounded by her mother's well-tended flowers and the delicate scent of the jasmine, and wondered at the clear young redness of the geraniums and at the bay glinting at that moment with the early sun, and wondered why such beauty could not wash her pain away.

She studied herself in the large, gold-rimmed mirror – her dress deep blue like the sea, her body almost curving, she noticed, her hair the colour of new chestnuts, as her mother had once told her. She stroked its straightness; her eyes – which were, curiously, her father's eyes, and yet on her face – reflected her pleasure. They moved away and focused on someone standing behind her, looking at her with the same pleasure and saying, 'How pretty!' Eleni turned round and saw her father, who repeated, 'Very beautiful!' and hastened away. Her eye followed his quick, silver-clad figure as he threaded his way through the guests; he ran up the wide staircase with the lightness and elation of a soul – her eyes following him, losing him, finding him.

Her father's new department store jumped in dazzling fragmented patterns in and out of the large mirrors. Crystal chandeliers were redoubled, playing with white light, the well-dressed guests were multiplied, and the splendid merchandise made infinite. She walked amongst the downpour of foreign faces talking and inspecting animatedly, unstoppably. They paused only to take, with dilated eye, a richly stacked canapé from trays carried by arrogant abstemious waiters. She recognised from a distance her mother's new hat: the smooth velvet shadowed the lines on her brow and made her face look soft and pleased; the slanting and gathering on one side gave her a touch of feminine vanity, even frivolity. Eleni went near her, recognising with relief in that foreign sea her familiar, corseted curves. She was the centre of a circle of women with similar hats talking loudly and vivaciously all at once.

'Phantasmagoriko! Equal to any American department store! Supermarket, I tell you! Hollywood!'

'Is it true, Mrs Anastasia, that there is going to be a fashion show? A beauty contest?'

'I heard that even the cinema men are coming! It's not true, is it, Mrs Anastasia?'

'Imagine being in the movies and all our friends seeing us! Like Hollywood stars!'

'Tell us, Mrs Anastasia, are the contestants beautiful? They won't parade in swimsuits!' They looked round for beautiful half-naked girls, and cameras, filling the place with a symphony of laughter.

Men's voices calculated in intimate tones costs and profits.

'Gigantic venture! Risky, terribly risky.'

'They say he borrowed huge amounts from the National.'

'That's how he moves – by leaps. And always lands on his feet.'

211

Eleni was slipping through the crowd, when a hand, small, gloved, gripped her, and pulled her into a nightmare. She was surrounded by a plump arm and heavy perfume mixed with the spicy smell of sweat.

'Look how our Lenaki has grown! Already a little woman. And so suddenly! Only yesterday she was a mere child, and now . . .'

The hand did not loosen its grip; the face, chubby and dark with small round baby features, came near; it shone with perspiration which had collected in tiny opaque powder globules. A pair of red lips landed resoundingly on her cheek: then a perfumed handkerchief rubbed off the kiss. Eleni turned her head to avoid the woman's breath, and shut her eyes, unsure whether the hand would strike, or stroke, whether the memory was of pain or of love – which came back to torment or to delight?

The gloved hand pushed her into a group of people and stayed on her shoulder. 'Look what we have here!' she cried triumphantly, and a group of men and women turned and looked at Eleni. 'Who would have said that she would become one day a human being, a proper little woman, in all respects . . .' There were reciprocal smiles and agreements. 'Yes, she is pretty in her blue dress, suddenly she looks a girl, ready for a husband.' Their voices became louder. 'And who will be the lucky one, eh?' They looked mischievously at a big, large-cheeked young man, standing solidly in ample stay-ironed American trousers and jacket, and exuding a fresh spicy smell; he gave his mother, who came up to his shoulder, a plump smile, then resumed his serious inspection of the shop. 'And what a handsome dowry!' Gregoriou had said publicly, 'The new shop is for Eleni.' The gloved hand slipped round Eleni's waist. 'Who knows what may happen one day? I may yet make you my daughter-in-law. Lenaki has got the dowry, my Dinoulis has got the American degree – not many bridegrooms in Saloniki have American degrees, and in business administration! How would you like having me for a mother-in-law? Eh, Lenaki?' Dinos smiled confidently and in a businesslike manner continued his calculations with his father. His father turned to the group with amusement. 'I wouldn't mind having Lenaki for a daughter-in-law, and also Gregoris' new shop for a bonus.' Fat laughter reverberated: Eleni thought of Dinos's fat thighs chafing against each other. She noticed that the woman had crumpled her new dress, and almost broke into tears.

She slipped free from the gloved hold and walked through the crowd looking for her father. She saw an immensely fat and extraordinarily short woman sitting, with her thighs far apart, on a chair that supported only a very small proportion of her body; she was out of breath as she took long deep puffs at a cigarette, which she then exhaled with vehemence, so that a continuous stream of smoke came out of her nostrils. She looked at the world with grudging, malevolent curiosity, as if thinking it was not worth the bother, and thinking of all the unsettled bills and unkept promises, of dowries not given, of properties mortgaged and lost, of deceitful lawyers, careless doctors, thankless children, unfaithful husbands, beautiful women, burned dishes, undigested meals. A current of new worry ran through her body as it alerted to the trays of food sailing through the room: the small eyes quickly negotiated distances as flesh rippled and quaked blindly, with expectation.

The Mr Tax Inspector was surrounded by a group of businessmen: his eyes, raven black, swooped down and tore off pieces of the beauty and success round him. The ample volume of his wife's bosom throbbed with pleasure. Their daughter stood nearby, her body silently, sulkily growing into her mother's image; the young Minister stood at attention, astonished whenever his voice broke into a part shrill, part hoarse bark.

At the top of the stairs Eleni saw her sisters exhibiting their new bare-shouldered dresses and their fiancés. Mr Tryphon, his face rounded and polished with good feeding, was explaining to Sophia the finances of her father's shop. Her dark face was turned up to him with feminine submissiveness, while her eyes registered the furniture and fabrics. The fiancé detected the approaching tray and, without stopping his peroration, stretched a long dextrous arm over people's heads. Words and crumbs got tangled, rhetoric was baulked by appetite, and appetite, choked on its own excess, bulged out in a pair of bewildered olive-black eyes, and stopped dead in a mask of agony, rage, and frustration. His petite fiancée was moved with concern and restrained impatience.

Eleni gazed at the couple, the woman and the man, the sister and the brother-in-law, gazed at that love and marriage-to-be, at what had lodged in her home, and felt without a home.

The other couple stood nearby. The man with the jeep wore a broad-shouldered padded jacket tapering down to a narrowness at the hips that created the impression of an inverted triangle. He raised and bent forward his padded shoulders, as if to look down on the world from a supernatural height and breadth. He wore his polaroid glasses. The Clark Gable moustache covered his mouth, from which a permanent cigarette hung. The frequent guttural sound of sarcasm, and smirk of universal contempt, seemed to be without particular point. His plump and fair Kaliopi looked up at him with a face tense with pleasure, womanly subservience and animal fear. She looked as if she was there to accept, with exquisite delight, all the manly contempt he was prepared to heap, for no clear reason, upon the world. Her face twitched from the pressure of confused, unknown emotions. Eleni gazed in astonishment at her tormentor in torment.

Gregoris inspected his army of well-groomed shop assistants displaying the new merchandise with self-respecting discretion. You would think they are partners, the way they pose. The muscles of his face quivered with impatience. They smile, they say the right words, but where is the feeling? Where is their heart? He wished he were each one of them and did their job as only he knew how, and spoke with flair and with gusto – and sold.

He serpentined nimbly through the important guests, the pillars of society, greeting them with affability, noting potential financiers and clients, paying compliments to their bejewelled wives, the true galantuomo – but he could not stop, he had to be everywhere at once, he had to hold together and to himself this moment of success, of arrival. He could not waste it in words, trust it to others, the air and light crackled ready to shatter. He ran, flew to different parts of the store to contemplate his promised land, but the guests, noisy and greedy, were in the way, blocking and crowding his vision. He observed them eat, and his mouth salivated, imagining through other people's busily masticating jaws the flavour of success. 'Eat!' he said. 'There's plenty!' He was big with generosity. But will you buy? His eyes observed arms stretched towards food trays, stretched cheeks: and the ends of his own abstemious mouth pulled down in displeasure. Would they buy? Dissatisfaction gnawed him. He looked with disdain at appetite surrounding him Hydra-like with incalculable mouths.

His family should be with him at this moment of success, but where were they? Scattered. Anastasia sulking. His elder daughters had eyes only for their – lovers: the word squeezed through his teeth. Unloving thoughts welled up in him but he pushed them aside: not on such a day. And Eleni, he was giving her up too: she was moving away, leaving him, she was not his, really his, as she was once. But this department store was his, and it was the envy of the gods. It had everything in it his heart ever desired.

He looked for Aslanoglou. He saw him sitting on his own, not eating, his big body undergoing a subterranean upheaval with each breath. Gregoris worried a moment about his friend's health – how could a heart support all this flesh? He tried to guess from his expression what Aslan thought of the shop: he wanted to see pleasure on his face, appreciation. Aslanoglou leaned back, and the delicate French chair gave little panicked shrieks and creaks as the large benevolent mountain of flesh expanded; furniture and people suddenly looked mean. But he was unaware: his pleasures were in a faraway motherland, of herbs and spices, open to the air of Mount Ararat and to the breezes of the Black Sea. Gregoris turned away impatiently. Aslan cannot hear very well, that is why he's sitting on his own, he is getting past it, he never really put his heart in it. But Gregoris could already see his friend's heart rise, and raise in its own slow steady rhythm ocean waves of remembered and desired satisfactions. Gregoris, fed by his compatriot's presence, turned his mind to other worries.

Her father's face was haggard now. He looked to Eleni like a bird swooping down but not touching his prey. His cheeks, hollowed by abstemiousness and a hunger, made his mouth look large and his lips full with appetite. The delicate bones, the leanness, belonged to a man who refused worldly pleasures, but his vagabond eyes were alert for the material chance. They might appropriate instantly: or pause and stare with innocent curiosity.

Eleni saw his features mobilise as he flew down upon Mrs Marika from Smyrna, more beautiful than ever. She, inviting and evading, rolled black long-fringed eyes, and let honey trickle from her smile. She moved towards him, her walk a melody, her voice an angels' choir. Her curves, perfect semicircles, her waist a bracelet, a ring. Each ringlet of hair a promise, a miniature pleasure, a flight, a tiny intimation of paradise.

Eleni watched from a distance: she could not hear what they said, but saw in their faces the animated duet, and almost felt the quiver of pleasure in their bartering of desires and refusals. Her own desire was to stop the encounter, and thinking of herself as her mother's emissary and her father's guardian angel, permanently, she walked towards them, to appropriate him. She held his hand with love, and without trust.

'The cinema men! The cameras! They are going upstairs.'

Eleni was pushed forward by the crowd.

'Keep a place for me – and for Kyria Papadopoulou!' a voice called in agony.

'What's happening upstairs? Are they giving things away free?'

'Yes, yes, they are giving free clothes.'

More anxious people joined the crowd. Was it true they gave things free? They became a crowd of starving, homeless people pushing for escape, survival, the promised salvation. Hats were dislodged, women's sandalled feet were crushed by men's shoes, men's feet were stabbed by stilettos, buttons uprooted, blood-puffed faces exploded.

The fortunate and the resilient secured seats, on which they sat with triumph and relief; tired buttocks abandoned their belligerence and overflowed maternally the edges of seats; clothes and hats were rearranged; tired, perspiring faces uncrumpled, secure in divine providence. But restless eyes still measured the situation, exchanging confirmations with others who were seated, and recriminations with those standing with rage-ravaged faces at the back. Eventually all faces were turned towards the closed, gilded doors, moved by communal desire – for further and ultimate pleasures.

Small toiletry mirrors came out of handbags, faces were powdered, lips reddened, cheeks rouged, smiles practised; eyes concentrated on judging the image in the glass which reciprocated with equal judgement, both slowly softening in mutual approval. The mirrors were put away, the smiles of coquetry and self-satisfaction remained on the faces, that were now armoured against the world. Women studied each other's faces and made comparisons; glanced at men's faces for reassurance. The men stretched up their necks to free them from the noose of their ties.

Attention was directed to the cameramen, shouting orders at each other; the strong lights transformed the room into a theatre. The Latin American melody from the new loudspeakers brought softness and romance; women gave up faces and bodies to its sensuous rhythms.

The door opened wide like the gate of paradise and a young woman walked into the light and the noise. A big, burgundy-lipped smile sat startled on her face. Her broad-hipped body, in a full-skirted dress the colour of her lips, searched for the rhythm of the music as it balanced its weight precariously now on this now on that stiletto heel. Her face and smile turned rhythmically to right and left while her eyes flew to the camera that pursued her; with each step the dress danced on the round plump calves. The spectators' senses were stroked complacently by the woman's smile and movement. Some, intrigued by the mysterious roving eye that transported people and events into instant fame, gaped at its blank stare.

The woman slowed her gait before a semicircle of important, well-groomed men, who sat back in amused judgement. Eleni discovered her father in their midst and watched him through eyes narrowed with accusation. She could hardly bear to see his face

216

mirroring the lasciviousness of the woman parading before him, for him. He stretched his arms, the owner of the shop and the world.

A man whispered passionately into a microphone, which carried his voice, intimate, caressing, to all ears; he held its small metal head near his heart, and every now and then with an elegant dancing movement of the arm he whiplashed away its long tail that coiled round his feet. He sang his admiration for the beautiful woman disappearing, and again for the new beautiful woman appearing. She was short but had the dignity of a goddess. She touched the back of her head and tossed her hair, casting threatening glances at the audience that made them thrill with delight. The next woman, tall and blonde, took restrained steps in her restraining suit, knowing she had class, and Europe. The next was childlike, in a simple cotton dress, all impudence and cheek. She was followed by a shy romantic beauty in white, followed again by a large *femme fatale*. Eleni observed her father's face registering the feminine beauty that moved before his eyes.

The man with the microphone cooed, rhapsodised, flirted and sang; he tormented and wooed his creature with the metal head and long tail, which in return tried to trip him up. He tossed the occasional compliment to women in the audience, who looked back at him meltingly. He conjured with his words women and more women, and the same women, in different clothes and faces and colours and poses, who inspired words and more words while the music played and the camera's eye swallowed everything.

Eleni heard her father's name. The camera turned its hard eye on him, all heads turned to him; the bright light lit his eyes examining the women that moved in front of him, dressed by him and for him. The dresses, the shoes – the voice announced – the jewellery, the perfume and the lingerie were merely a sample of the new lines on display here – in the new Gregoriou department store, the first department store in Saloniki. Eleni's eyes travelled from him to the women, carrying on their bodies his shop. She caught sight of her sisters, mimicking expressions, swaying their bodies to the music. She sought out her mother, and read in the tightness of the lines between her plucked brows the betrayal and the wrong.

The moment of choice. The lights twitched brightly, the cameras raised their lids, the compère lassoed the long tail of his words in a fling of apotheosis. The women froze in twists of beauty.

'The Bride of Smyrna! The beautiful, charming, Miss Roula Zoum-boulaki is unanimously chosen as the Bride of Smyrna.' The cameras, the lights, the music, the flowers – her father surrounding the woman, her father posing with her, offering her presents from the shop, dresses and dresses, a kiss . . .

Eleni saw herself in the woman's dress, her own rightful place – the Bride of Smyrna. Like angry birds flapping their large wings at her, her mother's eyelids punished her.

The woman's heel broke, her body stood lopsided, ridiculous. People laughed. Her lipstick, from all the kisses, was smudged across her face. The flowers Father gave her lost their heads. Before everyone's eyes her white bridal dress lies torn and dirty on the floor, tripping her as she tries to run to hide her nakedness, and falls. The smudged lipstick is a bloodstain. Eleni turned her eyes away: her sisters were locked together, for ever, each holding triumphantly the other's uprooted hair. The fiancés intervened, but too late – one of them was swelling up like a balloon and rising to the ceiling where he stayed suspended; while the other, blind behind his glasses, and flayed by his own sarcasm, was wrung and throttled by his muscles. The metal-headed snake tightened coiling round its master. Eleni, terrified, looked at the beautiful fabrics hanging in shreds. The cameras were shooting the spectators, the floor was strewn. The flames embraced the shop, the dressed and naked bodies. A Smyrna in flames running after her father stretched to him her arms. In the end everything drowned in the flood, the floating bodies coming together and separating in a quiet dance, Eleni's own body burning and drowning in the sweet coolness of the water, she glimpses herself in the darkness of her father's warehouse dressed up, the Bride of Smyrna, admired and loved. Her father, unharmed, strokes his hair back. Her mother's body bursts out of its corset and overflows, filling her with pleasure.

Eleni leaned against the wall and imagined she was alone in the room, quiet, looking out of the window at the afternoon sunlight, waiting for her lover, tuning with delicate attention her lute.

· 9 ·
The Refugee

ELENI RECOGNISED the sound of Kaliopi's heels carrying the weight of her full married body and leaving their marks on Mother's parquet floor; then the moan of the springs of the large deep armchair. They were followed by the soft rub of Mother's slippers; she sat with a softer noise, and a sigh. The voices were pleasant and comfortable: her sister's high-pitched, histrionic; her mother's intimate, with a permanent complaint in it these days. Her voice resembled her body which, unsupported by the corset, looked smoother in its curves, and smaller; her breasts hugged her body closely, her legs and arms were thinner, her face tired. Quite frequently now Eleni put her arm round that unprotected small woman. In her sister's voice, vibrating through the rich over-furnished apartment, Eleni saw the large breasts uplifted by the lace-frilled, wired-up bra, pointing at the world like bastions of matrimony. Her puffed up, lacquered hairstyle sat like a starched bonnet round her face, smoothed and sun-pinked by a light film of make-up. The black pencil lines pulling the corner of her eyes upwards and the whitish cyclamen lipstick were marks of her new social status – of a married woman frequenting the fashionable tavernas and charity tea parties, travelling occasionally to Europe, entertaining in her brand-new, European-furnished flat other socially successful couples.

Eleni listened to the voices of the two women while her eyes scanned the various triangles on the page of her textbook. The solution was there, in the shape, on the page, but it eluded her. Her sister's voice became animated as she described the reunion of her class.

'Poor Myrto hasn't married yet – without a dowry, what does she expect? She's a nice girl, clever, always top of the class – for all the good it does her. Twenty-two, and she looks thirty! Thin, bookish, unsocial . . . Still, better her than Lina: since Leandros left her, she's going from bad to worse: now she's seeing Kostas, she believes he will marry her, but I am afraid she is deceived. Kostas comes from a good family. Why should he marry someone else's remnants? You know, they say that Leandros had her. And once a woman is had and left by a man, then it's all downhill, isn't it, Mother? She is branded. I don't know, for all her good looks and dowry and family name, I don't see any man wanting to marry her. Play around with her for a while? Yes. But when it comes to marriage, they want to be the first. And it's right, Coulis is right. A man can have as many women as he likes, in a way he should, Coulis says, because he is strong, he is a man, he has nothing to lose, on the contrary, a lot to gain. But a woman, once she loses her virginity, she is fair game, she is a harlot. Coulis, who met a lot of women, says they are all harlots. Young girls, he says, who are still at school, the way they dress, the way they look at men – he thinks the new generation is lost, corrupt. He really believes, Mother, that all women, with very few exceptions, are harlots. And unless they have a husband to keep tight reins on them . . .'

Mother remained quiet. Eleni blushed, the sword of married virtue swung over her head. She tried to disentangle her mind from its sinfulness, and apply it to the secret symmetry of the patterns on the page, the clear and simple lines.

'Geranoui came too – you remember her, the Armenian girl who married someone twenty years older. Well, with such a nose, what could she hope for! She looked withered, poor girl. He doesn't let her go out, or buy new clothes. We all felt so sorry for her, and promised to go and see her. Stella showed up near the end. She is still engaged to Vangelis. It must be, what – five years now? Waiting for his sisters to get married, for his father to die and leave him the shop. Well, that's what he says, and she swallows his lies as if they were manna – she was always naive.

'And by the way, mother, I had better warn you about Eleni. Someone – who should remain nameless, but certainly a friend and well disposed towards our family – saw her with a boy, walking openly, on the street in broad daylight. Well, I don't know about you, perhaps you don't care about your name and reputation, but I have to defend my husband's name. And I can't have her, the little – embarrass us and disgrace us. The name Korizis is known all over Saloniki, I should say Macedonia. And I am honoured to bear it. Well, how do you think I feel when I am told that my sister is seen out with this and that boy? Where will she stop? She has already taken the wrong path. It's these university ideas she's got into her head. Do you realise the sort of place the university is? Full of whores and communists – if she goes to the university, with all the free life and free love they preach there, you've lost her. I don't want her to be my sister, do you hear?'

Eleni heard her mother speak quietly; she went closer to the door. 'Father says she is not going anywhere. He wants her to go to the shop as soon as she finishes school. She's got the brains, and they need a cashier.'

'With the kind of reputation she's getting, she'll need brains – and a job. Coulis warns me about her. He says, your little sister gives the wrong impression. Her eyes look around too much, and she has an impertinent tongue. All these ideas about emancipation, and univer- sities, and literature, and that garbage . . . People get the wrong impression, they talk. Coulis is right, mother. You'd better tighten the reins. "Your little sister has got liberal ideas," my mother-in-law told me the other day, the poisonous shrew! "Doesn't your mother keep an eye on her?" She dug in her poisonous tooth. "You were lucky," she says, "that my son decided to marry you, and had the wisdom not even to let you finish school. Why does a good girl and a wife and mother-to-be want all these letters to give sails to her head?" Well, she is a shrew, but she is right. Those novels have been the ruin of her . . .'

'Mmm, your mother-in-law! Since when does that light-brain tell us how to raise our children! Eleni does very well at school.'

Eleni knew she had Mother's support. She had said, 'Don't worry about the university – I'll talk to Father.'

The doorbell startled her. Sophia's voice was pointedly sweet, and mother sounded on guard. Eleni listened to the women's voices with the greedy attention of the outsider. She was divided between joining mother and daughters, not to be left out, and remaining in the room that used to be the three sisters' room and was now her own. She looked round it with satisfaction. The bookcase all to herself, the desk, the one bed, her own, the white lace curtains, the Turkish kilimia with their woven geometry. The women's voices outside became angry and she realised she was not missing any motherly or sisterly love. She stayed in her own room, which was flooded with the warm afternoon light, and gazed into the pattern on the page till her mind was submerged in its secret symmetry. That light brought her as always to the outskirts of the city, not far from the walls, where the refugee shanty towns sprawled without end. They – she and a man whose face was not clear to her and who had no name – stood facing each other, saying sweet words and playing and hiding their faces in each other's shoulders, now and then saying the same words, and exclaiming: 'What

221

a coincidence – what a wonderful coincidence!' She thought: this is what making love is like, as they both took their clothes off and stood naked in the middle of all that dereliction in the warm afternoon sunlight. They loved each other with agreeable whispers for the entire long sunlit afternoon, surrounded by burned-out houses and dilapidated walls, and heaps of stones, until one, two, then more old women in mourning came towards them and put their oriental rugs down, woven in the looms of Anatolia, and sat – refugees in a foreign country – and watched the lovers in their happiness. The lovers never stopped making love, even when the policeman approached and said, naturally, to the women: 'Don't you see they are making love? Why don't you pick up your rugs and camp some-where else – and leave them in peace?' Eleni remained in that peace, while the mother's and the sisters' voices outside her room became angrier and angrier.

Sophia was demanding the rest of her dowry, insisting that Kaliopi had been given a larger dowry; her own flat was smaller, her shares gave very little profit, Tryphon needed money now to start his office. And the piano – why should it stay for Eleni? She too played the piano – but Kaliopi shouted that she needed the piano for her singing. 'What singing?' Sophia hissed. 'And those pieces of furniture – they are back in fashion, they're antiques and cost a fortune. And for whom are you keeping all these embroideries? Eleni? She doesn't appreciate their value. You promised me this Romanian embroidery.' Kaliopi was panting in agony, then there was a noise of something falling, Eleni ran out, Sophia and Kaliopi were standing with a piece each of their mother's embroidery. Mother sat back crying.

'Take it. Take everything, before the courts take them all. Dowries! Your father has no more dowries for you. He is losing everything, the creditors are already after us like crows.' Her daugh-ters stood with the torn pieces in their hands, looking at their mother in horror. Eleni, at the door, wanted to go back to the warm after-noon sunlight: but she was held by the sight of her mother grabbing the pieces of embroidery from her daughters and hugging and kissing them. 'I made it with my own hands – my dowry, my youth. I am a daughter, and where is it all gone? Cruel, ungrateful daughters.' She kissed her torn embroidery as if it were a beloved lost baby. Eleni noticed that the rings and bracelets were missing from her mother's hands. She wanted to kneel to her and kiss her hands, but instead she lashed out, blind, towards her sisters and with wordless, centuries-old rage she hit, hit, hit, hit, hit.

222

Eleni concentrated on the rectangular patterns of empty, pale floor where her mother's rugs used to be. The china cabinet was made larger and lighter by its empty, glassy reflections. The black furniture, bare of embroideries, stood elaborate and inflexible in the naked flat that lay open to sea and mountain breezes. The Gregoriou family sat on the straight-backed chairs in an imperfect circle. Father sat on the edge of his chair with taut legs and back ready to spring. His skin was pale, almost transparent, stretched on the bones of his face; his nose was thin, long, rapacious. His glance raced about the room accusing, threatening, ordering, expecting, looking for help or escape. The one-day stubble darkened his face and reminded Eleni of early fears; but his forehead, tall, arching back, encroaching with elegant symmetry deep into his smooth silvery hair defined for her his permanent power and authority. Her father's head contained her in its smooth, elegant cavities.

The economist Tryphon pontificated. He advised bankruptcy; and agreement with the creditors to pay 40 per cent – he would still be a rich man. Father listened to him with contempt. Sophia supported her husband with vehemence, and with the confidence of their alliance she upbraided her father. Mother, a grey strand of hair ready to fall across her face, moved back and forth in quiet rhythmical lament. 'What is this evil destroying our home! Katastrophe, katastrophe.' Kaliopi was divided between comforting her mother and looking at her husband's sceptical, sarcastic face with admiration. When his turn came, he repeated with fatigued superiority, 'I told you, I warned you, you hired too many people, you tried to run too many shops, the interest was too high . . .' Kaliopi seemed moved with pride in her husband's true words, that brought her mother a new crisis of tears. Irritated by the way Father ignored her husband, she complained: 'And what about the rest of our dowries, and what about your promises?'

'According to Tryphon's scheme, the dowries will be saved.' Sophia, guided by her husband's nods, explained the details. 'You can give us our property, Dad, before you declare bankruptcy.'

Eleni looked at the iron bar across the door: it brought memories of the Occupation, of the Civil War. It had not been used for many years and looked out of place in this flat, so modern and open. She did not know mother had kept it: was it to keep the creditors out, or herself in? She had to get out. She wandered down to the waterfront where the air was full of healing, and life all sweetness. One by one, each in her turn, supported by Father, they jumped into the boat which rocked crazily

223

with each new weight; her sisters sat side by side, Mother rested her head on Father's shoulder, he had his arm round her, stroking, teasing. Eleni sat opposite them, her fingers furrowing the water. Tsik tsik tsik – the girls broke the pumpkin seeds, eating the heart and spitting out the shells. The boatman sang of the old home – I Smyrne, mana, keyete – while Saloniki was in flames from the setting sun. The boat sailed round the bay, never left it, never stopped rocking.

Eleni noticed the two square pieces of old blanket with which, one for each foot, mother polished the floor. They lay waiting at the door. Her sisters and their husbands passed each other papers with lists and numbers, solicitors' documents, contracts, powers of attorney. Tryphon was explaining to his brother-in-law, Coulis; Kaliopi listened with suspicion. Mother had stopped listening; her body comforted itself with a rhythmical rocking back and forth. Father paced up and down the room, wild. 'Keep your documents and lists and solutions, I am not paying in percentages and I will not go bankrupt. I will pay every single one of them in full, plus interest, if that takes my last drachma and leaves us starving. But I will come out of this with my forehead clean.' He slapped his forehead with passion. 'Keep your shrewd solutions for yourselves.'

Sophia stood up and pointed at her father. 'You madman, you are not only destroying yourself, you are destroying all of us.'

'At least, give us the rest of our dowries first,' Kaliopi whimpered.

'Never!' Mother's voice filled the room and made everyone stop.

Kaliopi looked at her mother horrified. 'You are behind all this. You told him not to give us our dowries.'

'Out of our home. Out!' Mother's voice was hoarse. Father held his head in his hands.

'You are responsible for this. He always listens to you, and you control him. In your quiet way you always take the decisions.' Kaliopi's passion persuaded everyone in the room, almost Mother herself. 'And now, you decide not to give us our dowries, to go back on your promise. God has eyes, and can see every single one of your deeds.'

'Out of here.' Mother leaned her head back, her eyes shut. Eleni felt, again, Kaliopi's conjuration of the dark powers spreading fear and guilt through the room. A lump of guilt in her stirred to life. Even Mother's silent tears seemed tears of guilt. With blind faith in her righteous fabrications, Kaliopi continued, merciless.

'You were always jealous of us – because we are young, and pretty, and have entered a higher social class. You, with your preferences and distinctions, you always made us quarrel. Me, me! You were always

224

unfair to me. You gave special favours to your firstborn and special favours to your baby. What about me? Who was to love me?' She turned to her husband's embrace. Eleni's own tenderly nurtured tree of remembered injustices came to instant blossom.

'Collect yourself,' Sophia ordered, but Kaliopi was invigorated by the maternal succour she received from her husband and came back at her mother with new force.

'And you will end up with the entire department store in your name. Shrewd, very shrewd!'

At the mention of the department store, Father jumped up in bewilderment and took in, in panic, the new enemies around him. Instantly the fear turned into attack.

'Get your wives out of here.'

Mother was mourning, 'Ach! Ach!' Gregoris turned, from wife to daughters to sons-in-law. With knife-sharp formality of estrangement he said, 'Please. Do me the favour. Stop meddling in our affairs. Take your wives out of our house.'

'One moment, Father,' Sophia's husband interrupted.

At the word 'Father', Father reddened.

'The department store is your life-saver.'

Gregoris looked at him with contempt, suspicion; the others attended with hope. Kaliopi had momentarily forgotten her grudges.

'No one can touch the department store, Baba,' Sophia mediated. 'You'll come to an arrangement about the rest of your property. But your biggest asset, the building itself – an entire block, the best property in Saloniki, in the heart of the city – that remains intact.'

Gregoris looked her up and down: a cold sarcastic smile measured her ignorance, her impudence. 'So you learned something from your husband, the great economist, and you think you can teach your father to run his business.'

'Yes, yes, you are a great businessman, the greatest in Saloniki. But you need advice right now. You should listen to your lawyers, you should listen to Tryphon, no matter what you think of him. At least his advice is free.'

'Lawyers! Economists! Business administrators! All scoundrels! I have spent a fortune on lawyers, and look where they led me. Impostors! Working for the other side! On two payrolls! Don't tell me about lawyers, they brought me to this!' He gesticulated, ready to leap. Kaliopi looked at her brother-in-law accusingly. He smiled, infuriating his father-in-law. Mother had sunk into a private unhappiness.

Sophia pounced. 'Don't change the subject. Never mind what you think of lawyers, now you need them and you need us, and you will listen whether you like it or not.'

Her father raised his arm; Kaliopi intervened, pushed Sophia away, and coaxed her father back to his chair. He sat with his head raised, not listening. Tryphon was again explaining, with forced patience, intricate ways to avoid paying, labyrinthine escapes, suspect salvations. He was drawn with pleasure into his calculations, which he concluded by extolling the blessings of a shrewd, well-organised bankruptcy.

'Out! Snakes! I fed and raised a viper, insulting her own father and bringing this beggar here to insult me. Me, the most respected businessman in Macedonia, to deceive colleagues and clients, to stain my name, to furrow my brow, to live the rest of my life in shame! Bankruptcy! Do you know what you are saying? Do you know what this means to a merchant? Not to dare to look my colleagues in the eye, not to dare appear at the market? To condemn the name Gregoriou – my father's name, and my grandfather's, and yours, Sophia, you thankless dog – to shame, to death!' Gregoris was armed with dignity, protected by the saint of shopkeepers, watched by a long ancestral line of keen-eyed merchants, inspired by the young volatile god of all merchants, Hermes. He was prepared to fight the world. 'Perhaps that's what you do in your village, perhaps those are the ways of your Greece. Where I come from, a businessman has some beliefs which he holds sacred. He has honour, and the word honour means something. And I prefer to see myself destroyed, dead, rather than tread on those sacred articles that my father bequeathed to me. I prefer to see all of you, the whole world, destroyed first.' He was consumed with his own force, and new visions. 'I will pay all of my debts, to the last drachma, with interest and interest on the interest, in double and in triple, but I will pay. Even if that leaves me homeless and bare, as homeless and bare as when I arrived in this country, only a young boy – but God be my witness, I will start all over again, I will start from nothing, as I did at the Katastrophe, as I did after the war, and after the Civil War. God be my witness, I will start from nothing, travel round the villages in Macedonia, with a donkey – not a car, a donkey – and create a fortune that will make petty, wily little manipulators like you, parasites on people's miseries, cringe. And then your wives can claim the rest of their dowries and more. Their father will provide royally for everyone.'

'And what will you do with the department store? Sell it in order to pay up?' Tryphon swallowed the insults and persevered.

'Yes, I will sell it and pay up, all my debts.'

'You'll have to sell it for half its value, even less. They know you need cash. They'll knock you down.'

'Let them. It's mine and I will do what I like with it. I will give no account to anyone.'

'It's not yours – it's in Mother's name,' Kaliopi reminded everyone.

'You haven't the right to do what you like with it,' Sophia scolded him. 'You owe Mother a good living. She has worked at your various shops like a slave. She has suffered all your megalomaniac craziness. It's all right for you, you thrive on your adventures, but look at her, aged before her time. You owe it to her now to rescue what you can. You owe us the rest of our dowries. You owe Eleni a dowry – an education at least.'

'He has no say in that building.' Kaliopi was triumphant. 'None whatsoever. It's in Mother's name, and she decides. No one can force her to sign anything. Do you hear, Mother? He cannot make you sign. I'll make sure he doesn't. And I'll make sure you take the right decisions.'

There was something invincible in Kaliopi's passion – as if she were a possessed Kassandra, or inebriated Pythia – that made everyone pause. Her mother lay back, wilted by her daughter's heat.

'Mother, you will not let him persuade you,' Sophia implored. 'Tryphon has been like a son to you, you will have to let him advise you. You will have to listen to what the lawyers say. Your own life, and Father's life, depends on this building. With the rents alone you could live royally.' Her mother remained immobile, tears ran down her cheeks. Father paced quickly to the door, examined the iron bar, came back to his seat. He looked at the people round him, calculating their threat that increased every moment. 'Eleni, bring your father a glass of water.'

'Of course, Mother will act according to her lawyers' advice,' Tryphon answered for her.

'The lawyers' advice, not yours!' Kaliopi emphasised. 'I know what advice you would give her.'

'Please, Couli, do me the favour to tell your wife to shut her mouth! This is no time for hysterics. Please restrain her.' Sophia's contempt had authority; Kaliopi was speechless, indignant.

'We too know something about business, Mrs Tryphonidou.' Kaliopi's husband answered contempt with contempt. 'We deal in dollars, real capital, not in poor drachmas, and I believe we should have a say.'

Father shook his head in unutterable derision. He took the glass of water from Eleni's hand, absent-mindedly. 'Sit down,' he ordered her, 'Stop disappearing into your room. There.' Eleni sat.

'Why don't you tell them, Gregori?' mother sobbed. 'Tell them, tell them.'

'Tell us what?'

'Tell them, Gregori.' Mother was now crying freely.

Gregoris' eyes raced about the room. 'I have nothing to tell anyone. I don't give accounts to anyone.'

'Mother, what should he tell us?' Sophia asked with threatening sweetness. 'What should we know, Mother? You tell us.'

'The building is not in my name. It's in his name.'

'You are lying!' Kaliopi shrieked.

'Mother, it can't be true!' Sophia tried patiently to help her mother remember better. 'Mother,' she repeated, and the reprimand and threat in her voice chilled the heart. 'Think well! How is it possible? We were together, we planned it, we had made the appointment with the solicitors, in the evening, you remember? Mother, stop crying! You remember?'

'I never went to the solicitor. I waited and waited, all dressed up, until late in the evening.' She spoke between her sobs. Father was exercising his fingers, his hands; the muscles of his face moved with extreme energy and intensity. 'He came with a bottle of champagne, and said, "Let's celebrate! It's signed and finished." "What is signed and finished, Gregori?" I asked. "Where have you been? I have been waiting all evening!" "We didn't need you," he said, "I bought it in my name, much the best." And he kept wanting to kiss me and make me celebrate with him, and he was saying "It's all for you anyway," and I pushed him away, "You are drunk, Gregori, you have been drinking!" "Just a glass," he said, "with the other party and the solicitors, for the good luck," he said . . .' She broke into uncontrollable sobs. They were speechless. Father looked at his wife as at a newly recruited enemy and traitor. Then defiantly at the rest of them. Eleni knew those words, although she had hoped they could be revoked, and remembered that night. Now it was all said. She sank in her seat, relieved. The dusk inside compacted and weighed like clay, and the summer sun was mercilessly bright outside.

Kaliopi was crying like a baby in her husband's arms. 'He destroyed us all!' Sophia and her husband were out on the balcony discussing the legal implications: 'If we act immediately and backdate it, we might persuade the court . . .' Through her tears Kaliopi looked suspiciously in their direction: she quietened her sobs to hear what they were

228

saying. Father sat forward on his chair, his face and hands were busy in a vehement dialogue with someone. He looked suspiciously at the conspiring pairs of daughters and sons-in-law, then at his wife sitting back in her armchair with her eyes shut, defeated. Every few minutes he asked Eleni to bring him a glass of water, which he did not drink. He would hold his head between his long elegant fingers, tightening like a spider on its prey. These men and women around him were planning the final details of his Katastrophe. Look at their eyes, preparing for the looting. He must find a way to get them out of his house before they destroyed it. They looted his shops, now they will loot his home, their own homes are furnished with his wealth, even the clothes they wear. Their hungry bodies, their eyes asking for more, their big fat udders shaking shamelessly, advertising their shamelessness, touching everything, everyone, always in the way. The way they rub against their husbands, hang from their lips, hungry, all of them hungry for it. Women, daughters, they were my Katastrophe. Eleni too, look at her, indifferent as a stone, to me but not to others. Her eyes – the same greedy look. She will end up like the others.

'Eleni, where's your mind? Do you care what is happening to your father? Are you my daughter? Do you understand this pain?'

Eleni sat next to him, frightened by his pain which she tried with all her strength to keep out. Her eyes looked back at him abstractedly, without tears: if she let it in, she would sink and drown under it, she would be burned by it with him. She clung to fragments of pleasure and love that travelled hither and thither round her with the tide. The boat swayed on the waves, she and her lover leaned against the embroidered cushions, protected from the sun by the white canvas canopy flapping in the sea breeze, hiding their faces in each other's shoulder, kissing and laughing and saying sweet things to each other.

'It's not too late.' Sophia and her husband walked into the room decisively. 'You can still save the building, Father. You can write it in Mother's name, or anyone else's, now, it's not too late, but we have to do it immediately.' Her father's face confronted her with cold hostility. 'Tryphon, explain to him.' Tryphon sat down importantly. 'A glass of water,' he ordered. Mother signalled to Eleni, she went grudgingly; he started describing his plan with studied slowness. Kaliopi and her husband listened with small eyes. Gregoris uncoiled, alert: they had come out in the open, they were set to take his building from him, they had thought out the smallest details, and this man of course is at the centre of it. He studied his attack without hearing the forked words, his thoughts turning quickly to find a way out.

Mother stopped her quiet lament and listened to Tryphon. He was moved by the ingenuity and logic of his scheme: the more his listeners hung from his lips, the more he spoke with selfless passion. Sophia had abandoned her austerity and pleaded coaxingly with her father. 'Dad, please, Dad, do it for Mother's sake. We don't want any of it, you've given us enough. Do it for mother's sake, and for your own.' Mother, at the dawning of hope, broke into profuse tears.

Father looked around him, surprised by this abundance of family feeling; his eyes seemed to say 'You're so right! Such caring sons and daughters! Why hadn't I noticed before!' His face had softened, he shook his head with attention and understanding.

'My children.'

'You agree then, Dad? You understand this is the only way.' Sophia and Kaliopi competed in securing an agreement. He moved his head resignedly and leaned back in the chair. He was tired. He wanted peace. While Sophia discussed the details with her husband, Kaliopi tried to cheer her mother, but Mother hesitated, she glanced doubtfully at her husband sitting back with his eyes wandering sadly round the room. Eleni noticed the shadows of regret travelling in his face.

'I'll ring the solicitor.' Sophia went to the telephone. 'He can come now and draft the documents.'

Father looked at her with shock. 'What solicitor? What documents?'

'The documents, Father. To convey the property to Mother.' Sophia walked towards him, her mother was frightened of her.

'Gregori,' Mother almost cried, 'You agreed.'

'Father is tired.' Tryphon was conciliatory, patronising. 'Let me explain to him . . .'

Gregoris stared at him in rising fury. Abruptly, he got up. 'I have to go to the shop. I cannot waste my day with you.' He was at the door, fighting with the iron bar.

'What shop, at this hour?' Sophia shrieked. 'You're not going anywhere. You're staying right here. You're not taking a step outside this house until you sign the documents.' She advanced towards him, as the rest of the family got up and drew close.

He struggled with the bar, it would not move as he wanted. He turned to them, his back against the door. 'Out of here – out of my sight,' he howled, 'all of you.' The faces stayed immobile. 'Take them, Anastasia, before they tear me to pieces.' He clutched the iron bar.

'Go, get out. Let them go, Gregori. Come, come away from the door.' Mother pulled him to her.

'I am tired. I need some rest, Anastasia. Like vultures they fell on me.'

Sophia said to Mother, 'We'll come tomorrow with the solicitor.'
Gregoris stared at his daughter.

'Anastasia.'

She followed him into the bedroom.

Tryphon lifted the iron bar. 'I've got to eat,' he said to his wife.

They walked out; with a sudden flash of invention Kaliopi gave
Eleni, standing at the door, a strong push as if she were to blame for all
this.

Eleni went to her room; she locked the door behind her, they might
come back. She listened for noises: the flat was quiet. She held her head
between her fingers, like her father, wanting to collect her thoughts,
which scattered in all directions. She looked round her room, where
she kept locked up her loves and pleasures, and made sure nothing was
missing: her books, the plants - they were dying in front of her eyes,
she watered them and looked for instant life. She went to her drawer
and pushed her hand among the clothes, washed and neatly folded by
Mother. She reached deeper in the fine, cool material, to the right, to
the left, she turned the contents upside down, threw them on the floor,
pulled the rest of the drawers out; she pulled up her bedcovers, turned
the mattress upside down, went through her books. In a mania of hope,
hopelessness, impotence she tore through the room looking for her
money.

She sat in the midst of the heap of clothes, books, drawers,
bedcovers, holding in her lap an empty envelope, in which all that day's
unhappiness had gathered. She broke into loud, angry tears. Her life,
the world, lay about her in pieces. When her mother walked into the
room, Eleni leapt at her and grabbed her by the shoulders.

'My money. It's gone. My school fees are gone. My school. My
degree. My scholarship to America. My life, my life, my life, my life is
gone.' She shook her mother by the shoulders. 'Do you understand
what that money meant to me? Do you care? Mother, I need that
degree.' She was yelling. Mother tried to shut the balcony door. 'I can't
have the scholarship without the degree. I want, want, want my
money.'

Mother started crying. 'What scholarship? What are you talking
about, Eleni?'

'You took it! He took it! No, I know, my sisters took it. No, Mother,
you were the only one who knew about the money, and knew where I
kept it. You took it, didn't you, and gave it to him. And yet you knew I
had to have it for my school.' She was yelping. Then a new rage. 'I

231

want it back. I want my money back. It's mine. I worked for it, I taught all the fat, spoiled, hateful little children of Saloniki, pampered by their fat, spoiled, hateful mothers, taught them "This – is – a – book, this – is – a – pencil," until I could vomit. I suffered all the fat people in Saloniki for this money, my school fees, the scholarship.'

'I had to give it to him. The creditors, Eleni, they are falling on us like locusts. They come to the door. I don't answer. I put up the bar and hide. I've given everything away. Our china, my jewellery, the furniture, the rugs.' Eleni fell limp on her mother, who was small and weak, smaller and weaker than herself, for support and protection, knowing there was no more support and protection.

She lay on the bare mattress, suffocated by the airless knowledge of her bereavement, that had no comfort and answer: she pressed her face into the soft, dark smothering of the pillow, wishing with all her rage that there was no comfort. Immobilised by lovelessness, she wanted the world drawn into this desolation.

Gregoris wandered through a city of domes and minarets, looking for his home. The muezzin's prayer to Allah rose into the shriek of a war siren, signifying the arrival of armies. He tried to run, but his new shoes were tight and heavy. He lifted his feet with difficulty and took slow, painful strides. He asked strangers if they knew where his father's shop was, but they looked at him as if they couldn't hear him. And that filled him with loneliness and sorrow.

He had not noticed all those people lying on the ground, until he stumbled on their bodies, an endless sea of bodies reclining on beautiful oriental rugs. He asked whether they had seen his family, but the reclining women – he had not noticed before that they were women – only smiled. They turned away and shut their eyes, and one by one they died. When he looked back, all the women of Ionia lay dead on their priceless rugs, that had come to full colour in the early sun. He wished with all his strength to reach his father's shop, where he would be safe from the armies gaining ground all the time, but the cemetery of women stretched like a hushed bazaar, unending, before him, and his feet, so heavy and painful, made him stumble and fall, while the galloping approached.

He opened his eyes in bewilderment: he lay paralysed, gripped by the pain of the dream that sat on his chest and spread its roots throughout his body. He lay, unable to release himself from such pure sorrow; he craved home, and there was no home.

A woman's warm, heavy body next to his reminded him that he had a wife and daughters and a shop, more than one shop, in another, in this country; and reminded him, adding new life to the ancient fear and sorrow and unanswered craving, that he was going to lose everything.

'Are you awake, Anastasia?'

'I cannot sleep, Gregori.'

'I dreamt that I was young. I dreamt of home.'

'Tell me your dream, Gregori,' she whispered conspiratorially.

He told her, in the dark.

'It's good to dream of the dead.'

They lay whispering in the dark until the old misfortunes took the shape of present ones.

'We are losing our livelihood, Anastasia.'

She sighed. 'Perhaps your parents are looking at you, protecting you.'

He got up and walked about the room, looking for something in the weak reflection of the street lights. He opened the door of the wardrobe, pulled out drawers, searched in pockets. He became agitated, Anastasia sat up.

'What is it, Gregori? Have you lost something?'

'Nothing. It's nothing.' He took his briefcase out to the balcony and went through his papers, holding them up one by one and peering at them. Anastasia came to him, her hair hanging in a long grey braid.

'Gregori, what are you looking for?'

'Please. Please leave me, Anastasia. I am putting my papers in order. Am I allowed to put my papers in order? In peace?'

Anastasia stared at the crumpled papers littering the balcony floor: a piece of paper, looking like a receipt, rested lightly on one of her plants. 'Gregori! At this time of the night!'

'Please, leave me, all of you. I am sinking, I am drowning, wife – do you understand? Do you understand that this is the end? Katastrophe!'

She tried to help him collect his papers.

'Go. Please go.' He grabbed the papers from her hand and pushed them into his briefcase.

She lay in bed making stifled sounds. 'That building has the curse on it. It ruined Demoulis, and now it is ruining us. It destroys everyone who touches it.'

He went back to bed and lay next to her.

Eleni was woken by a sorrow whose cause she could not remember. Devastation slowly materialised and fell on her like fine ash. She was sinking into the feathery shroud of a long, sorrowful lethargy punctuated by her parents' voices which created momentary nightmares. Daughters, parents, fathers, circled about her head enticing her with their fear. Daughters became figures became words embroidered on her parents' white linen sheets, stitch by stitch, by mother's versatile hand, spelling the secrets of the universe, if only she could spell and break this spell of sorrow.

Laboriously her eyes crawled with the thread, following the embroidered words, each word weaving its own promise of meaning; while the end of the thread was unravelled, and unravelling with it the words, figures, children, in quick tap-dancing movements pulled by an invisible hand. And while her glance is still on the first word, stilled by the fear of the end of the thread, unravelling fast and racing to meet her and pulling the word, her first word, right from her eyes, and leaving her bereft.

'Father, help me – our shop is burning!' Gregoris shouted as the water from the buckets rose into a sea around him. But out at sea was a splendid boat decked and draped with the finest fabrics. Its sails were silk, and sang as they flapped in the wind, giving the boat speed. Gregoris swam after it because his home, and shop, and family, were all contained in that splendid ghostly boat sailing fast through the Aegean. They were all there, mother and wife, father and brothers and daughters. Iordanis the town-crier and messenger of war was the captain, clanging his cowbell made of gold, giving orders; strangely, he became Aslanoglou. Mother-in-law, gigantic in her voluminous petticoats billowing in the wind, as tall as the masts and sturdier, was the second-in-command. The children, like seagulls, were perched on the masts, gazing at the sea and waving. His father and mother waved to him, telling him how to swim – 'Faster, faster.' His father unrolled a bolt of silk and threw him one end, but it became one with the water, and slipped through his fingers; while he could only dog-paddle – like their puppy Hector, barking to him now from the stern of the boat. He was heavy and tired, and left behind, sinking. 'I am sinking, drowning . . .' But the boat with all the beauty and love of the world on it sailed fast away.

Anastasia tended and comforted her ailing husband like a mother until dawn: and soon after dawn, with a new and frightening energy and force, Gregoris sprang up and in a few minutes he was at the door – in his Sunday suit with his briefcase containing, with difficulty, his entire life in paper. Anastasia, barefoot, in her nightdress, called after him from the balcony. 'I've got work to do, business to finish,' he answered, as he walked away energetically. She watched his young, disorderly gait in the early deserted street.

Eleni was pulled out of sleep by voices. She pulled back, wanting to stay in that element where wishes and fears so fluidly materialised or dissolved. She sought in that healing sea of revelations her anonymous lover and pulled him to her, pulled him into the boat for one more round of the bay, pulled him and made him lie on the cushions with embroidered seagulls, but he was melting – oh how she was losing him! – into the harsh August light, and breaking with her parents' voices into scattering splinters of love.

Streets and balconies were still deserted, windows shuttered, kiosks armoured with wooden boards as if in a state of siege. A young boy walked drowsily, carrying a tray of fresh sesame rolls; Gregoris bought one and asked him how old he was.

He recognised from a distance Aslanoglou's mother, the Karamanlou, sitting on the balcony smoking her hubble-bubble; the rest of the street was still asleep. She's still alive, he thought with indifference.

Kyria Haridia peeped through the partly open door; she undid the chain and, holding her dressing gown together in self-protective modesty, let him in.

'Kyrie Gregori!'

Aslanoglou appeared at the bedroom door, hot and dishevelled in his loose woollen underwear, looking like a gargantuan baby.

'Bright and early, Gregori! With the birds! Haridia – coffee!'

He took his friend to the reception room. Even the pre-war velvet settee, and the tapestries on the wall portraying almond-eyed hanoums in blossoming gardens, exuded the hot, musty smell of Karamanli pastourma.

Gregoris looked suspiciously towards the balcony, where the old Karamanlou sat cross-legged on a chair in her black pantaloons, peering at the world through dark slits; the only sign of life was the muffled noise of her hubble-bubble. Aslanoglou tapped his ear – 'She cannot hear.'

Gregoris pulled out of his briefcase quantities of paper, which he examined in agitation.

'Gregori, things are bad –'

'They are destroying me, Aslan. It's the end.' Gregoris looked like a bird, concentrating its aim in the last few moments before it plunges in its fatal swoop. 'You can save me. Only you can save me, Aslan. Look, I have all the deeds here, surveyors' reports, city plans.'

'What are you saying, Gregori? What are all these papers?'

'My home, Aslan! Four storeys, in the best position in Saloniki, right on the waterfront, beside the White Tower, what more do you want?'

Aslanoglou looked puzzled.

'I don't want some barefoot scoundrel living in that palace. If I am to lose it, at least let it go to a friend. Aslan, I am selling you – I am giving you – my home! I need money.'

'Never, never Gregori!' Aslan looked at the blasphemous papers lying on the table. 'Not your home, Gregori! Where will you live? Think of Anastasia! It will kill her.'

'I need the money. The creditors, Aslan, are eating me alive! Do you understand me? Have it, have all four flats for whatever you can give me – in cash, promissory notes, anything.'

'Gregoris, this is a crime. I can't do it. And I don't have the money. I am in difficulties myself from the devaluation. There are other solutions. Listen to me.'

'Is it no, then?' Gregoris said impatiently.

'Because I love you, Gregori. I'd do anything else, but put these papers away, please, for your own good – and for Mrs Anastasia.'

Gregoris gathered his papers in a fever of disappointment and shame. The veins along his temples were swollen and blue; his eyes, enlarged by lack of sleep, were focused on something not in the room. The muscles of his jaw were chewing something to extinction. 'It's no, then.'

Aslanoglou held his arm. 'Promise me, Gregori, that you will not sell your home. Promise your friend.'

Gregoris nodded absently, hurrying to the door – just as Kyria Haridia appeared from the kitchen holding, disappointed and puzzled, the tray with the coffee.

He stood for some time outside the modern flat of the tax inspector. There were angry shouts inside. The daughter came to the door in tears; she had her mother's generous physique but not her height. She was followed by a young man in his underwear, perhaps younger but much taller. 'I told you I wanted my shirt ironed!' he shouted. 'How many times have I got to tell you to shove it into your stupid head?' He gave a curt greeting to the visitor and then harangued his mother, who was fussing with his shoes. 'Mr Gregori!' she exclaimed with restrained politeness, and returned to her son who had grabbed his shoes from her hands. 'Women – they're good for nothing!' His mother collected the shoe-polish and brush from the floor with meek pleasure and pride in the true male man she had raised. 'When our Minister is angry, the whole world must keep mum! I always said he would be a leader of men!'

'Ah, Gregori!' the tax inspector said curtly. He inspected his son with pleasure. 'When are you meeting your friends?' He spoke to his son as man to man. 'Our Minister here, Gregori, is already hobnobbing with generals' sons.'

Gregoris stood at the door clutching his briefcase. 'He has grown!' he said with thin cordiality. 'I remember him when he was a real terror.'

'He still is, he still is,' his father boasted. 'A true holy terror, eh, Minister? We'll show them one day!' He confirmed his pride in his son with a manly slap on the back, which the son took like a man.

'I have come on important business,' Gregoris offered. Seeing the cautious expression on the host's face, he hastened to dissolve any suspicions of wanting to borrow money. 'I have an offer, a proposal to make to you, Antoni.'

'Coffee,' the tax inspector shouted sourly to the women, and asked Gregoris to come in.

Gregoris spread his papers on the glass top of the low modern table – surveyors' reports, city plans, contracts . . .

'Come to the point, Gregori. Why are you showing me all these papers?'

'My home, Antoni. My lovely home. The best location in Saloniki. I am offering it for sale. A unique opportunity!' The tax inspector remained unmoved. Gregoris hesitated; he couldn't understand. Those apartments had been the envy of the tax inspector and his wife. Every time they visited, they would stand on the balcony and say 'Ah, this is real property! Paradise! Sanatorium! Smell the oxygen! It cures the tuberculars and brings the dead back to life! Your most clever deal, Gregori!' And now, he was cool as a cucumber.

The tax inspector said nothing. Gregoris went through the city plans. 'You see this empty plot at the front. It will become a park, with gardens, trees, a pavilion.' Gregoris' voice was ready to break into a thousand pieces as he portrayed the little paradise, that he had to lose.

'I have to sell it, Antoni. I need the money, to save the shop.'

A long stretch of silence. Gregoris hung on its delicate thread; he was already lowering the price in his mind.

'These plans, Gregori, are old,' the other man finally declared, with quiet assurance. 'You got them when you bought the property? I thought so. They are out of date. You may put them away. There is not going to be a park. They are going to build a theatre – the National Theatre of Northern Greece. That brings the value of your property

237

down, Gregori.' He let his visitor register the shock. The Mrs Tax Inspector came in with the coffee; she asked after the Gregoriou family while her eyes scanned the papers on the table. Gregoris thanked her mechanically and gulped down the coffee in one go. It burned his tongue and palate: he welcomed the pain.

Gregoris looked at the dark man from Peloponessos – the snake, he was thinking, the parasite, when I was rich he was always at my table, he would have starved if it weren't for the baksheesh he got from me and the other merchants, and now he thinks he is Prime Minister.

The tax inspector finally tossed off a price, with indifference, almost contempt, concentrating on his coffee – it cut all thought in Gregoris. He had no home, to sell, or to live in. He had no shop. No dignity.

'I'd rather burn it.'

'As you prefer.'

Gregoris started putting the papers away. This was the end. His face creased, his eyes ran back and forth, trapped; something was tearing in his lungs.

'I accept,' he whispered, and felt dead with shame. He heard women's excited whispers behind the door. 'I would be grateful for a tiny advance, I happen to need cash desperately, the creditors – to clinch the agreement, in good faith, between friends . . .'

He put a wad of money in his pocket, without counting it; he signed a piece of paper without reading it, and ran out.

The heat took his breath away. He put down the briefcase to wipe his forehead. His handkerchief: he could not find his handkerchief. Ah, here it is: he wiped his face with relief, and looked for shade. He remembered with alarm his briefcase, looked at the passers-by; he had put it down of course, he picked it up and tried the latch. The shop was saved for the time being, that was the important thing. His home – he would buy it back from Antoni when he could, he would understand; no, that Peloponnesian would squeeze blood out of stone, he had squeezed his own blood from him. Gregoris' head was hot with anger. That was no price, it was a kick in the belly. The thought of the tax inspector and his fat wife sitting on his balcony, enjoying his view, made him howl. They took his home from his own hands, they took the bread out of his mouth. He should have dynamited the place rather than give it to them. He did not even count the deposit they gave him. He clutched his briefcase, lifting it to weigh the value of the money. It would keep him going. There were steps behind him, he clasped the briefcase tightly and hastened his own step. Perhaps they had been following him all day. Perhaps the tax inspector had telephoned them and told them about the deal. No, the telephone was cut off. He had to hide the money. He could not go home. He turned a corner, the steps still followed him, he would refuse everything, they had no right to make him sign. But he couldn't walk the streets all day carrying this money. The shop, he would hide it in the shop. He disappeared into a doorway and waited. The money would be safer on his person. He opened the briefcase, held the envelope tight and put it into his inside pocket and felt it against his heart. He stroked his hair with his free hand, it was in place, he continued his journey.

This sun, this heat! It made him weak and tired. His feet were swollen and hurt at each step. The briefcase felt full of stones. He tried to take a deep breath but there was no air; he panted shallowly, his lungs hurt from the effort. A whining whispering noise came out of his chest as if it were someone else breathing. He listened, it sounded like a stifled crying. That was what took all the air from him, he thought, and caused the pain in his chest. It brought back the dream – which, as he remembered it, inhabited the streets and buildings of this foreign city, where he walked, an alien.

Wily, he thought, but I outwitted them. They had foreseen everything, come to an agreement with the creditors and organised the entire takeover down to the smallest detail. They even had solicitors ready. Daughters! But the shop was safe now and locked, and he had the keys in his pocket. He only wished he was in the shop, and could hide the money and himself in the dark and the coolness, and lie down behind the counter in the back room and rest. He felt his pockets, the keys were not there, someone had stolen them. No, they would not go so far. But the keys were not there, and without the keys he had nothing, he was nothing. He turned his pockets inside out – his wallet, empty, and papers, what are these papers? A promissory note, the bank book, his handkerchief, they were all here, the money was here, but the keys, who had taken his keys? The noise! What was this shrill screeching noise, they are police sirens – they've sent the police after me. With all his property in his hands he tried to run, papers fell on the ground, he crouched down to gather them, felt his money, it was secure in his pocket. The sirens had surrounded him, he looked up and said, 'My papers, excuse me, one moment.' He saw he was surrounded by cars, people were gesticulating and shouting at him through open windows. 'Couldn't you find another place to stop, my man? You decide to stop in the middle of a roundabout to search your pockets! Kyrie Eleison, good Christian man! You've stopped the entire traffic! It's a miracle you weren't killed.'

Gregoris crouched over his papers while the hooting and the shouting multiplied. If only that noise would stop, then he could concentrate, and put his affairs in order, all he wanted was peace, and some time, and a place to be: his keys, he had to have the keys to his shop, if they would only let him stay in his shop, he would put everything in order.

Someone was approaching: they were going to arrest him. No, they'd come to take his papers. 'These papers are mine, please. Ah, thank you. And I thought you wanted to take them away from me. How foolish. Thank you, thank you. There. They are safe now. Yes, I think I can find my way to the island.' He stood on the pedestrian island and tried to put his pockets and his thoughts and his affairs in order, while the hooting and shouting subsided and the normal traffic hum resumed.

I have to get away from this heat, and the stench, to clear my mind. If I can get to the waterfront – where there is some breeze. That's where everyone is going. The boats are taking the people away. The sound of his voice helped collect his thoughts.

He hurried along the waterfront to join the crowd quarrelling with the captain of the boat.

'What do you mean you cannot take anyone yet?' a man in a suit demanded. 'Look how many we are. We are a full load, and more.'

'That's the regulations. I cannot take anyone till two o'clock.'

'Two o'clock? Who wants to swim at two! We'll report you to your superiors for obstructing the public services. We'll have you fired.'

'Why don't you go to the devil!'

'Do you know to whom you speak? You are speaking to someone, to a paragon of this community. I have the means and the acquaintances to have you destroyed.'

'It's a matter of life and death,' Gregoris kept repeating; people gave him strange looks.

He pushed his way through the crowd and joined in the general anguish to get a place in the boat. Women and children first, of course. But the boat was big enough, with the Virgin's help they would all get in. With the Virgin's help – he crossed himself – we'll all be saved. There will be room for everyone, otherwise it is between the fire and the knife: the fire and the knife and the water.

'Kyrie Gregori, I didn't know you for a swimmer? Where's the family? Caught the early boat?'

'Good afternoon. Yes. The family are well.' Gregoris peered at the man cautiously.

'How will you find them, Kyrie Gregori? We are told it's the end of the world, Judgement Day, at Agia Triatha! Mother loses child and child loses mother. Halasmos Kyriou.'

Gregoris agreed politely. Who was this man? He couldn't remember. Perhaps one of his shop assistants, in Kapnohori. Perhaps he was from the homeland – yes of course, he has a shop in Mouryes. What does he want from me? He felt his pocket, the money was still there. He sighed with relief. 'Excuse me, I have to go now.'

'But, Kyrie Gregori, I thought you were waiting for the boat!'

'The heat, it's getting stronger. Excuse me, excuse me, please. I have to go.'

'Kyrie Gregori, Kyrie Gregori, do you want me to say anything to your family, if we see them? Kyrie Gregori . . .'

Gregoris wound through the crowd politely, desperately: 'Please, make way, excuse me . . .'

He did not know how he found himself at the church of Agios Minas, his Patron Saint. He guided my steps, he thought, and crossed himself. Agios Minas would help him, enlighten him, and save him from the Katastrophe.

He knelt on the floor weakly, and prayed. 'Help me, save me, Agie Mina who protects all merchants! My little Holy Mother, show your miraculous pity!' The relief and pleasure of the dark cool shade, and the quietness and emptiness of the church, and the silent holy images on the walls looking at him with compassion, made him weak with tiredness, slowly melting on to the floor like a candle, dissolving in tears.

When he stood up, and looked for his handkerchief in his back pocket, no, the handkerchief was not there, but – the miracle had happened – the keys! The shop key was here!

'The vagabond! Playing hide and seek with me, eh?' Such profusion of thanks, such jubilant dialogues with all the Saints, such promises to the Holy Mother from her child, her cherished son, Gregoris – who ran, flew, to his shop.

And once he was in, refreshed, regenerated, saved, surrounded by his possessions and blessings, the beauty of his life, he was ready, like a good son, to get down to work, start all over again, as he had promised the Holy Mother. He walked round the shelves and touched the fine delicate fabrics, the satiny, warm, mahogany wood; he went upstairs, the jewels glittered in their glass case, the ready-made dresses hung in mute elegance. He came down the palatial stairs of his department store bearing his life's blessings. All he wanted to do now was sit in a corner of his shop, quietly, and rest. He was saved, and he was tired.

241

He sat, and watched from his corner his father unfolding endless stretches of silk; the tender noise silk made! How soft it felt on the lips, what feminine scent!

'Gregori! What happened to you?' The sudden light, and noise, and all those people, wife, and daughters, rushing into his shop, made him crouch on his chair with fear. They were all round him, talking, advising, explaining.

'Father, our last chance, for your sake, for Mother's sake, sign the papers, save the shop, the building.' Sophia was begging, and at that moment he was quite clear that she meant it for his own good; they all meant it for his own good. They were his daughters, his family, and he loved them. There was little Eleni, too. He was filled with love for all of them. 'Forgive me, forgive me, Eleni, for taking that money. I needed it, my child, it was a matter of life and death. But look,' he took the envelope out of his pocket, 'here, my child, how much money do you need? Your father will pay, for fees and degrees and scholarships, whatever your heart desires. Your father will take care of you. We have plenty of money now, and we'll have more and more. We are saved!' He was tired, but pleased, peaceful. 'And you, Anastasia, you have been a good wife to me . . .'

Anastasia went and knelt by him, and held his hands.

'Gregori, where did you find this money?'

'I cannot give you my shop, Anastasia. It is my life. It is my soul.'

She clasped his hands in hers.

'I sold our home, Anastasia.'

Kaliopi fell on Sophia's shoulder. Sophia looked at her Father with lasting unforgivingness. Eleni looked at the separated members of her family.

Mother got to her feet.

'Sophia. Kaliopi. Eleni. You may go now.' She stood over Father, spread her protective arms round him. Her daughters hesitated. 'Your father is tired.' He nodded in agreement. The ghosts were vanishing. Their daughters walked out of the shop without a sound. Gregoris put his arms round Anastasia's body and let his head rest on her breasts. 'My wife!'

'We'll be all right, Gregori.' She pulled a chair and sat next to him. 'You and I, Gregori, will start all over again. You are such a good merchant, the best in the whole of Macedonia. We'll go to the villages together, and start from the beginning. And I'll not leave your side.'

· 10 ·
Love's Room

'I'VE GOT the key to a room. Do you want to go?'

'Yes.'

They walked through the tin-can shanty town beyond the walls. Women sat knitting, or embroidering, in front of bullet-riddled doors; miniature vegetable gardens grew by dilapidated walls; chickens ran in and out of houses making a racket, a woman was crying to them – ko ko ko. Girls played hopscotch in narrow dirt alleys. A mother was stirring a pot on a small oilstove in front of her door; a small child sat on the ground nearby with her hand between her legs, and an expression of alarmed discovery on her face. An old woman lay asleep or dead on a wooden bed under a mulberry tree, a young woman came out and covered her with a blanket. In the churchyard, a quilt-beater was beating and airing with his large bent bow mountains of cottonwool; housewives sat round him with heaps of pillows and quilts and mattresses, exchanging pleasantries as they waited for their turn; the quiltman's harp-like instrument made a curious music of lingering vibrations and soft thuds as it filled the air with white tufts floating like snowflakes in the warm afternoon light. The women stopped their conversation to gaze at the lovers as they went by, the lovers had eyes only for each other. A group of boys followed them part of the way.

The lovers passed by the public oven, disused since the Germans burned in it the men and the women. They passed the Yiadi Koule prison in the city walls. The turkish baths, always full of women washing. They walked through the north city gate, passed the Monastery of Vlatathon – beautiful peacocks ran round the yard making ugly noises (if we were to marry we should marry here they both thought but said nothing). They strode downhill through the old Turkish alleys, catching the scent of roses behind walls. The sea at

243

their feet was still and blue, the boats were waiting. But there was no breeze.

They entered the dark hall of a modern building; the young man took a key out of his pocket and unlocked the door of the concierge's room. They stretched their arms in the dark and found each other. There was a smell which she could not define – perhaps of old wood, musty walls, used bed-linen, old mattresses, something burnt. But she liked it, because, she thought, this was the smell of love. The young man struck a match; they saw quickly an unmade bed – the sheets looked unclean, but she did not mind – and a chair next to it with a small oil lamp sitting on it. A small shuttered window. He struck another match and another, and finally lit the lamp while she watched. They sat together on the edge of the bed while the burning lamp filled the air with soft murmurs and made the walls of the room tremble. She imagined ghosts had crept in and were breathing her air: she recognised with pleasure the airlessness of love. And its secrecy, when they took their clothes off and lay next to each other. And its vulnerability, when their hands touched each other's bodies. The cottonwool layers of smell absorbed, with relief, even the memory of her own name and the memory of those voices that all her life called her by that name. She took off the cross she wore round her neck and the bracelet with her name engraved on it, which her parents had given her for her birthday, and placed them on the chair with a smile of mischief and blasphemy. She leaned back on the pillow thinking of seagulls flying overhead. She looked up at them, and at a black spot on the ceiling directly above the burning oil lamp, in order not to hear the voices of people outside the room going in and out of the building, in and out of the elevator; and the voices of the ghosts taking the air from her mouth and body. Children and brides burned like upright Easter candles in the middle of wheatfields, while armies and cities crumbled into the sea. Childen lying on marble altars under a father's knife, while armies and fleets waited to sail: Hera and Zeus bargained their love-making over the destruction of nations, drunk with eros and the scents of crushed flowers.

The lovers could not tell how the oil lamp keeled over and rolled on the bed and threw them to the end of the tiny room clutching each other in terror while the bed went up in flames. In terror of being burned alive they fought and smothered the fire with pillows and blankets and clothes, till the fire died leaving a black smoke blending with the blackness of the room and suffocating them. They covered each other's mouths with their hands to stop each other coughing, and crying, and laughing; they covered each other's mouths with their mouths and remained motionless in each other's arms, contorted in silent agony, and love, charred at the moment of love.

'Mama, I can see light in the little room. I can smell something burning.' The voice of a young girl: Eleni could have sworn it was hers.

'I can't smell any fire. Where do you see the light? Come along.' A familiar woman's voice.

'I can see it through the shutters. Can't you see? Under the door. Can't you smell the fire? There are people in there.'

The lovers, at the mercy of mother and child, held on to each other. Their mouths sealed each other's silence.

'You are making things up.'

'I heard the voices.'

'Voices! You are hearing voices.'

They went into the elevator: a shudder, and the machine hummed its way up.

The lovers dressed in the dark, in secret tears, touching wistfully each other's bodies as they covered them and slowly lost them. She remembered at the last moment the cross and the bracelet. Their clothes smelt charred, they were probably blackened, but no one could see, it had already turned dark outside.

After the long stillness, there was finally a sea breeze. They walked in each other's arms down to the waterfront, the breeze became cooler and livelier. They stood at the edge and watched the moving shadows in the water, wondering what they were, and looked at the boats waiting, and at the row of silent fishermen holding their lines, while next to them small fish danced with sudden leaps and pirouettes in and out of their tin cans as they died.

· 11 ·
A Sea Breeze

THEY ARRIVED in Athens the day before the boat sailed. The three wandered in a daze from office to office at Pieraeus trying to deliver – with trepidation – a large chest containing Eleni's home: embroidered linen, icons, towels portraying the Acropolis in tufts, a thick kilimi, woollen blankets for the freezing winters of America; and bottles of Metaxa and ouzo as presents – 'You cannot arrive in a foreign country empty-handed.' Mother had packed all her art and tearful care in her daughter's chest.

Relieved of the chest and the officials, Father announced he would take his women sightseeing. Ahead of wife and daughter he climbed the sacred rock of Acropolis in big exuberant strides: he skipped and hopped from stone to stone as the two women far behind negotiated the climb, and the long trip ahead. Father was impressed by the sight of all the tourists wandering around doing nothing. 'It must be important, our little Acropolis, for all these foreigners to leave their work and come from the ends of the world to see it! Eh, Eleni? You know about these things from school. Did you see the Japanese, Anastasia? Had you seen Japanese before?'

He hurried them round the Parthenon, telling them this was one of the seven wonders of the world; the others were the Colossus of Rhodes and the Hanging Gardens of Babylon, and the Statue of Liberty in New York – Eleni would see it, and the Niagara Falls, and send them photographs. He pointed out Lykavittos, where he promised to take them in the afternoon by the Teleferique – 'Have you been in a Teleferique, Anastasia?' He described the little box with the three of them in it hanging up in the air thousands of metres above the ground, and was pleased by his wife's fright. He tried to find the big avenues where the important shops were, the large department stores, but

Mother was in tears. 'Never mind, Gregori. Let's not think of those things now!' He tried to comfort her, 'I'll give you another such shop, bigger and richer, you'll have all your rugs and all your crystals back.' 'Please, Gregori, stop,' she implored, and Eleni said 'Come, Father, show us the rest of the Acropolis.' But Father was looking pensively now at the damaged wonder of the world scattered about him.

Eleni led him by the hand to the sturdy caryatids. He was impressed by them, to please her. 'Imagine resting a whole roof on young girls' heads! And not a sign of tiredness! What art! What an idea! Our ancestors must have had genius to think of this! Now you, Eleni, you are educated – tell us about it.' He looked at his daughter, hungry for pleasant answers, she put her arms round him and her mother. Her mother looked dazed, sad, tired, from all the preparations for the journey; her father was so thin and also young-looking, his exuberance so brittle. They sat on the parapet, in the warm September sun, and gazed at the tourists, hypnotised by the foreign looks and sounds. Father was proud his daughter knew languages: he too, he told them, had started to learn English when he was planning to go to America to look for relatives and make his fortune. 'So what are they saying, Eleni? You should go and talk to them, you should practise your English. You should tell them you are going to America. Tell them you have this scholarship for the university.' He sat up, in readiness for the journey ahead of her. 'Ask for their addresses, Eleni. It's useful to know someone when you go to a foreign country. Not as I came to this country – a stranger amongst strangers.' Mother started crying, and he comforted her. 'Don't be a child, Anastasia! Before you know it, the year will go and she will come back to us. I'll take you to see her, at Christmas!' He entertained the idea brightly, briefly, Mother sighed with disbelief: the promise left all three empty.

They remained sitting on the parapet, close together, while groups of tourists came and went, and the September sun journeyed through an immaculate blue sky. Mother sighed as she looked at her daughter, whom she was losing, and at her husband, trying with all his strength not to be lost. Eleni noticed that the sun had pinked her mother's cheeks. Her father sat with his head lowered: his face was engraved with thin lines, his eyes wide open and not seeing, fixed on the stones. To bring him back to her Eleni talked. She told them the story of Lord Elgin, and how he bought the frieze from the Turks and shipped the marble all the way to England, and how all the English people came to see them. Father attended, with strong interest.

'Did he sell them, Eleni? He must have made a fortune, the rascal!

Buying them for a hunk of bread from the stupid Turks and then opening a museum and charging a good fat entrance fee!' He looked at the Acropolis and at the crowds of tourists with new appreciation. His eyes raced among the stones and through quick calculations which made them sparkle. 'Clever, very clever,' he kept muttering as he counted the tourists and the drachmas they could fetch. With love Eleni saw in her father's face the new plans already drawn up and signed: himself the owner of the Acropolis, staffing it with trustworthy people, exhibiting it to advantage, the world in his pocket! 'Tourism' he murmured, shaking his head, his eyes lost in new understanding.

'Well, this is nothing to the antiquities we had at home, Eleni. That coast is full of antiquities, all Greek, of course. But did we know their value? Troy – you learned at school about Troy, Eleni. Ah, we would go and play over there. Some foreigners were digging, we thought they were crazy – "Parlez-vous français?" we said, but I think they were German. My father knew their value. The Golden Fleece! Do you know the story of the Golden Fleece, Eleni? A terrible story, my child, but very didactic, very didactic! I suppose you don't know it, Anastasia. You see, Jason was Greek, he came from your part of the world. He and his sailors, the Argonauts, as they were known, they sailed all the way to our coasts, to Ionia, which was there of course before Turkey was even a glimmer in Allah's eye. They were rich lands, Anastasia mou! Gold mines! And the myth goes that Jason and his sailors came to steal the Golden Fleece, an untold treasure kept by a powerful king. Well, only a child wouldn't see the symbolism of the story. The fleece was not only a fleece, Anastasia mou: it meant all the riches and treasures of the land. Anyway, Jason made the king's daughter, Medea, fall in love with him. But Medea was a witch and wouldn't stop at anything: she stole the Golden Fleece from her father and gave it to the foreigner and sailed away with him.' He gave a sigh. 'Wait, the worst is to come. The poor father sailed after them, and Medea, cruel as she was, what did she do? She cut her little brother in pieces and scattered them in the sea.' Mother covered her eyes in horror. 'Don't, Gregori.' Eleni listened. 'The broken-hearted father stayed behind to collect all the pieces of his son, and in the meantime his daughter with her lover escaped and sailed back to Greek waters. But the story continues. The foreign land, this land, was not kind to her, she was always a foreigner – but that's another story, too terrible for your ears.' He got up.

The air was getting chilly, they moved into the museum. Mother and Father stood hand in hand in front of the statues, at a loss amongst the guided tours. Eleni wandered into a room that was almost empty, where the solitary statues of the young girls had all the air and light to themselves. The smile dawning on their faces made their young arms, bound to their bodies by the marble, seem ready to move forward. Eleni was held by that smile and by the knowledge that she had not loved anything in her life as she loved what was in front of her: the young, contained body, the leg hesitantly forward, the arms in the eternal knowledge and pain of their bond to the body: the smile, reflecting something perhaps intimate, perhaps open to all eyes. She looked for the secret bond between that smile and the constrained arms, and wondered whether the smile gazed at a freedom that the arms could not give. She wondered at those bodies and faces, at the artist who with innumerable gentle accurate blows moved a leg forward while preserving the balance of the ponderous stone, and who first shaped a smile out of stone; she wondered at the invention of a smile and as she did so, creation with its rivers and birds came close and crouched in her hands.

In the evening they went to a taverna near the sea, where they ate fresh mullet and drank retsina; in the cool dusk they talked about the journey and about home, about the future and the past. Mother gave Eleni last-minute advice – to keep warm, America was treacherously cold, she had seen photographs of their cousins in Vancouver looking like Eskimos lost in the snow. 'But Mother, Pennsylvania . . .' She must keep the icon over her bed, and keep the cross and the blue eye always pinned on her underwear, and look after them like her own eyes. Did she have the family photographs safe? And that cheese pie and the koulourakia, they would last her for days if she kept them cool. And the dollars, she had hidden some dollars among her blankets in the chest. 'Keep everything in the chest, you know how forgetful you are, like your father, but don't forget us, Eleni.'

'The addresses – have we given the child the addresses, Anastasia? As soon as you arrive, Eleni, you should look for your cousins in Detroit. They are the daughters of a second cousin of my father's, whom I haven't seen since before the Katastrophe. They will look after you like their own child. Their father grew up with my father, they went courting together.' He paused, then remembered, 'And this address – Panayiotis Photiou, he was the son of our neighbours, younger than me. I don't know how he survived, the only one out of five children and the youngest. A compatriot gave this to me and said that Panayiotis is a rich man, in Chicago, he owns his own petrol station, and is always happy to see other Greeks and help them in moments of difficulty. Tell him you are the daughter of Gregoris Gregoriou, son of Georgios Gregoriou, the shopkeeper next to the barber's shop. His mother used to come to our shop. Tell him about Iordanis, how we ran after him and he clanged his cowbell at us. He will remember!' Eleni promised she would look for them all, and held her father's and her mother's hands. Mother was crying again, and Father tried to cheer her up.

'You know, Anastasia, our Eleni is going to have her own cinema in her room.'

Mother looked offended. 'Oh, Gregori, I don't know how you can be in a mood for jokes!'

'I swear, Anastasia! Everyone has their own cinema at home, don't they, Eleni? You want to see *Quo Vadis*, you see *Quo Vadis*, you want to see *Gone With the Wind*, you lie back and watch *Gone With the Wind!*'

'Let me be, Gregori, I am not in the mood.'

'Ask Eleni!' He enjoyed his wife's scoldings.

'It's true, Mother, they all have televisions in their houses.'

Mother had softened.

'Have some fresh fish, my little wife, and a sip of retsina, and listen. In America they have dinners, ready and wrapped, which you put in the oven without moving your little finger, and in a few minutes it's all ready and served, and you have it in front of your cinema, and you are a king.'

Mother shook her head in disbelief, and looked at Eleni; Father made her drink some more retsina, and made Eleni drink, and they all felt light-headed. 'You see, Anastasia, everything in America is made of plastic. Plates and cups are made of plastic, and clothes and shoes are made of plastic. Bottles are made of plastic – you drink your retsina from the plastic bottle, you throw it away, you are a king. You eat your mousaka from your plastic plate, and throw it away. Dirt cheap, no washing up, you are a queen.' He ordered more retsina. Mother objected weakly, 'No, Gregori, we shouldn't have any more to drink!' But Father was already flying and Eleni, rosy-cheeked and giggly, was flying with him.

'Our new shop, Anastasia mou, will be full of plastics. Eleni will buy them cheap and send them to us, and we'll fill Greece with plastics.'

Mother looked frightened. 'I don't want to know about shops, Gregori, please.' But he was inspired. 'All these tourists, Anastasia mou, they won't only want to go to the Acropolis – they'll want to go to our nice beaches. They'll need plastic slippers for the beach, sayonaras they call them, they'll need plastic sheets to lie on, sunglasses, sun hats. This is the new era. The dawning of the new technology, the new civilisation.' He drank to it, and Eleni drank with him and Mother was forced to take a sip.

At the next table they started singing nostalgic songs, and father and Eleni soon joined in. 'Londra, Parisi, New York, Voudapesti, Vieni . . . Ah, Eleni mou, no city compares with Athens, but whoever wrote that song hadn't seen Smyrna. A true aristocratic city. Athens is a village compared to Smyrna.'

Through the rest of the evening Father talked about home, and the sweetness of his youth. The harvests and the grape seasons, and the long lazy summers by the Sea of Marmara. His mother's voice travelled through the orchards.

The three of them, arm in arm, walked through the streets of the city silently, all the talking and singing left behind.

They were still quiet the following day as they wandered round the white transatlantic boat as big as a city, with its own restaurants, cafés, bars, promenades and swimming pools. When the visitors were asked to leave the boat, mother and father hurried to the gangway in alarm.

The two of them seemed small, standing on the pier. The harbour and the entire city was receding from Eleni; the water rushed in between her and her homeland in quick iridescent whirlpools, followed by dark shadows coming together and almost touching each other, and moving apart. Mother was waving her scarf and Father waved his arm with determination. They called to her, but the noise, and the rock-'n'-roll music, and the breeze, that had just arrived in sudden powerful gusts after many days of stillness, took their voices away.